Moonshine Promises

JOHN VAN RYS

RESOURCE *Publications* · Eugene, Oregon

MOONSHINE PROMISES

Resource Publications
An Imprint of Wipf and Stock Publishers
199 W. 8th Ave., Suite 3
Eugene, OR 97401

www.wipfandstock.com

PAPERBACK ISBN: 978-1-6667-1261-2
HARDCOVER ISBN: 978-1-6667-1262-9
EBOOK ISBN: 978-1-6667-1263-6

JULY 14, 2021

Some of the stories in this collection were originally published in journals: "Dome" in *The New Quarterly* (volume 147, summer 2018); "In the Hills and Valleys of *Perche*" in *The Dalhousie Review* (volume 99, no. 3, autumn 2019); and "Nether Lands" in *Blank Spaces* (June 2021).

Illustrations (c) 2021 Rosalinda Perez. All Rights Reserved. Used with Permission.

Moonshine Promises

For April

Without her, none of these stories would have seen the light

In loving memory of Keith Van Rys and Russ Smith

"Well shone, Moon. Truly the moon shines with a good grace."
—WILLIAM SHAKESPEARE, *A MIDSUMMER NIGHT'S DREAM*

Contents

Acknowledgements

C.S. Lewis is reputed to have written, "You are never too old to set another goal or to dream a new dream."

(Dear Reader, as this isn't a scholarly book, I'm not going to supply a footnote for this quote. After all, you can find it on the Internet. That's where I got it. To be precise, my wife shared it with me in a Facebook post. On Facebook, we're friends.)

Anyway, I think I'm that guy Clive is talking about here. In December 2016, I was fifty-five years old. Over the years, I'd been whining to my wife April that I wished I could find some time to write fiction. Undoubtedly tired of what she called my "ceaseless whinging," she said, "Why don't you write a story and give it to me as a Christmas gift?" Being of Dutch descent, I jumped at the chance to save money on presents and started writing. Every holiday, birthday, and anniversary became an excuse to write another story and exercise frugality at the same time. Eventually, I didn't need excuses to do either.

About a half year after I started writing the stories, though, my father died. Then a year later, April's father passed away. What had started out as comedy threatened to turn tragic in the wake of these deaths, which were small personal catastrophes to us. The memory of our fathers somehow inhabits these stories, and I believe they're better for it.

So I offer *Moonshine Promises* in their honor, but dedicate it first of all to April, grateful for the misadventurous life together that gave rise to these tales. Next, I thank my kids. (I hear my dad's voice saying, "Children, not kids. Kids are baby goats.") To sons Matt, Tony, and Charlie, daughter Beth and son-in-law Ren, thank you for inspiring your fictional doubles and allowing me to play with them liberally. Looking farther, I thank my extended family for their inspiration and support: my brother Nick, someone who's perfected the pregnant pause; my sisters Tracy and Wendy for finding me funny, in spite of the pest I was as a teenager; and their husbands—John who helped us wake up from our home-reno nightmares, and Steve, who for decades kept asking me how the novel was coming along, a cattle prod that has at last produced results. And yes, I thank the woman who gave birth to me. Mom, thanks for doing it: I know it was a pain, almost as big a pain as I've been ever since.

(Dear Reader, as this is my first published collection of fiction, I have many other people to thank. Please bear with me to the end. I promise for my next book, if there is one, that I'll just write "Ditto" or "See my first book.")

I have so many colleagues to thank. First and foremost, Hugh Cook—mentor, colleague, and friend. His feedback and advice on these stories have made each one infinitely stronger; any weaknesses still existing are entirely my doing.

To my English Department colleagues at Redeemer University (Deborah Bowen, Karen Dieleman, Ben Faber, Jonathan Juilfs, and Doug Sikkema), I couldn't ask for better ones. Thanks for your encouragement and for reading stories I couldn't resist sharing, like a father with cellphone video of his child screeching away on the recorder at a school recital. Ditto to my part-time colleagues: Bill Fledderus, Thom Froese, Jantina Ellens, and Judy Robinson. Special thanks to Ray Louter for his expertise on motorcycles and Friday-the-thirteenth parties at Port Dover, Ontario, and to my egg clients at Redeemer for enduring my egg yolks.

But still more thanks is due. To Brent van Staalduinen and Liz Harmer, much younger writers who offered great encouragement and advice, as their own writing blossomed into print. Thanks to my past colleagues at Dordt University, whom I still count as friends. Some of the events that inspired these stories happened among them in Northwest Iowa during fifteen years there. Special thanks to Mary Dengler for responding so positively to several of these stories and to Dave Schelhaas, who long ago told me in response to another set of my mock department-meeting minutes, "You should be writing humor." It took a while, Dave, but I got there. To Verne Meyer, thank you for putting up with my quirky humor for almost thirty years, as we worked on sober textbook projects.

(But wait, Dear Reader, I'm not done! Don't turn the page yet!)

Along the way, I received much encouragement from Mary Darling, Ted Harris, Tracy Ware, Katherine Quinsey, Gerald Lynch, Chris Erickson, Janae Sebranek, and Hilary McMahon; and through their writings, from Heather Sellers, Anne Lamott, and Annie Dillard. I want to offer a special thanks to editors who accepted stories from this collection for their journals: Pamela Mulloy and Emily Bednarz at *The New Quarterly*, Anthony Enns and Lynne Evans at *The Dalhousie Review*, and Alanna Rusnak at *Blank Spaces*. Your acceptances offered me a lift when I needed it.

Naturally, I have to thank all the English teachers and professors who inspired in me a love of language and literature, of poetry and story: among too many to list, David Bentley, Donald Hair, Richard Stingle, and Stan Dragland from the University of Western Ontario, and Mr. Ashdown and Mr. McKeone from Sir Wilfrid Laurier Secondary School in London, Ontario. In the company of these inspiring teachers I put my own creative writing students at Redeemer, thanking them for their contagious energy and dedication to the life of the imagination.

Finally, I thank the good people at Wipf and Stock, who took a chance on this late-blooming, old-dog writer. It's been a delight to work with you.

(By the way, Dear Reader, I couldn't leave that quote from C.S. Lewis alone. It turns out that the Internet wrongly attributed it to him. Go figure! The Internet. Wrong! I may complain to my Internet service provider, possibly stop paying my bill. The quote is apparently from an inspirational speaker and writer named Les Brown.

Once again, my wife has led me astray, as she has from the very beginning.)

A Note to My American Readers: *Timmy's* in these stories refers to Tim Hortons, a coffee shop you can find in every small town and big city in Canada (stores sometimes right across the street from each other). The phrase *May two-four weekend* refers to Victoria Day, a holiday on the Monday before May 25, originally in honor of Queen Victoria, now a long weekend typically celebrated with a two-four (24 bottle) case of beer.

Illustration and Design: A special thanks to Rosalinda Perez for her playful illustrations, both on the cover and inside the book, and to Matt Van Rys (son numero uno) for his creative and practical input into this whole project.

Funding Support: I would like to thank the Research Office at Redeemer University for supporting *Moonshine Promises* with a grant in aid of publication.

UNDER THE HONEY MOON

Evan had been too embarrassed to buy condoms at the drugstore. He'd gone during lunch hour at school, but couldn't bring himself to pick up a box, just stood staring at it for several minutes—as if it were a girlie magazine broadcasting his intentions. The clerk at the cash register reminded him too much of his mother. He could hear her "tsk tsk" as she rang him through; she'd ask for his ID, call it fake when it showed he was eighteen, say "You're just a baby. What the hell are you doing with these?" He could see the disappointment in her eyes.

He'd taken Sex Ed at William Lyon Mackenzie King Secondary School (WLM-KSS for short, like a vanity plate). The school was on the south side of London, the working-class side. Not England's London, of course, but Canada's London, a sprawling midsized city planted in southwestern Ontario farm country, a city with its own Thames River—a replica that in size and flow showed fitting colonial deference to the original.

In class, he'd even practiced putting a condom over a banana, so he knew better than to let his little man go exploring without a raincoat on. Looking back now, he chastised himself for not asking around at school to see if there was a black market for prophylactic devices. Or for not bicycling across the highway, the Four-O-One, to the truck stop there.

The rumor was they had a coin-operated machine in the washroom. Why would truckers need condoms, though? He imagined liaisons on the road, burly truckers making very special deliveries before rolling farther and farther down the highway, free and sexually satisfied birds heading to Detroit or Toronto. Or were they tomcats prowling from one end of the country to the other?

He stood before the rows of condoms in their sensuously-colored boxes, waiting for the clerk to take her eyes off him. If she did for a moment, he might slip a box down his pants. He had money to pay for them. That wasn't the point. He glanced up; she was watching him, suspicious, he was sure. Turning red, he fled the store empty-handed, mumbling something about being late for class as he passed the clerk, her arms crossed. He felt like he'd been in flight ever since.

So now, three months later, he and Mae had fled London. Cause and effect, he thought, as they sped down Highway 4 approaching the town of Flesherton. They were in a borrowed 1972 Chevy Nova—eight years old by then. Evan remembered from Grade 9 Latin that "nova" meant "new," feminine singular of "novus." And all of this did feel new, driving, sitting close beside Mae, who was definitely feminine and singular. But he'd heard too that "*no va*" in Spanish meant "doesn't go," so he was worried.

He and Mae were on the run, two lambs on the lam. That morning, they had eloped. They tied themselves in knots, got hitched to the same wagon, walked down a very short aisle at the London courthouse. And now they were running to Beaver Valley where they planned to hide out and honeymoon at the Talisman Ski Resort, offering discounted rates in July since it was off season. Every few seconds, he checked his rearview mirror to see if they were being chased down—either by the cops, the morality squad, or Mae's dad in his Happy Hearth Upholstery and Furniture Repair truck.

As Evan drove through this unfamiliar landscape of hills and pine woods and rock outcroppings, his left thumb played with the wedding band on his finger, fretting at it. He'd never worn jewelry of any kind, not even a watch. The closest thing might be his wire-rimmed glasses, which slid down his nose in the heat and needed to be pushed up periodically. How did I get here, he thought, then corrected himself, *we*. Mae's left hand with its ring rested lightly on his thigh. "Are we there yet?" she asked, squeezing his leg. He could feel her vibrating beside him, stretched tight like a rubber band.

How big would the fetus be, inside her, at three months? A little peanut? How about a hazelnut? When he asked her, she said about three inches. That big, he thought. Already.

Just a month ago, they were sitting side by side on the grassy hill at the back of the grade school Mae had gone to. School was out, the parking lot and playground empty. The hill sloped down to the narrow pathway leading to the larger boulevard that separated the half of the subdivision where Mae's family lived from the half where his family had their house. We come from opposite sides of the boulevard, they'd said to each other. We're star-crossed lovers—except it was streetlights in their case. They'd both had to read *Romeo and Juliet* in Grade 9 English. They agreed it was stupid to die for love like that. The lesson? Always check your lover's pulse before you kill yourself. It saves a heap of trouble.

"It's for sure," she said. "I'm pregnant."

He knew she'd gone to her family doctor, worried about missed periods. In that moment, the sky felt like a hazy gray roof above him, the air numb and still, a mirror to his insides. After some moments, he said, "How much?"

"What do you mean, how much? You're either pregnant or you're not. That's how it works."

He could sense her irritation. Or was it fear? Was she worried his flight instinct would kick in, that he'd abandon her rather than stand and fight? "Sorry, I meant how far along."

"The doctor said two months."

His mind went back to a Saturday morning in her bedroom, her parents both at work, her sister asleep in the next room. His hands and lips and tongue traversed and trespassed her body, hers his. Shy of each other, they hid in the tent made by her blankets, not even fully undressed. He's sure he was still wearing his socks—white athletic socks with two red stripes around the top. The elastic was limp, so the socks drooped down to his ankles. Aroused and alarmed, they went all the way, as the kids said then, or almost. "I guess we shouldn't have trusted the withdrawal method." After a few moments, he added, "What else did the doctor say? Did he offer you any advice?"

Mae turned to face him. "You mean did we talk about an abortion?"

"No, no, that's not what I meant. At least not just that." He wouldn't look at her. "I meant everything. Options. Choices. Your health, the baby's health. Keeping the baby, giving it away . . . ." His voice trailed off.

"Or getting rid of it."

"That's a choice. I mean, how do *you* feel about it?" He knew what his family and church felt about it, at least as a moral abstraction. He knew how he was *supposed* to feel about it. But faced with it, it was so tempting, wasn't it? Such a simple solution, good riddance. Everything would go back to normal, after. But he couldn't even finish the phrase in his mind, *Good riddance to bad rubbish.*

"How do I feel about it? It feels like you're dumping the choice on me, washing your hands of me and the baby. That's what it feels like." Mae's voice was rising. "Well, I'm having this baby with or without you." She was close to tears, moving to get up.

"Wait! Don't." He gripped her hand and turned to her. "That's not what I meant." After a moment, he added, "I don't know what I meant." She settled back onto the grass, letting him hold her hand, fingers twined together so tightly it hurt. The moment stretched out, thinning as he considered what might be coming for them. Confessions to their parents, who would be angry and, perhaps worse, disappointed in them. A serious talking to by his Dutch-immigrant parents, worried especially about his education. The news spreading mouth to ear, especially in church—where premarital sex was almost the unforgivable sin, not the sin against the Holy Spirit, whatever that was. Looks and awkward conversations. Labels and categories. Teen pregnancy. Out-of-wedlock. Bastard, if the baby were a boy. What was the label for a girl born out of wedlock? Bitch? He didn't think so. Something worse? He didn't know.

He saw ahead of them a shotgun wedding: Mae's dad, ex-military, standing behind them in the church aisle with his weapon of choice, maybe even a bazooka, a tank outside just in case. Evan in his cut-off jeans and Supertramp T-shirt, a grenade down his pants with a string attached to the pin, Mae's dad holding the other end. Evan's mop of hair sweaty and heavy on his head. Mae in her sexy blue tube top and short shorts, Daisy Mae. The church full of guests smirking and winking knowingly, her clan on the left, his Dutch-Canadian clan on the right, "If she ain't Dutch, she ain't much" running through their minds.

As the moment stretched thinner and thinner, he did the math. After all, he was a math whiz in school, part of the 98 plus club. *Mutual attraction + reciprocal desire + shared passion = pregnancy = a baby = an unintended consequence = a human being, one among billions = a walking, talking addition to Earth's overpopulation problem = a tiny burping and pooping and peeing solution to Canada's falling birth rate.* Fatherhood for him, motherhood for Mae. Parents suddenly, like their own parents.

Where did love fit into the equation? He'd have to sort that out later. He'd just finished Grade 13, Mae Grade 12. They'd graduate in the fall, after he'd started his first year of university. He had $10,000 in the bank—he'd saved virtually every dollar he'd made, starting with his paper route. Enough to make a start. On what, exactly?

The future now felt like a tidal wave bearing down on them, standing together on an empty shore with everyone else on higher ground. "Let's elope," he said.

"Elope? Like just run off and get married? Like not tell anyone? Like right now? Are you crazy?"

"Crazy like a fox," he said. And cowardly like the lion from the Land of Oz. Practically a Munchkin. "Think about it. It's the perfect solution. Get married now, apologize later."

"They'll kill us. They'll hate us. They'll never forgive us."

"Your dad's gonna kill me anyway when he finds out you're pregnant. At least this buys me some time." He paused, then added, "I don't mean we need to do it right this second. We need to come up with a plan, and keep it secret for now."

He looked closely in Mae's face, searching for some sign there. Could she see the fear and uncertainty in his eyes? He tried to hide it.

Finally, she said, "Alright," and squeezed his hand hard before relaxing her grip. As if relieved, she lay back in the grass, and he followed her, feeling the blades tickle his upper arms. Plotting their escape could wait, even if for just a few minutes. They studied the sky in silence; it felt low to the ground, barely above his face.

Now, it was just a month later, and they were turning up the long driveway to the Talisman. After passing through Flesherton, they'd headed north into what was obviously ski country. Before turning, Evan had paused to take one last look in his mirrors—no sign of pursuit. He breathed more easily after they were around the corner, as if they'd found a secret passage into a hidden realm. Surely they wouldn't be caught now.

In Beaver Valley, hills rose to the west, ski slopes bright green ribbons lacing the landscape, like waterfalls undulating from the peaks. As he drove their borrowed 1972 Chevy Nova toward the Talisman, they passed through a golf course. A few duffers were out on the links. Then the lodge came into view—the central chalet straight out of Evan's Alpine imaginings with its high peak, deep brown woodwork, and gingerbread trimming; three-storied wings to the left and right like a beehive for workers on holiday. Behind the chalet, the ski hill rose to meet the western sky, the sun dipping toward it.

At the check-in desk, they were greeted by a middle-aged woman with bright blond hair, frizzy with grey roots. Her name-tag said Annie.

"Names?" she asked.

"Mr. and Mrs. Mulder," he replied. It sounded odd to say; his parents were Mr. and Mrs. Mulder—not him and Mae.

When he and Mae were plotting to elope, they'd talked about names. After all, it was 1980, not the Dark Ages. Mae had said she might keep her name, Miller, or she might hyphenate it, Miller-Mulder, so their baby would be Johnny or Janey Miller-Mulder. Evan had pointed out that Mulder was actually Dutch for Miller, so Miller-Mulder would be redundant. They thought how strange it was that their last names were essentially the same, that it had never occurred to them until that moment. Maybe they were distantly related, somehow their ancestors connected across the North Sea. They hoped they weren't committing incest in some way, but no, the blood test confirmed they were safe to have sex together, at least in that sense. Mae suggested he might consider changing his name to Miller, since they were in Canada now, not Holland. English was the parlance here.

Why not change it to French? he retorted. After all, it's also an official language. They would be the *Meuniers*. But, she replied, there's the masculine-feminine thing in French. He'd be *Meunier* but she'd be *Meunière*. That would be so confusing, especially if they had both boy and girl children. Children, he'd thought, more than one? He hadn't looked that far ahead. In the end, he argued that Canada was officially multicultural—Trudeau had made it so in 1971—so Mulder was a perfectly good name. She'd said she'd let him win that argument, but it would be the last one. He shouldn't get his hopes up.

Annie seemed to be looking at him and Mae skeptically. He laid his left hand on the countertop and flashed his wedding band. Out of the corner of his eye, he saw Mae smiling up at Annie. "That's right," she said, "Evan and Mae Mulder—newlyweds."

Annie's face brightened. "Well, congratulations! And welcome to the Talisman for your honeymoon. You're a couple of young pups, aren't you? Can I upgrade you to our bridal suite?"

"No, no," he replied quickly. "We're on a budget, I'm afraid."

"Will that be Visa or Mastercard? We need a credit card to book you in."

"Actually, we'd like to pay cash. Is that possible?" The truth was, neither he nor Mae had a credit card. They weren't even sure how to get one, and they were pretty sure they wouldn't qualify. They were practically still kids. So Evan had gone to the bank and withdrawn $1000 from his savings. He was carrying a wad in his wallet; the rest was hidden, rolled up in some underwear in his luggage—a pair of black boxers with red hearts on them he'd bought at Eaton's for the occasion; embarrassed, he'd told the clerk they were a gift for his brother, who was getting married.

"With cash, anything's possible," Annie replied. "You'll just need to pay for both nights up front." The transaction completed, she passed them their room key and added, "Enjoy your stay at the Talisman." She winked at them mischievously. "I don't imagine we'll see much of you two young pups the next couple of days, but dinner will be served at 7:00 o'clock."

Their room was small but cozy—windows with an eastern view, a couple of alpine photos on the walls, and a double-bed. "We have a couple of hours before dinner," he said. "What would you like to do?"

"I know what you'd like to do," she replied. Soon they were in bed, undressed. "Wait," Mae said, "Can you check the room for cameras?"

"Cameras?"

"You know, hidden cameras. Some places they do that sort of thing. I don't want to be in somebody's private porno film."

Suddenly suspicious, he pulled back on his underwear. It was tricky because he'd already gotten hard, though the thought of cameras helped him go limp pretty quick. He went over the room methodically, checking especially the photos for peepholes and the lamps for hidden microphones, the smoke detector in the ceiling for a camera eye. As he dropped his underwear once again, it got tangled around his ankles and he tumbled onto the bed as he tried to extricate himself. He assured Mae it was safe as he slid under the sheet. Big Brother wasn't watching them.

They removed their glasses—hers with the big tortoise-shelled rims, seventies style. Their passion waxed to the full, and they had marital sex. They were still shy of each other's bodies. He felt like he was fumbling into love, but at least this time he remembered to take off his socks.

After, they lay tangled together for some moments before Mae said, "It's hot, and I'm sleepy now. Why don't you roll over and we'll have a nap before dinner?" But he didn't sleep. He listened to Mae's breathing as she slid into slumber, watched her chest rise and fall, longed to touch her breasts again, but resisted. I've just had sex with a married woman, he thought. I'm a married man having sex with a married woman. Of course, she's my wife, so it's not adultery. Then why does it feel illicit in some strange way, sex with a pregnant married woman? Is it this hotel room? We've consecrated our marriage; we've christened this bed. Of course, we don't have our own bed yet. He looked forward to consecrating it when they did. He studied the ceiling's woodwork, looking for patterns and messages in the knots.

It was just that morning they had eloped, but it felt worlds away, a different lifetime. Once they'd decided to do a runner, they plotted their escape. His friend Perry and her friend Nora would stand up with them, and Perry would lend them his car. They'd kept their siblings out of it, thinking not just of loose lips but of future blame from their parents. Evan researched the legal requirements; together, he and Mae snuck away to get the license. Mae remembered that Nora's family went every winter on a ski holiday to the Talisman; Nora could make the necessary arrangements for their post-elopement hideaway. The few weeks of carrying around these secrets—of Mae's pregnancy, of their elopement plot—made Evan feel like a stranger in his own skin, jumpy.

That jumpiness reached pitch point the night before they eloped. He and Mae had been talking for more than an hour on the phone, until his dad's impatient looks and curt complaints told Evan it was time to get off. He'd never fully gotten used to these almost nightly calls with Mae once they started going steady. Before, he'd never had a phone call lasting more than a couple of minutes, but for months they had been pouring words into each other's ears until they said goodnight.

After hanging up the phone, Evan had lain in bed staring at the ceiling for an hour or more, thoughts piling on top of each other, a weight transferred to his chest—the night hag, a succubus. When he finally slept he dreamt he and Mae never made it to the courthouse, intercepted by her dad and a platoon of his army buddies, all outfitted with bayonet-tipped rifles. They marched Evan and Mae through Hookerville—the street lined with prostitutes, pimps, police, and johns, like a parade—to the Western Fairgrounds, where crowds were screaming on the rides and playing carnival games. In the stadium, Billy Graham was waiting for them. He called them little lost lambs as he began the ceremony. Mae was now wearing a white dress so puffy it was like a large, three-tiered wedding cake, he a neon-blue tux with wide lapels, a baby-blue shirt with frills falling down like a waterfall, super-wide bellbottom pants, and blue suede platform shoes. He heard a voice like his mother's yell out that

Mae shouldn't be wearing white—she was a Jezebel. When Billy Graham asked whether anyone objected, Mae's former boyfriend Brad Reynard jumped up and yelled that his penis was one inch longer than Evan's, so Evan had no business marrying Mae; he'd never keep her satisfied. The crowd—mostly strangers but also filled with family and fellow students and teachers—laughed uproariously and pointed at Evan with one hand, gripping their groins with the other. Strangely, that was the end of the ceremony—no vows, no rings, no kisses. He and Mae were marched to the National Travelers Motel for the reception, right beside the Beef Baron strip club. As he and Mae sat alone on low stools at the head table, they wore dunce caps. Strippers pranced into the reception hall and began performing table dances. Some guests were scandalized, others mesmerized. Evan awoke in a sweat, hand around his penis, his groin soiled from what had turned into a wet dream.

That morning after their parents had gone to work, he and Mae left behind notes. He wasn't sure what Mae's said, but his read *Dear Mom and Dad, I'm madly in love with Mae. Call me crazy, but we're getting married this morning. Don't worry about us, though. We're going away for a few days to celebrate. Be back Thursday night or Friday at the latest. Love, your normally sensible son Evan. P.S. I got Mae pregnant. You're going to be grandparents. Congrats, Oma and Opa! P.P.S. Don't worry, I'm still going to university in September.* He was counting on their not reading this note until he and Mae were fully married and hiding out at the Talisman, where no one could change their minds or undo a legally binding and consummated ceremony.

The civil ceremony was a quick affair in the old courthouse, within one of its gothic rooms before a justice who blandly fed them their vows, like he'd seen it all before. It hardly seemed worth it for Evan to put on his light-blue Sunday suit, Mae her yellow sundress with the sunflower belt at her waist. Her dress made him think of butter. They'd stopped at the downtown market for a bouquet of flowers; their clothes and these flowers seemed the only splash of color in the room—two pots of fake red geraniums not to be counted—as he and Mae promised to love each other until death put a kibosh on the whole affair. They picked up their signed and sealed marriage certificate from a clerk wearing cats-eye glasses on a string around her neck. After quick and teary but somewhat sheepish hugs with Perry and Nora, they headed north out of London. He'd looked in the rearview mirror virtually all the way to Beaver Valley.

When Mae woke from her nap, they made love again—this time more slowly. They were sore when they showered together, gently washing each other and kissing in the somewhat weak stream of water. When they were done drying each other, he put on his new black boxers with the hearts on them. They made him feel almost sexy when Mae called him "lover boy" in response. He retrieved a small gift box from his luggage and presented it to her. She opened it and pulled out a bird, a glass bluebird of happiness. As she studied it, she said simply, "Thank you. It's beautiful." She hugged him, a somewhat fierce, hard hug that compressed his rib cage.

Before they entered the dining room, he surveyed it to make sure it was safe—no father-in-law waiting to force-feed him humble pie, or something worse. He gave Mae the all-clear. They found the room sparsely filled—mainly middle-aged couples still in their golf togs after a round. There was one family with two children, girls who looked to be eight to ten. They were still in their bathing suits, their hair damp. Their parents were in shorts and T-shirts, looking distracted and somewhat morose. Evan had put his wedding suit back on, Mae her sunflower dress. He felt overdressed, out of place for this first formal meal as husband and wife. The hostess led them to a table near an elderly couple, who were intently studying their menus. The man, crowned with a rich headful of grey hair with yellow streaks that looked like lightning bolts, wore a bright blue-and-yellow checkered sport coat with a yellow ascot at his neck, a bright blue shirt, yellow slacks, and white loafers. The woman looked like a gypsy to Evan—long dark gray hair, black blouse with plunging neckline revealing deeply tanned and wrinkled cleavage, a colorful skirt in peacock design flowing to the floor, rings on both hands, large hoops in her ears, bright silver necklaces, bangles on her wrists. Evan imagined them a deposed king and queen of some small eastern European country.

"Let's order something special," Mae said as they studied the menu. "To celebrate. It's not every day we elope." He glanced at the couple to see if they were listening. They gave no sign of having heard.

Mae chose barbecued salmon and scallops, he rainbow trout—a dish he associated with northern rivers, outdoor life, cottage country, adult leisure. These felt like adult meals—serious eating, healthy. He was only mildly regretting his choice as he carefully pulled apart the flesh to avoid the sharp bones—a choking hazard his mother so worried about she rarely cooked fish, and when she did she carefully picked out the bones for him and his brother and sister. There were awkward silences as he and Mae chewed. He glanced at her and then out the picture window overlooking the green ski slope. He watched cumulus clouds drift to the east, realizing he was still shy and nervous of her, in spite of how they spent the afternoon, in spite of her being three months pregnant. He suspected he might always feel this way before her.

He was lifting a fork full of peas to his mouth, concentrating on keeping the pile of little green globes balanced on the four stainless steel tines, when he saw out of the corner of his eye movement beneath the table of the regal couple near them. The man had removed his loafers, the woman her sandals. They were gently rubbing each other's feet and calves. Startled, Evan spilled the peas into his lap and onto the floor. What he was witnessing felt unbearably intimate. As his empty fork hovered, he turned to Mae. She practically choked on a mouthful of salmon, pulled her napkin to her face, and struggled not to laugh behind it. He began fishing the peas out of his lap back onto his plate. He looked around. All the other diners were focused on their own meals, their own company. They hadn't noticed his dining disaster. The elderly couple continued to eat their soup as if nothing was happening beneath their table. Perhaps they didn't realize their tablecloth didn't reach the floor on that side. Evan caught them for one instant looking up from their soup spoons. He was sure their eyes were twinkling. He leaned over to discreetly pick up the peas on the floor and deposit them in his napkin. One had rolled all the way under the elderly couple's table. They continued playing footsie, oblivious to the pea. Evan couldn't take his eyes off it, afraid one of them would squish it. He watched the gentleman's socked foot travel up to the woman's thigh, her skirt riding up to expose her tanned legs. He bolted upright before he saw more. After the man dabbed his napkin on his lips, he leaned towards Evan, winked, and said confidentially, "You should have seen us before this damn arthritis set in. Quite the show then."

Evan smiled weakly in reply and turned to Mae. When she looked at him quizzically, he slipped off his shoe, began rubbing her calf, and nodded his head in the couple's direction. After a moment, her face filled with understanding and she glanced at them stealthily. Guarding the side of her mouth with her napkin, she whispered, "That's so sweet, at their age." She took off her own shoe, and began rubbing his calf.

What had he just witnessed? And what was happening now? Feeling Mae's stockinged foot slipped under his pant leg, he sensed he would never get enough of Mae, of such touch, of such love. This is folly, he thought. Pure folly. Maybe even something greater—lunacy. We're just a couple of lunatics. They carried the feeling back to their room when their meal was done.

~

The next morning, sunlight filled their eastern windows when they finally opened the curtains. On alert, Evan did a quick survey of the parking lot—no Happy Hearth van. Safe for now. The elopement night over, their plan was to fill this day with honeymoon activities, all the clichés they could think of—tennis and golf and hiking in the woods, lounging by the pool with fruity drinks. They were sure that's what newlyweds did, and why shouldn't they? They had an itinerary, and he was determined they'd stick to it.

After breakfast, they donned their gym clothes—still bearing the logo of the WLM-KSS Lions. When their school teams lost, which they often did, their opponents would call them the WLM-KSS Lambs, then baa loudly, mockingly. He and Mae picked up rackets and balls from the rec office and headed to the tennis courts. The elderly couple from last night were already there, outfitted for Wimbledon, though Evan noted the man continued to sport a cravat, union jack design this morning. The couple paused in their play to greet Evan and Mae warmly, and now introduced themselves as the Laurences, Larry and Caroline Laurence. Laurence Laurence, thought Evan, how odd. As if in reply, Larry said, "Yes, I know it's a strange name—a joke in my family. I'm actually the third Laurence Laurence in a row." Caroline added, "It's so strange I simply call him L." With that, the Laurences returned to their game. They played a lively match that belied their age, while Evan and Mae chased balls they'd hit way out of bounds or into the net. They repeatedly apologized to the Laurences when shots strayed into their neighbours' court. After a half hour of hacking and running, he and Mae had worked themselves into a sweaty lather, while the Laurences still looked fresh. When they asked him and Mae if they'd like to play doubles, Evan declined the invite, faking a cramp in his thigh as he hobbled off the court. Larry replied, "You young folks need to learn to pace yourself, get a good night's rest." Larry and Caroline chuckled and waved their rackets before starting a new game.

Evan and Mae collapsed on the bed in their room for a half hour. He was mildly disappointed—their first honeymoon failure. Once they'd recovered, though, they changed into jeans and T-shirts, returned their tennis rackets, and picked up golf clubs. It was quiet on the links, since it was still fairly early on a midweek morning. He'd seen golf on TV and thought it didn't look too hard. He secretly believed he'd be good at it. It was all about math and physics, his specialties. They took a few practice swings at the first hole, then teed up. When Mae hit the ball, it dribbled onto the fairway. He laughed and she told him to shut up. When he approached his ball, he imitated the posture of the pros he'd seen on TV. His first swing was all air, no contact; he did a pirouette, pulled around by the momentum of the club. Mae laughed and said, "That was God." Evan looked around to see if anybody had been watching. And there they were, the Laurences. He quickly lined up beside the ball again and took another swing. The ball dribbled off the tee onto the fairway at an odd angle—a slice he thought it was called. He and Mae grabbed their bags and headed down the fairway before the Laurences arrived.

The next twenty minutes he and Mae spent hacking at their balls, creating divots, trying different clubs, moving along at the pace of ten or twenty yards per swing. To speed things up, they started hitting their balls at the same time. With each whack, they looked back to see more couples and foursomes arriving at the first tee. When he and Mae deposited their balls in a creek that crossed the fairway before the first green, they'd had enough. Embarrassed, they retreated from the fairway, making way for the real duffers. As they walked back up to the lodge, they watched Larry and Caroline launch straight and true drives across the creek. When the couples passed each other, Evan noticed that the Laurences were wearing polo shirts and caps with golden bear logos, Larry a golden bear cravat. The clubs they were pulling carried the Jack Nicklaus signature, too. "Happy to give you a few pointers later," Caroline offered. "I was a club pro before I retired."

"Thanks," Mae replied. "But we're only here for another day. I think you'd be wasting your time on us."

Evan and Mae passed a foursome of men next up at the first tee. One smart aleck quipped, "There's a second course out by the pool you kids might want to try. Mini putt-putt. More your speed, by the looks of your game." His partners chuckled at the joke. They appeared to be in their thirties, clean-shaven and short-haired, beginning to develop a slightly paunchy look in their bright shirts and checked pants. Likely businessmen, Evan thought. Capitalist pigs.

He smiled in return and said, "Thanks. We'll check it out." But he was red in the face. *You kids*, the guy said. Kids are baby goats, Evan thought. It was a language lesson his dad gave him any time he used the word to mean children.

"Pricks," Mae said as they headed back to the lodge. "Big mouths and tiny dicks, that bunch."

They flopped on the bed back in their room. "We were bad," he said. "Very bad. Embarrassingly bad. Strike two on our honeymoon itinerary. Golf is definitely not our game."

"If you ever take it up like those jerks and turn me into a golf widow, I'll kill you. First, I'll divorce you, then I'll kill you." They were married now. *Divorce* had suddenly become an important word in their vocabulary. *Murder*, too.

This time, they rested for more than an hour before they roused themselves for the third event on their honeymoon itinerary—a hike through the wonders of nature. By then, it was getting close to noon, and they soon discovered their hike was a bad idea. Not only that, but they'd taken the hilltop trail, hoping to reward their effort with a breathtaking view. Mae had brought her camera and was hoping to chronicle their life together from its very start. But they were out of breath half way up, sweaty and hungry, resting on a log. Evan heard someone coming up the trail. He feared it was Mae's dad and prepared to hide behind the log, inside it if it was hollow. His father-in-law's spies might be anywhere and everywhere. Who did it turn out to be? Why, Larry and Caroline Laurence, wearing hiking outfits and boots, sporting walking sticks in their hands and binoculars around their necks, smelling potently of bug spray. Larry wore a camo cravat. Was he ex-military? An old army buddy of Mae's dad sent as an advance scout to locate Evan and Mae? From under floppy hats, the Laurences greeted them. "Onward and upward," Larry encouraged them, in the tone of a high school coach. "There's no better feeling than reaching the summit and surveying the world you've conquered."

How many summits had this super couple reached? "We're right behind you," Evan replied. As the Laurences continued up the trail, Evan and Mae slapped mosquitos biting their necks and arms and legs. When the Laurences were out of sight, he turned to Mae and asked, "Ready to turn back?"

"Damn right," she replied. "The only summit I'm ready to conquer is a pool-side lounge chair."

They spent lunch scratching their mosquito bites, then donned their swimsuits and hit the pool. The only people there when they first arrived were the couple with the two girls. Evan and Mae were self-conscious, Mae in her leopard-print one-piece and he in his too-tight tiger-stripe trunks, a big-cat obsession from his days eating Frosted Flakes for breakfast. Tony the Tiger was his childhood hero. His trunk and legs were completely white, the only tanned skin his arms and neck from his summer job at a nursery.

They splashed about in the pool for a respectable amount of time. When the girls asked Mae to play Frisbee, Evan did a few cannonballs off the diving board before drying off and sunning on a lounger. This is more like it, he thought, as he watched Mae toss the Frisbee to the girls, whose parents seemed just as preoccupied and morose as at dinner the night before. Was this what married-with-children looked like? he wondered. Mae had one of these creatures growing inside her, and she wanted more. He was sure he and Mae would never become as distant as this couple appeared, as separate. Could they?

"Honey, I'm going to get us drinks," he said to Mae. *Honey*, how domestic the word felt in his mouth, how sweetly married it sounded.

"No alcohol for me," Mae replied, adding "Honey" at the end. Was that a slight note of mockery he heard in her voice?

He chose a Shirley Temple for Mae. For himself, he went crazy and ordered a Margarita. Except on a school trip where he tried whiskey and got sick, he'd never had more than a beer—and that was just once when he was sixteen working for a summer on a dairy farm. When he got back with the drinks, Mae was stretched out on a lounger, soaking up the sun. "This is more like it," she said as she sipped her Shirley Temple.

"That's what I thought," he replied. "See, now that we're married we think exactly the same thoughts. Pretty soon we'll have just one brain between the two of us." His drink tasted so fruity, he downed it too fast. Right away, he started to feel light-headed, as if he was beginning to float.

"Didn't they ask to see your ID?"

"Nope. I must look very mature."

"In your case, looks are deceiving. You know you're breaking the law."

"That law doesn't apply to us married men."

While they were dozing in the afternoon heat, sufficiently lathered in sunscreen, they heard a couple of loud splashes. When Evan opened his eyes, it was to see the Laurences swimming laps, goggles and caps on. This time, Larry wasn't wearing a cravat. Perhaps he couldn't find a waterproof one. "I'm getting worried," Evan said to Mae. "Do you think they're stalking us? Maybe they're spies sent by your dad."

"Don't worry so much. You'll make yourself sick."

At that moment, Annie the desk clerk came out to the pool carrying a tray. She stopped beside Evan and Mae, blocking the sun. "Good news, newlyweds," she said loudly. "Here are your complimentary honeymoon drinks." She placed another Shirley Temple and Margarita on the table beside them. "And I'm happy to inform you that you're receiving a free upgrade to the bridal suite. As we speak, your luggage is being moved. Here's the key to paradise, young lovers." With that, she winked and retreated to her post.

"Your honeymoon!" It was the two girls, who swam over to the side of the pool after hearing Annie use the word. "That's so romantic," said one, with her hands over her heart. "Tell us all about the wedding," said the other.

"We didn't actually have a wedding," Mae replied. "We eloped. Just yesterday." She had to explain to the girls what eloping was and how she and Evan had gone about doing it. As he listened, he noticed that the girls' parents appeared to be growing concerned, even alarmed at the explanation. Possibly they were afraid Mae was putting ideas in their heads. When they told the girls it was time to get out of the pool, their daughters raised a stink, attracting the attention of the Laurences in their laps. They swam over to the side and asked to be filled in.

"Young love," Larry sighed. "Is there anything more beautiful, anything filled with more *joie de vivre*, as they say in gay Paris." He pronounced it pear-ee. "Just a couple of love birds, hiding out at the Talisman."

"I knew something was up with you two. I remember exactly what it felt like with L here when we first fell in love." Caroline's smile was knowing. "We couldn't keep our hands off each other, could we L? Remember that first night in Paris…."

"Such *sensualité*, such *passion*. That's the Paris effect," Larry raved. "That's Paris, Ontario, of course. We couldn't afford to honeymoon in France."

"Girls, out of the pool, now!" It was the alarmed mother, clearly seeking to avert revelations about the Laurences' sex life, or perhaps she was troubled by their use of the French language. After the family left, Caroline continued, "She's rather uptight, isn't she? Puritanical, even. Nothing wrong with cultivating a healthy understanding of sex among children." She went on to regale Evan and Mae with tales of Laurentian sexual adventures at various Paris, Ontario landmarks, where they honeymooned four decades earlier. Larry Laurence III was smiling and getting misty-eyed as he listened. When Caroline was finished, he sighed, "Damn this arthritis! It's getting harder and harder to perform such amorous feats. Just yesterday—"

Caroline interrupted. "L, these young lovebirds don't need to hear about that. We don't want to give them any ideas. They might try it themselves and get injured." She added, "You two enjoy that honeymoon suite. L, be a dear and get me my towel." Looking straight at Evan and Mae, she confided, "We need to go back to our room and have a 'nap' before dinner." Her eyes were full of mischief as she climbed the ladder out of the pool and sashayed around to where Larry had retrieved their towels.

Left alone, Evan and Mae sat quietly for some moments. Mae spoke first. "Wow, I'm trying to get those images out of my head, but it's not working."

"Me too," he replied. "Mind you, they must be doing something right. They've been married for forty years." He'd made a mental list of the sites and positions she'd described. Perhaps one day he'd suggest them to Mae. It couldn't hurt, but they would need to do some fitness training first.

In unison, they sipped their fruity drinks. His second Margarita was giving him a significant buzz. He was sure now he was floating, floating to Margaritaville. It was mid-afternoon, and the bright sunlight reflecting off the pool water, along with the tequila, was giving the world a golden glow in which he believed it impossible his father-in-law would ever find him, in which his father-in-law was no longer real. After another half hour of basking, he said to Mae, "Let's go check out this honeymoon suite. Aren't you curious?"

"It's probably just got a king-sized bed. I wouldn't get your hopes up." She rose from the lounger, wrapped her towel around herself, and slipped on her flip-flops.

The bridal suite was on the west side of the resort, top floor, overlooking the ski hill. In his tipsy state, Evan felt like he'd floated up to it. As Mae unlocked the suite, he noticed that the windows were covered in thick curtains. When he mentioned this to Mae, she took a quick look and said they were called black-out curtains. He offered to carry her across the threshold, but she declined it, given his current state, saying she didn't want to end up sitting for hours in the Emergency room of some unfamiliar hospital. When she flipped on the light switch, the room

took on a reddish glow. They discovered that one of the lamps had a red
bulb in it. The room felt like the inside of a body. In the center the room
was furnished with a large heart-shaped bed, covered with deep red bedding, including silk sheets and pillows in various shapes and sizes, some
elaborately fringed. The walls were papered with a psychedelic design—
one he imagined might be found in a Playboy Club. On the walls were
large photos of blonde ski bunnies, each one of them topless, along with
blond men, also topless, to show off their hairless, highly muscled torsos.
Evan imagined they were the Swedish ski team.

Facing the bed was a large TV, the largest he'd ever seen. When he
turned it on, the first thing the screen showed was adult movies for rent.
He quickly snapped it off. When he opened the top drawer to the TV
cabinet, he saw that management had supplied a library of adult magazines for the stimulation and entertainment of newlyweds. He was embarrassed but also titillated, so much so that he slammed the drawer. He
gave Mae a running commentary on what he was finding as she herself
surveyed the room. When he opened the bottom drawer, he was startled
to find a video camera, a tripod, and blank tapes. He pulled out a set of
instructions and a cost list for newlyweds to memorialize the consumma-
tion of their marriage, whether they chose to do an amateur video or hire
the services of a professional videographer. When he showed Mae the
equipment, she said, "Not on your life," and added, "Come check out the
fridge." She picked up a sheet and read off the foods provided, all of them
considered aphrodisiacs. With each one she named, she located it in the
fridge or in the cupboard above it: chocolate and oysters, of course, but
also watermelon slices and strawberries, figs and chili peppers. A bottle
of champagne was chilling in an ice bucket on the counter.

Through an open door past Mae he saw the bathroom, red-tiled
with a hot-pink heart-shaped tub the main attraction. "Look at this," he
said, taking Mae by the hand into this holy of holies. His and hers plush
robes, jet black, hung on hooks. On the vanity counter between the double sinks sat what looked like a large fertility god with an enormous penis
stiff at attention; Evan had never seen such woody wood on a wooden
statue. It could be useful for hanging a face cloth or storing an extra roll of
toilet paper, he thought. To complement the fertility god, both sinks had
a ceramic Venus-on-a-clamshell soap dish—soft pinks and flesh tones
of the naked goddess contrasting the woody god's walnut hue. Evan and
Mae looked at each other in companion heart-shaped mirrors above the
sinks. In the corner of the counter sat a tray full of bottles in purples and

blues, lotions and oils at phallic attention. "I wonder," he said, "if there's any surface of this room where someone hasn't had sex."

Mae surveyed the room. "Not likely," she replied. "I hope they disinfect the room after each couple." Slightly stunned, they returned to the bedroom, which to Evan was taking on the feel of a giant womb, the bathroom a giant vagina. Side by side, they sat on the bed, slipping slightly on the slick covering.

He noticed a basket on the nearest night table. When he looked closer, he saw it was filled with condoms of all varieties and sizes. Too little, too late, he thought, as he returned the basket to its spot. "I guess we won't be needing these." He opened the drawer, naively expecting to find a Gideons Bible. Unsteady, he was feeling the need to find his moral footing again, or maybe to read to Mae from the Song of Songs, those verses about twin fawns and grape clusters and pomegranates. (He'd never seen pomegranates. Maybe he would substitute them with apples when he read that verse.) What he pulled out of the drawer instead of the Bible was a book called *The Kama Sutra*. On the cover, a man and a woman who appeared to be Indian lay in each other's arms and looked off in the distance. How exotic, he thought. Maybe it was like a Hindu Bible. He flipped it open to a page in the middle. "Whoa!" he said, then slammed the book shut.

"What?" Mae said. "Let me see." When he passed her the book, she began flipping the pages. "I've heard of books like this. Like *The Joy of Sex*. My mom and dad have a copy in their bedroom."

"Your parents have sex?"

"Very funny."

"Your dad's ex-army. He probably does it with military precision, like a machine gun."

Mae paused at a page with a particularly complicated-looking position. As she turned the page sideways, she asked, "How do they do that? Wouldn't something get broken?"

"I didn't know this was what grown-ups got up to." He looked over to the other night table. "I wonder what surprise we'll find over here." He crawled across the slippery bedding and piles of pillows to pull open the drawer. Inside, he found a range of odd looking gadgets, each sealed in plastic with the word "sterilized" stamped on the package. "Look," he said as he pulled one out, "a massager."

When Mae finally pulled herself away from the page in front of her, she said, "Uh, that's not exactly a massager, at least not the kind you think."

"No, then what is it?"

"A vibrator."

"A vibrator? What does it vibrate?"

"You know."

"No, I don't know."

"You know. Down there, for a woman. Her va-gee-gee."

"Va-gee-gee? Ohhhhh." The light went on and he dropped the vibrator on the bed. He looked further into the drawer and tried to imagine what services the various tools performed, matching tool to possible body part. At the bottom, he found a set of furry handcuffs. He thought of his paranoia about the cops chasing them down, catching them in this honeymoon suite—a Las Vegas LSD hallucination—and dragging them back to face the father-in-law music. He slid off the bed to engage the lock-bolt and put on the chain. He found a chair, propped it under the door knob, and returned to the bed. Maybe he and Mae could handcuff themselves to the headboard, like protesters. When he looked for a likely spot, he found instead a coin slot beside a knob. The sign above it said, "Magic Fingers Vibrating Bed." And above the sign he noticed for the first time a large art print. He could tell from the style that it was a reproduction of a page from *The Kama Sutra*. Mid-coitus, the man and the woman seemed to be looking out at Evan, so much as to say, "Think you're a big enough man to try this, lover boy?"

"I think we should get this book," Mae said as she continued turning pages, rotating them sideways every once in a while. "Maybe it's complimentary with the room. You should ask Annie at the front desk." Mae dropped the book abruptly in her lap. "I bet this room is filled with hidden cameras and microphones. I bet some of those movies you can rent were made right here in this room. We're going to have to do a thorough sweep, or I won't be able to sleep here, let alone try out some of these positions."

Evan started surveying the room, eventually looking up at the ceiling. For the first time, he noticed above the bed the mirror, heart-shaped and as large as the bed itself. Then he noticed the large rectangle of mirror above the sofa, remembered the mirrors in the bathroom, including the mirror tiles by the hot-pink heart-shaped tub with the water jets. He thought about the video camera, the oversized TV like a large electronic altar, the magazines. Did people really want to watch themselves while they were doing it? Catch every angle? Record every move, every moan and groan? Images multiplied in a hall of mirrors?

To assure Mae the room was safe, he went around it twice. He removed the chair under the door knob and used it to make sure there was nothing fishy in the ceiling, either. Mae was studying *The Kama Sutra* the whole time. "That's enough book learning," she said. "Let's try out this upgraded bed." He quickly wedged the chair back under the door knob.

As he watched her remove her leopard-print swimsuit and slide under the sheets, he growled like a tiger, then dropped his own suit around his ankles. "Just a minute," he said. He found his pants and searched the pockets for some change. He put a pile of quarters on the bedside table and fed four into the Magic Fingers. The bed started vibrating as he too slid between the sheets and snuggled up to Mae. "Kama Sutra," she whispered, her breath like warm feathers on his face. "Kama Sutra," he whispered in reply. They were two young lovers inside a vibrating silk sheet sandwich. As they began, she gave him instructions. The problem was, between the silk sheets, the vibrating bed, and the Margaritas, they had trouble keeping their balance and connecting. Instead, they slid around on the heart and collapsed in a tangle of limbs. It took some serious coordination and concentration to finish.

After, they lay together for a few moments facing each other. All he wanted to do was touch her hair, her face, her lips as they caught their breath. When Mae rolled over to nap, he lay on his back looking up at their image in the heart mirror. He remembered from Biology class the diagram of the heart. Mae's head lay on the right atrium, her body on the right ventricle; his head and body the left atrium and ventricle. He remembered the diagram was confusing because left was right and right was left; it showed the heart from the front, not looking out from the heart-owner's chest. Now, the mirror reversed the image so that he could see the looking-out image of the heart.

Here he was, an eighteen-year-old kid, lying on a heart-shaped bed with a girl who just yesterday was his girlfriend, his steady, now his wife, he her husband—in a room that felt like a womb. A heart in a womb, such strange physiology. Like the heart growing in Mac's womb, their child's heart. He thought about *The Kama Sutra*, about Mae's instructions and the concentration and coordination he needed to complete them. He was getting a sense that he had husbandly duties, obligations to perform, a wife to keep satisfied. His own satisfaction wasn't the only concern, it turned out, not by a long shot. He didn't know if he was up to it.

He studied in the mirror above the bed his ribby chest and his mussed up hair, before turning toward Mae. He looked at her neck, the curve of her bare back, the shape of her buttocks beneath the sheets. She was inches away but far off in sleep. His chest constricted. His ribs ached with what he saw, what he felt. He never knew happiness was this painful.

When Mae awoke, they bathed in the heart-shaped tub before getting dressed for dinner. They'd contemplated staying in their room and simply nibbling on aphrodisiacs, but decided they needed a real dinner, given their honeymoon itinerary workout. It turned out one of the phallic-looking bottles on the bathroom counter was bubble bath, so they'd filled the tub. Mountains of bubbles overflowed onto the floor when they tried out the jets. They were wearing wigs and beards of bubbles when he said, "I could get used to this honeymoon lifestyle."

"Yeah, but it can't last forever."

"Did you know that once upon a time people thought honeymoons were dangerous for women? It's true. I read about it in a book. Thought I should know what we were getting into. Doctors were worried the honeymoon would be too hard on the woman, given her natural frailty, and I think the morality police frowned on it because of its focus on the woman's sexual initiation."

"Sounds like a bunch of sexist BS to me. Remember on our first date—that bike ride—you told me people once thought it was dangerous for women to ride bicycles for similar reasons?"

"And look how that bike ride turned out."

Mae splashed water and bubbles in his face. "I don't remember ever doing it on a bike. More of that Adam blaming Eve shit. Typical."

"Hey, don't kill the messenger," he replied. "The original reason it was called a honeymoon is also a bit strange. It might have to do with the queen honey bee hanging out with the drones for a month after she's born, collecting a lifetime's worth of sperm from them before returning home to spend the rest of her life laying eggs. Or it might have meant the month after the wedding—you know, a lunar cycle, when the newlyweds were the most affectionate and loving and happy—the waxing of the honey moon—followed by the waning of those feelings into normal married life."

"I wish you wouldn't research everything. Besides making you sound like a nerd—which you are—it kind of spoils things." She put a large pile of suds on his head.

"It's just a theory," he replied, blowing bubbles at her off his palm. "It isn't fate. Our lives don't have to turn out that way." For him, their love was waxing right now, and he couldn't yet imagine its waning. "I believe that. That's why I got you a bluebird of happiness—a promise between us." He didn't realize he was making promises he couldn't possibly keep. He didn't yet know that their love would wane, or that it would wax and wane again and again over the years.

"It's been lovely, this honeymoon," she said. "But you know we have to go back, and that's not going to be a holiday."

"Why go back? Why can't we just keep going, make our life somewhere else?"

"We can't run forever. Eloping is one thing; disappearing is another. Besides, my dad would eventually track us down. Better to face the music."

"More like a court martial, I think."

"Don't worry. They don't do firing squads anymore."

When they went down to dinner that evening, they dressed casually. He felt like himself again. But when they entered the dining room, they were surprised to see balloon bouquets of red and pink hearts, flowers on every table, paper ribbons running between the ceiling lamps. They were even more surprised—and confused—to see a couple of home-made banners strung up inside the entrance. "Congratulations on Tying the Knot!" read one, the other "Happy Anniversary!"

Annie greeted them, while the rest of the diners stood and applauded. "You didn't think I would keep your secret, did you? We couldn't let you love birds run off without a proper party."

"But happy anniversary?" Mae asked.

"Oh, it's a double celebration," Annie replied. "The Laurences happen to be celebrating their fortieth anniversary this week, can you believe it? They're still like newlyweds." The Laurences were waving at Evan and Mae, and waving them over. Together, they'd sit at the party table, the table of honour. Larry and Caroline were already wearing party hats. When Evan and Mae arrived at the table, the Laurences hugged them and gave them cheek kisses—both sides—something very new for Evan, very Parisian. Larry was wearing a white cravat with a pattern of small red hearts on it. There were party hats for Evan and Mae, as well. The elastic felt tight beneath Evan's chin, and he couldn't help feeling self-conscious in his cone-shaped party hat. It felt more like a dunce cap, the table they were at more like the corner of a school room.

Soon, though, they were listening to Larry and Caroline talk about their travels—not just to Paris, Ontario, but to other towns named after English and European cities. There was London, of course, Evan and Mae's hometown. But there was also Stratford and Norwich here in Ontario, along with dozens of other places, including a small town with the lovely name of Windermere. There were Wembley and Keswick, Alberta; Derby and New Brighton, British Columbia; Lancaster and Wickham, New Brunswick; Penzance, Saskatchewan. The list went on and on. They talked about their travels from one end of Nova Scotia to the other, connecting virtually every city, town, and hamlet to some place in Britain. "What a province!" they said in conclusion. "What a country!"

During dinner, there was the tinkling of glasses, and calls for the couples to kiss. After dinner, there was even cake to cut, and the couples had their picture taken together with their hands on the knife, Mae and Caroline in the middle, Evan and Larry on the outside. Eventually the tables were shoved aside and Annie brought in a boom-box and a handful of tapes. She popped in Elvis Presley, and the young and old lovers were clapped and hooted onto the floor as Elvis sang about fools falling in love. While the Laurences danced smoothly and elegantly, Evan turned Mae around in a circle with his awkward, Dutch Calvinist hips. He was a fool, and he knew it, but everyone was clapping anyway. When he took a rest, he watched Mae dance with the two girls from the swimming pool. He felt his face shaped into a silly grin at the sight.

But Annie had another surprise after an hour of dancing, when the sun had set and the moon was up. It was movie night at the Talisman, and they were showing the classic film *Bringing Up Baby*, starring Cary Grant and Katharine Hepburn. The title gave Evan a jolt. Did they know somehow that Mae was pregnant? But no, it turned out Baby was a tame leopard. "Such a great film," Caroline said as it opened, "L and I just love screwball comedies, and this is one of our favorites." Screwball comedies? Evan had never heard the term, but he sat beside Mae, holding her hand to start, then placing his arm around her shoulder. Soon they were laughing at the misadventures and confusions and zany antics of David Hurley in search of that intercostal clavicle for his Brontosaurus and Susan Vance in search of David, both of them in search of the tame Baby when they mistakenly find a wild leopard from the circus. What a circus the whole movie was. He and Mae and everyone together, even the parents of the two girls, laughed till it hurt, and then laughed some more.

After, when the lights came back on and Evan was catching his breath and wiping his eyes, he thought this too was happiness, laughing so hard it hurt and squeezing drops onto your cheeks and turning to your lover to share it all. To love Mae and Susan Vance and Katharine Hepburn all at the same time. To find yourself in the middle of a farce, to mistake wild leopards for tame ones, to be in search of one thing—a fossil bone—and find something else unexpected—a woman—that turns out to be exactly what you needed in the first place.

Evan and Mae talked about the movie all the way back to the honeymoon suite. As they paused before the door, he said, "Look, in the sky, it's the honey moon." And it was—a small white disk reflecting the sun's light over the landscape and onto the threshold where they stood together. They carried the light and the laughter into the room and into the bed when they climbed between the sheets.

"I think we should watch more of those screwball comedies." It was the next morning. He and Mae had checked out of the Talisman, and they were in their borrowed 1972 Chevy Nova heading back to London, heading back to face the music—and he was sure it wasn't going to be an Elvis song, except maybe "Jailhouse Rock." On the dash, Mae had placed her bluebird of happiness, facing forward to the road ahead.

"So far, our marriage is a bit of a screwball comedy," she replied. "So why not?"

Inside their luggage sat a snow globe wrapped in tissue paper. They'd picked it up from the gift shop before leaving. In the globe was a miniature horse-drawn sleigh with a miniature family travelling along a snow-covered road through a wood. In the background of the scene beyond the forest was a ski hill with tiny skiers riding the lift and others descending the slope. Shaken, the globe turned into a winter wonderland—or a blizzard. It depended on how vigorously things were stirred up. The base read simply "Talisman."

They'd also stowed *The Kama Sutra* in their luggage. They said to each other they were just borrowing it for now. They were sure Annie wouldn't mind. But maybe it was the latest transgression in their life of crime, two little lambs living like Bonnie and Clyde, waiting for the hail of bullets. Evan kept checking his rearview mirror, worried that Annie might have sent the local sheriff after them to retrieve the book and demand payment for that complimentary upgrade to the bridal suite.

The rain began to fall as they drove back through Flesherton. He was beginning to think they were safely away with their stolen sex manual when Mae said abruptly, "Pull over. Now!" He looked ahead and checked his mirrors, afraid. But he responded to her urgency by braking to a quick stop on the gravel shoulder. Mae opened the door and began vomiting. He put the car in park, searched the glove box for some tissues, and found only a crumpled napkin. When she'd finished, she sat up and pulled the door shut. She looked pale. Her face and hair were wet from the rain, or possibly from sweat brought on by her retching. She took the napkin and said weakly, "Thanks." After wiping her mouth and forehead, she added, "Morning sickness. I thought I'd gotten lucky and skipped it since I'm already three months along."

"Sorry." He didn't know what else to say.

"Why are you sorry? It's not your fault." She reflected a moment. "Well, maybe it kinda is. Thanks for knocking me up."

"Guess that's the end of the honeymoon," he joked.

She picked up the bluebird off the dash. "So you're already breaking your promise?"

"Not on your life," he replied. "But that baby suddenly got real, and now I'm worried. Worried sick, in fact."

"You're supposed to say that everything's going to be fine."

"Everything's going to be just fine, as long as I'm not killed by your dad. If I can survive him, I'll be able to handle anything, even bringing up baby." With that, he pulled back onto the road. Mae turned on the radio, placed her left hand lightly on his thigh, and cradled in her right the bluebird of happiness.

Through the rain he looked ahead, not just down the road but to later in the day and the coming weeks and months and years—confrontations with their parents, explanations to their siblings, the adult responsibilities of finding a place to live and setting up a home and paying bills, the start of university, and high school graduation in November. He had a vision of Mae crossing the stage when her name was called. Would it be Mae Miller they called, or Mae Mulder? Would she walk ahead of him, or would he go first, given the alphabetical arrangements of these things? He saw her as the audience would see her, in a red maternity dress, her belly big in profile, a blood moon. Her body was saying, "Go ahead. Look at me. Screw you and your judgements, all of you." He liked to think he would walk that proudly across the stage, for one moment heroic and defiant in spite of his shyness, embarrassment, and shame.

As he was mulling over the possible outcomes of this day and the next, he saw in the distance a familiar vehicle. As it drew closer, he was certain. "Oh, shit," he said.

"What?" said Mae, who'd been humming along to the radio with her eyes closed.

"Oh, shit! Oh, shit! Oh, shit!" The Happy Hearth Upholstery and Furniture Repair van was bearing down on them. Evan shut off the wipers and slid down in his seat, as if that would make him invisible. But as the van came parallel to them, he saw that while his father-in-law was driving, it was his own dad in the passenger seat. At that very moment of passing each other on the road, their two fathers appeared to be consulting a map and engaging in conversation. He and Mae were safe for now.

"Thank you, Jesus," he shouted as he sat back up, flipped on the wipers, and pressed his foot on the accelerator, "for performing that little miracle."

"What are you talking about," Mae said. "The little miracle's happening right inside me. Has been now for months."

NETHER LANDS

Evan wished Aunt Hennie and Uncle Pete had ordered more than one portable toilet for Sophie's wedding. He was in a long lineup for the Johnny-on-the-spot, and almost out of time. Ahead of him and behind, it was mostly his Dutch-Canadian relations—red and blond heads chatting and laughing, their hair an inheritance on his dad's side of the family, the Mulder clan.

During the outdoor ceremony, his bowels had betrayed him—knotting up and burbling loudly, to his own embarrassment and Mae's mortification. He'd made it to the end of the ceremony, then rushed to the lavatory, finding only temporary relief. The reception was now in full swing, and this was his third trip, each one brought on by a powerful urge from his nether regions. He counted the heads in front of him—six. *Please hurry*, he thought, as he performed the potty dance.

He was tempted to head into the woods but knew no spot was secluded enough. He might stumble across a teenaged cousin making out with her date, or, God forbid, an aunt and uncle doing the same. He feared bearing witness to wife swapping. Worse, an attractive stranger might catch him with his pants down, his white but hairy butt cheeks exposed to her—and maybe to poison ivy, which he couldn't remember how to identify.

Around him, he caught snippets of conversation lubricated by wedding wine.

"It's certainly different, isn't it, holding the wedding here. You'd think the church was good enough. It was for us."

"True," replied a second voice, "but it's beautiful here. It's like an outdoor church. All creation is holy."

"I'm sure I smell some holy shit from that farm over there," said a third.

A fourth voice chimed in. "Not to mention church is too dry. No drinking. No dancing. Give me a wet wedding like this one. So much the better if it's open bar."

The third voice quipped, "Yeah, Uncle Pete's the man. He's got the Midas touch. Bet he turned water into wine just for the occasion."

"There's a good reason we didn't allow drinking and dancing in our day."

From the party tent, Evan heard dishes clinking, loud laughter, and the insistent beat of a huge hit from a few years ago. Robert Palmer was singing about being addicted to love, his voice flooding the countryside. An image erupted in Evan's head—red-lipped music-video sirens in skin-tight black mini-dresses, fingering guitar strings. In that summer of '88, the song was big on the wedding circuit.

His cousin Ellie's husband Harry emerged from the toilet, smiling and straightening his belt. "All yours," he winked to the red head next in line. "My sincerest apologies" was his warning. Five more to go.

Aunt Hennie and Uncle Pete could certainly afford more than one portable toilet now. They'd made their fortune manufacturing and importing Dutch treats—windmill cookies, chocolate letters and sprinkles, Gouda cheese, peppermints, salty black licorice. These treats had Dutch names Evan couldn't pronounce, words that involved a lot of throat gravel and spit. In church, people sucked either the salty black licorice, called droppies, or peppermints. His theory was that droppie suckers were into predestination, while pepperminters erred on the side of grace. His family were peppermint people, thank God.

Within the family, Aunt Hennie and Uncle Pete were the immigrant success story, moving out of a tiny house in Old London to a rural property with a sprawling home hidden at the end of a winding lane through the woods. Uncle Pete had the house built into a hillside. At the front, it was a modest single story, but in the back it rose three stories, with balconies, a patio, and a kidney-shaped pool overlooking a lawn that opened onto southwestern Ontario pastureland—the ideal place for an outdoor wedding. Evan remembered visiting their old house when he was a child—a tiny cottage with asphalt siding, lit by the green-filtered shade of maples. Along with his older brother Jeff and younger sister Annalise, he would play street hockey with Sophie and her two brothers. Now years later Sophie was a woman, and wedded.

For Mae and himself, Sophie's wedding day had started with an argument. Like most weekends, he'd had work spread over the kitchen table. He'd been at Wheel and Barrow Chartered Accountants for three years now, after getting his accounting degree and certification. For reasons he didn't examine, he'd become blindly driven by his work. The workaholic habits he'd cultivated as a student seemed to have carried over into his job—no end of clients, always new projects to take on. He was drinking a cocktail of drive and anxiety.

When he should have been in weekend mode—Saturday chores, attention to seven-year-old Alex, time with Mae—he'd had his face buried in paperwork. At the very least, he should have been getting ready for Sophie's wedding.

"Do you have to do that today, of all days?" Mae was exasperated. It was a note that sounded more and more in her voice. He knew he was ignoring it at his own risk.

"I just need a little more time. This has to be done by Monday."

"Something always has to be done by Monday. I've made Alex a sandwich. Do you think you can keep an eye on him? I've got to get ready." Mae had followed these clipped sentences with an expectant pause before turning away. Impatiently, Evan had gotten up, turned on Saturday cartoons, plunked Alex at the coffee table with his sandwich, and returned to the kitchen table.

As he listened to the sounds of Mae showering, though, he couldn't concentrate on the papers before him. His stomach churned, a cramp formed—signs of stress he'd been ignoring for months. And next month, they'd be married eight years.

Theirs wasn't a traditional wedding, like Sophie's. They'd eloped because Mae was pregnant with Alex. Still teenagers then, they'd stood before a justice of the peace in a Spartan room decorated with gaudy plastic geraniums in red vases and made promises binding them until one or the other's death.

People talked about the seven-year itch. Was that what he and Mae had been going through—their honeymoon in Beaver Valley long forgotten, the heart-shaped bed in the bridal suite a dead memory because of marital cardiac arrest, *The Kama Sutra* covered in dust on the bottom shelf of a night table, their collection of screwball comedies ignored in their cases? They'd started with all the ingredients for a disastrous marriage—teenage pregnancy, time and money pressures, family strife. They'd survived some intense fights early on—thrown food (including a carrot to his forehead), tossed clothes, and packed suitcases—but he'd thought they were through the rough patch once he'd graduated and started working. But maybe, obsessed with work, he'd created nothing but boredom. He'd grown up in a house where dancing and movies and bars were taboo. Were fun and romance foreign to his DNA, atrophied emotional muscles?

He and Mae had begun trying for a second child, only to learn she'd developed secondary infertility—a bitter irony, a cosmic joke, given how easily she'd gotten pregnant before. They'd endured testing and treatment, and they'd grown tired. Sex had become a means to an end, and the end wasn't in sight, might not even be believed possible anymore. He'd once heard a radio DJ call sex mommy-daddy dancing. Lately, he and Mae hadn't been doing much of a simple mommy-daddy two-step, let alone a full Argentinian tango.

Maybe that's why Mae had started clubbing again with friends—single women—from her old job, when she was supporting him through school. Some nights, she'd come home in the early morning hours, still drunk. She'd said it was harmless fun—a little dancing and drinking, a lot of girl talk. Still, he was worried.

Mae had emerged from the bedroom wearing a new summer dress with a flower pattern. Her dark hair, still damp, fell down her back in a long French braid, leaving a wet spot between her shoulder blades. She carried a light green hat to shade her brown eyes at the outdoor service. She was a bewildering addiction. He felt it but didn't know what to do about the craving.

He went to the bedroom to get himself ready and discovered she hadn't laid out his suit and tie—something he thought gave her pleasure to do.

They had dropped off Alex with Mae's parents for an overnight visit and made a silent drive into the countryside. At Aunt Hennie and Uncle Pete's, he'd greeted family with a fake smile, pretend cheer hiding the turmoil inside. He could feel the gap between his body and Mae's, the distance between his empty hand and hers.

They'd crossed the lawn to a flower-clad arbor and rows of white chairs, taking up seats near the back. The remaining seats were soon filled with summer dresses and suits, the women's hair neatly beneath hats. A string quartet began playing, the groom and groomsmen took their places at the arbor, and the bridesmaids came forward and fanned to the left, a perfect balance to the groomsmen. A flower girl scattered rose petals down the aisle. Sophie, tall and slim and blond beside Uncle Pete, floated in her sleeveless wedding dress to the side of her fiancé, Rob, a rose petal clinging to her hem. Evan didn't know what to make of Rob, but was mildly annoyed by his ponytail. An ungenerous judgement, Evan realized. He himself had long hair, shoulder length, feathered, and parted down the middle, a hangover from the seventies.

Uncle Paul had officiated. Every Dutch-Canadian family had at least one minister in those days, and Uncle Paul was liberal-minded enough not to balk at a wedding outside the church. So Sophie and Rob exchanged their vows and rings in the golden afternoon sunlight, framed by the arbor. It was then that Evan had felt the first burblings. When Uncle Paul launched into his wedding homily, the burblings turned into louder bubblings. As Uncle Paul spoke glowingly of love's patience and persistence, Evan's gut was seized with pressing cramps.

When he'd returned from his first foray to the portable toilet, he discovered Mae had wandered off. He found her with his family—brother Jeff, sister Annalise, and his mom and dad. They were by the wedding party, who were being immortalized by the official photographer as well as family and friends. Mae was judging shots with her 35 mm Canon.

"Stand with your sister and brother," she'd said, "and I'll take a picture of the three of you." After she shot them, his mom offered to take a picture of him and Mae.

"Mae, dear, pull in your stomach," his mother said. Mae offered a frozen, closed-lip smile and then pinched his waist as his mother clicked the shutter. When developed, the photo would capture Mae's tight smile and his startled, pained expression.

They'd headed to the reception tent and found their table laden with wine. He poured a glass of white for Mae and red for himself. Mae downed hers and held it up to be refilled, but he sipped his slowly to test its effect on his digestion.

"Evan," his mother confided, "did you notice Rebecca Postma's here? Mae, she just had her third child, can you believe it, a girl this time. I invited her to stop by our table for a visit." While his mother believed in the sanctity of marriage, she saw some marriages as more sanctified than others. His to Mae wasn't on that list, given Mae wasn't Dutch and they were bound by a secular rather than a sacred knot. His mother had hoped he would show an interest in Rebecca, whose family owned a Tim Hortons franchise.

Rebecca was at that moment navigating her way to their table. She greeted everyone and dropped into the chair beside Evan. He felt embraced by perfume. "So good to see you! How's your little boy? Pour me some red, will you?"

Evan obliged. She leaned past him to tell Mae about her own two boys who drove her crazy and the baby girl she had had two months ago. Stuck between Mae and Rebecca, he'd felt himself overheating. When Rebecca placed her hand on his wrist, Mae gripped his knee and squeezed. The two touches created an electric current, a jolt that met in his middle and shocked his bowels. As he excused himself, Rebecca called after him, "Save a dance for me!" Fleeing, he heard her explaining to Mae that her own husband had two left feet. Mae replied, "Well, Evan has two right feet. Maybe they should get together."

When he'd returned from his second odyssey to the portable toilet, the wedding feast had begun. His senses were assaulted by food, everything from shrimp to prime rib to roasted vegetables and potatoes. He tested his appetite with tiny bites washed down with sips of wine. Mae asked how he was feeling, then turned to Annalise before he could answer.

He survived the tinkling glasses and kisses, the toasts and the speeches. When the party turned to dancing and swimming and games, he stayed at the table alone—it was all a bit too much to stomach. Jeff and Annalise and Mae had gone off to play some softball at the encouragement of his cousin Leonard, his hair a red flame leaping off his head. Evan could see them across the lawn in the direction of the pasture. Mae's kicked-off sandals lay in the grass, her hat beside them.

His mom and dad had stepped onto the dance floor. When he was a kid, he thought they'd never danced before. What was he seeing now? Everywhere, jackets and ties were being shed, sleeves rolled up, buttons undone, hats and shoes cast aside. Outside the party tent his younger cousins had invaded the pool. Their wet skin and hair glistened as they splashed and dunked each other. Cannonballs sent waves over the side.

Here and there, cousins who'd brought dates were engaged in more serious play—chasing and holding, stealing kisses. It was a gene pool. They were all splashing in it, he and Mae too, up to their necks.

He looked across the lawn to where Mae was swinging the bat in her bare feet. Her swing was late and high above the ball. He loved that about her—she was game to play, but no athlete. Lenny was now giving her pointers on stance, grip, and swing. As she held the bat, Lenny wrapped his arms around her from behind, placed his hands over hers, and rotated her body through a practice swing. Gigolo. The name came unbidden to Evan as he watched. He never liked Lenny, thought of him as a lady's man who'd had several girlfriends and just as many messy break-ups. He watched Lenny take Mae through another practice swing, no daylight between their bodies. Evan felt his cousin delivering him a low blow, his nether regions doubling over in reply. Evan had then propelled himself to the toilet for his third trial.

He was close now—next in line for the lavatory. He continued his potty dance until the door opened on his Aunt Helena, who emerged in queenly fashion, as if descending from a throne, and paced by her subjects with a nod and a regal wave. With this blessing, he latched the door and unleashed his bowels and bladder, shamed by the loud sounds echoing off the fibreglass walls. Sweet smelly relief, at last. Third time's a charm.

He sat and he thought. When he went back to the party tent, he'd find Rebecca and take her onto the dance floor, trying to make Mae jealous. An inspired plan? Foolish, no doubt, but it was all he had. Sheer lunacy.

The DJ was starting "Stuck with You" by Huey Lewis and the News when Evan returned to the tent. He saw Mae at their table, Lenny close beside her. Evan found Rebecca and invited her onto the floor. He began moving in herky-jerky fashion. His limbs were not his own, they felt foreign. His hips were stiff machines lacking lubrication. What he was doing was more like marching than dancing. He was dancing to the beat of a different drummer, alright. I should have had more wine, he thought, as his face reddened. He watched Mae obliquely for her reaction. She leaned into Lennie and said something into his ear. They got up and moved together onto the dance floor close by.

Rebecca grabbed him by the hands and twisted him side to side. "You need to loosen up," she said. She came in close and moved her hands to his hips, rotating them in sync with hers. He felt her hands sliding dangerously close to his butt. His glutes tightened in reply.

Throughout the song, over Rebecca's shoulder he caught glimpses of Mae and Lenny. Lenny's a good dancer, he was forced to admit. Lenny was saying to Mae "Dance me loose, dance me loose" as he moved to the music. At the end of the song, the couples were dancing side by side.

Without a pause, Foreigner's "I Want to Know What Love Is" started up. Rebecca pulled Evan close, and Mae did the same to Lenny. Lenny buried his head in Mae's neck. He was practically guzzling her up, his hands drifting down her back lower and lower. Evan had enough. Elbows out, he danced right into Lenny.

"So sorry, Lenny," he said as he took Mae's hand. "I'm such a klutz. Do you mind switching partners? I'd like to dance with my *wife*." He put special emphasis on the word, whether for Lenny or Mae, Rebecca or himself, he wasn't sure.

Rubbing his ribs, Lenny replied, "By all means, I surrender the floor to the lovely lady's house-bound." Then turning to Rebecca, he added, "I'd be honored, milady, to lead you astray." He bowed his flame of red hair, then slow-danced her across the floor. Evan was sure he heard Lenny murmur "Dance me loose" as he went.

Evan turned to Mae. She said, "Real smooth. You must be feeling better." When she put her hands on his shoulders, he placed his on her hips and began leading her in circles. He felt like an awkward teenager at a school dance, just as he had on their honeymoon. Maybe he always would. Addicted, he placed his cheek against hers and smelled her skin, her hair.

"Great song," he said. It was reaching the point where the choir joined in. "That's the New Jersey Mass Choir," he added. "Interesting fact. When Foreigner recorded this song, the choir gathered around the band and together they said the Lord's Prayer. True story." Evan was an encyclopedia of such irrelevant trivia.

"You're so awkward," Mae replied, "You haven't got a prayer, so just shut up and dance." He did both, as a disco ball shed light around the tent and across their bodies.

When they got home that night, they were all over each other, undressing as they got in the door. They didn't make it to the bedroom. He dumped his work off the kitchen table and lifted her onto it. There, they performed the mommy-daddy dance.

A couple of months later, Mae was by then pretty sure it was that night or the next that she conceived their second child.

"See," he said, "that's what they're afraid dancing leads to."

The Jelly Cupboard

W̲hen Evan was first faced with building a jelly cupboard, he was puzzled. He'd never heard of one, let alone seen one. Mae had signed him up for a night course in woodworking at their local high school, given him a picture of a jelly cupboard cut out of the Sears catalogue, and said, "I want you to make that for me."

In the picture, the jelly cupboard appeared to be about five feet tall, two to three feet across, and eighteen inches deep, with a glass door. The finish looked to be maple, though he was no expert on finishes. Through the door glistened dozens of mason jars filled with preserves—pickles, relishes, jams, and of course jellies. Cornucopia, he thought, though he couldn't tell from the picture if the jars were real or fake. He wondered where the Sears catalogue people had gotten all those jars and how much they had cost. It also looked like a lot of work, growing that food to fill those jars to pack such a large cabinet, not to mention the work of making the jelly cupboard itself. It would all add up.

He had studied the picture carefully, weighing what response might be right, the one that would mean the least amount of work for him while still keeping Mae happy. They were sitting together at the kitchen table on a Saturday morning late in June. This was back in 1991; he'd turned twenty-nine just a few months earlier. "Don't you think I should start with something simpler? How about a toaster tray? It would take care of the crumbs on the counter." He was thinking, a small rectangle of wood with some trim around it—I might be able to handle that.

He pushed the picture across the table to Mae, got up, and refilled his mug from the coffee maker, adding a splash of cream from the fridge. He looked out the small window into their postage-stamp yard, which backed onto a mirror-image yard of a clone house on the neighboring street, a chain-link fence dividing the two. A blue bike and an orange trike lay tipped over in the grass.

He returned to the table. Mae had picked up and was studying the picture. On the wall behind her hung two black-and-white photographs of wild horses from Sable Island and the Alberta foothills. Even before they got married she talked about her love of horses, said these were places she one day hoped to go. She slid the picture of the jelly cupboard back across the table to him. "I have complete faith in you." He couldn't tell if she was being sarcastic or serious, maybe both. "Besides, you know how women love a handy man, a guy who can swing his hammer. Might be good for our love life." She took a sip of tea, then added, "You'll be fine."

He didn't feel fine. He felt the opposite of handy, in all the ways possible. He didn't own a single tool, had rarely used one. He'd never seen his dad use a tool, ever. When Mae needed something fixed in the house, she had two choices. If it was big, she called their landlord. If it was small, she called her dad. Evan's father-in-law, now there was a handy man—ex-military, adept at renos and repairs, working out of a brightly lit shop in his basement.

As Evan looked down at the image of the jelly cupboard, he imagined losing fingers, maybe a hand or something more precious, to a power saw. He considered the chances of a splinter lodging in his right thumb and getting infected, gangrene marching past his wrist to his elbow. Radical amputation would be needed to save the rest of his body. He briefly indulged a vision of Mae's face etched with lines of guilt. He imagined their two kids, Alex and Lizzie, weeping over his lost limb, which he would display in an enormous pickling jar on top of the offending jelly cupboard. He wouldn't have enough fingers to count on anymore, so his accounting career would be over. Besides, he couldn't imagine anyone wanting a one-armed accountant, a bean counter with an unbalanced body. Looking up, he said, "Okay, I'll risk life and limb for you."

"My hero" was Mae's sarcastic reply.

~

That's how Evan Mulder found himself in the woodworking shop of WLM-KSS each Wednesday evening in August, about a decade after he and Mae had graduated from the school in the early 1980s.

During high school, he'd never set foot in a shop class and rarely visited that part of the school. He was all brain, no brawn—firmly on the academic train track, math obsessed. The plan was to graduate with honours from Grade 13 and earn an accounting degree from his home-town university, frugally saving money by living at home with his Dutch immigrant parents. Then he'd settle safely and permanently into Wheel and Barrow Chartered Accountants, a firm renowned for coddling the investments of London's many millionaires, the largest density per capita in those days, before the age of dotcom fortunes.

At least, that was his plan—until Mae. They met when Mae worked with his younger sister Annalise on a science project. The girls' model rocket was a dud, taking a quick nose dive after liftoff. Mae just laughed at this flop, unworried about her grade. "What goes up must come down," she said. "Just sometimes sooner than expected." She'd turned to Evan. "Could you rescue our rocket for us?"

He knew he had it bad for her when he biked past her house fifteen times before working up the nerve to stop and ring the bell. A skinny teenage boy with a heavy mop of hair, he asked her in a sweat if she wanted to go for a ride. "With you?" she'd said. Her brown eyes laughed—slightly mocking—behind large tortoise-shell glasses, framed by brunette hair in a bob cut. Together they meandered side by side along their subdivision's streets, young trees staked on front lawns of bungalows, semi-detached homes, and row houses. On the busy roads of the adjacent industrial park, he rode behind her, a gentleman, admiring the view of course, smitten.

Less than a year later, she was pregnant.

He'd been too embarrassed to buy condoms at the drugstore. At her news, visions of a shotgun wedding filled his head, the experienced fingers of Mae's dad on the trigger. "Let's elope," he'd said. Their parents weren't exactly ecstatic when they found out, but Alex's birth as the first grandchild on either side settled the rough waters a bit.

After eloping, Evan and Mae had moved into a small, one-bedroom attic apartment on Queen Street. Single-minded and stubborn, he toiled away at his accounting degree, aiming to prove to their families that he and Mae could make this marriage work. His tool was a Texas Instruments calculator, his materials numbers on spreadsheets. He tuned out Mae and baby Alex, drawn to the comforting logic of ledgers.

There were strains—between him and Mae, within the family. He ignored them. Part of it was Mae feeling outside the Dutch cluster he grew up in. She'd heard someone say, "If you ain't Dutch, you ain't much."

Half-joking, she'd said to him once, "You know your mother believes I raped you."

"No, she doesn't." His denial, he knew, did nothing to resolve the blame game.

"Yeah, I tied you to the bed and forced myself on you, stole your precious Dutch seed. Did it with handcuffs—tools of the trade."

"Sounds like fun."

"You're such a dog."

When they began trying for a second child, though, nothing happened. Mae had developed secondary infertility sometime after Alex's birth. "This must be God's idea of a joke," they'd say to each other. Sometimes, Evan wondered if it was a punishment. Other times, he took it as another sign he just wasn't handy enough. Then Lizzie came along as a surprise, eight years after Alex, after they'd rented a house in their old subdivision, after they'd given up on fertility treatments. "She's a miracle," they would say to each other.

But now that Mae had two children, a boy-and-girl set, he suspected he had outlived his usefulness. Maybe, he thought, this woodworking course could make him a handy man. He remembered a *Three's Company* episode in which Mr. Roper, hounded by his wife for lots more sex, asks Jack for advice about how many "shelves" a man should be expected to put up for his wife, and how regularly he had to do it. Those old shows used such comical euphemisms for sex. What exactly, thought Evan, did Mae want? Was it just a piece of furniture, or something more?

～

The fluorescent lights in the WLM-KSS woodworking shop starkly lit up an array of hulking grey machines—saws, planers, drills, grinders, lathes—sitting still and silent. At that moment Evan didn't know their names, but he could imagine what power they held. Everywhere he saw blades, sharp edges, teeth, wheels—all of them eager to mangle his flesh, sever his appendages.

He stood at the edge of a group of five men, all with their arms crossed in that universal male first-encounter pose. They wore plaid shirts—the late-eighties, early-nineties uniform of both working-class men and university undergrads—and gripped one or two sheets of paper outlining the projects they wanted to make.

He was alarmed to recognize one guy from their student days, Brad Reynard. Mae had told Evan she'd had one boyfriend before him, nothing serious. It was this Brad. Evan had asked her to clarify what "nothing serious" meant. She'd said they'd dated for a few months, but when Brad farted after asking her to pull his finger, she dumped him. That explanation satisfied Evan for a while, but he was unsettled by a cryptic comment Mae had once made early in their marriage when they were talking about penises. The subject came around to Brad's peter versus his. "Long and thin gets it in," she'd said. "Short and thick does the trick." What was he to make of that? He imagined Brad's dick as snake-like, a hooded cobra waving about, while his own was a small furry mammal with frightened eyes. He wanted it to be a mongoose. Another time she'd said, "You're a grower, not a shower." He supposed that was meant as a compliment, but he couldn't be certain.

Brad sidled over and introduced himself. "Hey, Allen, isn't it? I remember you from high school—the glory days."

"Evan, actually. Yeah, seems a lifetime ago now, doesn't it?"

"How's Mae?" Before Evan could answer, Brad continued, "You two ran off and got hitched, didn't you? Made for quite the story at school. Everybody was talking about it. Yeah, Mae was a great girl. We had some good times when we were young and foolish."

You bastard, Evan thought. Now you're just plain foolish. An idiot. A dink.

But he couldn't help feeling unsettled. A pinprick of worry and jealousy settled in his chest. To cover it, he said, "She's great! We did get off to a rough start there, but now we've got two kids, Alex who's ten and Lizzie two." He glanced at Brad's hand, noting the absence of a wedding band. He saw from Brad's project plan he was hoping to build a gun cabinet. Evan stood a little taller and straighter, not to be cowed by Brad's Burt Reynolds moustache and big head of 1980s hair. Gesturing toward Brad's hand, Evan added, "How about you? Not married?"

"Nope, Mae completely ruined me for other women." After pausing, Brad added, "Just kidding, man! To tell the truth, I've been divorced a couple of years. Marriage was just cramping my style. Guess I'm a bit of a rooster. Why stick with one hen when there's a whole flock out there?" Evan offered a weak smile at this joke. "That's why I'm building a gun case," Brad continued as he showed Evan the plans. "Gotta keep the shotgun handy when foxes are trying to get in the hen house." Brad laughed at his own joke.

"You're into hunting, then?"

"Yup, whatever walks on two or four legs—wild turkey, deer, coyotes. Depending on the season, I usually get out every couple of weekends with my dad. Maybe you and your boy should come out with us this fall. What's his name again?"

"Alex. Thanks for the invite. I'll think about it. Though our weekends are usually pretty busy with family stuff, plus hockey." Alex wasn't in hockey, but right then and there Evan decided to sign him up.

"What's your line of work?"

"Accounting. How about you?"

"You're a bean counter, eh? I'm in the insurance game—home, auto, life." He pulled a business card out of his wallet and passed it to Evan. "I could meet with you and Mae any time to go over what you need, especially now that you've got two kids. As a husband and a father, you shouldn't leave your loved ones exposed to risk. Lots of dangers in the world out there." Including you, Evan thought. I won't risk bringing you into my home, you turd.

Brad leaned over to look at the plans in Evan's hand. "What's your project?"

Evan had taken the catalogue picture and turned it into a line drawing with detailed measurements and notes. He'd considered buying a CAD program to develop even more accurate, to-scale plans with blow-up drawings. He reddened slightly as he looked at their drawings side by side. "I'm making a jelly cupboard." It sounded like a confession. "Mae asked me to make it for her birthday. For the kitchen."

"Anything to keep the wife happy," Brad replied, offering Evan a grin and an elbow bump. "Let me know if you need any help in that department. As far as the ladies are concerned, if you can't be handsome, at least you can be handy."

"Good one," Evan said. He recognized the joke as stolen from a new show, *Red Green*. "So far, thank goodness, no complaints in that department."

"Of course, I can tell you from personal experience it's sure better to be both."

Their instructor appeared at that moment and cleared his throat. "I'm Bob Wright," he said. "Welcome, gentle men, to shop class!" He paused between "gentle" and "men" for emphasis. Perhaps, Evan thought, it was a private joke or a dig reserved for Bob's normal crop of high school students. He noted that Bob had all his fingers, both eyes, both ears, and his whole nose—surely a good sign in a shop teacher. Or was it? Wouldn't a real shop teacher have wounds to prove he'd been in the battle, that he'd literally put skin in the game?

Bob went on to explain and demonstrate all the machines, stressing the safety rules the men needed to follow. "Don't want to send you back to your better half in half," he joked. "Our goal is to make you handy, not handless." The men laughed dutifully.

Bob then reviewed the men's plans and got them started on picking out their materials and taking the measure of things. When he got to Evan's jelly cupboard, Bob took him to the Aspen planks where the wood was stored along the wall in orderly sections. "Aspen's similar to maple, but softer," he said. "It'll be a better wood to learn with." Evan examined and felt the planks, their smooth blondness and dark knots where branches had once emerged from the tree's trunk and limbs. He chose the best one-by-eight planks he could find, and got to work on measuring and cutting. He carefully guided spinning blades along pencil lines, hands out of harm's way. Sawdust clung to his clothes and skin, floated into his hair, filled his nose.

When he got home that evening, he found Mae sitting quietly in the living room, enjoying the summer evening's semi-dark, sipping wine with the TV off, the kids already in bed. "How'd it go?" she asked when he turned on a light. "Obviously you're still alive, but let me see if you've got all your limbs."

He held up his hands and wiggled his fingers. "Things are taking shape," he said. After pausing, he added, "You won't believe who was there. Brad Reynard, your beau from high school."

"Brad? You're kidding. I'd never call him a beau. He's not the type."

"You're probably right. I got the impression he's a real dink eyes."

"Dink eyes? That's a new one. You shouldn't have said that. You know I have a terribly visual imagination. Now I'll never get that picture out of my head."

"Good."

"Anyway, how's the old fart?" She laughed at her old joke.

"Divorced," he replied. "Apparently, he dumped his wife a couple of years ago to move on to greener pastures, a larger hen house, something like that."

She laughed again, this time with a darker edge. "Is that what he told you? The liar. That's not what I heard. Amy left him. There were rumors of other women. And worse."

Evan looked at the dark rectangle of the living room window, where a sliver of moon hung in the sky. How did she know this about Brad and Amy Reynard? Had she been keeping tabs on him all these years? "Worse than fooling around?"

"Just rumors. Nothing else. I won't repeat gossip."

⌐∿

The jelly cupboard took shape during the remaining Wednesday nights in August. As Evan worked on it, he developed a healthy respect for what those hulking gray machines could do. With Bob's guidance, Evan constructed the sides, top, bottom, and shelves by cutting down the Aspen boards with the miter saw, ripping some with the table saw, sanding them, then joining them with little biscuits glued into aligned hidden grooves cut in the sides of the boards. As he clamped the boards tight side by side, he thought about the hidden joints that held things together, making them strong and smooth. Bob then showed him how to connect all the parts with housing joints that allowed one piece of wood to be set into another. He loved the other name for a housing joint, dado. It sounded almost like daddy-o.

Evan needed to be patient and precise working with wood. He liked that. His hands and muscles grew accustomed to pulls, pushes, and turns as he learned what tools could do. Soon enough, the jelly cupboard had a face and a door, along with modest molding as a crown. It just remained to finish the cupboard with a maple stain and satin varnish, followed by setting the glass in the door and attaching it with bronze hinges to the cabinet.

All this time, he kept an eye on Brad and the progress of his gun cabinet. They man-bantered and joked around. Sometimes Evan was tempted to reveal what he knew about Brad's failed marriage, to put Brad in his place, but he held his tongue, worried Brad might be the vengeful type, spiteful. A real dink eyes. Instead, a half-friendly competition evolved to see whose project would turn out better, Evan's jelly cupboard for Mae or Brad's gun cabinet for his hunting rifles. He stole glances at Brad's work, occasionally walking by his cabinet to judge how the piece was shaping up. Several times, Evan turned around to find Brad right there behind him—sometimes with a hammer, other times with a screwdriver. Was it Evan's imagination, or was Brad wielding the tools in a slightly threatening way? "Looking good," Brad would say and walk away. On the last Wednesday night, when they were varnishing their work, Evan thought things looked neck and neck.

"Well, gentle men," Bob announced at the end of the evening, "let's have a look at your handy work." He led them from project to project, commending each student on the strengths of his work and offering one or two pieces of advice for how the construction might be improved. When he came to Brad's gun cabinet, Bob praised the cuts and joints, but encouraged Brad to be more patient with his finish work. Evan's jelly cupboard was last. "You could use a little less glue in the joints—it's squeezed out here and shows through your finish a bit. But the construction is solid—great proportions. As a cabinet, it's both useful and handsome. That's the goal with whatever we make. It should be practical, but it should look good, too."

Evan thanked Bob and looked at the jelly cupboard. For a month, he'd focused on the details—getting the measurements right, calculating the width of the saw blade into his cuts, making sure the biscuit grooves matched in the planks he joined together, rubbing the stain evenly into the Aspen wood. Those details were important, necessary. But until that moment he'd missed the big picture—what he'd really been making for Mae. It was more than a piece of furniture; it was something to furnish their lives, but he didn't understand how exactly.

Brad walked up to him after Bob's review of their projects. "Great job on your jelly cupboard," Brad offered, looking it over. "I bet it'll make Mae happy."

"Thanks," he replied. "I hope so. Your cabinet turned out great, too. It'll look really sharp with your rifles in it."

"Now that it's done, I'm actually thinking of giving it to my dad." Evan look surprised and Brad continued. "He's the one who taught me to hunt as a kid. Made me the man I am today. I should thank him for that."

"Makes sense." Unsure what else to say, Evan's gaze rested on the gun cabinet before passing to Mae's jelly cupboard.

Evan let the varnish dry for a day before returning to WLM-KSS. He inset the door's glass with sharp metal triangles pressed deeply into the wood with a flat-tipped screwdriver, then hinged the door to the cupboard. He had removed the seats from their Voyager minivan and brought along Alex. With Bob's help they were able to slide the cabinet onto the blanket covering the floor of the van. After shaking Bob's hand, Evan drove home, taking corners carefully so that the cabinet didn't shift and the door stayed shut.

When he backed into the driveway, Mae came out to help. Together, they strained to pull out the jelly cupboard and carry it into the kitchen. There, she supervised his and Alex's maneuvering of the cupboard into a corner, properly angled. The whole time, Lizzie danced around the kitchen. She stood in the corner where the cabinet was going, then raced out at the last second. She crawled under the table and laughed among the chairs before finally climbing onto the jelly cupboard's bottom shelf. Alex shut the door on her until Mae reminded him that the glass door could easily break. Mae sent the kids into the backyard, telling Alex to mind his sister.

"It's beautiful," Mae said as she ran her hand over the smooth finish on the top of the cupboard. "You did a really nice job. I mean it. Thank you."

"No problem. Tomorrow, I'll get started on that toaster tray."

Mae laughed. "And now that you're so handy, I'll get started on my honey-do list."

"I thought you already had one." He started showing Mae how the jelly cupboard was put together. "Did I ever tell you that my opa in Holland was a cabinet maker?" He opened the door to show her the inside. "Apparently, he and Oma had to get married, too. Like us. It's like an open secret in the family. They had nine kids."

The next day, he left the offices of Wheel and Barrow Chartered Accountants early. He went out of his way to visit a Home Hardware store, where he wandered the aisles. He started with the woodworking tools, then moved on to the wood trim, nails and screws, electrical, plumbing, heating, and paint. He even wandered down to the farm and country section of the store, curious about shovels and horse tack and chicken feeders. He considered the possibilities, what might be made and grown and cared for. How their lives might be furnished with such making. In the end, he bought a hammer, a handsaw, some pliers, and a set of screwdrivers. He picked out a sturdy black and yellow toolbox in which to house them.

At home, he greeted Mae and put his new toolbox on the kitchen table. He pulled out the hammer and waved it about. "I'm pretty good at swinging my hammer now. I'd be happy to show you later."

"I suppose you want to play handyman and housewife."

"I can wear a tool belt to bed, if you like." After he put the hammer back, he saw that Mae had been busy filling the jelly cupboard. Instead of jellies and preserves, though, it contained decorative dishes she had long kept stored in the attic. He noticed old-fashioned tins, a platter from her grandmother, a teapot cottage, and an assortment of china teacups and saucers she had picked up at yard sales. On top sat a snow globe, a glass bluebird, and a framed photograph of him and Mae with Larry and Caroline Laurence, a couple they'd met on their honeymoon.

"It looks great," he said, "but I had no idea that's what you wanted it for."

"A girl's got to have her secrets."

"You've got secrets? I thought you told me everything."

"Everything's on a need-to-know basis."

"Is it?" He went to make tea, automatically checking the backyard for the kids. As the kettle began to hum, he thought about the horses on the wall. A vague vision of a home in the country began to take shape. He'd keep the vision to himself for now.

Turning to Mae, he asked pointedly, "I need to know what's up with you and Brad, with him and Amy. What's the story, the big secret? What's worse than cheating?" That pinprick of worry and jealousy was sitting there in his chest. He needed to know. He thought it might help him understand what Mae wanted, what she needed.

"You need to know, or you just want to know?" When he didn't answer, she went on. "What's between Brad and me is just ancient history. As for him and Amy, I told you it's just rumors, though somewhere in the bad blood between them is the truth."

"You know what the Good Book says, 'The truth shall set you free.' Maybe that's what's needed."

"I'm not sure I buy that. Some things are better left unsaid. Once out, the words are out for good and just hang around your neck like dead weight." She looked at him leaning against the sink with his hands buried in his pockets, then said, "You really want to know? What's worse than cheating is getting another woman pregnant when your own wife wants babies, but you're too damn selfish to give them to her. That's what's worse."

Evan was stunned. Shit, he thought. "Seriously? He had a kid with another woman? Okay, that's definitely worse. Was he already such a dick when you were going out? I really can't understand what you saw in the guy."

"Why are you so obsessed with him? It's really simple. He chased me. I was flattered. I was just a teenager, remember. I wanted something—call it attention, affection, love, I don't know—and I thought at first he had it. It started off good, but then." She stopped.

"Then what?" It sounded like something more than a pulled-finger fart joke.

"Then he got too handy. He was all hands. He pushed me too far, too fast. I couldn't stop him. I've never told anybody, but I broke it off after that."

Her words were even and measured, but Evan could sense the hurt, free floating as a phantom limb. After a moment of silence, he said, "God, I'm sorry. What a jerk."

"Are you talking about him or yourself?"

Her question startled him, but after a moment he said, "Take your pick, I guess. I shouldn't have pushed you to tell me. I shouldn't have been so jealous. But he's clearly a jerk, a real asshole. If you want, I could take the biscuit cutter to his balls. I know how to use one now."

"That's a bit harsh, isn't it? I appreciate the offer, but all this happened a long time ago. Before I knew you, remember. And he was a teenager, too. We were both teenagers. He has to live with what he did."

"Bull shit. I'm not sure he's living with it at all. Look at his marriage. The other women."

"Yes, he's done a lot of damage. That can't be undone. But I have to believe there's more to him, that some time down the road regret will catch up with him. It's too easy to just turn him into a monster—even if it's just dink eyes, as you called him—and let him off the hook that way."

"You go ahead and believe that, if you want to. I'm just glad you got away from him. If you hadn't, nothing would be the same—you, me, the kids." For a moment, he glimpsed a life without them. The vision filled him with a strange dread, like the safe, almost pleasurable fear created by a horror movie.

"I'm just glad you got up the courage to ask me out for that bike ride."

The kettle was whistling. He watched her for a few seconds, then turned and filled the pot, steam rising into his face. He set the toolbox aside and placed the teapot on the table between them. He retrieved cups and saucers from the jelly cupboard, along with a small pitcher, which he filled with milk from the fridge. Before sitting down, he awkwardly hugged her from behind, his chin resting on her shoulder and his arm wrapped across the top of her chest. When he sat, he reached for her hand. She let him hold it, but didn't return his hand's pressure for some moments. Eventually she squeezed and then released. "Sorry, I don't want to be touched right now." His body felt foreign to him. Would he always feel this clumsy, this graceless?

They sat quietly until the tea steeped. He could hear the kids' voices in the backyard, the squeak of the swing set. After he poured a measure of milk in each cup, Mae filled them to the brim with tea, the white deepening to a warm brown.

She took a sip and returned to the thread of her thoughts. "I know you thought you were chasing me when we went for that bike ride. The truth is, I chose you when I first met you at your house. I was chasing you. You didn't know it at the time, but you were in big trouble."

"I suppose that's the good kind of trouble—love trouble. But you could have warned me."

"What would've been the fun in that? Some things you need to figure out on your own." After a moment, she added, "I think love's more art than science. You just learn by doing it."

As he sat and sipped, he studied the jelly cupboard and its contents, and he thought about how this piece of furniture now filled a space in their lives. He tried to take the measure of things as they now stood between himself and Mae, but found it beyond reckoning.

Early Birds

"Alex, it's time to get up for your paper route." Alex moaned in reply, rolling over to tighten the blankets around himself. "Come on, we've got to get going, or you won't be done in time for school."

Why did I sign him up for a paper route? Evan wondered on days like today. It was 5:30 on a biting January morning. He could hear the wind whistle around the house as he went downstairs to the kitchen to grab a glass of orange juice and some preventative vitamin C tablets. You can't be too careful, he thought, as he chewed. Out the window, the backyard was bleak, the kids' swing set dim in the weak light thrown by streetlights on the next street over, one of the streets on Alex's route.

He knew why he'd signed up Alex for the paper route. Because he himself had one when he was a kid. His own dad thought it was good for him to get started on his work life. "You need to learn responsibility," his dad had said. "It will build your character, not to mention some muscles and stamina. You're too skinny." And like his dad, Evan thought it would be good for Alex, too. Of course, making a little money was good—no harm in Alex learning the value of a dollar. Evan and his dad would agree on that.

Evan remembered those times when he was twelve and thirteen. He had an after-school route delivering the *London Free Press* evening edition. Back then, there was a morning edition, too, but a different carrier delivered that paper. Back then, he was sure the paper was much heavier and his route uphill in all directions. Back then, he had to collect money from his customers each week, going door to door and bringing all the cash back for his dad to count. He remembered the huge Saturday papers and his aching shoulders. He remembered having a paper left over sometimes and having to backtrack to figure out which house he'd missed. He remembered his hands, sore and cold and black from the ink.

Now, Alex had a route for the one daily edition of the *Free Press*, the morning edition. The previous summer, Evan had built for Mae the jelly cupboard that sat in their kitchen. It was in that woodworking class he'd met Mae's former flame Brad Reynard, a Burt Reynolds type. After that, Evan decided it would be good for Alex to have a route, just as he did, even though Alex was only ten. He wanted his son to grow up strong and confident so he could stand up to the Brad Reynards of this world. No bully was going to kick sand in Alex's face if Evan could help it.

Mae didn't agree with Evan about the paper route. When they got Alex's paper bags, she had to shorten the straps to keep the bags from dragging on the ground—proof positive to her that Alex was too young and too small for this kind of work. Not only that, she didn't want her ten-year-old little boy out by himself at 5:30 a.m. So every morning, six days a week, Evan got up at 5:30 to deliver papers with his son. They walked down opposite sides of the streets on Alex's route, heat or cold, rain or snow or fog, dark or light depending on the time of year. And this was their first true test of winter weather, early January.

Why did I sign him up for a paper route? Evan asked again as he bundled himself up. The answer he'd conjured was cold comfort.

They walked silently side by side to the street corner where the papers were dropped off for several routes. It was so cold their boots squeaked on the snow and the exposed skin of their faces began to tighten over their muscles going stiff. Their eyes teared up behind their glasses—Alex had gotten his four years earlier when he started school. Their noses began to run. Evan felt the frost begin to form on his beard and eyebrows. A cold and high winter moon shone down on the dry snow.

At the drop site, they located their bundles, loaded them into their bags, and counted them. Lifting Alex's bag, he put it over his little son's shoulder and smoothed out the strap so it wouldn't dig in like a rope.

Alex leaned his body against the weight. When Evan had his own bag ready, they walked over to their first street, Courtland (all the streets were named after apples), and began their deliveries, Alex on the right side, him on the left. And so it went, their silent trek each morning. He kept an eye on Alex, making sure he was okay, making sure he wasn't missing customers. Sometimes, though, Evan zoned out, sleepwalking from house to house.

When they were at the end of Courtland, they met up again to walk up to the next street, McIntosh. "My feet are frozen," said Alex.

"Mine too," he replied. "Keep it up. We're half way done. Tomorrow I guess we better wear two pairs of socks."

"My hands are frozen, too."

"Here, take off your gloves and blow into your hands."

They concentrated on blowing, which wasn't really helping. He knew there was a church at the corner of McIntosh, so he thought of that as a goal. It helped to divide the whole route into stages this way, like stations on a pilgrimage.

Ahead on the church corner, a large maple tree was coming into view out of the darkness. It was stripped of leaves, but wasn't empty. He grabbed Alex by the sleeve and stopped him. He whispered, "Look!"

"What? Where?"

"In the tree. Do you see?" Perched on a large limb was an enormous owl, pure white with flecks of black on its feathers. "It must be a snowy owl," he whispered. "I can't believe it's this far south. Let's walk slowly and see how close we can get."

Together, they stepped forward, walking as calmly as they could. The owl looked straight at them, unblinking, its yellow eyes rimmed with black, black pupils at the centre. Its black beak was pointed at them.

When they were within thirty or forty feet, the owl spread its wings and lifted off from the branch, circling around behind the church, vanishing into the darkness. "Awesome." They stood for a few more moments, until the cold jolted them into moving.

They continued their deliveries up McIntosh. They were on the back half of the route, getting closer to home and warmth with each step. Their target now was the children's park, empty of swings in the winter, the wading pool drained of water.

As they closed the distance, he heard above the wind a ruckus. It grew louder with each step. When the park was in sight, the source of the noise became clear. The large cottonwood tree in the park, orange-lit by streetlamps, was filled with crows. They were perched on the upper branch tips so the tree was on fire with their noise and motion. He and Alex stopped to watch and listen to the cold chorus. As if at some signal, the crows erupted from the tree and flew to the west, leaving a trail of noise that faded as they did into the darkness.

He and Alex had been lightened of their loads, though he still felt the ghost of the weight in the ache of his shoulders. He asked Alex how his shoulders were doing. They were about the same. All was now quiet except for the squeak of their boots.

When they entered the house, their glasses immediately fogged. He felt the warmth begin to defrost his face, ice melting into moisture in his beard. When Alex was out of his woollies, he ran off to wake his mom. "Mom, you won't believe what we saw this morning!"

As he put on the kettle, Evan saw again those early birds. He considered the company they'd offered to Alex and himself. Of all the reasons he'd signed up Alex for a paper route, this was one he'd never imagined. The money Alex was making seemed a pittance in comparison.

Evan was happy, though, when they moved to the country that summer, where the houses were too far apart to make a paper route for Alex practical. Evan didn't miss it, not even a little bit—though he would never admit that to his own dad.

POSSESSION

"Please don't wreck anything else." That's the note Evan and Mae found written on the bathroom mirror. They were doing a walk-through of the old farmhouse they were taking possession of in three days. The lettering was in red—whether marker, lipstick, or blood, it was hard to tell.

He looked around at the rust-stained bathtub, the peeling floral wallpaper, and the pool of water at the base of the toilet dampening the old wooden floor. What's left to wreck, he wondered.

He had tried to talk Mae out of buying this dump by convincing her it was possessed—she'd been seriously disturbed by watching *The Amityville Horror* when she was a teenager.

She was the first to react. "Who do you think that's meant for? Maybe she wrote it for him? Or maybe it's the other way around. It couldn't be for us, could it?"

"Hard to say. Might be a message from the resident poltergeist."

"Very funny. Don't get started on that again." He was shocked to see his smirk in the mirror behind the lettering, and checked it before Mae noticed. He considered the first word in the message. Was it simple politeness or a desperate plea?

The seller, Jace Tifflin, wasn't around for the final walk-through, and his common-law wife and son were nowhere to be seen. But Tifflin's realtor, a big-bellied, handlebar-mustached brick wall, was fixed outside the bathroom door. At the last minute, Evan and Mae had learned their own realtor couldn't make it, as he'd suffered a stroke and was in the hospital. Evan tried hard not to interpret their realtor's medical catastrophe as their own personal disaster, as their typical hard luck—hard luck that had started when Mae got pregnant with Alex, luck Evan thought might have changed when he built the jelly cupboard last summer and started dreaming of a life in the country.

They squeezed past the pot belly and continued the inspection, Evan feeling dazed and disturbed. They found his sister Annalise and her husband Todd in the kitchen, where a broken fan with a dull bare bulb hung tilted from the ceiling, wiring exposed. Cupboard doors were ajar and the sink was filled with dishes. Nowhere was there any sign of packing.

Three days, Evan thought. Just three days.

"Maybe it's better upstairs." Mae sounded unconvinced, but they climbed the stairs anyway, with the handlebar moustache wheezing behind them. In the bedrooms they were met by tipped over dressers, beds tilted from the walls, and clothes scattered across the floors. It was as if the furniture had been hit by a tsunami.

"Everybody's got their own method of packing, I guess." One of Todd's gifts was making disaster comical.

"This is not good. Not good at all," said Annalise. "There's no way they'll get their stuff moved out by Saturday."

"Not to worry, not to worry." The mouth situated below the handlebar moustache produced these words and punctuated them with laughter. "Jace Tifflin'll get it done on time."

"What about the water? Did he manage to get that fixed on time?" Evan wanted to inspect the water system in the basement. Tifflin had agreed to get it repaired before the walk-through. Without a working purifier, the water from the well wasn't safe and smelled horribly of rotten eggs. Evan and Mae had both grown up on city water they'd taken for granted, so "not potable" was a phrase they'd had to learn when they started looking at old farmhouses.

The handlebar moustache led them to the basement. A wrench was perched on top of the first tank in the system. It was obvious from the leaks and the extra parts scattered on the cement floor that Tifflin had tried to fix it himself—and had inflicted more damage. In three days,

Evan thought, we won't have safe city water magically pouring from our taps anymore. "What the hell are we supposed to do about this?"

"I'd hold back some money till it's fixed," Todd said. He picked up a couple of metal rings off the floor and checked how they might be pieced together.

"A couple a hundred oughta do it." Tifflin's realtor tried to sound appraising, as if he sized up repairs all the time.

"I'd hold back at least a couple of thousand, if I were you." Though Annalise was his younger sister, she seemed to him more practical and worldly-wise, or at least more suspicious, maybe even cynical. Hard-nosed, he thought. For a moment, he imagined her nose as a sharply pointed iron wedge splitting the handlebar moustache and its owner in half. Evan wanted that nose in his business, prowing through every obstacle.

Evan would remember this conversation later and wish they had held back $10,000, rather than the $500 they settled on. For many years it would be a common refrain during his ritual bouts of regret.

The basement had a rock foundation more than one hundred years old, the house having been built the same year as Confederation. He had learned that the mortar back then was filled with horse hair. How they collected it and what they mixed it with, he didn't know, but he imagined the mortar as both strong and soft. It felt chalky when he touched it, though he couldn't see any horse hair.

He looked around at the debris of someone else's life, someone with the strange name Jace Tifflin, someone he had never met. Someone he and Mae were depending on for the largest transaction of their lives.

So far, the transaction wasn't going well.

An assortment of machine parts was piled in one corner of the basement. In another, pink fiberglass insulation sat molding, damp and smelly. They'd have to get a dehumidifier running down here, not to mention a sump pump—another piece of practical wisdom from Todd. Cans of hunter-green paint, jars of nails, and a scattering of tools populated some wood shelves propped on cinder blocks. The floor in front of the shelves was covered with their overflow—odds and ends of wood trim, lamps missing cords, rusty saw blades, a roll of what looked like telephone cable. In fact, most of the floor was covered, except for narrow pathways kept somewhat clear. Evan navigated these hunched over to avoid banging his head on the ductwork and tangling his face in cobwebs. Beyond the furnace two unplugged chest freezers were pushed against the wall. Mae and Annalise walked over to check them.

"I wouldn't open those if I were you." Todd's warning came too late. The stench of rotting food billowed out, causing Mae and Annalise to stumble away, coughing and grabbing onto each other as the lids dropped shut. Evan covered his mouth and nose with the top of his shirt, approached one of the freezers, and lifted the lid to discover the bottom filled a couple of feet deep with black liquid. Vague shapes, even darker, were submerged within this cesspool.

"Animal or vegetable—it's hard to tell, maybe both. I don't think it's a body, but who knows. Could be the remains of the original owner."

"Not funny, Evan." He could tell Mae was upset. His joking was over the line. Passive aggressive behaviour, she'd call it.

He dropped the lid and tried to stop the rolling of his stomach. "Let's get some fresh air and check the barn."

Within the closed-in porch he and Mae found their kids playing with a pile of cast-off molding. Alex was watching Lizzie, as instructed. "We're going to check out the barn. Want to come along and see the barn cats?" Evan sensed Mae's invitation as a scheme, a maneuver to make their kids happy about moving to this place. Clever girl, he thought. He considered—for just a moment—taking the kids into the basement. Would giving them nightmares be considered child abuse, he wondered.

On the way to the barn they passed the back mudroom door. They could hear Tifflin's dogs barking behind it, and it was shaking as they lunged against it. Just as Tifflin's realtor was assuring them there was nothing to worry about—the door would hold—the bottom of the door gave way and a pair of German shepherds muscled their way out.

"Stop! Stand still!" For once, Lizzie listened to Mae's commanding voice. The dogs slowed and circled them, barking until they stopped at Lizzie. They were the same height as her face, which they sniffed and licked. Lizzie just laughed and scratched their ears until the handlebar moustache collared and stowed them inside the house.

"No harm done," he said as he re-emerged. "Absolutely harmless. A couple of big babies, really. Let's check the barn." He strode past them all, his moustache leading the way. He seemed determined to complete the walk through and if at all possible save the deal and collect his commission.

In some ways the barn was an extension of the house—cluttered and cobwebbed. But Evan expected this and it didn't bother him. In fact, the barn was the one thing he liked about the place—remnants of animal smell, old hay in the loft, massive beams joined by wooden pegs, the classic shape of the hip roof, the empty horse stalls he imagined one day might be occupied. Hell, the wiring and lighting in the barn were better than in the house, though the tack room had some funky electrical work that made him suspect it had been used for a grow-op.

A noisy, smelly herd of swine in the sty beside the barn dampened his enthusiasm a bit. The sty had been rented out by Jace to a neighbor, a Dutch farmer. Soon enough, though, the pigs would be gone, the smell would dissipate, and they'd have a paddock. He could imagine the smell of hay and horse manure already.

They emerged from the gloom of the barn into the harsh sunlight, the walk-through over. They silently loaded into the minivan—a Plymouth Voyager—and rolled down the pot-holed laneway to the road, Evan doing his best to navigate around the deepest craters. Tifflin's realtor followed in his Dodge Ram, bright red, clean, and accented with lots of chrome.

"Well," Annalise broke the spell. "It'll be interesting to see what we find here in three days." *We,* thought Evan, that's a good sign.

"Anyone know the local sheriff?" Todd asked. "His number might come in handy in case you need an eviction notice. After all, possession is nine-tenths of the law."

Evan hoped it wouldn't come to that. He'd never had any serious dealings with the law—whether cops or lawyers—and the few times he'd been pulled over for speeding he had enough guilt and common sense to show regret for his violation and respect for lawful authority.

Now with his and Mae's search for a home, they'd had more dealings with bankers, realtors, and lawyers than made him comfortable. He always felt at a disadvantage, as if he was being scammed in some way and they were enjoying it, glee masked by their serious faces. He told himself he was just being paranoid, that these people were offering him a service and expecting to get paid for it, that was all, but he couldn't shake the feeling they were in the know while he was in the dark. Not to mention that the whole process made him feel vulnerable, exposed to errors, accidents, and even incompetence he couldn't see coming. And strokes, for that matter. He hadn't felt this vulnerable, this paranoid, since he'd eloped with Mae and honeymooned at the Talisman, looking almost the whole time in the rearview mirror or over his shoulder for the cops or, worse, his ex-military father-in-law.

Up until this point, he and Mae had been renters—starting way
back before Alex was born. They'd started out camping in the basement
of Mae's parents' house for a few weeks, until they found a small attic
apartment to rent on London's Queen Street. Her dad wasn't especially
pleased about taking in Evan after what he'd done to and with Mae, his
oldest daughter. During those few weeks, Evan avoided her father by
picking up as much overtime as he could in his summer job working
in a plant nursery. As he helped customers cultivate their gardens and
landscape around their houses, he imagined pregnant Mae at her folks'
home. Harbored, cloistered, or trapped—he wasn't sure exactly how she
was feeling. Her father was more than happy to help them move out.

After some months in the attic apartment, they realized they'd need
something better with a baby coming, so in November they moved to
the second floor of a three-story walk-up apartment building closer to
university. It was convenient for Evan since he was working on his Accounting degree. When Mae starting waitressing at a downtown restaurant eight months after Alex was born, she could walk to work.

Their windows looked out on an empty building that had been a
convent at one time. It was rumored to be occupied by homeless men,
derelicts in a derelict building. He imagined them peering out their
windows into his, the sheer curtains failing to give Mae and himself the
privacy they needed. After the illicit passion that led to their marriage,
they were now learning to be at home in the pleasure of each other's bodies. This was disturbed by his imagining these down-on-their-luck men
watching Mae approach her climax above him, possessed by it. When he
encountered such homeless men on the street, he avoided their eyes for
more than the ordinary reasons.

Just once did he meet such eyes. He'd taken a load of clothes down to
the basement laundry room. Awkwardly holding the basket, he opened
the door to find a young man, probably about the same age, prying at
the coin basket with a screwdriver. They looked at each other for a brief
moment in silence. For his part, Evan was too surprised to say anything.
What he saw in the young man's eyes was something hunted, something
stony but restless.

Then the spell was broken. The young man barged past Evan, elbow-
ing him hard in the chest and holding up the screwdriver as a warning.

He was glad when he graduated and got a job at Wheel and Barrow
Chartered Accountants, as it gave them the freedom to move. He and
Mae found a house for rent in their old neighborhood in south London

near the highway—a split-level with three bedrooms and a family room. They were trying hard to have more kids, but it wasn't working. Ironically, given her first pregnancy, Mae had developed secondary infertility. Evan sometimes wondered if some damage had happened to her womb during her pregnancy with Alex, but what did he know? He knew only it was empty and Mae felt it. He tried to fill it, he really did. They carefully timed their sex now, attentive to any signs of ovulation, but without success. They tried to distract themselves from the empty third bedroom by turning it—temporarily, they said—into a home office and sewing room, but they never really fooled themselves or the house.

Then seven years after Alex was born Mae was surprised to learn she was pregnant with Lizzie. Evan moved the office furniture into the basement, took the crib down from the attic where it had been banished, along with the dusty change table and diaper pail. He put a gate at the top of the stairs, and the highchair at the kitchen table. On the wall above it were Mae's photos of horses from Sable Island and the Alberta foothills.

It was when Lizzie was two that Mae signed up Evan for that summer carpentry course at WLM-KSS, the school they'd gone to as teenagers, and he built her the jelly cupboard for their kitchen. As he constructed the cabinet, a strange door opened within him. Maybe it was working with the wood. Maybe it was the thought of jellies and other preserves. He felt urged to leave the city and set up some sort of country life. He convinced Mae by talking about space to grow, tire swings for the kids, old houses with real character, picture-book horses in a picture-book pasture. Hell, he could've turned his spiel into a great article for *Country Living* or *This Old House*, complete with glossy photos.

So he and Mae had started travelling the county roads around London with the realtor his in-laws had once used. That was before Ralph from ReMax had his stroke, of course. Though it was about twenty years since the 1970s farm crisis, many farm families still hadn't recovered and never would. A lot of land had been bought up by the government or sold off to bigger outfits in the move to factory farming. As a result, Evan and Mae looked at many houses so rundown as to be almost unlivable. Houses without furnaces. Houses with toxic insulation inside their walls. Houses with old, wavy-glassed windows and slanted floors. Evan felt they were travelling back in time when they approached these tall farmhouses, the sandstone brick darkened by decades of weather, and then crossed the threshold onto worn linoleum.

Annalise and Todd were with Evan and Mae when ReMax Ralph showed them this house, the house they were now going to take possession of in three days. Mae thought the house had a lot of character. Annalise agreed. They both saw the potential. Todd, a handy guy who knew a lot about electrical work, plumbing, and construction, listed off the problems he saw. But when he caught the look on Annalise's face, he quickly added there wasn't anything that couldn't be fixed. Evan was sure, though, that when they were descending into the basement he heard Ralph mutter, "money pit."

None of them foresaw that the one problem that couldn't be fixed was the seller, Jace Tifflin. They'd learned from Ralph that Jace was the sole owner of the property. His common-law wife had no say in the matter, no influence as far as they knew. So when the date of possession came, moving day, with all the legal paperwork and bank documents signed, with Evan having lined up friends and family to help, he was afraid of what he'd find when he rolled up the driveway with the first load of boxes and furniture.

Jace was gone. His wife and his son were gone. The dogs were gone. Much of the furniture was gone. The message was gone from the bathroom mirror. Left behind was a mass of construction material in an upstairs bedroom, an old tent and some boxes of discarded clothing in the attic, cold ashes in the wood stove, rotten water in the taps, and a basement full of junk including the two freezers—along with a lingering sense of the lives lived here, damaged now and displaced. Outside, a derelict pick-up truck was parked by the collapsing shed, which was also filled with metal castoffs. That day, they didn't even bother to go out to the barn.

"Well," said Todd, "It's better than I expected, but I'd still talk to your lawyers about getting Tifflin to clean up his mess." Having had his say, Todd pulled out the ramp on the U-Haul, set it on the top step of the side porch, and began lugging boxes into the house through the glare of the hot July sun. Mae directed them to pile everything in the family room until she and Annalise cleaned. By day's end, the rooms were populated with boxes, some with their lids already open, along with furniture placed tentatively, awaiting final arrangement.

With family and friends fed and thanked, beds assembled, and the kids finally asleep in this strange house, Evan and Mae plopped down their tired bodies on a couple of kitchen chairs and shared a beer. They hadn't yet found the bottle of wine they'd bought to celebrate. Several cats, banished from the house after spending the day trespassing through the open door, mewed at the windows. Flies lazily circled the single light bulb below the ceiling fan.

Evan looked around the kitchen, his eyes settling on the empty jelly cupboard before turning to the darkening sky outside the window, where a half-moon hung in the sky. Half full or half empty, he mused, then said, "Well, we're now the proud owners of a fixer-upper, plus an albatross of a mortgage. What do you think?"

"I think we've made a mistake."

"What? I thought this was the house you wanted."

"It was. It is. And it isn't. Now that we're in it, we're really deep in it, if you know what I mean." Mae paused. "Forget it. I guess I'm just tired. It doesn't feel like home, like it even belongs to us."

"It'll just take some time."

"And a shitload of work."

"Can you make it work, though?"

"I have to, don't I?"

"It'll help to get everything unpacked and in its place."

"It might be better just to blow up the place and start over."

"It already kinda looks like a bomb went off." He paused. "I'll call Tifflin's realtor on Monday and see if I can get him to clean up his shit and fix the water."

"Good luck with that."

Evan had booked two weeks of vacation around their moving date, so the week following their move was filled with unpacking their stuff— lugging and shifting boxes and furniture, along with fighting to get shiftless Jace Tifflin to shift himself and his possessions. It started with an unreturned phone message to Tifflin's realtor on Monday, left after the phone company had come to hook up the phone.

"Hey, you've reached Danny Drake! I can't come to the phone right now, likely 'cause I'm makin' someone's real estate dream a reality. But if ya leave a message, I'll get back to ya soon!"

As the machine beeped, Evan felt his chest tighten. He recited the message he'd rehearsed: "Mr. Drake, this is Evan Mulder. We moved into Jace Tifflin's house on Saturday, and I'd like to talk about the state he left things in. What he promised to do isn't done, we still don't have safe water, and his stuff is everywhere. We need something done."

When Evan hadn't heard back from Danny Drake by Tuesday afternoon, he called again, leaving what he hoped sounded like a firmer message, one that mentioned lawyers. He suspected, though, that what he hoped was a firm message sounded hollow on the recording, easy to dismiss by someone like Danny Drake busy making real estate dreams a reality.

Evan was surprised, then, when on the Wednesday morning a truck rumbled up the driveway, turned around on the lawn, and deposited a large dumpster near the mudroom door.

He approached the driver who was sliding the dumpster off the truck bed using the hydraulic controls. "Hi. What's with the dumpster? Are you sure you've got the right place? I never ordered it."

The driver didn't pause on the hydraulics. "You Jace Tifflin?"

"No."

"Sure?" The driver studied Evan for a moment. "He's the guy ordered the bin. If ya don't want it, just call that number on the side there. They'll send me back to pick it up. But right now, I'm told to deliver a bin, I deliver a bin." The dumpster boomed as the near end hit the ground. The driver returned the truck bed into place, then retrieved paperwork from the cab showing the order had the right address and Tifflin's name on it.

"If I sign this, do I have to pay for it?"

"Only if your name's Jace Tifflin." The driver paused and studied Evan again. "Sure you're not Tifflin?"

"I'm sure of it, absolutely. My name's Evan Mulder. At least, it was last time I checked."

"Then no need to sign. Tifflin did and put down a deposit. He'll have to pay the rest when we haul off the garbage to the dump and get it weighed."

As the truck rumbled down the driveway, Evan studied the dumpster. He didn't know they came this big. It looked as if it could hold all of Tifflin's stuff and then some.

The bin stood empty until the middle of the Thursday afternoon, when a pick-up truck bounced up the laneway and reversed into position beside it. When they heard the truck, Evan and Mae came to the porch door, curious about their visitor. A tall, thin man stepped out the truck, let down the tailgate, and then, unsure for a moment what to do next, headed to the mudroom door.

Evan and Mae emerged from the porch and intercepted him.

"Hey, there. Can we help you?"

"Hope so. I'm Jace, Jace Tifflin." He held out his hand. Evan found Jace's grip strong, his hand rough and wiry. His smile seemed genuine enough, though it exposed a couple of missing teeth, the remaining ones nicotine-stained like his fingers. His long hair was gathered in a loose ponytail at the nape of his neck.

As Evan and Mae returned his greeting, Jace surveyed the house and the property around it. "Sorry about the mess, especially when you came to see the house the other day. Funny story that. We'd had a break-in, see, so we were told by the cops to preserve the evidence. We couldn't do anything till they were done."

Evan exchanged a glance with Mae. He could tell she was equally dubious of Jace's story. "I hope it turned out alright. They didn't take anything valuable, did they?" Her concern covered her disbelief. Mae believed in letting people preserve their dignity. It was one of her mottos. Evan had frequently heard her say, *The least they can do is leave them some dignity.*

"Not that I can tell. They just made a mess of things. Must've heard my dogs scratching and barking to come in and decided to get while the getting was good. My dogs are real territorial. They don't take kindly to trespassers."

"Well, I hope they catch whoever did that to you." Mae turned to Evan. "I think I hear Lizzie. She must be up from her nap. It's so hard to sleep in this heat. Nice to have met you, Jace."

"Likewise." As Mae made her way to the porch door, Jace continued. "I've got a little one myself, Jace Jr.—six next month." He paused to pull a pack of cigarettes and lighter out of his shirt pocket. Before lighting up, he held up the cigarette and said, "Mind if I smoke?"

"No problem. Go ahead." Evan had never been tempted to smoke, had never even tried a puff. He just didn't understand the habit.

"Thanks. Seems like there's no place anymore to light up. Pretty soon the government'll make it a law you can't smoke in bars. Next thing it'll be your car and your own home." Jace lit his cigarette with a puff, then took a drag and exhaled. The smoke drifted around Evan. There was an awkward silence during which he debated whether he should side with Jace against the government. Then Jace continued. "See the bin arrived."

"Yeah, yesterday morning. What's the plan?"

"Thought I'd finish cleaning up my stuff. You know, sorting what to keep and what to dump." Jace took another thoughtful drag. "It's kinda hard, 'cause a lot of the stuff is from my folks. They used to farm all this land around about here till they lost most of it, bought up by the government. You've got what's left."

"So you grew up here? I didn't know that."

"Yeah—kinda hated it back then and got away as fast as I could. Went out to Alberta for a while. Actually played minor league baseball for a few years, pitcher, until I blew out my shoulder. Came back to take care of my folks—they're in a home in London. Drive truck now. Been trying to fix up the place for a few years, but it's hard going when you're on the road all the time. Not to mention my folks couldn't keep the place up. You're welcome to whatever materials you find, if you can use them."

Evan knew from talking with Ralph that Tifflin needed pretty close to his asking price just to break even, to pay his creditors. Ralph had hinted too about strains between Jace and his wife. No wonder, Evan thought, given the situation. He felt a bit bad for undercutting that price, but, hey, Ralph had said buying a house required tough negotiation.

Jace returned to his original thought. "It'll take some time, but I should be able to get my stuff cleared out by next week."

"What about the water?" Evan was reluctant to push the point, but they needed the system fixed. As it was, they were getting by with bottled water. That couldn't continue.

Jace leaned in confidentially. "I've got a plan. See, I've got some base-ball memorabilia I'm sure is worth a lot of money, stuff any baseball fan'd pay good money for. Fact is, I got a baseball signed by the one and only Fergie Jenkins. Met the man himself. Great guy. More than that, I've got a program from the Jays' home opener back in '77, their very first season. I was there with my dad, April 7, 1977, in the snow at Exhibition Stadium. Great day. Magic."

"That's amazing," Evan said. "I'm a huge fan. They're having such a fantastic year, I can see them going all the way."

"Damn straight. With Carter playing like he is, it's going to happen. Anyway, back in '77 my dad had a cousin that worked for the Jays, see, so we got into the clubhouse after the game. Met all the players—Bill Singer and Dave Lemanczyk, Ernie Whitt and Dave McKay. The whole gang. Remember Doug Ault, got two homers in that game? But I didn't just meet them, no sir. I got nearly every guy to sign my program. That's right. Gotta be worth a bundle now. Once I find the ball and the program, I'll sell em—should get me at least a couple a thousand—and I'll get the water fixed, right as rain."

Evan listened to Jace's plan and felt his heart sink. He recognized a longshot when he heard one. He knew there was little hope of getting Jace

Tifflin to fix the water. Evan accepted that he and Mae would have to find the funds themselves.

He met Jace's eyes for a moment when Jace had finished. There was something familiar there, though he couldn't say what. Something hunted about his look. It would haunt Evan for a long time to come. "Okay. Just let me know when you've got the money." He watched Jace finish his cigarette and toss the butt onto the grass, grass that once belonged to Jace and now belonged to him—as much as grass could belong to anyone. The butt sent up smoke signals that couldn't be deciphered. "Well, I'll leave you to it. The back door is open, and so's the door to the basement. Let me know if you need any help lifting things. I'd be happy to help move things along."

"No need for that. By the way, if you're looking for a little cash yourself, you might check with the county about that shed." Jace pointed to what passed for a dilapidated garage, the end walls leaning in and the roof line bowed in the middle. "A couple a years ago a lady stopped by, said that shed was the original schoolhouse from the crossroad to the west. Said it doubled as a church in the pioneer days, too. If you make some noise about it, you might get the county to pay you for it—you know, a historical monument. Maybe they'll want it for a museum."

"Thanks. I'll look into it."

For the rest of the afternoon, Evan and Mae heard Jace tramping up and down the basement stairs, shifting things around, hauling keepers out to his truck and tossing discards in the dumpster. All this while they themselves continued to unpack, to settle in. The first booms were soon followed by more muted crashes as the bin began to fill up. They could hear his footfalls until well after dinner, Jace sorting his family's possessions in a house he no longer owned. It was an eerie and unsettling feeling for Evan, to have his and Mae's house—which didn't yet feel like theirs—occupied in this way, Jace Tifflin rummaging below the floor.

When they finally heard the rumble of Jace's truck heading down the driveway and then gearing up as he turned right onto the county road, Evan and Mae checked out the basement. Given all the activity they'd heard going on, there was still a discouraging amount of junk. They headed up the back stairs and out the mudroom to check the dumpster. With all the stuff left in the basement, there was a surprising amount already in the bin. Evan wondered if junk multiplied as rapidly as cancer cells or rats.

That was the last they saw of Jace Tifflin. They'd hoped he'd come back to finish the job, but when his truck headed west down the county road he became nothing but a ghost to them.

After several weeks, Evan made a half-hearted attempt to find out where Jace was through the lawyer who had handled the sale for Tifflin, but the lawyer either didn't have Jace's forwarding address or wouldn't give it. As far as the lawyer was concerned, the deal was done and there was nothing more to it. One of their new neighbors heard a rumor that Jace, his wife, and Jace Jr. were living in a cottage down by the lake, but Evan never found out where.

What happened is that mail started arriving for someone named Chase Teflon. What a ludicrous name, Evan thought. Chase Teflon. Jace Tifflin could've done a lot better choosing an alias was his initial thought. What kind of business was Tifflin-Teflon mixed up in? It couldn't be any good if he was using a fake name like that. At first, Evan wrote "Previous owner" and "No longer at this address" across the envelopes and put them back in the mailbox by the road, the post sitting in a barrel filled with rocks. After a while he didn't bother and just let the overdue bills and threatening notices pile up near the wood stove, still unsafe to use. He knew that was what they were. He found them substantial and weighty, a good stand-in for the ghost of Teflon-Tifflin.

It was during this time of giving up on Tifflin-Teflon that he and Mae called Annalise and Todd, along with the rest of the moving crew, and asked them to come out one more time. Together, they hauled the freezers out of the basement and dumped the contents behind the shed. They lined up the freezers beside an old fridge, a washer, and a stove on the lawn. They made a burn pile of broken furniture. They dumped boxes of junk into the bin.

But they didn't stop with Jace's stuff. "The bin's here. Might as well use it" was Mae's reasoning. So they went room to room through all their worldly possessions, thinning out the accumulation of a decade of married life.

"Let's keep it a while longer," he suggested to Mae when their help was gone. "We can use it to get started on some reno work, and maybe to clean up the barn. It's the least Jace can do for us."

About a week later, a pick-up truck again bounced up the driveway. He and Mae were working outside on more clean-up and thought for a minute it might be Jace, but no, it was an older guy, his shaved-bald head shining in the sun, his Harley T-shirt tight across his chest and biceps.

He walked toward them, looking around, and held out his hand. "George Tifflin. Here's my card. I'm in the salvage business. I noticed you folks moved in and thought I'd stop by to see if I could help. These old farms can have a lot of stuff that's just been lying around for years, decades even."

Evan interrupted. "Did you say Tifflin? Maybe you know the guy that used to live here, Jace Tifflin?"

"Matter of fact, I do. I'm his uncle. Sorry to say though I haven't seen him for years."

"No?"

"We had a falling out. Happens in families. I wouldn't want to bore you with our dirty laundry."

"We've been curious about the history behind the house. Wouldn't mind hearing the story, if it's not too painful for you."

"Afraid it's an old one. It was the late seventies. Times got tough and we were struggling to keep the land in the family, to keep up the farming. My brother and his wife, Jace's folks, they were in a bad way. And what does Jace do? Goes west to play baseball, of all things. Waste of time. And while he was gone, they went under and had to sell up. Practically had to give it away to the government. But that's not the worst of it. Five or six years later, he shows up like the prodigal son, expecting to be forgiven. Before the year was out he'd gotten the house for himself and shipped them off to some retirement home in the city. I couldn't abide by that. Gave him hell and we haven't spoken since." He paused to look around. "And now he's lost what little was left."

Evan felt mildly uneasy. Mae's refrain *the least they could do is leave them some dignity* ran through his head.

"I'm sorry for your family's troubles," Mae said. "I have to say we've had our own problems with Jace."

"I expected as much. That's really why I'm here. I'm out of farming and into salvage. What I do know is junk. The least I can do for you is take care of all these old appliances and any other metal you got lying around."

Evan replied, "Sure, take what you want."

Mae jumped in before he could give away the farm. "There's some stuff I'd like to keep, so we'd need some time to set it aside."

"No problem, no problem. Let's say I come back next Saturday. That'll give you a week. Did I give you my card?"

As mail for Chase Teflon piled up, George Tifflin came and hauled away several loads of old appliances and other metal scraps. At least it's all getting recycled, Evan thought. Eventually, he called to have the dumpster hauled away, filled to the brim with Jace's castoffs and their own. Evan called the county office about the dilapidated shed, but they had no record of its history as a settlement school and church. He and Mae spent a Saturday knocking it to the ground.

Though they were settling in—even Alex and Lizzie were starting to sleep regularly—flotsam of Tifflin's past continued to float into view. One day in the fall, Evan and Mae were scouting the countryside, not really looking for Jace, when they came across a dirt road marked "not maintained" that trailed off into the bush. It was named Tifflin Road.

Evan and Mae had come to see that many roads in the area were named after settler families, early generations who had carved the farms out of the bush, graduating from log homes to large brick houses if they were successful—at least until a couple of decades ago.

As the sign for Tifflin Road diminished in his rear view mirror, Evan thought about the Tifflin generations linked to his and Mae's house, the men and women and children that had occupied it and furnished it with their ordinary hopes and troubles, wearing away the linoleum. The past several weeks, troubles at Ipperwash over land claims had dominated the news. The Natives were restless, tired of broken treaties and stolen land. That seemed far away, on one of the other lakes—Lake Huron—but it made Evan realize that before the Tifflins, there were others on the land he and Mae now owned. He'd taken possession without knowing a thing about it.

Some might say it didn't matter, that taking possession was about today and tomorrow, not yesterday, about gaining legal title to the land, but he wasn't so sure. When they rolled up the driveway, the house now looked occupied to him, not just by his family but by the ghosts of Jace and all the other Tifflins, by Natives whose old paths were blocked by the buildings he now owned, whose old hunting grounds were now fenced off. He was unsettled. He wasn't so sure he was entitled to the place.

As the fall deepened, the pile of Chase Teflon's mail sitting beside the cold woodstove grew. "You need to do something about that stack of mail," Mae said.

"You're right. I'll take care of it." He knew she meant him to drop it all off at the post office, deal with the confusion, and maybe report Tifflin's Teflon alias. But Evan pulled on his barn coat and gloves against the cold, took the bag outside, and started a fire in the burn barrel. He slowly fed Chase Teflon's mail into the flames. Maybe he was breaking the law, but Chase Teflon didn't exist, did he? He felt he was doing right by the man who called himself Jace Tifflin.

In early December, Evan was getting the Christmas decorations out of the attic for the first time in their new house. He noticed that boxes and furniture were beginning to pile up—out of sight, out of mind, just like in the basement. When he went to retrieve a nutcracker that had tumbled off the edge of the attic floor where it met the roof boards, he discovered a box that must have been jammed there and forgotten some time ago. He opened the lid to find a baseball and a home-opener program, both of them signed just as Jace had said.

But that wasn't all. There was a tarnished silver baby spoon with a rabbit on the handle, a child's worn-out baseball glove, a few shells and smooth stones, and some coarse hair tied in a knot, hair Evan assumed was from a horse's mane or tail. And there were photographs, many of them taken on the front porch of the house—pictures of Jace on the first day of school, framed by the wooden door. As Evan flipped through the pictures, he watched Jace grow younger and younger. There was one that must have been of Jace and his dad at the home opener, grinning with arms around each other in front of Exhibition Stadium.

The last photo was of a baby in a christening gown, held by his mother who was in turn held by the father of her child. And the three at the center of the tableau were flanked on either side and even behind by a host of others, men and women of all ages. So here were the Tifflins, placing their hopes in God and the latest Tifflin, baby Jace.

As Evan lifted the photo to look closer, he noticed below it an old document. At the bottom of the box he found a copy of the original deed to this property and much of the surrounding land, the Tifflin homestead.

He surveyed the objects and photos and papers piled outside the box. All of this, he thought, has come into my possession, whether I want it or not. So many lives, so much lost. Wreckage. Jace was gone and wasn't coming back for any of it.

Evan carefully returned everything to the box and closed the lid. Soon, when he couldn't stand the cold in the attic anymore, he'd show it all to Mae.

A Beginner's Guide
to Getting Plastered

"What a ball-less chicken shit!" Mae shouted after the Sears home-reno salesman as his truck picked up speed heading down the gravel drive to the county road. She and Evan were standing side by side on the lawn off their side porch.

"Proves my point, though, doesn't it?" Evan couldn't help it, pushing into *I told you so* territory. He and Mae had been back and forth over the long list of renos their old farmhouse needed. They'd lived in it about a month, and Mae was fidgety, unsettled.

She was having none of his lip. "All I wanted was an estimate, not his kidney or his first-born child. It's not even like I expected him to do the work himself." She had set up an appointment for an estimate about their windows and doors, their roof, and the siding on the back side of their house—just to get an idea of what would be involved, what kind of cost they were facing.

The salesman had looked at the house for little more than a minute. He'd barely gotten around the house when he'd said, "There's no way we can take on a job like this!" and hustled back to his truck.

Now his Dodge Ram—bright blue, lots of chrome—kicked up a blast of gravel as he turned right and headed back to London. Evan imagined the salesman at one of the many bars the city offered, recovering from the shock of seeing their house. He saw the guy perched on a stool, red-rimmed eyes shedding tears in his beer as he quietly got plastered, seeking solace in drink. Evan was sure the salesman was counting himself lucky to have escaped a country nightmare. That's what he and Mae had bought, and here they were standing beside it—*Canadian Gothic*, minus the American pitchfork.

"I don't know why you want an estimate. It's not like we have any more cash to throw into this money pit."

"That joke's getting old—and less funny every day. You might be happy living in a hell hole, but I'm not. I need to turn this place into a home."

"Who said I'm happy?"

Mae turned back to the house, annoyance flinging outward like sparks from every step she took. She disappeared through the old wooden door, painted hunter green. Broken glass was patched with a greying piece of plywood.

Though Evan had turned to follow her, he hesitated. In the month since they'd moved in, he'd been possessed by doubt and regret, blaming himself for pushing this dream of living in the country. They'd been worn down, maybe by all the dumps they'd visited with their realtor. This house seemed a mansion by comparison. Mae had seen potential in the place, with its high ceilings and substantial woodwork, even though it was badly run down and poorly maintained by the previous owner, Jace Tifflin, who had started a number of reno projects but never finished anything. Evan could feel the defeat when he walked from room to room.

We should have listened to our realtor, he thought. ReMax Ralph was the one who muttered "money pit" after leading them through the half-finished upstairs bedrooms, the main floor's disastrous kitchen and bathroom, and the ancient, low-ceilinged basement.

That was just this past March, but it now seemed a lifetime ago. In the harsh, unflattering light of an August noon, the house looked like an old hag. There was something monstrous about it. One half of the house was two-story sandstone brick, a looming structure pockmarked and blackened by more than a century of southwestern Ontario weather. Both the floor and roof of the front porch were sagging, making a toothless grin facing the road.

The back half, presumably added some time after the brick structure was raised in 1867, was a low and squat appendage, sided with clapboard going rotten and green-black with mold. The roof was covered with decaying black shingles, patched in places with dull tin sheets. Here and there bare patches of roof board were showing through.

All the windows were old and ill-fitting, the panes wavy and bubbly glass, as if they had cataracts. The ill-fitting doors were as draughty as the windows. On windy nights the front door simply blew open. Around the whole house were overgrown shrubs—lilacs, snowball bushes, forsythia all gone wild, cedars planted too close to the foundation and now crowding the brick and blocking the lower windows. On the east side, a plum tree planted beside the house climbed to the second story. With the slightest breeze the branches tapped against their gothic-arched bedroom window. He swore he sometimes heard the tapping even when the air was fully still.

He stood now on the opposite side of the house, facing the door that had swallowed Mae. Reluctantly he entered and paused as his eyes adjusted to the inside gloom. The family room he stood in was dominated by rough eight-by-eight posts and beams added at some time in the house's history to prop up the second floor. Everything wooden was painted hunter green—not only the posts and beams, but all the trim around the windows and door, the door itself, the wainscoting on the walls, the baseboards, and the sheets of plywood that separated this back part of the house from the front. Jace Tifflin had obviously been aiming to turn the house into some sort of a lodge or den or man cave.

Evan walked into the kitchen looking for Mae. Hunter green paint—it must have been on sale—cloaked the wood trim in the kitchen and dining room and even the staircase spindles going up. In all the bedrooms, Jace had attached wainscoting to the flat and slanted portions of the ceilings. He had stained some a dark walnut and painted others—again hunter green—to match the baseboards and deep window frames. In several places this woodwork was disturbed by cloudy water stains and crackled paint, injuries from rain leaking through the roof or penetrating the draughty windows, or from summer heat and humidity cooking the finish.

From the kitchen Evan could hear Alex and Lizzie playing upstairs. It sounded like Lego blocks for Alex and horses for Lizzie. Evan saw the living room door closed against him, knocked, and entered without waiting for a reply. Mae was sitting in the far corner of the couch, her face hidden by the most recent issue of *This Old House*, a magazine she'd started reading the past few months. Evan settled into the couch's other corner. He sat silently, unsure how to begin.

He didn't understand what was happening in the space between them, which seemed now to be occupied by a wall growing brick by brick. The living room door closed against him was one sign of it; her restlessness was another. Before the move, things had been strained. Since Lizzie had been born, Mae had shown less and less interest in sex. She complained that he was a passive partner in their marriage, and accused him of passive aggressive behavior when they disagreed. It was true; for some reason he didn't understand, he hated conflict, avoided it as much as he could.

For his part, he wondered what had happened to the girl who got pregnant, eloped with him, and ran off for a memorable honeymoon at the Talisman. He had a momentary vision of that bridal suite. Where was the girl who'd shared that crazy room with him? He wanted her back. He wanted her to step up, to get out of the house again. She'd supported him through university with waitressing and retail jobs, then quit to focus full-time on being a mother to Alex and trying to get pregnant a second time once he graduated and got his job at Wheel and Barrow Chartered Accountants. Lizzie was three now, old enough for daycare. They could use the money. He'd thought she believed in women's lib. When he raised the point, she argued it was because of women's lib she could choose being a mother as her career. That's what she wanted to do, she didn't have other ambitions, and she had the studies to show she was right about the developmental importance for children. She'd told him, you're the accountant, you make the money work.

He'd thought moving to the country might change things. How naïve. He'd tried to be bold and decisive, to give them a fresh start—and they'd landed in this pit of a place. It was enough to drive a man to drink, he'd often thought. Not Margaritas, like on their honeymoon, but the fact was he was actually drinking a lot more than he normally did. When he got home from work, he grabbed a beer before supper just so he could face the house. He might have a whiskey or two late in the evening, after he'd half-heartedly puttered at some project. Sometimes another after Mae went to bed.

Without lowering the magazine, she asked, "Can I help you?"

He launched into what amounted to a rehearsed speech, something he'd been mulling over ever since Mae started pushing her reno projects.

"I don't mean to be a stick in the mud. But I thought we agreed we'd move slow on the renos—you know, do the repairs that absolutely needed to be done, do the rest when we had time and money." He'd secretly been hoping to delay any serious renos for a couple of years, a decade or more if he could get away with it.

Mae didn't move the magazine. "You agreed to that. I didn't."

"What about just doing some painting to spruce things up? Get rid of the green. Beige is a great neutral color. Wouldn't that be enough for now?"

She lowered the magazine into her lap. "Ever heard of a white-washed sepulcher? That's what a bit of paint will do to this place. Or to be more blunt, in terms you'll understand, throwing good money after bad." She paused. "Besides, you might be beige, but I'm not. I won't have a dull beige wall in my house."

So now I'm dull, he thought. Mr. Beige. He decided to try a different tack. "We're already in the middle of one big project. I don't think we should take on anything else—there's the time and energy and cost to think about."

"You know the bathroom absolutely had to be done. The toilet was practically falling through the floor, for crying out loud. Besides, we've made a lot of progress on it. It's just the finish work left, so we should be ready to tackle the next project. If we stop now, we'll lose our momentum. Before you know it we'll be sixty and still sitting in the same leaky boat."

"But to fix this boat we need our ship to come in." As he said this, Evan knew that the leap wasn't logical, but he needed to bring up the money. "To be honest, I need a break from this God-forsaken place. I'm starting to hate it. Everything's broken. It's a nightmare, from the bats in the attic to the beetles in the basement. It's driving me to drink. Right now, I wish we were back in our old house, back in the city where every-thing works." What he didn't admit out loud, of course, was that it was his idea to move to the country in the first place.

"Ready to give up, are you? To run screaming from the house and drown your sorrow in a pitcher of beer?" Mae got up and tossed down *This Old House*. "Help me move the couch."

"What? Why? You want to rearrange the furniture—again—right now?"

"Just shut up and do it."

As he helped her slide the couch away from the wall, he noticed for the first time the sledgehammer leaning in the corner. How long had it been there? When had Mae brought it in the house? *Why* had she brought it in? How come he hadn't noticed it before?

The wall behind the couch separated the living room from the laundry room. This wall had a strange bump in the middle, a bulge that made no sense. Evan had taken to joking that there might be a body in there, maybe one of the original builders. The poor man had been swallowed up more than a hundred years ago by the hungry maw of the house.

"Stand back," Mae warned and then swung the sledgehammer. Plaster crumbled and wood splintered as the hammer punctured the wall. Mae pulled out the hammer and swung it again and again and again.

"Careful! There might be wiring or plumbing in there."

Mae passed him the hammer. "Your turn." He gripped the handle, measured the weight, and swung. The crunch and collapse of the wall was gratifying. He felt the adrenaline, the release of some steam from his pressure cooker self. This was intoxicating. As he took more swings to widen the opening, it became plain the bump hid an old doorway that had once joined the two rooms.

"You wanted to know what was there. Now you know. Nothing to be afraid of."

"I wonder why they covered it up in the first place." It felt as if the house contained secrets, a history within and behind the walls. He took one last swing to see if he could dislodge the stud that had been installed in the middle of the doorway. The wood gave way with a shudder. A moment later he and Mae heard glass shattering and falling to the ground from the bedroom above them—Lizzie's room.

They stared for a moment at the living room window, stunned. "What the hell." Evan dropped the sledgehammer on the pile of rubble they'd created and headed to the stairs. He took them two at a time.

Standing in Lizzie's doorway, he saw his daughter perched on the window ledge looking down at the fallen glass below, her forehead and nose pressed against the wobbly glass, a plastic toy horse mid-gallop in her right hand. The upper half of the window, its gothic arch, was a vacancy, humid August air billowing out the animal-print curtains Mae had made for Lizzie. The entire window, its wooden frame and four glass panes, was missing, dislodged by their hammering and tumbling out of the rotten casing, the hunter green paint unable to seal it shut.

Instinctively, Evan said nothing. He didn't want to startle Lizzie. He covered the floor in a few rapid steps and grabbed her off the window ledge.

When he turned, Mae was standing in the doorway, her face white. He passed Lizzie to her and turned back to look at the window. "God, that was close," he said. For a moment, he imagined the lower sash giving way and Lizzie tumbling onto shards of glass on the ground below. "I guess some things can't wait," he admitted.

That afternoon, he took a couple of hours to board up the top half of Lizzie's window with a piece of plywood and screw the bottom half to the frame. For good measure, he covered the whole window, frame and all, with an old piece of wire fencing held in place by sturdy fencing staples. Lizzie couldn't climb onto the window ledge anymore. *My daughter's room is now a prison cell,* he thought. *Not good.* It took him a few drinks to get over it.

But Evan wasn't ready to capitulate—to the house or Mae—at least, not yet. He could be a stubborn Dutchman when a certain lunacy seized him, a cheap one too. Typically, when he sobered he realized he was just a Dutch Don Quixote tilting at windmills. Until then, he was in the grip of a kind of folly, at war with everything.

To keep the front door from blowing open at night, he guarded it with the heavy metal knight Mae had picked up a number of years ago at a yard sale. With its back to the door, the visored knight stood at attention with its shield and halberd.

To battle the infestation of flies, Evan hung yellow sticky traps in virtually every room and relished the flies' buzzing death-knells. Never mind that the strips were full and useless within a couple of days and the infestation back to full force. Or that he, Mae, and the kids often walked into them. Or that their dog sometimes sat and barked at the buzzing.

To battle the whining and stinging of mosquitoes at night, he lathered himself and the kids with Deep Woods Off and sprinkled their bedding with vanilla extract. It must have been more like a basting, for in the morning their faces and necks were itchy with stings. But he told himself he was winning the war, if not the nightly battle.

One morning, he and Mae woke to find their bedroom window covered with wasps warming themselves in the early sun—on the inside of the glass. He took the vacuum hose to them and sucked a dozen or more into the vacuum bag, which he gingerly removed and destroyed in the fire pit. He inspected the outside window trim and discovered two active wasp nests. He waged war on the invaders with cans of foamy wasp spray—nests in the window frames, nests in the eaves, nests in the attic.

To combat the oppressive heat, he bought expandable screens and portable fans. Wedged between the window ledge and the bottom sash of each window (except for Lizzie's, of course), the screens gave some relief—when there was a breeze. When a heavy wind gusted, though, they invariably popped out and the sash crashed to the ledge with a bang. He moodily carried fans from room to room, the simple effort adding to the sheen of sweat that made his shirt cling to his back. At night, at least, the whine of mosquitoes was drowned out by the drone of fans in their bedrooms.

When heavy summer rains drenched the house, he draped old towels on the soaked window ledges and manned the bailing buckets beneath the ceiling leaks. Sometimes he stood at the front window and watched the sheets of water roll off the humus-clogged eavestrough, the house's own waterfall.

When he heard a rattling in the chimney pipe leading from the wood stove in the family room, he donned his barn gloves, cautiously opened the door enough to see and reach in, then gently grabbed a struggling sparrow. He released the bird outside and returned to the stove, angry to find five dead birds among last winter's ashes. He cleaned out the stove and, though fearful of heights, climbed the roof to cap the chimney with a screen. He'd have to hire someone later to inspect whether the stove was even safe to use. He suspected not.

When the kids broke through a piece of rotten plywood on the front porch, he viciously took a pry bar and the sledgehammer to the steps. He wrapped caution tape from one worn post to the next to prevent anyone from getting trapped in the porch's jaws. When he stood back, the yellow and black tape seemed to add a crooked leer to the toothless grin. He felt he was losing his grip.

Late one evening as Evan was doing some of the finish work on their bathroom reno—installing some baseboard in the tight spots beside and behind the new toilet—he heard Alex yelling upstairs. "Dad, Mom, there's something flying around in my room!"

Evan was exasperated at the interruption and yelled from the bottom of the stairs, "Are you sure it isn't just a bug? It's probably a big mosquito, one that migrated from Manitoba. They're as big as birds out there."

"Very funny! I'm serious, there's something flying around, and it's too big to be a bug." Alex's voice sounded muffled, as if it were coming from under the blankets.

Mae joined Evan at the bottom of the stairs. "You better go up and see what it is. Take a fly swatter with you. It could be a horse fly."

When he got up to the landing armed with a pink swatter, Lizzie was standing in her doorway, curious about the commotion. He listened at Alex's door and heard an unusual whooshing sound within. "I'm going to open the door now, Alex."

At first, the light in the hallway made the darkness of Alex's room impenetrable. What is that sound, Evan wondered. Before he had time to consider further, two bats, confused by the light, flew out the doorway into the hall. He felt the breeze of their wings on his scalp as he ducked and yelled, startled and afraid.

"Lizzie, back in your room and close the door! Alex, stay under your covers!" Evan had a momentary vision of his children with bats tangled and struggling in their hair. It might be just an urban legend, but he didn't want to risk it. With the bats swooping, making an unpredictable circuit from one end of the hall to the other, he crawled along the floor to the stairway, pink swatter in hand, then raced down two steps at a time.

Mae was in the living room reading *Country Living.* "What's all the commotion?"

"Bats!"

"Bats in your belfry, how appropriate. Go get Lizzie's butterfly net. You might be able to catch them and get them outside that way. And please close the door until it's safe."

He rushed to the mudroom, pulled on his barn coat and raised its hood, then placed Mae's wide-brimmed straw hat over the hood and tied it under his chin with the red ribbon. He grabbed his barn gloves and found Lizzie's little blue butterfly net. It didn't look up to the job, so he also grabbed a corn broom and the metal lid of a garbage can.

Thus armed, he cautiously ascended the stairs. He first saw the shadows of the bats crazily sliding across the walls and floor as they continued their circuit around and in and out of the hall light. Sweating beneath his armor, he sat on the top step, looked up at the wheeling bats, and considered what to do next. Should he try to catch them with the net or swat them with the broom? A good swat would likely kill them.

The bats paused in their flight and landed on the screen Evan had installed in the hall window. Stilled, they were surprisingly small, with their large ears, furry bodies, and leathery wings that looked like arms. Perhaps they were tired, he thought. Maybe they were more confused and afraid than anything else. Even more afraid than he was. To them he was Evil Evan, not Even Evan—the friend to all animals he fancied myself, even to those critters invading his house.

The light, he thought. What an idiot. He reached up and turned off the switch, leaving only a patch of moonlight on the floor. He heard the bats take flight right away, swirling back and forth in the hallway, looking for an exit. He felt one land on Mae's hat and crawl along the brim. He fought the rising panic and gently brushed the bat away with his gloved hand. After a short pause to calm his nerves, he crawled along the floor to the window. With the bats whizzing above him, he stood and opened the lower sash its full height, removed the screen, propped open the window with the broom, and stood back. His eyes had adjusted enough to the gloom that after a minute or so he saw the bats find the opening and return to the night sky. He quickly reinserted the screen and lowered the sash, then peered out in search of the bats, only to find himself momentarily mesmerized by moonshine.

"All clear," he shouted eventually.

Alex and Lizzie emerged from their rooms, and Mae came up from the living room. She had rolled *Country Living* into a tube. "Just in case," she said, "there were more bats in your belfry." She bopped him on the head for good measure. They stared at him in his barn coat and Mae's hat, armed with net, broom, and shield.

"Funny daddy" was Lizzie's judgement.

"Silly daddy" was Mae's comment.

"Cool outfit, Dad," Alex said. "Can I wear it to bed? Except Mom's hat. I'll put on my bike helmet instead."

Evan checked Alex's room to investigate how the bats had gotten in. There was no obvious opening. The screen was in place, and Alex's window still had both a top and bottom sash, unlike Lizzie's. There was no crack or crevice in the ceiling wainscoting that might lead up to the attic. Were they here all along? More likely they squeezed through some small crevice in the loose-fitting window, but why would they want in?

In the years that followed, he would have to deal with the occasional bat in the house. He was always startled, unnerved. But when he was outside in the dusk of summer evenings, he would pause in whatever chore he was doing to watch and admire the bats swoop and circle, feeding on insects. He liked to imagine the bats were daytime's barn swallows transformed by moonlight, their flight seemed so similar.

The next morning, Evan was working—or pretending to work—at his sober job in his air-conditioned office at the very sober firm of Wheel and Barrow Chartered Accountants. ("You can count on us," was the practice's motto.) The state of the house and his marriage was an enormous distraction that kept pulling him away from the spreadsheet before him. He pictured Mae and the kids sweating it out at home, where so much was unsettled. For starters, there was Lizzie's broken window, with its bars. There was that hunter green paint everywhere accusing him of his less than manly stature. And then there were the holes in the wall, holes plural. Every couple of days when he came home from work he would discover that Mae had punched another hole in a wall, just to see what was behind it. The walls were beginning to take on the texture of Swiss cheese.

He pulled the Yellow Pages out of his desk drawer, found the section on waste disposal, and ordered the largest dumpster he could. He used the same company Jace Tifflin had used when cleaning up his junk, in the week after Evan and Mae had already moved in. It was just a couple of weeks since Evan had had Jace's dumpster picked up. After Jace's short-lived attempt to clean up, Evan and Mae, with lots of help from family and friends, had finished the job, more or less. On Jace's dime, they'd also thinned out their own stuff and gutted the bathroom.

Now, Evan realized, he needed to use his own dimes to exorcise the house, maybe to protect his family from it. He needed to save it, and to salvage his marriage.

He put away the Yellow Pages and called his sister Annalise.

"Sis, I need your help again."

She was unfazed. "I wondered how long it would take."

That Saturday, an army arrived—Annalise, her husband Todd, Evan's brother Jeff, a bunch of Evan's redheaded cousins (Lenny included), even his father-in-law Archie in his Happy Hearth van. They carried hammers, pry bars, and shovels into the house. They moved furniture out of rooms and unscrewed the kitchen cabinets from the walls. They donned dust masks and colorful bandanas, then began smashing at walls and ceilings.

Plaster hidden beneath several layers of wallpaper crumbled. Small chunks and huge sheets of the chalky stuff crashed to the floor and raised a fog of dust. What had been created by workmen more than a century before—the soft, smooth plaster hardened on top of hundreds, maybe thousands of pieces of lath—came down over the course of one long day.

Evan, Mae, and the whole crew shoveled the broken plaster into buckets, then dumped it out of windows onto chutes they'd rigged up. Bucket after bucket slid into the dumpster. What they couldn't reach by chute they carted to a wheelbarrow outside, then rolled it through the dumpster's opened doors into the bin.

Upstairs, they pried the hunter green and walnut wainscoting from the bedroom ceilings, exposing cracked and stained plaster. With the supporting wainscoting gone, much of the plaster plummeted to the floor.

In room after room they pried the lath from the studs, each piece of lath held by old iron nails with rectangular heads. They gathered lath by the armfuls, salvaging intact four-foot pieces and setting aside broken shards for the burn pile.

As the day wore on, they cleared out the kitchen, the dining room, the living room, the laundry room, and all of the bedrooms. By day's end, the brick structure was gutted. The work crew were plastered—covered in dust, chalky ghosts. Fed and lubricated, the sweaty army retreated into the night, leaving Evan and Mae to parlay with their house and each other.

All was now exposed—the old wiring, water pipes and drain pipes, duct work running within walls and between beams. It felt like the inside of a body, not exactly that womb-like honeymoon suite at the Talisman, but something with a skeleton, with circulatory and respiratory and digestive systems, and various organs.

"It's really quite amazing," he said. "Look at these studs. They're true two-by-fours, if you measure them, not planed down at all. And look at those massive beams. They've got to be true two-by-tens or twelves. Just think of the craftsmanship that went into this place."

"The house definitely has great bones. I mean, look at the brick walls." Mae walked over to the dining room wall and examined the now exposed brick. Given how thick the walls were, they'd speculated it was a double layer, tied together with bricks turned sideways every so often. Todd had heard of this construction method common before modern framing made it unnecessary. The beams above, joists for the second floor, were set directly into the brick walls. It was disconcerting to learn that between the plaster walls and the brick was no insulation, nothing, but opened up in this way, Evan and Mae at least knew what they were dealing with, what they were facing.

He turned to her. "You're quite the sight," he said and brushed some plaster dust out of her hair. He looked around and added, "There's no going back now, I guess." He studied a pile of rubble on the dining room table. Over the course of the day, Mae had gathered a variety of objects—trophies, she called them, and mementos. There were several pieces of wallpaper she'd salvaged from chunks of plaster. Some of the prints were floral, others more formal and elaborate Victorian designs. Layer by layer, these likely went back, he thought, to the house's original construction. Mae had also collected several iron nails of various sizes, from the inch-long ones holding the lath to the studs to three- or four-inch spikes. Each had a rectangular head with a smaller rectangular body that tapered to a fine point.

"Yeah, we're in it for the long haul, deep in the doo-doo," Mae replied. "So where should we start?"

That night, he didn't have an answer. He knew they'd have to do it right. He didn't want to rebuild it all in vain, so they'd have to do some serious planning. He also knew they'd have to do a lot of the work themselves.

"Maybe *This Old House* will have the answers," he said. "Isn't it like the renovator's Bible? You grab your magazines and I'll check if the show's on PBS tonight."

In the coming weeks, Mae ordered sets of how-to videos. Many evenings, they'd watch encouraging and confident DIY celebrities—some of them TV couples, either truly married or just video spouses, it was hard to tell—explain how to install insulation, replace a worn electric plug, install a kitchen sink, hang a door, put up drywall and mud the seams smooth. On and on it went, domestic bliss achieved through DIY. They placed the videos on a shelf next to their collection of screwball comedies.

During this time, Evan got curious about plaster, having broken up so much of it. He learned that plaster was typically comprised of lime, sand, and water. Sometimes horse hair was mixed in to strengthen it. Older plaster might be made with a clay base and contain straw and manure. He wasn't sure about the plaster they'd pulled out of their house, but he did wonder what they had breathed in and ingested during demolition.

He was alarmed to learn that asbestos had sometimes been used in plaster, rarely, but in the time before its dangers became known. To be safe, without telling Mae he mailed a sample of their plaster to a laboratory in

Toronto. Two weeks later, he was relieved to receive a report assuring him their house's plaster wasn't toxic. The report was silent about horse hair, straw, and manure.

He would share the asbestos scare with Mae only many years later, when he could at last reflect more soberly, with something close to nostalgia, about renovating their house. After all, for better or worse, they were about to dedicate their lives to it.

DOME

Evan normally slept like a baby. Obviously, he thought, the guy who first said that about babies hadn't met any—certainly not his and Mae's. As infants, both Alex and Lizzie were light sleepers whose wails through the baby monitor jolted Evan awake. Most nights, now that the kids were both a little older (eleven and three), he contentedly slid into bed beside Mae. He was on the side nearest the door, as he'd been ever since they eloped—twelve years back that he liked to call a lifetime. He would rub her back or scratch it for a minute, whatever she wanted, then kiss her neck or an ear. Maybe he'd test whether she was interested in something more. If not, he rolled over and nodded off in short mea-sure—less than a minute, if Mae's calculations were right. She'd shared this exasperating number with friends and family. Like the kids, she was a light sleeper who might take an hour or more to settle for the night. Evan frequently boasted to anyone who would listen that he fell asleep so easily because he had a clear conscience. His father-in-law once suggested it was a sign of having no conscience whatsoever.

But for more than a week now, Evan had woken up from a recur-ring nightmare. He was high up, hanging onto the edge of a dome with his left hand. The sky was a brilliant blue vault above him, populated by

circling birds he couldn't quite identify—maybe eagles or vultures riding updrafts. Below him was a vast expanse of thin air, a gaping space
terminating in an asphalt parking lot filled with cars, including their
1988 Plymouth Voyager minivan. He knew in his dream that this was the
Houston Astrodome, though he'd never been to Houston and had only
ever seen the dome in television images from baseball games. He didn't
know why it wasn't the SkyDome, which would make more sense given
that he lived in Ontario and was a Blue Jays fan. Like their minivan, the
SkyDome was now about three or four years old—a youngster loomed
over by the imposingly mature and upright CN Tower.

In the dream, Mae hung from his right hand, her grip painfully
tight, and he felt his left hand slipping from the lip of the dome. His fear
of the height was paralyzing. There was the horrifying moment of release,
his grip on both Mae and the dome lost, their rushing down to the van
or its rushing up to them, he couldn't tell. He erupted out of the dream, a
sudden reversal of gravity that jarred all his internal organs.

Like the biblical Joseph, Mae had been busy analyzing the dream
for him. Over breakfast the first morning, she offered this probe, reading
imaginary tea leaves in her cup: "Maybe you secretly want to dump me,
but because you come from a long line of Calvinists you're afraid of the
guilt you'd feel, so you're punishing yourself through an act of suicidal
self-dropping. Maybe you really believe you're going to hell, you good old
Puritan, you. And the road to hell starts in a stadium parking lot. Maybe
hell *is* a paved parking lot." As a fan of Joni Mitchell, he had to agree with
Mae about the parking lot, but he protested the rest.

One night before bed he was watching a baseball game in the family
room and she suggested this tie in, blocking his view of Joe Carter's at-
bat: "In your heart of hearts you really want to be a professional baseball
player rather than an accountant, so you're experiencing an identity crisis. You're trying to climb into the Astrodome to get on the field, where
a game's obviously going on, but I'm a drag on you. I might as well be a
ball and chain in the dream, tied to your wrist and weighing you down.
I'm killing your dream." Finished her diagnosis, she plopped down beside him on the couch, just in time for them to catch the ball descending
sharply over the center field wall. "Did he just get a touchdown?"

On Saturday afternoon, they headed out to do some shopping, Alex
and Lizzie in the back of the van. As Evan drove, Mae offered this in-
terpretation: "Maybe it's all about the van. You're experiencing anxiety
about whether it's going to start each morning, worried about whether

we can get another year out of it. You're even deeply ashamed of it. It emasculates you. What you really want is a sports car with a blonde in the passenger seat, so you're willing—in the dream, of course, I'm not saying you'd do this in real life—you're willing to drop me on the van so that it'll be destroyed by the impact. It's a small sacrifice, but you want the insurance—both for the van and me—so you can get the fancy car and the bimbo. Problem is, you end up destroying yourself too and never get the car of your dreams. The saddest thing for you is you can't collect any of the insurance because you're dead." Evan checked the rearview mirror to see how closely Alex and Lizzie were listening. Certain they weren't, he asked Mae if she knew any blonde bimbos.

One night after sex, they were sharing a bar of dark chocolate. Musing between squares, she spun this psychoanalytic web: "The dome, I think, is actually a giant boob. After all, you *are* a boob man. You're trying to scale the boob like a mountain climber, but it's not one of my boobs so I'm holding you back. Secretly, you want to have an affair with a single-breasted Amazon warrior—possibly that Rebecca Postma your mom wanted you to marry—so you're trying to drop my two boobs like a couple of hot potatoes to get your hands on at least one of that hussy's boobs. You know, a boob in the hand is worth two in the bra." Finished, she started licking the chocolate from her fingers, her skin wearing a sheen of moonlight. He protested that she was already more Amazon warrior than he could handle—why would he want another? But that night when he dreamt, the dome took on a fleshy look and feel that strangely heightened his fright.

The next morning, they were in the bathroom getting ready for the day and she picked up the bluebird of happiness off the window ledge. While he was shaving, she mused, "Maybe it's all about those birds. They're way up high where you want to be, unafraid in their natural element, but your arms aren't wings and you can't get to them. You really want to be a bird, not an accountant—sounds like a Daedalus and Icarus thing. It could be one of those birds is your father, and you're afraid he's completely forgotten to make you a set of wings, too. Of course, things didn't end too well for Icarus—would have been better if he'd been afraid of heights, like you." Evan appreciated Mae's ability to recall myths learned in high school and make sense of their own lives from them.

"Or maybe the birds represent astronauts way above you in orbit— out of reach because I'm gravity in your life and won't let you lift off. After all, it *is* the *Astro*dome, and Houston is all about NASA. That's it—I'm your gravity, pulling you into the grave—get the connection, gravity-grave—and you're not happy about it. The whole thing's a harrowing experience for you." He'd never thought of being an astronaut, though he did build a model rocket in high school.

"Or given your upbringing, maybe those birds are angels, and you're looking for them to rescue us. Could even be that one of them is the Archangel Michael, you know, like your middle name. If my memory's right, he's quite the warrior, leading God's army against Satan and defeating old Lucifer, fallen archangel that he is." As Evan Michael Mulder's razor stalled and hovered in midair, Mae put down the bluebird and started brushing her teeth, seemingly satisfied with her latest explanation. He stared into the mirror at his half-lathered face. He sought the archangel there, but couldn't find him.

Now, a few days later, he was both amused and disturbed by Mae's dream readings. Maybe in some of them she was too close to the truth. There had to be some reason he kept having the dream, some warning knot in his mind or cautionary tale sent by the universe. What he did know for sure was that his old fear of heights had kicked into high gear, that he was afraid of developing vertigo. He felt haunted and hunted by disaster.

What goes up must come down. He'd known it since childhood. After all, he grew up during the Cold War, the arms race, the race to the moon. Rockets escaping earth's gravity. Rocket men bounding on earth's pockmarked satellite. Rockets raining down from the sky. All those countries with all their missiles, all their bombs puncturing the skin-thin dome of blue surrounding the Earth. He remembered that most of the atmosphere was within just ten miles of the Earth's surface, the rest thinning out to nothingness at 300 miles. The drive from their farmhouse to the nearest town, Windermere, was about ten miles. That was all. He imagined driving ten miles straight up, and falling back down, the van stalling before he achieved the balance point of orbit. The van's impact blew a crater in the pasture. He imagined himself in the crater, trying to see over the lip of upturned earth.

He dwelt on painful falls. Years ago, Alex falling forward off his tricycle and smacking his mouth on the cement sidewalk, on their way home from the dentist no less. At the top of the stairs, Mae grabbing Lizzie's ankle to prevent a tumble after she had squirmed out of her mothering arms. His cousin Martha's husband Andy, a construction worker who fell to his death from the top of a high rise he was working on.

He remembered watching the Challenger Space Shuttle explode, over and over on the news. It wasn't that many years ago, five or six—seventy-three seconds of glorious flight against gravity blown apart by something as simple as failed seals. Seven lives consumed by fire, raining down to earth. What remains couldn't be identified buried in an Arlington Cemetery monument, the remains of the shuttle sealed underground in abandoned Minuteman missile silos. He thought of the model rocket he built in high school, how simple and innocent it all seemed then.

Now, he was on guard, on high alert. He was cautious on stairs and escalators, stayed clear of windows and balconies, gripped railings in elevators. He considered trimming the legs on the kitchen table and chairs so they were closer to the floor, maybe learning to eat reclined on pillows, Roman style. He checked the weather forecast for meteor showers. Whenever he was outside in the yard, he kept one eye on the sky for hail, lightning, tornadoes, descending planes, errant hot air balloons, and freak flying fish. In the car, he kept the other eye out for sudden sinkholes. Even barn swallows and birds on wires became potential dive bombers. To protect Alex and Lizzie, he'd pulled down and hidden the ladder to the barn loft. He was mulling over whether he should dismantle the play center, or maybe get a truckload of foam installed beneath it and around it. Or maybe he should just clothe the kids in bubble wrap.

If the dream didn't go away, he'd dismantle all their beds and leave the mattresses on the floor. If the news stories didn't change, he'd start digging a bomb shelter.

"You can't avoid it forever. If we don't do it soon, they'll collapse from the weight." It was a Saturday morning early in September, and Mae was trying to cajole Evan into cleaning the eavestroughs before they were filled with a fresh load of leaves from the Silver Maples, Kentucky Coffees, Weeping Willows, and other Carolinian trees that surrounded their old farmhouse. They were finishing up their bathroom reno by painting the wainscoting together. It was tight quarters, but they were managing. The dream had subsided in the past few weeks. It came a little less frequently, but it continued to hover just outside his consciousness.

"Maybe we should let them fall off and pay someone to put up new ones." He knew this was a lame idea, but he couldn't think of a better one to get himself out of this bind. He needed a *deus ex machina* to intervene. He'd settle for an archangel.

"After all the money we've put into the house this summer, you know we can't afford to hire someone."

"Guess I'll have to rise to the occasion."

"That's a groaner." She paused in her brush stroke. "Don't worry, I'll help. If nothing else, I'll break your fall if you tumble from the ladder." He imagined losing his grip, his balance faltering so he was pulled into a backward drop that knocked Mae to the ground in a cartoonish splat.

The summer of his nightmare was the summer they bought this old hobby farm and left city life behind. Maybe, he thought, the house was the source of his nightmare. Maybe the house *was* the nightmare. The house needed a ton of work, years' worth, and so far they'd gutted it of a dumpster-load of plaster and lath. What was exposed were comfortingly massive beams and joists, but also the insides of a double brick wall— without a shred of insulation. The outside had been neglected for years, if not decades. He'd had to block off the porch because the floor boards and railings were rotten, as was the roof. The gutters were filled almost to the brim with humus, a mixture of shingle grit and decayed leaves, and the downspouts were clogged. Rain just washed down the roof and over the eaves, creating waterfalls that dug a channel in the ground below. In several spots, plants were growing out of the gutters, including a maple sapling. If he didn't act soon, he might have a forest on the roof. But if he was careful, maybe he could transplant the sapling from the gutter to the ground. After all, it was a free tree.

He could hear the kids outside on the tire swing suspended from the large maple on the southwest corner of the house. He kept forgetting to check the rope.

"I bought a gutter scoop from the hardware store for the job," Mae mentioned before hammering down the lid on the paint can. He admired her "get it done" energy, and realized she was trying to ease him into the task, if not cure him of his fears.

"Seems like they've got tools to fix almost everything." Except for phobias, he added in his head.

The truth was that he'd much rather watch the ball game this afternoon than ascend the ladder to the roof. The Jays were close to clinching a pennant. They were contenders for the World Series. Parked on the family room sofa, he might escape the gravity of his situation for a few hours. In this weather, the dome would be open. He'd watch the sunlight slide slowly across the field. He'd witness the ball obey the magic spin placed on it by pitchers. He'd measure the varying parabolas of line drives, pop flies, and home runs. If they started on the eaves before lunch, maybe he'd be able to catch part of the game.

"Where's the scoop? I'll get the ladder and meet you at the front. Let's start with the porch, since the roof's a bit lower there."

Measure one foot out for every four feet up. Make sure the feet are firmly seated. Stay off the top three rungs. He chanted this three-line mantra as he leaned the extension ladder against the right end of the porch eaves. He'd researched the rules, found the advice he needed in *This Old House.*

He began to climb, Mae's arms on either side holding the ladder firmly, then realized he'd forgotten the scoop on the ground. Mae had to let go to retrieve and pass it to him. He twisted awkwardly to receive it. Continuing, he felt the give and sway of the aluminum ladder under his weight. At the top, he looked down momentarily. Mistake. He knew it wasn't far, but the distance felt neck-cracking. He got his momentary panic under control, crooked his left arm around a rung, concentrated on the full gutter before him, and started scooping and tossing debris with his right hand.

"Look out below," he yelled too late, as a scoopful of humus rained down on Mae.

"Shit! That's gross! Damn it, Evan. Can't you be more careful?" He was unanchored when she let go of the ladder to brush dirt out of her hair.

"Sorry." He held his breath and studied the porch roof until she was ready to steady him again. And so the work proceeded. He cleaned the portion of gutter within easy reach from right to left, carefully dropped the debris directly below the ladder, descended slowly keeping his eyes forward, moved the ladder a few feet to the left, tested the distance and the seating, waited for Mae to hold both arms of the ladder, and then ascended. Again and again and again.

When they were two-thirds across, Mae said, "Time to break for lunch." At last. *Terra firma.* He felt it as he walked away from the ladder. The ground had never felt so solid, so sure.

After lunch and kitchen cleanup, Alex and Lizzie headed back outside. "Coming, Dad?"

"Your mom and I'll be out in a minute." Mae had gotten engrossed in a novel and needed to finish the chapter. He considered cleaning up the gutter debris scattered on the ground and planting the sapling, but decided to check the starting time of the ball game instead. He found a pregame show about the Jays' run for the title and was soon deep into stats. He enjoyed watching replays of big strike-outs by Jays pitchers and bigger home-runs by Jays sluggers.

Over the commentary and the crack of bat on ball, a sound began to register. A kind of scuttling on the roof, as if there was an animal up there—a squirrel? A raccoon?

Alex was at the door. "Dad, Dad, Lizzie's on the roof! I told her not to climb the ladder, but she wouldn't listen!"

Evan yelled for Mae and in a moment they were both at the base of the ladder. Needlessly, he told Lizzie not to be afraid. After all, she was walking back and forth on the rotten porch roof, enjoying herself immensely.

"You go up and get her. We'll get some cushions in case she falls." Having issued orders, Mae pulled Alex into the house with her and they began emerging with couch cushions. As Evan carefully ascended the ladder, checking his panic, they arranged the cushions along the ground below the roof line, went back in, and dragged out the twin mattresses from Alex's bed and Lizzie's.

At the top of the ladder, he tried to coax Lizzie over so he could bring her safely down. Nothing doing. Even when Mae commanded, "Elizabeth Maria Mulder, you go to your father this instant!" Lizzie stubbornly parked her bottom on a patch of rotten shingles. There was no help for it. He had to get on the roof. He saw above her the roof's main expanse, with its steep pitch. He pushed away his fear that she'd retreat to this higher ground as he got closer.

Mae and Alex both held the ladder now. Evan broke a rule by climbing onto the second rung from the top. He had to so he could step onto the roof. His heart thumped and his head buzzed during this awkward maneuver. For a moment, he felt completely vulnerable, balanced on a thread, thin air all around. He found his footing but then decided to get down on his hands and knees, lowering his center of gravity and distributing his weight better. He started crawling to Lizzie. He slid and shifted on the crumbling shingles, feeling the give in the soft, rotten wood as he closed the distance.

When he got to her, he carefully flipped himself over and sat beside her. They held hands as he paused to calm himself. He focused on the ladder's top and encouraged Lizzie to shimmy down to it with him. She began laughing, like it was a game they were playing together.

At the ladder's top, he helped her turn around onto the top rungs, keeping a firm grip on her hand. Mae was already far up the ladder, with Alex holding it at the bottom, so Evan let go of Lizzie's hand as Mae guided her down, nested between Mae's chest and the rungs. When Mae was safely on the ground with Lizzie in her arms, Evan began his own awkward swivel off the roof onto the ladder's second rung.

"I told her not to climb the ladder," Alex was assuring his mom.

"Mommy, he's telling a lie! He told me to!" Right away, Alex protested his innocence. Mae started grilling him and was quickly engrossed in negotiating the dispute.

Both Mae and Alex had now let go of the ladder. As Evan planted both feet on the rung to begin his descent, the ladder began sliding to the right along the eave. Instinctively, he reached for the gutter and gripped it with both hands as the ladder clattered to the ground. Surprisingly, the eavestrough held, perhaps because it had been relieved of most of its weight of humus, of its clumps of sod and its seedlings.

Hanging there, he looked up. In his line of sight, swallows dipped and swerved across the blue dome, all of them oblivious to his predicament, except for one. One swallow flitted above him, almost hovering. Strangely, this calmed and comforted him. Grateful, he looked down at Alex's mattress below him. Off to the right, he saw the maple seedling he had removed before lunch. I should plant that today, he thought, or it won't stand a chance. His right hand slipped its grip and he was hanging from his left hand, his center of gravity swaying his body to the left. Strange, he thought as he swayed, how this moment echoed his dream. Or did the dream echo this moment?

"It's not far." Mae was encouraging him. "If you just let go, the mattress will break your fall."

Yes, he thought, it's not far. He realized that it was only a five-foot drop, maybe six. He wasn't much higher than the outfield wall at Sky-Dome. If he were a center fielder leaping to catch the ball going over the wall, robbing the batter of a home run, he'd be almost this high and he'd come back down, unharmed, a hero.

He let go.

Mae and the kids gathered around and helped him to his feet. They were all laughing now, relieved that everyone was safely on the ground.

More than that, they'd all been startled by his perfect landing and roll, like a skydiver.

For a moment, his eyes met Mae's. "That was close," she said.

He was shaking as the adrenalin subsided. "Too close for comfort." Thinking of the dream, he added, "Too weird for words."

Together, they cleaned up the pillows and mattresses. Then he and Mae got back to the gutters. They worked smoothly, in rhythm, while the kids swayed on the tire swing, the rope taut against their pendulum motion, except for the pause at either end of their arc. Mae decided to take some turns on the ladder, and he held it firmly for her. Grit rained down on him, but he'd been smart enough to wear a ball cap.

As he held the ladder, he thought about the dream. Was that it? Was that all? A coincidence, a premonition, a case of *déjà vu* all over again? Would life contrive such a joke against him? Then guiltily, he considered how a small lapse in attention almost led to tragedy. Some dream, he thought. Some dream. He still feared the high tumble, the slipped hold, the snapped rope, the missed catch, the momentary transgression. He was still on the lookout for dangers raining down on life's parade. But his fear felt contained, no longer grave. The sky, it turned out, wasn't falling—at least not today.

As they were finishing, clouds thickened. He sent Alex to get a shovel and then planted the maple seedling near its parent so that, he hoped, one day their branches would intertwine.

Now Mae was back in her book, and the kids were upstairs building Lego towers. He heard repeated crashes, bursts of laughter. He was catching the end of the ball game when he heard the rain begin, first a few drops on the east windows, then a steady thrum on the roof. He turned down the TV to listen. He heard the water sliding smoothly into the gutters and downspouts; it gurgled onto the grass.

He was wrong about the dome. They'd closed the roof for the game, obviously paying more attention to the forecast than he had. With the sound still down, he wondered what rain on the dome sounded like, and what kind of gutters were needed for a roof that big.

It was the bottom of the ninth, and the game was tied. There was a man on first for Joe Carter, with two outs. He planted his feet wide apart. When he swung, the ball silently leapt off his bat, following a beautiful trajectory within the bubble of air below the dome's roof. Confidently, he tossed his bat aside and began trotting the bases while the dugout emptied to meet him at home plate.

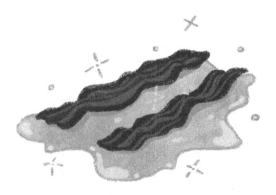

HAPPY AS PIGS

Wedding anniversaries have been disasters for Evan and Mae, and their fourteenth was shaping up to be no exception. Mae was sitting in their 1988 Plymouth Voyager minivan, but they were voyaging nowhere. They were parked at the side of Highway 4 north of London, before Lucan and out of luck. The windows were down and the rear liftgate gaped open, letting in drifts of muggy, late-July air, as Mae fanned herself with a romance novel she kept in the van, just in case. Evan had removed his suit jacket, tucked his tie between two buttons of his white, sun-drenched dress shirt, and rolled up his sleeves. He was worrying away with a tire iron at the lug nuts on the rear driver-side tire, which was now nothing more than a deflated balloon pressed hard by the wheel rim into the shoulder gravel. He was aware of the cars passing him, moving over but still hitting him with blasts of hot air. No one stopped, even though this was the mid-nineties—a time before cell phones. He knew just enough to loosen the nuts before jacking up the van.

"How's it going?" Mae asked. She'd offered to help, but he didn't want her to get grease and dust on her dress, and he was afraid that in her heels she would tip in the uneven gravel and sprain her ankle. The dress was black, cut above the knee. The heels were black, too, three inches.

"Fine," he lied. One of the nuts was proving stubborn, a meddle-some metal bastard sent to ruin his day and his hopes of anniversary sex. He cursed a car that cut it close because of oncoming traffic.

Their date had started promising enough. True, Mae had said she'd be happy with a quiet dinner at home, followed by a Screwball Comedy and a Rom Com after the kids were in bed. She'd said why not make next year special, their fifteenth, by saving up and going back to the Talisman for a second honeymoon. But he wanted to treat her to a meal at the Mermaid Inn in Grand Bend, a tourist town on Lake Huron about an hour out of London. For him, the Mermaid was an emblem of love and leisure, of the privilege enjoyed by those above them in the social scale. He thought of the senior partners in the accounting firm where he worked, along with the clients it served. Mae told him to think about the money. Instead, he arranged for her parents to take Alex and Lizzie overnight. They were happy to, joking they didn't see enough of their grandkids now that Evan and Mae had gone country, moving out of the city to what his in-laws ironically called Green Acres.

While Mae showered, he packed the kids' overnight things, remembering Lizzie's favorite stuffy, a pig named Hamlet. When it was Evan's turn in the bathroom, she offered to lay out his light grey suit and white dress shirt, along with the cufflinks and tie she had given him for their anniversary. The tie was silk, with a red paisley pattern. The cufflinks were ebony, engraved with a silver E. The suit itself was practically new, since he rarely wore one to work at Wheel and Barrow Chartered Accountants anymore and resisted dressing up for church—when they went. He had told Mae he was forever scarred by his mom making him and his brother, when they were about Alex's age, go to church in matching powder-blue suits with wide lapels, red bow ties, bell bottoms, and blue-and-white platform shoes. What made it worse was that their family was always running late. He remembered filing in, destined to sit in the front pew, his face burning with embarrassment at all the eyes, everywhere. Anyway, that was what he told Mae when she encouraged him to dress a bit better on Sunday or even Monday mornings, to set an example for Lizzie and Alex. He suspected that behind her advice was a niggling, wifely dissatisfaction with him, but he filed the thought away in a part of his brain reserved for future self-improvements. Once deposited there, such thoughts rarely came out.

When he walked, towel-clad, into their bedroom, Mae was in black lace bra and panties pulling on her stockings. Lace, he remembered from last year, was the traditional gift for a thirteenth anniversary. It was a gift that kept on giving, he mused as he watched her. Having birthed two babies, she had earned some stretch marks, widened at the hips, and put on some flesh, all this after eloping with him fourteen years ago. He jokingly claims he did it to make an honest woman of her before telling her parents she was pregnant. Her dress was laid out neatly on the bed. When she'd bought the black dress she'd said every woman needed one in her wardrobe—perfect for parties, as well as weddings and funerals, which sometimes amounted to the same thing.

The black pumps were in front of the wardrobe mirror. Her chances to wear these heels were rare, given their lives right now. He recalled with pleasure when she had once worn them for him in the privacy of their bedroom.

He toyed with the idea of dropping his towel to show her how aroused she made him. He could imagine her laughing and scolding him, "Stick it in your pants." Instead, he turned away, quickly pulled on his boxer shorts, put on his white shirt, and struggled to do up his pants over the uncooperative bulge, the towel piled at his feet.

When done, he turned to find that Mae had slipped into her dress and the pumps. Standing in front of the wardrobe mirror, she asked, "How does this look?"

He could see two Maes, both her and her reflection, as she turned each way and smoothed the dress fabric over her hips and stomach. Her face, framed by hair she had recently been growing out, seemed dissatisfied with what it saw, brown eyes appraising their partners within the glass. She had started dying her hair auburn in the past year after discovering some grey. "You look good enough to eat," he said as he walked over and kissed her on the neck, inhaling the scent of her hair before beginning to nibble. He often craved her to the point that it hurt; he sometimes felt her to be an addiction. Yummy, like bacon.

"Don't be a pig," she replied, but didn't move away. "Can you zip me up all the way?"

"Only if you help me with my cufflinks." He'd never worn cufflinks before and was sure putting them on would involve a great deal of fumbling.

~

With an angry jerk of the tire iron, Evan had managed to loosen the last lug nut and was now jacking up the van. The gravel didn't cooperate, so the jack slid around until he had raised it enough to create pressure between the ground and the van's frame. He paused, got up, and went to double-check that the parking brake was depressed all the way.

He felt Mae studying his expression. "It's a lovely day for a drive in the country," she offered in her best British accent. Together they watched BBC period dramas on Sunday evenings.

"Nothing better for the lungs," he agreed, taking a deep breath and exhaling noisily in the manner of a gentleman visiting England's Lake District. Sweat leaked into his eyes and dampened his shirt so that it darkened and clung to his skin.

They had broken down beside a hog farm.

Not a modern confinement, a long and sleek and fully fortressed hog hotel where the pigs check in but never check out. No, across the ditch was an old-fashioned pig farm, swine running semi-free and half-wild in a large sty bound by a shabbily pieced-together welded-wire fence. On the hot breeze rode millions of poo particles, the air an invisible, aromatic mist invading the van, their clothes, their hair, their pores. Above all, their mouths, their noses. The curious pigs crowded the fence, the wire creaking as they jostled for position. Their dark eyes, almost human, gazed steadily at the van as their snouts lifted and fell, inhaling the scents of the van and its occupants. They made soft grunting noises as he dropped the flat tire into the back of the van and rolled the spare into position.

"You've got quite the audience," Mae said.

"Maybe they think you're a damsel in distress and want to rescue you."

"So I'm Little Red Riding Hood, you're the Big Bad Wolf, and they're going to sacrifice their bacon so you don't eat me?"

"More likely, they're hoping we'll toss them a treat. Most likely, we're the treat." He'd heard of people falling into pig pens and getting trampled and eaten. He imagined these pigs storming the fence to get at him and Mae, a Robert Munsch tale gone sideways into a horror story of some kid's mom and dad turned into a tasty, well-dressed meal. It would make for a gruesome scene in a B movie or a titillating headline in a trashy newspaper. "SWINE ENJOY GRUESOME ANNIVERSARY FEAST!" This porcine appetite for human flesh, he thought, gave a new twist to the insult, "you eat like a pig."

What was it about pigs? Hogs, sows, boars, cute little piglets. That'll happen when pigs fly, people said. Happy as pigs in shit, too. You're such a swine. You're quite the little porker, aren't you? Not exactly a compliment, he considered, to belong to this family. But he liked the earthiness of these words, and he knew that pigs were supposed to be more intelligent than dogs, that biologically they were pretty close to people. Of all farm animals, though, their manure stank the worst. So if he was close relative to a pig, what did that say about his own bowel movements, politely disappearing from his nether regions into the septic tank and weeping bed, where the grass was ever green?

He was starting to get hungry. He tightened the nuts in a star pattern, lowered the jack, and then repeated the pattern more forcefully to make sure the nuts wouldn't loosen while he drove. As he placed the jack and tire iron back in their compartment, he gazed back at the pigs and imagined pork chops, ribs, roasts, bacon, ham, sausages. Their pink snouts continued to rise and fall, their throats to emit soft grunts.

When he and Mae had found their acreage three years ago, it was populated by pigs. A neighbor farmer leased the sty from the owner, one Jace Tifflin, who had been clinging to what had shrunk to a hobby farm, about fourteen acres all told with an old house, a barn and pigpen, a pasture containing a few cattle. He remembered walking along the pigpen's fence to survey the property with Mae, Annalise, Todd, and their realtor. The pigs followed them noisily beyond a fence that didn't seem strong enough to keep them in. He didn't know pigs were that huge, that forceful in their bristly pink personalities.

When they checked the house, he and Mae agreed it had potential. Secretly, he was torn, both hopeful and afraid. He thinks now it was probably good he didn't know much about plumbing and wiring, plaster walls and insulation, or they never would have taken it on. It had turned out to be a money pit.

He later learned that both his mom and dad and Mae's folks, after seeing the house for the first time, had driven away almost in tears, lamenting, "What have they gotten themselves into?" And him an accountant, who should know better. It was embarrassing. Penny wise, pound foolish. Cheap about things where it didn't pay to be tight, spendthrift when he needed to be frugal. That was why he was driving a second-hand, four-cylinder minivan with air conditioning that blasted hot air out the vents. He knew the tires were worn but had hoped to make them last into the fall before getting new ones. He slammed down the van's liftgate, banishing the flat tire from his sight.

Yes, he thought, a money pit alright, but more than that. The first summer in their century-old farmhouse, they'd started to make it livable by demolishing much of the inside and dropping a bundle on the roof, re-wiring, and insulation. With the help of his handy brother-in-law Todd, he learned the basics of plumbing. And a good thing, too, because that first summer the toilet was pretty much ready to fall through the bath-room floor, it was leaking so badly into the basement below. While they gutted and redid their only bathroom, he and Mae rigged up a temporary outdoor shower under the plum tree growing wildly against the eastern brick wall of the house, using rope, clothes pins, brightly flowered shower curtains, a blue plastic kiddie pool, and a hose hung over a tree branch. Fondly he remembers showering outdoors with traffic passing on the county road. When the time was ripe, they picked and ate plums while warm water from the laundry room faucet pulsed through the hose, out the house, and over their often-tired bodies.

As he got back into the car, he said, "What I wouldn't do for a hose and a plum tree right about now."

She searched her purse and the glove box for some napkins so he could clean his grease-blackened hands before touching the steering wheel. Finding none, she said, "We'll have to stop at a store so we can clean up a bit. I'm pretty sure we stink to high heaven."

"I'm sure the smell will fade before we get to Grand Bend. After all, we've got to drive with the windows wide open in this heat. Besides, you always smell sweet as a rose, my dear, fresh as a daisy."

"Liar." As he pulled back onto the highway, Mae waved to the pigs, crying, "So long, piggy piggies!" As one body, the pigs jerked away from the fence and galloped back to the safety of the barn, squealing their alarm. "I would've made a great swineherd," she said.

In Lucan, he first stopped at a gas station to wash his hands and then found a drugstore where he could buy some wet wipes. Walking the aisles, he felt like Pigpen from *Charlie Brown*. He imagined a smelly cloud about him and in his wake. When the cashier remarked that he looked like he'd been through the ringer, he confided, "Flat tire." She offered sympathy as she placed the change in his palm and backed away slightly. Or did he just imagine it?

She pulled a tissue out of her smock, raised it to her nose, and asked through her hand, "Heading into the city?"

"No, the other way—to the lake."

"Sorry, I just assumed—dressed in your Sunday best and all, I thought, well . . . ."

When he returned to the car, Mae popped open the wipes, passed him some, and began cleaning her skin where it was exposed—along her arms and hands, around her neck, piling her hair against the back of her head to reach the nape and her upper back. She dabbed lightly at her face to avoid messing her make-up, then wiped the skin exposed in the V of her dress. "Maybe I should take off my stockings. The smell's probably clinging to them."

"Don't stop there on my account," he said. He reached across to help and got his hand slapped for his effort.

"Never mind. We'll never get to the restaurant if you get started on that."

Why not get started? he thought. He and Mae were trying to get pregnant again, so getting started went with the territory. They'd been trying, off and on, for five years. They knew it was a long shot, given that when Lizzie was born six years earlier it might have been their one miracle. Eight years after Alex and many rounds of tests and treatments, Mae pushed Lizzie out into the light of a May morning, two weeks late that felt like a decade. The next day, Mae wept with the relief of it. Her main desire, he knew, was to brood over a large flock of kids, so they were trying again.

What hurt her was that the problem was her ovulation. Long ago, they had his sperm tested. One March morning, he sterilized a glass bottle with boiling water, let it dry and cool upside down on a paper towel, then masturbated into it. He drove to the medical centre with the bottle tucked between his shirt and skin to keep it extra warm beneath his winter coat. When he produced the bottle and passed it to the lab tech, she read the bottle's label, *One a Day*, and started laughing, turning away to show the bottle to a co-worker behind her. Red-faced but smiling, he'd submitted his paperwork, asked when they'd get the results, and quickly left. It turned out he had plenty of healthy long-distance swimmers; Mae's eggs were reluctant, hang-back types.

At the time, he selfishly hadn't wanted it to be his fault, but he thought now it might have been better if it were. Maybe, he thought, that was why their anniversaries derailed—with too much pressure, celebrations turned into self-sabotaged moments arranged by the universe for its entertainment. Maybe, though, it was a guilt hangover from getting pregnant and eloping and running off to the Talisman, feeling they had disappointed their families. After all, they didn't have a real wedding, so why did they deserve a real anniversary? Or maybe, he thought, it was just bad luck, a comedy of errors beyond their control.

There was their second anniversary, when he gave Mae a bouquet of meadow flowers from the downtown market rather than store-bought blooms, along with lavender-scented writing paper—paper being traditional for the second year. Too late they discovered that Mae was seriously allergic to the lavender in both the bouquet and the paper. She suffered with the rash for more than a week. For their fifth anniversary, the year he gave her a wooden jewelry box, their sitter had to call them mid-meal because Alex had accidentally clobbered a neighbor girl in the head with a croquet mallet, requiring several stitches and profuse apologies to her parents. Then there was the tragic comedy of their seventh anniversary, the year Evan gave Mae the wool coat she still wears during winter months. On the way to dinner in Port Dover, Evan hit a large rabbit that raced onto the road. He felt bad, but what could he do? He didn't even have time to brake before the heavy thump. Parking at the restaurant, he was horrified to find the rabbit lodged head-first in the grill. An audience of diners watched as Evan pried at the rabbit with a windshield scraper until it popped out. Unsure what to do with the furry body, he ended up laying it gently on a patch of grass. For a moment, he considered checking whether *Lapin* was on the menu, making a present of his roadkill to the chef. Perhaps they'd get a discount on their meal.

More recent anniversaries had been little better. The year they moved to the farm, he developed blood poisoning from a blister that broke while he was tiling the bathroom. To save his deeply discolored and swollen left hand, they had to make several trips to the hospital for IV treatments. Last year, the year he gave Mae a lace runner for the dining room table and something lacy to wear, Lizzie tripped over a bundle of barbed wire in a patch of land they were cleaning up, resulting in several deep cuts and a trip to emergency for stitches—not her first.

He was reluctant to think what would happen next year on their crystal anniversary. He saw shards of brilliant, fragile glass shattered over the floor from a tipped tray, a pool of blood spreading from deep wounds to major arteries.

Mae wiped her neck one last time. He thought of the blood pulsing beneath the skin from her heart to her head and back again, blood flowing throughout her body, like the blood heart-pumped through his. He remembered the heart-shaped bed of the Talisman bridal suite, Mae on the atrium side, him on the ventricle. As he started the van and pulled onto the highway, he saw in the west a mass of black clouds streaming swiftly toward them.

That summer Friday evening, the Mermaid Inn was filled with well-heeled cottagers, beautifully tanned from month-long holidays at the lake. They were decked out in casual wear, though it was clearly top-brand. From the entrance, Evan saw rings and earrings glisten, pearls shine on golden skin, wine gleam within crystal glasses. He and Mae had arrived, though more than fashionably late. They'd been delayed not only by the flat but by the thunderstorm that pummeled them between Lucan and Grand Bend, sheets of heavy rain draping the car, windshield wipers unable to part the deluge. It was one of those summer storms that erupted along the lake in the late afternoon of a muggy day, storms that in their wake offered little to no relief. The rain slowed but remained steadily hard until their arrival, so that the dash from the van to the restaurant door had left them wet and noticeably disheveled, with clammy skin and damp, wind-blown hair.

He saw they were at the same time over-dressed and poorly attired, by Mermaid standards. When he began to apologize for their tardiness, the enigmatic host waved him off and ushered them to their table. It was located in the center of the restaurant. They were surrounded.

He remembered to hold Mae's chair and then took his seat across from her. He felt eyes upon them—those of the closest diners, first glancing up from their food and then exchanging knowing glances with their table companions.

Mae looked at him over her menu. "It's bad, isn't it?"

"I'm sure most of the smell is gone."

"Awkward," she replied in an undertone, coloring as their waitress appeared beside the table. She wore a gold nametag that read "Amanda" and appeared to be in her early twenties, with blond hair neatly swirled in a bun on the back of her head. She was noticeably pregnant, though not massively. Her white blouse stretched comfortably over her belly. She introduced herself and reviewed the menu with them, then stood at the ready with pen and pad. Periodically she rested the pen and her forefinger below her nose. Another bad sign, he thought. She was looking a bit piqued.

"I noticed your last name's Mulder," she was saying. "Does that mean you have a hog farm around here?"

"No, actually we drove up from London. Funny story. Had a bit of a misadventure along the way." He was ready to tell her about the flat tire and the pigs, turning it all into a comic calamity they could laugh at together, a kind of apology, but she interrupted, slightly flustered.

"Oh, I'm so sorry. It's just, I assumed. A lot of pig farmers around here are Dutch. Have you decided on your order?" Mae smiled at him and ordered the pork roulade. He chose tenderloin medallions.

Once Amanda left, he said, "I'll try not to spill my peas this time." He was remembering their first married meal at the Talisman, at a table beside Larry and Caroline Laurence playing footsie. That day, Mae was already three months pregnant with Alex.

"That would be good," she replied. "No need to draw more attention to ourselves. And I'm not playing footsie with you today."

"Oh, how the honey moon has waned."

"It started waning when I had morning sickness on the way back. It has that effect on romance. A bit of a mood spoiler, though I wouldn't mind going through it again."

When they had returned from eloping, the men and women at the nursery where he was working asked where he and Mae had honeymooned. "Beaver Valley," he'd said, and was confused when they laughed long and loud. Clueless, that's when he'd learned what beaver meant, and blushed.

When he came home from work, he asked Mae, "Do you know what beaver is?"

"Of course," she said, and explained.

He blushed again. "You knew all the time we were there on our honeymoon, and didn't tell me?"

"I thought you knew." She laughed when he told her how he'd learned what it meant.

He was blushing now at the bill Amanda had brought to their table. As he laid down his credit card, he imagined it melting when she went to use it. When she returned with the receipt for his signature, he saw Mae glance at Amanda's belly. He wondered if Mae longed to reach out and rest her hand there for a moment. It was not something he felt free to ask her. The moment passed when Amanda was called away to another table.

He had cash for the tip. As he laid out some bills, Mae encouraged him to double what he'd laid down. "She deserves it," she said, "putting up with our stink when she's pregnant."

Uncomfortable with the eyes and noses surrounding them, they had eaten quickly and skipped dessert. Not that it would have taken long to eat, given the beautifully presented but tiny portions. Having finished their scant rations, they now rose and filed out of the Mermaid, looking straight ahead and entering into a stiff, warm wind blowing off the lake.

"Still hungry?" he asked.

"Famished."

The rain had stopped and the clouds had passed, but the air was still heavy with moisture. As they walked toward the lake, they stopped at a chip wagon and shared a large order of fries doused in malt vinegar and salt. Mae dipped her fries in a small tub of mayonnaise, a habit she'd gotten from her east coast relatives. "We should have brought our bathing suits," he mused as they munched. "Then we could have cleaned up and cooled off in the lake. That was dumb."

"It's still worth a look."

The light lasted late into the evening, so the beach was still busy, mostly with teenagers. With the storm, families had packed up their gear and headed back to cottages, trailers, and campgrounds to play games, drink beer, and start fires if they'd remembered to keep their wood dry. Here, girls were lying on beach towels, resting on their elbows and watching through sunglassed eyes boys toss around a Frisbee, performing tricks for them. Couples jumped like dolphins into the choppy waves stirred up by the storm. Occasionally, young lovers tangled in the surf, playing at drowning. Down the beach on a secluded bench, two young men shared a large, colorful beach towel, one draping his arm along the slat behind the other.

The stiff wind pressed his and Mae's clothes against their bodies, bodies twice as old as the golden ones on the beach. Here, too, they were overdressed and out of place, but he took pleasure in the glow of Mae's face and the shape of her body in the evening sun.

"Well," he said, "the lake's still here. Seen enough?"

"No," she replied, "let's go in."

"Are you crazy."

"At least part way."

At an empty picnic table, he pulled off his shoes and socks, removed his jacket, tie, and cufflinks, then rolled up his sleeves and pant legs as high as possible. Using his jacket, he shielded Mae so that at last she could kick off her pumps, lift her dress, and roll off her stockings. To save them from getting snagged on wood, he folded them neatly and placed them in the inside pocket of his suit jacket. Together, they walked across the warm, wet sand and waded into the water where there was an opening among the young revelers. As each wave rolled in, he and Mae jumped hand-in-hand, trying to keep their clothes dry, but they still got drenched to their waists by the persistent crests. Who cares, he thought, as Mae laughed into the spray. Far past the breakers to the horizon, the lake glinted like wrinkled tinfoil.

They walked back to the van in their bare feet. Through the windows of the Mermaid, he saw that new couples had replaced the old. At their table in the center, a man in his forties was studying the menu through reading glasses, while his date (wife, girlfriend, mistress—Evan didn't know) was pointing to her menu and asking questions. Amanda was waiting on them.

When they opened the car doors, the pig smell was still strong. The van had been cooking in the heat with the windows closed. After opening all the windows, he took a small, wrapped box from beneath the seat where he had hidden it. The box was black, wrapped with a white ribbon.

"A gift for you, my lady," he offered with a knightly flourish.

"Thank you, kind sir." When she opened the box, what emerged in her hand was a small ivory swan in flight.

"It's an Inuit carving," he explained. "Apparently, there are several species of swan that migrate to the Arctic in the summer, where year after year mates nest and raise their young before flying south again."

"It's beautiful." She ran her forefinger along its neck and wings.

He'd made a habit of giving Mae small birds. There was the bluebird of happiness when they eloped, but sometime before Alex started school, it was a glass cardinal, and after Lizzie was born, it was a porcelain hen with chicks. During a work trip to Ottawa two years ago, he found a soapstone owl with a wise expression. Mae had distributed these around the house and occasionally moved them. They might be on the jelly cupboard in the kitchen one day flocked around the Talisman snow globe, then fly to an end table in the living room the next. Another day, they'd have migrated to the window ledge in the bathroom, or settled to sleep on her night stand.

"Let's go home," she said.

~

The van's tires crunched on gravel and rolled to a stop before their house. Ike, their Newfoundland mix, descended the porch to greet them, pee on the tires, and enjoy the smell of the van, while he and Mae went inside and began to strip off their clothes in the laundry room.

"I'll put on the kettle while you shower," he said.

On the drive home, Mae had held the swan in the palm of her hand, resting in her lap. She was tempted, she said, to hold it out the window so that it could fly beside the van, but she didn't want to risk losing it. Instead, she cradled it. By the time they passed the pig farm, the western sky was darkening and the eastern sky was filling with stars, the glow of the city ahead of them in the southern sky. They waved to the nearly invisible pigs.

"The kettle can wait," she was saying now. She placed the swan on the window ledge in the bathroom, removed her remaining clothes, and helped him with his. She took him by the hand into the shower with her, where they washed each other, the residue of the day draining into the weeping bed and nourishing the ever green grass.

After, they shared toast and tea on the porch beside the plum tree. Thankfully, the night breeze was strong enough to keep the mosquitoes away. The swan sat between them on the table, and Ike slept below it. They now lived far enough out of the city that, with no farm light, the Milky Way was bright above, except where low in the eastern sky the moon had risen and washed out the stars.

"Look," he said. "It's the return of the honey moon."

"It shows up once in a while, doesn't it?" She picked up the ivory swan. "Were there more swans where you got this one?"

"Yes, there were."

"Good. A swan is lonely without her mate. You need one, too."

Below the breeze, he heard remnants of bird call and a multitude of crickets chirping. Across the nearby bean field, fireflies sent out beacons to each other. Above, bats circled and swooped as they fed. He imagined the pigs bedded down for the night, lying close together in the cooling muck, their sides rising and falling in slumber. All around him, he felt the world filled with strong desires. Within himself, too. Within Mae.

"We can find her mate tomorrow before we get the kids."

"I'd like that."

They woke Ike, rose, and entered their home for the night.

IN THE HILLS AND VALLEYS OF *PERCHE*

for Allan Curnew

"This is not what I signed up for." Evan had made this claim many times—often in his head, occasionally aloud to his wife Mae.

He and Mae and their two kids Alex and Lizzie were standing in the middle of their pasture. It was a Saturday morning in January, back in 1998. The field was a brightly lit frozen plain, so bright it hurt his eyes. The barrenness extended beyond the field to the line of distant woods, a dull grey-brown thicket.

Finnegan was sitting in the pasture like a large dog, unable to get up on his hind legs. Flecks of blood stained the snow and mixed with the scattered manure, manure that also clung in frozen globs to his tail. From the pattern in the icy snow, Evan could tell that the horse, a black Percheron, had been struggling to right himself for a while—possibly all night. The other horses were safely sheltered in the paddock run-in, seemingly unconcerned about Finnegan's plight.

If a woman driving by hadn't alerted them, Finnegan would still be alone in the field. A Good Samaritan, the woman had said, "You have a horse that can't get up." And then left Evan standing at the door calling out to Mae, fighting the panic he felt whenever something wasn't right with the animals.

Mae had calmly taken charge. She'd directed Alex and Lizzie to get Finnegan's halter and lead rope from the barn, along with a horse blanket. As they now stood around Finnegan, Mae fastened the halter over his neck right behind the large triangles of his ears, in a spot called the poll. She then attached the lead rope to the ring below his chin.

"Lizzie, you help me pull. Alex, help your dad push him up from behind. But watch out for his hooves. And for God's sake be careful he doesn't fall on you."

Evan had his doubts. After all, Finnegan was a Percheron, a heavy horse. Though he had been skeletal when they got him, he could now weigh in at a ton or more. What help could four puny humans offer to right such a creature? On three, Mae began clicking her tongue and encouraging Finnegan to get up. They pulled and pushed as the horse first set his front legs and then rocked to get his back legs beneath him. Evan and Alex jumped back as Finnegan failed to find purchase and toppled onto his side.

After they tried several times, the horse was exhausted, warm air from his lungs steaming from his nostrils, vapor rising from his shaggy winter coat. "Lizzie, cover him with the blanket. Evan, it's time to call the vet."

Evan knew how this might end. He knew what it meant when a horse couldn't get up. It meant permanent damage to nerves and muscles, atrophy. He hurried from the field through the paddock to the house. A vet could be there by noon, the receptionist told him after listening to his explanation and checking schedules. He thought, high noon for Finnegan.

When Evan returned to the field, he was just in time to see Finnegan rise up onto all four legs in one massive effort. Though initially unsteady, he found his feet, shook himself, and, led by Mae, began walking to the barn. The horse's gait was relaxed, so leisurely that Evan thought he must have had no memory of the struggle he'd just gone through. Evan went to open the gate. Mae said calmly, "Thought I'd give it one more try."

Lizzie, almost nine, and Alex, just turned seventeen, were pumped by this victory.

"I gave a really strong pull, Dad. I'm sure that's what did it."

"No, Dad, I used basic physics to get him up. His back legs were slipping to the right so I pushed from the left. It was leverage, that's what it was."

"He's wrong, Dad. It was really my muscles."

"Twerp."

Mae walked the horse quietly through the gate, into the barn, and straight into a stall. She tied the lead rope to a ring and examined his legs for cuts. With a pick, she cleaned mud and manure and ice out of his hooves. She rubbed his body with a curry comb, working in circles to warm him, then began brushing ice and manure out of his mane and tail.

"I don't know if it was just the ice giving him trouble or something else."

Evan, worried about the money, said, "I'll go cancel the vet."

As if reading his mind, Mae told him he was being cheap. "It's your decision, but it might be good to have him checked out." She finished brushing Finnegan's tail and turned to the kids. "Lizzie, throw in some hay for him. Alex, make sure his water bucket is filled. He's probably hungry and thirsty. Poor guy, out there all night." Mae gently removed the halter and untied the lead rope. She left the stall and headed to the house without another word to Evan.

Before closing the stall door, he rubbed Finnegan along his back and rump, then scratched his neck. Looking into the horse's eye, he felt an inscrutable life looking back. Then the horse lowered his head to eat the half bale of last summer's hay Lizzie had just tossed at his feet.

By the time Evan got to the house, he'd firmed up his decision to cancel the vet. Finnegan's fine, he told himself. It's all good."

"Finnegan" wasn't the horse's original name. If he'd even had one, it was long lost. He didn't come with any registration papers indicating his lineage, his sire and his dam, and his succession of owners. He'd been rescued from slaughter the previous summer.

Evan and Mae had gotten a flier from Green Pastures Horse Rescue in their mailbox in August. Mae had looked it over and then stuck it with a magnet to the fridge. She'd said, "Might be worth checking out some time."

When she'd left the kitchen, Evan had pulled the flier off the fridge to study it at the kitchen table. He sat across from the two photos of wild horses, one taken on Sable Island and the other in the Alberta Foothills, the black-and-whites Mae had bought early in their marriage. Whenever they had moved, these were the first pictures she hung. They'd been fixed on this wall for about six years now, ever since they'd made the move from the city to this old farmhouse.

The flier showed before and after photos of rescued horses, suggesting metamorphosis from skeletal, head-hanging nags to filled-out, shiny-coated horses trotting with heads held high. All it took was donations so that Chelsea and her volunteers could buy the necessary hay and feed, maintain the farm, and pay the bills. On the back panel was the Green Pastures logo, which depicted a black horse wearing a white saddle blanket adorned with a red cross, led by a long-haired and fully-bearded cowboy who strangely seemed to be both wearing a sword and carrying a shepherd's staff. Below the logo was a photo of a smiling Chelsea Phillips in a tan cowboy hat, looking up at a chestnut horse she was holding by the halter. The horse had white markings on its forehead—maybe a star, possibly a cross, or just a splotch.

Evan liked the idea of rescuing animals. He didn't stop to think about who or what they were being rescued from, or what they were being rescued for. The animal rescue movement was something new— horse rescue, dog rescue, cat rescue, for all he knew mouse and elephant rescue. Animal lovers could foster all sorts of creatures, adopt them if they felt moved to do it. It seemed to him there had always been the Humane Society and the SPCA, but the animal rescue movement had celebrity glamour and promised moral reward. Something seemed to have changed between people and creatures, but the nature of that shift was unclear to Evan. Rising from the table, he found the phone and dialed the number on the flier.

It was that call which led Evan and Mae to rent a horse trailer a few days later and make their way in their pick-up—a mid-'80s grey and rusted F-150—to the Green Pastures stables north of London, near Lucknow. When he turned into the laneway, he saw a small clapboard house to the right dwarfed by a weathered hip-roof barn beyond it. A paddock off the barn had been divided to contain and separate upwards of twenty horses. Evan quickly counted about half that number as he put the truck in park and cut the engine. Many raised their heads in curiosity and nickered before returning to their hay. It suddenly occurred to him that the truck's engine was measured in horse power, though he didn't know the number. How many horses like these were under his hood? He'd have to check it out. As he and Mae climbed down from the truck cab, they were met by Chelsea emerging from the barn.

"Welcome to Green Pastures!" She held out her hand as she approached. "You must be Evan and Mae." Her firm grip seemed consistent with her wiry, muscled body, decked in muddy barn boots, tight jeans, and checked shirt, topped with that tan cowboy hat. Her neck and cheeks were beaded with sweat. "Let me show you around."

Before they entered the cool gloom of the barn, Evan noticed the Green Pastures logo painted above the door, plus the words "The Lord is my shepherd." When his eyes adjusted to the relative dark, he saw two rows of stalls flanking the central aisle. Two heavy horses—Percherons—were the sole occupants.

"I just got these big boys earlier this week. They were being auctioned for meat and I just couldn't let it happen. They deserve a forever home."

A forever home? In the catch-phrase he heard the rescue movement's vision.

Mae asked, "What do you know about them? What's their story?"

"Don't know much. Their owner got too old to take care of them, so they were neglected till he got put in the home. Then his people just sent them to the auction. They didn't even come with names."

Evan noticed then how thin and bony they were. Their necks were too slender and their shoulders too pronounced, as were their backbone and ribs. Their hips were sharp points jutting out of craters. Their heads and hooves seemed oversized extremities on their gaunt bodies, their black coats dull and patchy. "Do they even have a chance of making it?"

"I wouldn't have got them if I didn't think they did. With a lot of food and a little love, they'll be okay. God willing."

Evan thought a resurrection trumpet might be needed. At the very least a miracle. "What would one of them cost?"

"Slow down a bit," she said. "Tell me about yourselves and why you want a rescue horse."

Mae took the lead, talking to Chelsea one horse lover to another in what felt to Evan like an adoption hearing. Mae talked about their move to the hobby farm, the horses they'd bought, the set-up they'd built with their barn and paddock and pasture. Mae even pulled out some photos so Chelsea could see for herself. They were like two women talking about their kids.

"Okay then. Five hundred would cover what I paid, along with a donation to the cause. But the number's between you and your conscience." As Evan pulled out his checkbook Chelsea continued. "You don't know how many horses are neglected. Not just neglected but abused. The physical suffering is one thing. The mental and emotional torture they've gone through is something else. It's a sin! I mean, it damages their spirits. Sometimes it's just that their owner has died. Other times it's a farmer that loves horses but is down on his luck. It can even be perfectly healthy horses nobody wants just being sold for meat. The worst cases are race horses past their prime and just left to die. It's criminal!"

Evan passed the finished check to Chelsea and then turned to Mae. "Well, which one is it going to be?"

"It's tough to decide. I need to get a closer look, get a sense of their personalities." She went into each stall in turn, talking to the horses, approaching them calmly, rubbing them, checking their teeth and hooves. She haltered each gelding and walked him down and back up the barn aisle. Evan noticed now how tall they were, how smooth their gaits, their hooves as big as dinner plates.

"It's a tough call. Too bad we can't take both these boys." Mae glanced sideways at Evan. "Since I've got to choose, I'll make it this big guy. He's a sweetie."

"He is," Chelsea said. "Let's put him back in the stall for now. There's the adoption paperwork to do up at the house."

Her house was little bigger than a double-wide trailer, but inside whatever wall space was available seemed to be covered with photos of horses. Among these, Evan noted a Sunday-schoolish picture of Jesus carrying a shepherd's staff and a lamb, and another of Noah's ark, animals entering two-by-two, an oblivious unicorn in the distance. In a third, Jesus was riding a donkey past children waving palm branches.

Evan and Mae filled out the adoption application, answering questions about their horse experience, their facilities, and their financial ability to care for the horse. They supplied references and the name of their vet clinic in Windermere. They read the agreement section, promising to provide a loving forever home for their adopted horse, then signed the form and headed back to the barn.

Their adopted horse trailered beautifully for them. But as their truck and trailer rumbled out of the barnyard, Evan could hear their Percheron and the one left behind neighing to each other.

Once their rescue horse was in his new stall with food and water, Evan pulled their horse books off the shelf, set them in a stack on the kitchen table, and began reading about Percherons. He learned of the breed's misty origins in the *Perche* region of France during medieval times. He imagined them in the *Huisne* River Valley and on the Hills of *Perche*, working the fields and forests. He considered their story, generations of horses bred and raised by generations of people for work and war, for riding and meat. He saw them crossing the ocean from Old World to New, like the *Perche* immigrants who came to New France. He imagined them straining to pull plows and wagons of grain, carriages and trams in cities. He thought about the rise and fall of their fortunes as they were replaced by one iron horse after another—trains and tractors and trucks—with engines measured in horse power. He imagined a line of Percherons walking out to pasture after a day's labor on a farm worked by Mennonites, holdouts for the horse. And this story, this history, he realized, was in the bones and flesh of Finnegan, the emaciated horse in their barn.

Lizzie was the one who came up with the name Finnegan. She liked Casey's dog from *Mr. Dressup*. Evan remembered that some Native people called the horse Big Dog when it was first brought to North America. Finnegan was definitely a big dog.

As the weeks went by, he got bigger. His skeletal body put on flesh, his blotchy coat gained thickness and shine. At feeding time, Evan would call Finnegan out of the pasture, and the horse would lumber through the belly-deep grass to munch his measure of sweet feed. When his long tongue had licked the bucket clean, he would turn back to the field.

After Finnegan's trouble, they were more careful. They kept him in a stall at night and restricted him to the paddock during the day. "Pasture grass during the winter has no nutrition, anyway," Mae said. He had a couple of more episodes where he needed help to get up, but they managed those. He's just old and the paddock is slippery, Evan told himself.

On a Saturday morning in mid-February, he bundled up and went out to the barn to do his normal chores—feeding Finnegan in his stall and throwing hay into the run-in for the other horses. When he opened the barn door, his eyes took a moment to adjust to the relative darkness, even though he'd flicked on the lights.

In his stall, Finnegan struggled onto his front legs so that he sat again like a big dog, his back to Evan. He felt his worry about the horse escalate into something like panic. He looked over the stall door. Finnegan's back end was pressed against it, and scattered pine shavings and manure showed the extent of his struggle to stand. A stall post was splintered near the floor, undoubtedly the cause of the bleeding gash on the horse's hind right leg.

Evan leaned hard against the door and was just able to unlatch it. Finnegan's weight brought his rear end out the door so that it was no longer possible for Evan to close it. "It's okay, boy. Take it easy." He talked to calm himself as much as the horse. Finnegan offered a rumbling reply from deep in his chest. Evan retrieved the halter and lead rope from the tack room and climbed carefully into the stall over the prone horse.

He knew that attempting to right the horse in the confined space of the stall was dangerous. One kick, one fall, and Evan might be injured, pinned, or killed. But he had to right the horse. He couldn't let Finnegan stay down. If he'd been thinking straight, he would have gotten Mae right away, but such sound judgement evaded him. With the halter snug, he pulled back on the lead rope, clicking his tongue and encouraging Finnegan to get up as Mae had done. His clicking became more urgent as Finnegan struggled to get his back legs beneath him. His left hip smashed against the door post and his hooves kicked out against the stall wall. His whole body strained with the effort, as Evan's boots slid in the shavings and manure. Then Finnegan toppled backwards out the stall door, his flung front hooves narrowly missing Evan. The horse's prone body was now most of the way out of the stall.

Defeated, Evan unlatched Finnegan's water bucket from its hook and placed it before the horse. He silently watched the horse drink. He fetched a half bale of hay and placed it beside the water bucket. Finnegan buried his muzzle in the sweet grass and began eating.

Thinking hard, casting about for a solution, Evan did the rest of his barn chores, feeding and watering the other horses. Then he removed anything in the aisle he thought might injure Finnegan if he tried to get up, and latched the door closed behind him. He didn't know why he latched it. Did he really imagine that Finnegan would get up and wander out onto the yard, scrape through the snow to the grass beneath, and begin grazing? Evan walked slowly up to the house to talk with Mae and the kids. He knew this time he'd have to call the vet.

A few hours later Evan, Mae, Alex, and Lizzie stood in the barn and watched Dr. Rachel Stewart examine Finnegan. Since the morning, he'd moved about fifteen feet beyond the stall door and had turned completely in the opposite direction. When they'd come in the barn, he'd risen up on his front legs for a few seconds and then gone back down.

"So as far as you know he hasn't been up since some time in the night?" Dr. Rachel had her right arm encased in a plastic sleeve and was pulling manure out of Finnegan's rectum. She'd already taken his temperature and listened to his heart and lungs.

"He wasn't up this morning, for sure. I couldn't get him up. He's moved, but it doesn't look like he was ever all the way up."

Dr. Rachel felt around inside Finnegan. She talked quietly to the horse as he lay on his side, occasionally looking back and shifting his legs.

Finishing, she removed her arm and deftly pulled the plastic glove inside out as she stood. She was a tall woman with a muscular frame contained within her light blue coveralls, her name stitched above the breast pocket marked with the veterinary logo, a wooden staff wound round with a snake, behind a capital V. Her coveralls were tucked into green barn boots that came up to just below her knees. Her pale blue eyes were creased at the corners, her hair a short salt and pepper grey.

Evan noticed that the grey had deepened since her regular visit last summer, her hair even shorter than before. He remembered now. He'd read in the local paper about the death of her daughter. There was a picture of her in the paper around the time they'd gotten Finnegan. Melody, he thinks her name was, something musical sounding. The picture showed a grinning eighteen-year-old young woman, bright green eyes in a lightly freckled face, reddish hair pulled back in a ponytail. She'd died in a rock-climbing fall the summer before going off to the Royal Military College in Kingston. She'd dreamed of becoming a pilot.

Dr. Rachel seemed to be measuring her words carefully. "His lungs are a bit wheezy, but that's to be expected since he had the heaves when you got him last summer. His heart's good. His bladder is quite full, which means he hasn't been able to get up and urinate. Given the amount of manure, he's eating just fine. The problem, as best I can tell, is along his spine. The signals his brain is sending to his hind legs aren't getting through right. There could be a number of causes, but I believe he's contracted EPM, Equine Protozoal Myeloencephalitis. It's a neurological disease that explains the weakness in his back and his lack of coordination. Basically, it's an inflammation of his brain and spinal cord."

"How did he get it? Can it be treated?" Mae asked.

"He had to come into contact with Possum feces at some point. Possums carry the parasite that creates the inflammation. Because he's a rescue horse, it's likely he was poorly cared for in the past, which made him vulnerable. To know for sure, we'd have to do a blood test."

"And possible treatments?" Evan was the one to ask this time.

"I'm afraid it's progressed too far. If it had been caught earlier . . . ."

A jolt of guilt hit his stomach. "Like a month ago?"

"No. Much earlier. He probably already had it when you got him. There's no cure, but we could have treated the inflammation to prolong his life. Then again, those drugs are quite expensive."

They all stood silently as the diagnosis sank in. Evan felt himself part of a tableau—five helpless people around a fallen horse.

Lizzie broke the silence. "Does that mean he has to be put down?" She had wanted to come to the barn to watch. She was what Evan and Mae called horse crazy. She'd already decided when she was five she wanted to be a vet. Alex had quietly watched the horse the whole time. He maintained his silent gaze.

Evan caught Mae's eye. He understood the look. It was Mae who answered Lizzie. "I'm afraid so. It's what's best for Finnegan if he can't get up. He's only going to get worse."

Dr. Rachel came to Mae's aid. "When a horse can't get up, his nerves are damaged and his leg muscles start to die. You've given him a great six months. He's looking really good, and he got to spend his last months on pasture. It doesn't get much better for a horse."

"Kids, maybe you should go up to the house. You don't need to see this."

"I want to stay. To know what it's like. To be with him."

Dr. Rachel spoke to Evan and Mae. "I'll get what I need from my truck."

With that, they were alone in the barn with Finnegan. Lizzie knelt down to rub his neck and his muzzle. Evan couldn't look at Mae and the kids. He felt his throat constricting. When they lived in the city, the only dead animals he saw were squirrels run over, and occasionally a cat. Since moving to the country, he'd become familiar with the deaths of animals, with the wildness of life. A rabbit mauled by barn cats that needed to be put out of its misery. A raccoon surprised by the dogs when he let them out in the morning. Birds floating in the water trough.

But nothing like this. God, he thought, some farmer I am. If he were a real farmer, he'd have no qualms about the deaths of animals. He'd use a rifle to take care of it himself. He was a city wimp, a softie, an imposter.

He tried to tell himself that it was just Nature taking its course, the nature of things. But he wanted none of it. If this was its course, the channel in which it ran, he wanted out. He wanted some kinder, gentler landscape. Something like the river valleys of *Perche* he'd seen in photos. This was not what he'd signed up for.

But deep down he knew that was a lie. It was exactly what he'd signed up for. Married to Mae till death parted them. Having kids, raising animals—life and death, that was the deal. It couldn't be helped. A beautiful one-ton creature would thrive in their pasture and be brought low by a microscopic single-celled creature, a protozoa, a parasite hitching a ride in possums and their feces, now invading the horse he and Mae had rescued. Their care, human care, could do only so much, and no more. Neither physical strength nor physics could save the horse.

Lizzie got up as Dr. Rachel returned to the barn carrying a large needle and syringe. The fluid looked golden in the cold light. "This will be very quick," she said as she knelt by Finnegan's head. "He might give a small spasm, but that will be all. It'll be painless." Mae now knelt beside Finnegan and held his halter. Evan kept his focus on her calm face. Dr. Rachel cleaned a spot on the horse's neck, inserted the needle, and pressed the golden fluid into him. His prone head leapt up in a single jerk before returning to the barn floor. His legs relaxed, his body settled into stillness, and his eyes emptied. Dr. Rachel held her stethoscope to his chest. "He's gone," she said.

Lizzie knelt down beside Mae and struggled to remove the halter from Finnegan's head. She studied it for a moment before going to hang it by his stall. Evan wondered if they'd made a mistake letting her stay, letting her see.

He stayed behind when Mae and the kids headed up to the house. At the truck, Dr. Rachel gave him the name of a rendering service. "Some farmers just bury animals on their property, but it's best to properly dispose of a body that's been euthanized. It's the chemicals." After a pause, she added, "Sorry for your loss."

"And for yours," Evan added, shaking her hand.

She paused again. Pain surfaced in her eyes a moment and then was gone. "Thank you," she said, climbing into her truck and starting it up.

Jesus, could I be any more lame? he thought as he walked up to the house. Comparing a dead daughter to a dead horse.

Finnegan's body lay on the barn floor until the Monday morning, as the rendering service didn't do pick-ups on Sundays. It felt surreal for Evan to do the regular chores in the barn—throwing out hay for the other horses in the run-in as they milled about, and making sure the water bucket was full and the heater working. Finnegan's body was an island of utter stillness within this commotion, this flow of normal living. Evan knelt to touch the body—the muzzle, the hairy ears, the point on the neck where the needle went in, the dome of the belly, the plate-sized hooves.

He stayed home from work on the Monday morning to be there for the rendering truck. Mae, Alex, and Lizzie had all gone to school, Mae being a volunteer class mom. He was in the kitchen when he heard the rendering truck rumbling up the laneway, sounding its horn. He pulled on his barn clothes against the cold, then went out to meet it. He read the name "Riverside Haulage" on the door.

A man wearing a black toque, brown winter coveralls, and work boots climbed down from the cab when it came to a halt. He looked to be about a decade older than Evan—late forties or early fifties, grey hair escaping from his toque, several days of grey stubble on his face. "You got a horse to take care of? Where abouts is it?"

"In the barn."

"Shit, that's a problem. Your deadstock needs to be on the yard."

"Jeez, I'm sorry. Didn't know that. This is my first dead horse."

"Well, this ain't my first rodeo. Let's take a look. Maybe we'll get lucky." As they walked toward the barn, the driver added, "Colder than a witch's tit, ain't it?"

"That it is. Goes straight to your bones." Evan unlatched and slid the barn door open.

"Jesus, he's a big bugger, ain't he. Gonna be a sonofabitch to get out." The driver walked over to Finnegan. "Bet this fella made the ladies happy in his day." He was a gelding, not a stud, Evan thought. He decided not to point this out. The driver looked around, seeming to calculate distances and consider options.

"What do you think?"

"I can make it work. I'll back the truck up, bring the chain around that post so we can get him in line with the door. Once that's done we'll unhook and reattach the chain, then pull him onto the truck in a straight run."

Evan guided the driver as he backed his truck to the door, then watched as the man operated the hydraulics to lower the ramp and tip the truck bed. A stream of blood washed down the ramp into the barn doorway. "Picked up a fresh one at my last stop. Cow sliced its neck on a wire."

He unrolled the chain, walked it around the post, and wrapped it around Finnegan's stiff back legs, securing the chain with a large hook through a link.

At first, the hydraulics strained against Finnegan's weight, but with a lurch his carcass began sliding across the barn floor toward the post. As the body came in line with the door, the metal post—installed long ago to help support the massive weight of the hewn beam—came unmoored and clattered to the ground. The driver stopped pulling. "Holy shit—didn't mean to do that."

"No harm done," Evan said as he lifted the heavy post and set it aside. "Don't think the roof's coming down just yet."

"At least there's no need to take the chain off now." As the hydraulics hummed again, the chain lost its slack and pulled Finnegan toward the truck, the metal clanging against the ramp. Sliding through the doorway, his stiff body was pulled through the blood pool and his front hooves got stuck on the doorframe. Before the driver could stop the chain, the frame cracked and broke off the foundation. The horse's hooves popped free and his body inched up the ramp into the truck bed, leaving a smear of red on the snow from the barn door to the ramp. Through the rear doors of the truck box, Evan could see Finnegan's body come to rest on top of some dairy cows.

With the chain unhooked, the truck bed lowered into place, and the door securely latched, the driver produced the paperwork Evan needed to sign, along with the bill. Fingers cold, he signed the form and wrote out a check.

"Thanks for taking care of this."

"No problem. All in a day's work." With that, the driver climbed into his cab. As he put the truck in gear, he leaned out the window and said, "Really is colder than a witch's tit. Day like today, an old pecker needs to find someplace warm." With a laugh and a nod, he rolled up the window and rumbled down the laneway.

Evan took a breath and watched it escape into the air. He looked across the pasture, the county road, and the empty fields to the grey woods in the distance. The February sun was low in the southern sky and covered the landscape with a wintry light. The wind was picking up. Snow snakes were travelling diagonally across the road and through the fields. He watched the rendering truck rumble down the road, picking up speed as the driver geared up, disturbing the snow snakes. Nearer in the pasture, the horses grazed, scraping their front hooves through the snow to get at the winter grass.

He walked up to the house, thinking of Mae's warmth. She could be a furnace in bed. Even in the winter, she'd be satisfied with a sheet, a window cracked open for fresh air, while he needed to pile on the blankets. He missed her, though she'd been gone only a couple of hours. He thought of the *Perche* he'd seen in photos, of its forests and fields and valleys. She wouldn't be home until lunch, and he'd said he'd be in to work by then, back at his desk.

The dogs greeted him as he opened the back door and removed his barn clothes, the smell of Finnegan on them, probably the smell of the driver too, maybe the smell of blood. They ran to their empty water dish, looking at him expectantly.

As he filled the bowl in the kitchen sink, he stared at Mae's photos on the wall above the table. In black-and-white, they captured a moment's energy and grace in the lives of these wild creatures. For all he knew, these horses were also dead by now. He went over to the jelly cupboard and looked into the Talisman snow globe at the horse, the sleigh, and its occupants. When he picked it up and shook it, they blurred inside a swirling blizzard.

The dogs were dancing around him, impatient. Their water bowl was overflowing in the sink. He put the snow globe back, tipped some water out of the dogs' bowl, and put it down for them. They drank noisily as he poured himself a cup of coffee and took a sip. It had been sitting too long on the burner and was bitter. He went to the fridge for some cream to take the edge off it. When he closed the fridge door, he noticed the flier from Green Pastures, still held by a magnet. Setting aside the magnet, he took the flier to the kitchen table, where he sat looking at it, his hands folded around his mug for warmth.

He turned to the back panel with the strange logo and the photo of Chelsea Phillips in her tan cowboy hat. There was something about the way she was looking at the horse. There was something about the horse itself he didn't understand. A forever home.

He studied the Green Pastures phone number. He decided he'd stay home from work and wait for Mae. He wanted to tell her about *Perche*, the little he knew of its forests and hills and valleys. One day maybe they'd go there. For now, it might be enough to drive up to Lucknow that afternoon. Explanations needed to be offered, inquiries made. He drained his cup and went in search of the phone.

HEIRS AND SPARES

Evan was pushing a double stroller along the county road at the western border of his and Mae's hobby farm, heading north into a stiff November wind. His eyes were tearing, and he could only assume the cold wind was doing the same to Max and Arthur, though they were carefully bundled up for this Sunday afternoon walk. He stopped to check, pulled out a hanky, dabbed the boys' eyes, and continued on his way as they dozed. Sometimes, he and Mae called Max and Arthur the peanuts, partly because of their size and partly because Evan loved *Charlie Brown*. Or they were simply "the boys." In a couple of months, Max and Arthur would both turn two, about two weeks apart. At this moment, for Evan and Mae, the boys didn't have a middle name or a last name to stick to them. Their last name wasn't Mulder, though he and Mae wanted it to be.

The sun was shining brightly behind him in the fall sky, the light making the eastward flowing clouds pewter underneath but a glowing white around the edges. He and the boys walked in and out of moving cloud shadows. The wind agitated the dry ditch grass and cattails. He chose not to think that this might be the last walk he took with the boys.

He'd been pushing strollers, off and on now, for about twenty years. It had started with Alex, born six months after he and Mae eloped. In those early years, they had no car. While Mae worked as a waitress and store clerk to put him through university, he spent a lot of time with Alex. He remembered transporting Alex in chest carriers, backpacks, and strollers around London's downtown, its neighborhoods near the university, and its parks.

Already in their dating days, Evan knew that Mae wanted a big family. He jokingly told her he'd be happy with an heir and a spare to carry on his noble bloodline. But when he was honest with himself, he had to admit he hadn't given much thought to fatherhood. Mae's dream was of a large brood, big family dinners, a noisy house, and wholesale purchases of band aids. That said, she was no Stepford wife, no anti-feminist. She just knew her mind and her desires, the strong children she wanted to raise. The problem was that her biology didn't cooperate. After their quick and easy start on a family, Mae had developed secondary infertility—an irony he knew was a bitter herb lingering on her tongue. Her ovulation simply did not cooperate with their efforts to get pregnant again.

When they'd virtually given up, though, Mae was suddenly, surprisingly pregnant with Lizzie. Between Alex and Lizzie there was almost eight years of waiting. By then, the backpacks and strollers had been passed on or donated, Evan couldn't remember which, and he and Mae had moved back to the neighborhood where they had grown up in south London, near the highway. They had to buy all new baby transportation gear. That included a Plymouth Voyager minivan that made Evan feel decidedly middle-class, depressingly paternal, with its boxy shape, rows of bench seats, and four-cylinder engine. The van hadn't stopped him from walking a lot, though. He remembered Lizzie perched behind his head looking about, riding his back like a cygnet or a baby chimpanzee.

That was about twelve years ago. Evan was now pushing forty, and they'd gotten through the Y2K scare as they entered a new millennium, two thousand years after that celebrated birth in Bethlehem, the one with the virgin mother and the perplexing paternal arrangements. He and Mae had survived the turn of the millennial clock, but it wasn't yet clear whether they would survive Max and Arthur.

It had all started when Lizzie turned ten—May of '99. Evan could tell it made Mae restless. They'd been trying for almost a decade to get pregnant again, sometimes intensely and methodically, other times casually, as if they were trying to sneak up on it, to trick her ovaries. No luck either way. Perhaps all the talk of apocalypse at the end of the millennium did it for her. Maybe it was just Alex and Lizzie growing up.

Mae's restlessness continued through the summer and into the fall. One Friday toward the end of October, he came home from work at Wheel and Barrow Chartered Accountants after spending the day untangling the finances of a father-son plumbing business—all of it causing some tension in the family. He plopped down and stretched out on the couch in the living room, where Mae was getting in some reading before supper. Nothing strange there. She often had her face in a book. It might be a romance if he hadn't been particularly attentive to her of late, a mystery if he had. He often thought his attentions perplexed her.

"Lizzie," he yelled, "It's Dad. Can you please bring me a beer?"

"Your wish is my command," she yelled back from upstairs, then thumped down to the kitchen, double time. She was a child with just one speed—fast. He heard the clink of the bottle cap rattling on the counter. It took some moments before Lizzie appeared, holding out the beer to him. The neck of the bottle was filled with foam.

"Thank you, humble servant, but it appears that you've helped yourself to my ale. You're just ten, not twenty, you know. You're too young to start drinking."

"Close enough. I'm very mature for my age, practically a grown-up."

Mae jumped in from behind her book. "Don't rush it, Sweetie. I'm not ready for you to grow up."

"Mom, why are you reading a book about adoption?"

"What?" Evan sat up, dribbling beer down his shirt, and looked at the book. *The Complete Adoption Book.* "Are you serious?"

Mae kept the book up. "It's just research. We need to explore all our options."

Lizzie walked over, sat on the arm of Mae's chair, and looked at the book over her shoulder. "What's it say about adoption? I mean, where do the kids come from? Is it like the animal shelter when we got Ike, or the rescue place we got Finnegan?" As a family they'd adopted dogs and cats and horses. The name "Finnegan" still gave Evan a pang. He had thought rescuing animals might have filled something of the void Mae felt. How foolish of him, imagining that adopting animals was good enough.

Mae placed a bookmark in the book and set it aside. Lizzie took the opportunity to slip into her mom's lap. Groaning from the weight, Mae said, "Your dad and I still have to talk about it." Damn straight, he thought, as he steadied himself with a long draw of beer. It's something Mae had mentioned once or twice before in passing, nothing this serious. "But how would you feel about having a little brother or sister? Maybe two or three." He spluttered and coughed as some beer went down the wrong pipe. "Look, your dad's getting all choked up about it."

"I don't know, Mom. Little kids can be so annoying."

"I'll try to remember that."

He and Mae did start talking about it. They were still talking about it when Alex got home late that evening after going to a movie with his girlfriend Selene. When Mae told him what she was thinking, Alex said, "Does that mean I'm losing my bedroom? I know I'll be going to university next year, but I'd hate to lose bedroom privileges." He went to the fridge and grabbed the orange juice. "Mind you, since I won't be home much, maybe it *is* a great idea. A crazy idea at your age, though." He drank from the jug. "What's really great is Lizzie will get a taste of her own medicine, the little pest. See how she likes being the older sibling." He took one more swig and put the juice back in the fridge. "Come to think of it, I'll be more like an uncle than a brother. Weird."

Evan knew Mae was serious when she started leaving adoption books in his reading pile. "Start reading," she'd say. "You've got a lot of catching up to do." He felt time ticking, the clock running down. Was it the millennial clock or her biological clock, maybe both? He wasn't sure, but he struggled to finish *The Complete Adoption Book*. Then he got started on *Raising Adopted Children*. Part way through, he said to Mae, "I don't suppose there's an *Adoption for Dummies*, is there? That would make my life so much simpler."

"No short-cuts. We have to do this right." It was soon after this conversation—early in 2000—that Mae contacted the Catholic Charities Adoption Agency. What followed were meetings, interviews, forms, personality tests, home assessments. What followed was a foster care and adoption course. For four successive Wednesday evenings in June, they drove to their old high school, WLM-KSS, and sat at tables arranged in a horseshoe in a home economics classroom with about a dozen other nervous, hopeful couples. They told their stories to each other—couples who'd found no success with fertility treatments, ones who were hoping to help at-risk children by fostering, others planning an international adoption, grandparents who were trying to get their grandkids into their own homes because their own children had had these children taken away.

For four weeks they had homework—reading and worksheets. They listened to social workers and psychologists talk about frightening acronyms—ADD, ADHD, FAS. They learned about attachment disorders suffered by neglected and abused children; they were taught attachment practices and coping strategies. They heard pep talks about the enormous need for children to be taken into what the social workers called "a forever loving home." In the phrase Evan heard an echo of the language used by animal rescue organizations. He thought of Ike, their adopted Newfoundland mix, aging now, and Finnegan, their rescued Percheron, gone. How much more was he setting himself up for by adopting a child? Was he up for this?

At the end of the four weeks, they walked away with a piece of paper certifying they were approved to foster or adopt. The couples parted, wishing each other luck for the next stage—the waiting.

Yes, he and Mae were approved—but not everyone approved. They were approved—but not everyone understood. Family and friends had opinions, and were happy to share them.

"Aren't you getting a bit old to start with a little one again?"

"I think what you're doing is great, but you're crazy."

"Aren't you happy with the two God gave you? Alex and Lizzie are great kids. Maybe it's best you stick with two. It may be his will for your lives."

Evan thought about that will as he continued to push the stroller along the county road. He was leaning into the gentle incline of a small hill. At the crest he paused to catch his breath and make sure Max and Arthur were still bundled up. They were asleep, their heads leaning together. Ahead was Evan's goal—a bridge across a small creek. He thought of it as the boundary between home and away. It was what he looked for coming back from work; crossing the stream meant he was close to home, to the world where he was husband and father.

When he and Mae were waiting, he had to confess that occasionally questions and doubts beset him. He shared them with Mae a couple of months after they were finished the course. They were sitting together at the kitchen table having a tea break on a Saturday morning. "I have no doubts about this," she said. "I'm certain, but I need you on side or there's no point going forward." On the wall behind her, Mae's pictures of wild horses from the Alberta Foothills and Sable Island bracketed the serious expression on her face. "Do you know how hard it's been for me to give up on getting pregnant again?"

Evan hesitated and looked away. In the corner, the jelly cupboard he'd made for Mae almost a decade before held the dishes she'd gathered over the years for special family dinners and holidays. There was also a teapot cottage and a platter from her grandmother. On top sat two souvenirs from their honeymoon at the Talisman Ski Resort, a snow globe containing a family in a horse-drawn sleigh, and a framed photograph with four figures in party hats cutting a cake—such young versions of himself and Mae beside the Laurences, Larry and Caroline. Finally, he said, "You're committed, so I'm committed. I'll do whatever it takes."

"We don't have to rush into anything. Let's see what happens next. We may be waiting for months, even years."

They got the call in March of the next year—about eight months after they'd completed their course. Evan picked up the phone from the top of the jelly cupboard. It was their social worker Margaret from Catholic Charities.

"Evan, we have two boys in foster care. We need to remove them from the home quickly. Are you and Mae willing to take them?"

"Two boys? Let me talk about it with Mae." He knew already the answer was yes when he saw her face. She took the phone, and he listened as she asked about their names and ages, what she and Evan needed to pick up before the boys came, what the situation was that made it an emergency. Max and Arthur. Fourteen months. They'd be coming with just the clothes they were wearing. There were problems in the foster home that couldn't be specified. Beneath the conversation he could tell she was vibrating. Two boys, he thought. Not a child, but children.

The next day being St. Patrick's Day, the house was decked in green. A paper rainbow ending in a pot of gold decorated the family room window. After dinner that evening Evan, Mae, and Lizzie were waiting when Margaret and another social worker Evan didn't recognize walked up the porch steps with Max and Arthur. They were two little peanuts in sleepers, big heads and big eyes with thin little bodies. Mae received Max while he took Arthur. They were wide-eyed and silent. Evan imagined how strange, even frightening, this journey must be for them. Though it had been years since he'd rocked Alex or Lizzie, he felt the rhythm of gentle holding and swaying and talking come back to him.

Margaret had bottles of formula ready for Max and Arthur. Mae instructed Lizzie on how to warm them up properly. Margaret then explained that something had gone wrong at the foster home in the last couple of months. The foster mother was not coping well. Her own children were acting out in worrying ways, her husband was on the road for long stretches with his job, and she was still feeding Max and Arthur as if they were babies. She couldn't see how thin they were getting. She wasn't transitioning them to solid food. For their own health and safety, Max and Arthur had to be removed. A tough decision, Margaret admitted. Max and Arthur had been born two weeks apart in St. Joseph's Hospital, taken from their mothers because of addiction problems, and placed in the same foster home. The foster mother was the only mother they knew.

Mae took a bottle from Lizzie and began feeding Max. Lizzie gave Evan the other bottle. He brought the nipple up to Arthur's mouth and he took it without hesitation. The boys were sucking noisily as Margaret explained they could be introduced fairly quickly to solids, starting with soft foods like bread, oatmeal, and apple sauce. She said she would check how things were going the next day. She told Max and Arthur they would be just fine, rubbing their cheeks as she said so. Then she turned and left with her colleague, Lizzie closing the door behind them.

Mae placed Max in his high chair, and Evan followed suit with Arthur. When Mae broke up pieces of bread for the boys, they stuffed them in their open mouths and filled their cheeks. If Mae hadn't restrained them, they might have gone on eating forever. Such appetites, thought Evan. Such hunger. So much need in the world. Lizzie laughed at the sight. "They're a couple of chipmunks," she said. She grabbed the snow globe off the jelly cupboard and shook it up for them; their eyes widened. She put it down on the kitchen table and rushed off to find some toys.

The coming weeks were filled with adjustments, with remembering past habits and practices, with rearranging their lives to make room for Max and Arthur, who were quickly taking over the house. It was everything times two—feedings times two, play times two, naps times two, baths times two, dirty diapers times two, exhaustion times two.

For a couple of weeks it was tag-team parenting as he and Mae were knocked out by something flu-like, obviously from the foreign microbes brought into the house by the boys. It was all part of their invasion. Thank goodness Lizzie had her March Break for part of that time. Alex came home from university for a few days, as well. Together, they picked up the slack.

Busy boys, busy boys. They were such busy boys, they needed as many parents as they could get. On the move, they scattered their toys— Duplo blocks and balls, stuffed animals and potato heads, cars and trucks and trains—well beyond the family room. Max was quick with a smile and a laugh, Arthur serious and silent. When Evan arrived home from work, he'd see them at the family room window. They would climb up on the bench to look for him when the dogs started barking. There was Max's face crowned by the tight little curls of his short Afro—one of his birth parents was Black, the other White, Evan and Mae didn't know which. There was Arthur's face, thin wisps of blond hair on his round head.

By late spring, they were attached to the dogs, loved to play on the porch with the barn cats that came up to the house, and followed Mae around as she tended to the horses. When Evan got home from work, they clung to his legs or piled on him. He sang to them the songs he had sung to Alex and Lizzie, did his Swedish Chef imitation, took them for walks in the double stroller, a gift from friends.

In his walk he was now at the bridge. Before he turned to head back, he watched and listened to the water run through the culvert and wind its way to the west, where the sun was lowering in the November sky. Checking the road, he crossed to the other side and began heading back, facing any traffic that might come their way.

It was back in July, close to their twenty-first anniversary, that he and Mae got a call from Margaret. She needed to stop by for a visit. What she didn't tell Mae on the phone was that there had been developments, that a detour had been thrown up on the road to adoption. When he got home from work, Mae shared her worry with him.

After spending some time visiting with the boys, Margaret asked if she could talk to Mae and Evan privately. He asked Lizzie to take Max and Arthur out to visit the horses.

"The boys seem to be settling in really well. It's great to see." Margaret paused.

"They're pretty much in like dirty shirts now." He filled the gap while Mae sat tense beside him.

"There's no easy way to say this, but I don't want you to be worried because I don't think it'll amount to anything." Margaret paused again. "The foster mother has appealed our decision to remove Max and Arthur from her home. She wants them back. In fact, she wants to adopt them, Max for certain if she can't have them both." Another pause. "The department believes she doesn't have a legal leg to stand on. We followed our protocols to a T and documented everything surrounding the removal, but she has the right to appeal and that's what she's doing."

Evan looked at Mae as she stared straight ahead. He could tell that she was too pained to trust herself to speak. "What can we do," he asked. "What *should* we do?"

"Just keep doing what you're doing. We'll step up our home visits—including unannounced ones—and keep gathering evidence about how well Max and Arthur are doing here. We'll have them examined by a doctor to show that they're healthy and growing. The judge will see that their lives are on a good path now. That will help the case."

When Margaret got up to leave, Mae managed to thank her for coming, for telling them in person. She appreciated that.

"I really don't think we have anything to worry about. I'll keep you informed, but don't hesitate to call me if you have questions or need anything."

When he and Mae were alone, they hugged silently. He didn't trust himself for some time to look her in the face. When he was able to, he said, "I'm sure she's right. The foster mother wasn't taking proper care of them. The courts wouldn't risk the boys going back to her."

"But what if Margaret's wrong? When it comes to kids, it's the story of our lives. Nothing seems to come easy. I don't think I'll be able to handle it if this goes off the rails and they take the boys away."

"It'll never come to that, I'm sure of it." He tried to sound more confident than he really was.

"Promise?"

"Promise."

"Swear?"

"Swear."

They locked their fingers together, a ritual they sometimes practiced when pinkies weren't enough. He silently prayed that it would work.

In spite of their compact, they've been on this worry train for the last four months. Evan thought of this as he pushed the stroller homeward. There had been sharp curves, steep inclines, and dark tunnels along the way as Margaret kept them informed about this glitch, that wrinkle, another strategy.

In the middle of it all, 9/11. Evan was at work when the news broke. In the office, activity virtually came to a standstill as he and his colleagues gathered around the one TV to witness the horror, the collapse, the dust-covered tragedy, the seeming triumph of hatred as a handful of men, ideologues, attacked a system by destroying innocent lives. He wondered later, when the identity of the attackers become known, whether any of those men were fathers. How could they be? It wasn't to be fathomed.

For him and Mae, their private worry became overshadowed and weighed down by a global crisis, a tragedy that made them feel selfish and guilty within their own small drama. It was as if they were obsessed with a furnace malfunction when their neighbor's house was engulfed in flames.

Now it was all coming to a head tomorrow, when the judge rendered a decision.

As he pushed Max and Arthur homeward, he thought of their many mothers. What disaster happened, he wondered, in the lives of their birth mothers? What burdens did they carry from their child's absence? These women had given their sons life and a name. That was all they'd been allowed to do, maybe all they'd been able to do.

And what of the foster mother? He wanted to hate her, but he couldn't, not really. As much as he was able, he understood her desire for the boys, but he resisted that desire with everything he had. He was angry at her on Mae's behalf especially. He was angry about the mess the foster mother made or got herself into. He was angry about the damage. They'd learned from Margaret that part of the problem was the foster mother had clearly favored Max and neglected Arthur. Her appeal was showing this was still the case. Reaching out to Mae, his heart sought to surround and protect her mother dreams. He knew it was hopelessly old-fashioned to think it, even paternalistic, but she was the mother of their children, all of them, both born from her and held by her, the heirs of his body and not of his body.

As the stroller tires spun along the pavement, he thought too of fathers—the foster father likely on the road when he learned that Max and Arthur had been taken, his wife devastated. The boys' biological fathers—what were their sons to them? A product of passion? An unintended consequence? A sperm donation? A way to pass on their name, their genes? Or maybe an attempt to graft their lives onto the trunk of a larger family story? He thought back to Mae's first pregnancy, how everything might have turned out differently if he and Mae had made other choices, even the most drastic of decisions. Back then, he hadn't really chosen fatherhood. Being a father hadn't been part of his vague sense of his future, when he even really thought that far ahead. He had just wanted Mae, plain and simple. But here he was, with Alex and Lizzie and now Max and Arthur. Now it was what he wanted.

Tomorrow, the judgement would come down. As he neared the corner, he began chanting the Lord's Prayer in sync with the rhythm of his walking and the wheels turning. Strange as it seemed to himself, he'd resorted to these petitions because he wasn't sure what else to pray. It had been a while since he'd wrestled with the discipline of prayer, but he did remember something he learned long ago. Jesus' word *Abba* was more like *Daddy* than *Our Father*, so *Abba* he prayed. It was *Thy kingdom come* as he rounded the corner onto the road that led to their house, a stretch of pavement that worried him because of the heavy traffic that rumbled along it. He was intoning *Forgive us our trespasses as we forgive those who trespass against us* as a minivan bore down on them, travelling too fast. As it closed in, he saw in a kind of tunnel the driver talking on one of those newfangled mobile phones, the man's wife turning to talk to the children in the back seats. The car was straying seriously close to the gravel shoulder. Afraid, Evan veered the stroller into the ditch as the car's tires caught and kicked up stones. Both he and the stroller took a tumble. In the end, he was prone in the bottom of the ditch, listening to the van's engine fade into the distance and looking up at Max and Arthur strapped into the stroller sitting on its side. They were awake now. Their startled faces cracked into smiles that turned into laughter at this trick their dad had performed. *Abba*, said Evan. *Amen.*

It was lunchtime on Monday, and Evan sat at his desk to eat his PB and J sandwich, yogurt, and banana. He'd squirreled himself away in his office at Wheel and Barrow Chartered Accountants as much as he'd been able to, waiting for Mae's call and not trusting himself to be sociable with his colleagues. A cold rain pelted his window, at the edge of freezing into sleet. Often during the morning, his eyes had lost their focus on the words and numbers before him on his computer screen, his mind wandering to the window and the what-ifs.

He was waiting. He was waiting on his children as he had for much of the last twenty years. Waiting for Alex to come down the slide. Listening to the baby monitor, waiting for Lizzie to fall asleep. Waiting for the bathroom to be free. Waiting in Emergency for wounds to be stitched up. Waiting for Arthur to finish his supper. Waiting for Max to finish splashing in the laneway puddle. In the early days, waiting for the bus, waiting at the laundromat for clothes to dry. Waiting for school to get out. Waiting late into the night to hear Alex return with the van. Waiting for them to grow up, to play and dance at recitals, to walk across stages. Waiting for glasses to be ready, braces to work. Waiting for birth, now waiting for adoption.

He hadn't always been patient. He thought of his own father, of the waiting and worry he must have felt on Evan's account. Work as often a means, not an end. The whiskey each day after work, taken for medicinal purposes, his father said. The immigrant's dream of his children having a better life than his own, waiting for it to happen—a vision of kingdom come that could become a parody, when realized.

Last night's waiting was full, unsettled for everyone in the house. Something felt afoot in the November darkness. Arthur took a long time to settle for sleep, and a couple of hours into their own restless dozing, Evan and Mae were awakened by Max's crying, his sleeper and pillow and stuffed bear all soaked. *Deliver us from evil*, Evan thought. He hugged Max to counter whatever nightmare lingered in his child's mind, then changed him into dry PJs and brought both boys into bed with himself and Mae.

Even Lizzie was disturbed and worried last night. "Dad," she'd said, "Can you tuck me in. I'm cold." It was like when she was younger, when he read to her every night—from Dr. Seuss to Robert Munsch to Tolkien and so many more, as she grew up. Eventually the Harry Potter series. Now, they were each reading the books as they came out, following the orphaned Harry's adventures and trials, most recently in the Triwizard Tournament that happened in the *Goblet of Fire*.

Evan pulled his banana out of his lunch bag. As he was about to peel it, he noticed that the yellow on one side had brown lines etched in it. *Hi Dad. Love Lizzie* was the secret message that had revealed itself over the course of the morning, as the banana sat inside the darkness of his lunch pail. He smiled at his daughter's joke. Maybe he could save the peel, stop the browning somehow, and frame it on the wall. *Give us this day our daily bread.*

He was packing away his lunch pail when the phone rang. He saw from the screen that it was Mae, and quickly picked up the receiver.

"Is there news?"

She was crying, struggling to get the words out through it. Finally, she said, "It's all good." The judge had denied the foster mother's appeal. They were free and clear to adopt Max and Arthur.

"I'll be home soon." He couldn't say much more through the choking that he felt in his throat.

How strange, he thought as he put down the phone and wiped his eyes with his fingers and then the backs of his hands. *Thy will be done on earth as it is in heaven.* How strange it was to think of that will, of even desiring that will to be done. For weeks, Evan had been thinking the worst, preparing for the worst, expecting that Max and Arthur would vanish from their lives. But it hadn't happened. He felt like they'd thinly escaped some judgement. Was this the plan for all their lives—Max's and Arthur's, his and Mae's, Lizzie's and Alex's, even the foster mother and father and their children?

It's a muggle's life, he thought, as he watched the runnels of rain slide down his office window. He knew that he was all-in now, as he packed up to head home.

Bunches of balloons were tied to fence posts and swayed in the breeze. Cars lined the grass along the laneway, and Lizzie had festooned the trees with paper streamers. In the yard, tables were covered with blue plastic cloths, clipped against the wind, and covered with fruit trays, a punch bowl, cookie plates, and a large cake. Beer and wine coolers were chilling in one metal tub. At a safe distance, another metal tub sat filled with water balloons. It was a Sunday afternoon early in June, and Evan and Mae were hosting an adoption party for family and friends. Max and Arthur wandered the yard, shepherded by older children and carried around by adults. Evan and Mae didn't need to watch the boys, there were so many other eyes on them. In the garden, daffodils had given way to poppies and black-eyed Susans. The lilacs were in bloom and perfumed the whole yard.

Two months earlier, the adoptions had been finalized. Only then had he and Mae seriously begun talking names, not wanting to jinx what felt like a final trimester. What names would they stick to Max and Arthur? They soon decided to accept the first names given the boys at birth. The names now seemed right, as well as a doing right by their birth parents. But their middle names needed to be new, as they also took on a new family name.

He and Mae considered their own names and the names they had chosen for their birth children. Mae, French for May, the month named in Roman myth for Maia, the goddess of spring growth. Alex, defender of men, protector of mankind. Lizzie, consecrated to God, who is bountiful. And himself, Evan, a Welsh name meaning Yahweh is gracious.

But what went with Max, great spring, and Arthur, the bear king? For Max, they settled on Samuel, God has heard, a family name from Evan's side. Arthur became Arthur Callum, strong-willed or wise hound-lover, in honor of Mae's dad and his ancestry.

All the legal paperwork done, last month they went as a family to the Middlesex County courthouse, not the old courthouse where he and Mae eloped two decades before but the new one, a tall cement monolith rather than a faux castle. In a windowless courtroom adorned with blond wood, red upholstery, and official crests, the authority of the presiding judge made them a family in the eyes of the law. They had a photograph taken in which Max and Arthur sat on the judge's knees behind the elevated wooden bench, surrounded by Mae, Evan, Alex, and Lizzie. In another picture, their extended family squeezed into the frame. He and Mae also received official birth certificates on which the names Maxwell Samuel Mulder and Arthur Callum Mulder were inscribed, their birth names having disappeared as though they never existed, the names of the foster parents nothing but ghosts.

This morning in church, Max and Arthur had been sprinkled with water to make their names stick. Evan and Mae asked Margaret if she knew whether the boys had already been baptized. With Margaret uncertain, he and Mae decided dunking them twice wouldn't hurt, and their pastor agreed. In Evan's tradition, it was called baptism. In Mae's, it was also called christening. So they brought their new sons before the congregation, pledged to raise them right, and held them up for Pastor Newhouse to touch their heads three times with palmfuls of water from the font, tying their names to the Father, the Son, and the Holy Ghost. Unlike many infants, Max and Arthur didn't cry. Instead, they looked quizzically at the pastor and then around at the congregation with expressions like those they offered the night of their arrival at Evan and Mae's home. In celebration of their adoption and christening, the pastor preached on a passage from Romans. Nice touch, thought Evan. This guy knows his stuff. If adopted, then heirs.

Pastor Newhouse also knows his beer, and he was now enjoying a cold one as he chatted with Alex about his year at university and his summer job. Evan was content simply to listen. He excused himself to seek out Mae, and found her alone in the kitchen adding fruit to a tray that had dwindled. Together, they looked out over the full yard, pausing for the first time in a long day.

"It's really done," he said.

"I think it's really just beginning," she replied.

In the late afternoon, the party-goers headed off in their cars to their own homes and their separate conversations around their own family tables. He and Mae and Alex and Lizzie cleaned up the food but left balloons and streamers tied to the fences and the trees. There would be time enough another day. Evan watched Alex obsessively traverse the lawn to retrieve every bit of broken water balloon, enlisting help from Max and Arthur, who were more interested in the colors and textures of the latex. Alex had to constantly remind them not to put the balloons in their mouths, to the point where he sent them off to help Lizzie because of the choking hazard. Enough done, together they ate a light supper, mostly party left-overs.

Then Evan put Max and Arthur in their spring jackets—it could still get cool in the evening this early in June—and strapped them side by side into their double stroller. He headed down the laneway to the road, where he turned right and followed the shoulder to the crossroad, looking back over his shoulder periodically to check the traffic. As he turned the corner and walked toward the bridge, he didn't know what was ahead—tomorrow, next year, the coming decades. Perhaps if he did, he would turn around. Likely not. The sun lowering in the northwestern sky was casting shadows onto the road from the high ditch grass and the woods up ahead. The Lord's Prayer came to him naturally, its petitions in rhythm with his gait and the stroller's wheels. *Lead us not into temptation,* he prayed. *Deliver us from evil.* He kept on walking.

FEATHERS

Evan was about to be swarmed by a flock of teenaged girls. Any moment the bell would ring, the school doors would open, and hundreds of students would flow onto the sidewalks, over the lawns, and into the parking lot—a river of teenage energy, young horses straining at the harness of classes and homework, happy for the temporary release of the May two-four weekend. Soon he'd see his daughter Lizzie, with friends in tow. It was her sixteenth birthday, it was the Friday of the long weekend, and she was having a sleepover to celebrate.

He was waiting—bracing himself, really—in front of WLM-KSS and behind the wheel of a 1995 Odyssey. It was his second minivan, a replacement for the '88 Voyager he bought used in '89. He'd made the two stretch over the sixteen years since Lizzie was born. He had caved in to the pressure of paternity when he and Mae bought the Voyager, since they already had Alex, eight years older than Lizzie. They dumped the Voyager and bought the Odyssey in 2002 when they adopted Lizzie's younger brothers, Max and Arthur, three years ago.

He was parked in front of WLM-KSS, the same high school where he and Mae went in the second half of the seventies, the high school where they met, got pregnant, and then eloped to the Talisman Ski Resort in Beaver Valley. The high school where he built the jelly cupboard one summer more than a decade ago. The high school where he and Mae took their foster-adoption classes just a few years ago. He couldn't seem to get away from the place.

It was still a working-class school, teaching the kids of lunch-bucket parents living in a subdivision near the big and busy six-lane highway, the Four-O-One, at the south end of London—a medium-sized city with subdivisions sprawling outwards into southwestern Ontario farmland. It was about a half hour from Lake Erie to the south and an hour from Lake Huron to the northwest, plunked at the center of what looked on a map like a roughly nibbled wedge of cheese.

The bell sounded and there was a delayed reaction, a pause before the school's maw began emptying. He scanned the crowd for his daughter's face, the blonde hair with the tell-tale orange and purple tints—a phase, he told himself. As the crowd and the parking lot began to thin out, he started to fret. Had Lizzie suffered a social disaster? Had the girls she invited stood her up? He fought the urge to get out, roam the familiar halls, and take them down—just verbally, of course, in a fatherly sort of way.

He worried. She had transferred to WLM-KSS for Grade 10 after a bad year in Grade 9 at the high school in Windermere, the small town nearest their hobby farm. You'd think a tomboy like Lizzie would fit in, but no. Short hair, braces, and glasses, lizard-covered T-shirts broadcasting her fascination with cold-blooded creatures—she was soon a target for the popular girls, the mean girls, the nasty girls. In the edited version Mae had given him, Lizzie was in deep water for months. Mae refused to put up with it for another year and transferred Lizzie to WLM-KSS, drove her each day to the outside edge of the farthest bus route.

Lizzie was suddenly there. She and five girls burst through the doors. They were burdened with book bags and knapsacks and pillows and sleeping bags. They were laughing. One girl caught her bag's strap on the door handle and was jerked back. Another dropped her own possessions to rescue her snagged friend. The rescue earned a dramatic hug before they ran to catch up with the others.

The van was suddenly full—of voices, of bags, of bodies.

"Hi Dad! Thanks for picking us up."

"Pleased to be of service, your highness."

Before he pulled out, Lizzie introduced each of her friends by name. He greeted them all while registering their inverted faces in the rearview mirror. He tried hard to remember their names. He knew he likely wouldn't, as they melted into a mass of femaleness. He needed to say little else all the way home. The chatter was nonstop. The words sometimes flowed smoothly along a deep channel, then rushed loudly over rapids.

He avoided the highway on the way home. He could take a stretch of it but preferred the country roads, the same roads he travelled to and from work at Wheel and Barrow Chartered Accountants, the firm where he'd been for more than twenty years.

"What's that smell? Gross!"

"Look at those pretty cows! I'd like to have a pet cow."

"Is it true that chocolate milk comes from brown cows? I definitely want a brown cow. I could live on chocolate milk."

City girls, he thought. Of course, he was a city boy growing up—until he worked on a dairy farm the summer he was sixteen. That was part of a summer-jobs government program to put city kids on farms. He came back to the city after that summer, but the country stayed in him so long that eventually he and Mae moved to a hobby farm.

He crossed over the stream that signaled they were a few minutes from home. He could see the roofs of the barn and the house already in the dip beyond the corn field, the young plants popping out of the spring soil.

As he pulled into the laneway, the babble stopped. "This is your house?" It was an old farmhouse—a full two stories tall, yellow sandstone brick blackened by more than a century of weather. The second-story windows had gothic arches, including the window that Lizzie almost fell out more than a decade ago, when they first moved in and started renovating—a project still in progress. Some days it felt like they were re-fixing parts of the house they repaired when they first moved in. In fact, a large portion of the front roof was covered with blue tarps, the roofers having quit for the long weekend. A number of weeks ago an April storm had split the ancient maple on the southwest corner of the house, half the tree landing on their roof. Insurance was covering the damage, but still. He worried about the unsettled weather. It seemed worse this spring than ever before.

He'd forgotten how strange the house might look to girls from the suburbs, living in bungalows and split-levels and semidetached houses built barely thirty years ago, or just a few. "Welcome to the Erie Inn," he said, "located on scenic Erie Acres."

As he brought the Odyssey to a stop and put it in park, the girls erupted at the sight of the horses in the paddock, clambered out of the van, and ran over for a closer look. The startled horses galloped into the pasture. Flight animals, he thought. Sensible. Run for your lives. What was it about girls and horses?

The truth was that Lizzie had been horse crazy for more than a decade. She rode Western, going to horse shows to barrel race and pole tilt. She was now retrieving a halter and lead rope from the barn and calling the horses back into the paddock. They weren't cooperating, so she got the lunge whip and headed into the field. When she snapped the whip's tip on the ground, the five horses galloped in an arc around her and rushed through the gate into the paddock, snorting and kicking like yearlings. Alarmed, the girls jumped off the paddock fence where they'd been perched. "Holy shit!" was one's response.

Mae emerged from the house. She was ready to supervise phase one of her only daughter's sixteenth birthday sleepover—teaching the girls to groom and ride a horse. "Welcome, girls. Ready for a riding lesson?" As the girls gathered around Mae, Evan unloaded the van of knapsacks, pillows, and sleeping bags, and deposited them in the family room just off the side porch.

Max and Arthur and the dogs rushed past him, almost knocking him down. Through the screen door he heard the girls fussing over the boys. Lizzie introduced her little brothers as the twerps. "Be careful," she said, "they're double trouble."

"They're so cute," was the reply. They could be talking about the dogs, he thought—a friendly old Newfoundland and a hyper Lab-Retriever mix.

"I've got an older brother," one chimed in. "He's a jerk. He tickles me until I pee my pants. Sometimes he pins me to the floor and let's his drool almost hit me in the face before sucking it back up." Evan thought back to when he was a teenager, how he treated his own sister Annalise. He was a pest. He confessed it freely whenever they saw each other.

"All brothers are jerks, except when they're little like your brothers."

"I've got an older brother, too," said Lizzie, "Alex. He's okay but a little OCD."

"How old is he? Has he got a girlfriend?"

"Sorry, ladies, he's already taken. He eloped with his bitch girlfriend last Thanksgiving."

"Lizzie, watch your language. And don't mention that bitch face again." Alex's elopement was a sore spot still with Mae, maybe because she and Evan had eloped themselves. But that was different. She was pregnant with Alex. Bitch face wasn't pregnant at all, just staking her claim on Mae's first-born.

"How romantic."

"Not really. She's a Lydia." Evan recognized the name. Lizzie and her friends were obsessed with *Pride and Prejudice*. He'd sat through episodes of the miniseries every Sunday evening for months now. He kept meaning to read the novel to see what all this Jane Austen fuss was about.

When Lizzie was born, he and Mae had chosen the name Elizabeth because they loved the sound of it. Practically, it was also a family name and could be shortened a number of ways. He thought back to the labor room in the hospital. He'd done his best to coach Mae through her contractions, essentially a spectator to a miracle birth—a miracle at least for them, since Mae couldn't get pregnant for seven years after Alex. There were the hours of labor into the night and the sudden rush to the birthing room when dilation reached the proper measurement—10 cm was it? The doctor was paged and had just enough time to pull on her latex gloves to catch Lizzie as she slipped from the birth canal into a pool of light and air. He remembers the crying and the cleaning and the blanket wrapping before Lizzie was placed on Mae's chest. He remembers the next day in the maternity ward, Mae weeping with relief—supercharged on hormones—when their pastor visited to congratulate them and set a date for the baptism. He still sees baby Elizabeth sleeping in the plastic bassinette beside the hospital bed, Mae wiping her own red and blotchy face.

Within weeks, Elizabeth had become Lizzie—a pistol, a handful, a troublesome bundle of energy. When she started walking, there was no stopping her. She was a drive-by eater, a consumer of snacks. "Snack" was one of her first words.

Evan recalled that his role at Lizzie's sixteenth was that of humble servant, so he began checking the BBQ supplies. Mae had already set the dining room table, a three-layer cake the center-piece—soft pink and light green icing, a galloping horse perched on top.

An hour or so later, Mae and the girls and Max and Arthur burst into the house. Two girls carried Max and Arthur, who were wearing dandelion chains around their necks and on their heads. Two more girls had the dogs in tow. All the girls had flowers in their hair, and so did

Mae. All of them seemed to have scratches on their hands and arms. Evan imagined they'd been chasing the barn cats, trying to pet them even though they were feral.

The last girl was carrying a basket of brown eggs and exclaiming how beautiful the chickens were. "I didn't know white eggs come from white chickens and brown eggs from brown chickens. It must be like white cows and white milk and brown cows and chocolate milk." She paused to count the eggs. "A whole dozen! Living on a farm is so cool! My favorite hens are the Black Sex Link. They're so pretty." The other girls snorted at the name. Looking dreamily into the distance, the chicken lover said, "Their feathers shimmer like black and red foil." Emerging from her poetic reverie, she added, "That's the beginning of a poem I'm writing. I'll call it 'Fowl Beauty.' Maybe my mom and dad will let me get a couple of chickens for the backyard."

Evan knew feathers. He'd had lots of experience with them—from the soft down of the day-old chicks to the rich and varied plumage of hens, each breed wearing its own distinct suit, a natural fabric. He'd read about feathers—scientists' theory that they evolved from reptile scales, their marvelous structure of barbs and barbules and hooklets creating their light strength, the smoothness that invited a finger's touch, the beauty that made of them a keepsake. He was familiar with the different types—contour feathers for the body with soft down feathers beneath, flight feathers for wings and tails, special sensory plumes and bristles.

Mae told the girls to get themselves a drink from the fridge—there was water and pop—and then come back into the family room. He and Mae had set up a long table and chairs in the family room the night before, and the table was now covered with all sorts of crafting supplies—glue guns, glitter, feathers, paints, and more.

All the girls chose pop and guzzled it down as they walked back into the family room. One burp led to another, turning into a full-bore belching contest. Evan wasn't sure whether to be horrified or impressed. He stayed in the kitchen where it was safe and made some tea, listening as Mae led the girls in making decorative bird houses. She'd bought a kit for each girl and herself, along with all the materials needed to create a bird to sit on the house's perch—a dowel set below the oval hole, the house's front door. One side of the roof lifted up so that valuables could be stored inside—lockets and charms, private letters. He often called Mae a magpie, and each bird house would let these girls satisfy their magpie urges.

Girls and birds. Girls as birds. What was the connection, he wondered? He knew that British blokes called girls birds—he'd heard it on BBC. Here in North America, it was chick—she's such a hot chick. He knew he was dating himself with this. He doubted teenage boys called girls chicks anymore, possibly that they used ruder names. But why chick? What made a teenage girl a chick? He'd never called Mae a chick, couldn't stand the thought of some guy referring to Lizzie as one. He called Mae sweetie, even when she wasn't sweet. Honey, too. Not sugar or babe or baby. The drooling language of pop songs.

As he listened to the girls laughing and talking, asking each other and Mae for advice about their bird and birdhouse—how to glue parts so they would stick, which paint colors to use, what bits and pieces to bring together for maximum bling—he felt the full weight of female culture in his life. He wasn't a man's man, he knew it. He was comfortable living in a matriarchy. Mae occasionally called him a Momma's boy when she wanted to get under his skin.

It began there, he had to admit, with mothers. His Dutch mother, immigrating as a young woman after WWII, calling a vacuum cleaner a fuckem cleaner until the woman for whom she cleaned house corrected her pronunciation. Both his mom and dad came from big Dutch families, so he had a couple of dozen aunts, making family get-togethers loud and dramatic. There was his little sister Annalise, the object of his pestering, with her own growing pains, ones he hadn't understood. Then there were all the female cousins, some younger and some older, some modest and conservative, some not so much.

He remembered camping with his family at Lake Huron when he was thirteen or fourteen. Two older cousins came down from the city to the beach for the day, waded out into the water, and took off their bikini tops. Was what he felt then for his cousins love or something else? Was such love even allowed? He remembered Elizabeth Bennet's cousin Mr. Collins and his proposal of matrimony to her—marrying your cousin made foolish and comical and creepy.

Then there were girls in school. Confusing pre-teen puppy love. High school infatuations he hid. Flirting he never recognized for what it was. Confessions of attraction when a girl had moved on to someone else, having lost patience waiting for him to get a clue. All of it leading to a bike ride with Mae—eventually to three sons and a daughter, Lizzie. Mothers and daughters, he thought, they are a mystery to me.

As the girls finished their birds and birdhouses, he began barbequing the staple food of teenagers—hamburgers and hot dogs. He set out buns and chips and salads and drinks and condiments so the table was full, then stood back to let the girls chow down. And they were ready, piling their plates—no dainty bird appetites here. They went back for seconds, not saving enough room for cake. They ate several slices anyway.

By the time the girls were done eating, dusk was falling fast. They rushed up to Lizzie's room and returned some time later wearing period dresses, hair up and make-up on. Mae had searched for these dresses at second-hand stores and consignment shops. In the family room, the large beams and the wainscoting provided a fitting backdrop to the poses the girls struck as they settled to begin a *Pride and Prejudice* marathon. Their plan was to stay up all night and make it a true Jane Austen film festival, moving from *P&P* to *Sense and Sensibility* to *Emma* to *Persuasion*.

As the opening scene to *Pride and Prejudice* sounded on the TV, Evan and Mae began tidying the kitchen. "It looks like a bomb went off in here," Mae said. He heard pride and satisfaction in her voice.

At that moment, a blast of wind buffeted the house. It was so strong that it popped the screen out of the kitchen window and tossed it across the counter onto the island.

"What was that?" one of the girls asked.

"Probably my brothers destroying the house," Lizzie replied.

The gusts began slamming the first raindrops against the western windows and screens. Neither he nor Mae had noticed the clouds piling in the west, bringing on dusk earlier than expected. Now they rushed to close windows before the drenching began. The girls turned up the volume on the TV, trying to drown out the pounding of the rain and the wind battering the house. A mist invaded the family room before he could get the windows closed. "Not to worry," he said, "just a light spring shower to water you little May flowers."

"Dad, that's a groaner. Please don't embarrass me in front of my friends."

"But that's my job," he replied.

As if in answer, the wind and rain raised the volume to drown him out. At their peak, the power went out in the whole house—lights and television snapped off, plunging them all into darkness. Several girls started screaming above the wind and the rain.

He saw Mae's faint silhouette in the kitchen doorway as his eyes adjusted to the darkness. "It's okay, girls," she said, "This happens all the time. We have an emergency kit just for when the power goes out. I'll be back with it after I find the boys." She headed off, calling out to Max and Arthur.

"I've got to close the upstairs windows," he said. "We don't want you to drown. That would put a damper on the party."

As he groped his way out of the family room and into the kitchen, he heard a girl ask, "Could that really happen? Are we going to drown?"

Lizzie replied, "That can't happen—we haven't seen Mr. Darcy go for a swim in the pond at Pemberley yet."

He was feeling his way up the stairs when a brilliant flash of lightning illuminated the landing. He counted off three seconds before the thunder shook the house. There was more screaming, a lot more, below.

As he moved from room to room to close the windows, he walked through puddles, thoroughly soaking his socks. He hated wet socks. Never mind, he would change them and towel up the water when the job was done. Once he had secured all the latches, he listened to the rain drumming the roof and the wind lashing the house, now seemingly from all directions. The house was a lifeboat for all of them, women and children first of all. His job was to keep it afloat, to hold it together against the swells. Or maybe it was a nest high in a tree, and he had to keep it nestled in the branches against a forceful wind.

He sensed another sound above the rain and wind, a vibration. He returned to the landing and the sound registered louder—the tarps spread over the damaged portion of the roof were shaking and slapping at the wood. In the storm, there was nothing to be done, nothing he could do. Not to mention his fear of heights. He was comforted with the thought that in this weather he couldn't even attempt it.

As if in reply, one of the tarps broke free and began whipping wildly outside the hallway window. The vivid blue snapped in and out of sight until a vicious blast lashed the tarp's corner against the window's upper sash. The gothic arch was smashed inward, glass and wood and screen scattering across the floor. A chorus of screams from below merged with the wind and rain invading the chasm into an extended howl.

In his soaking socks, he walked gingerly across the glass-strewn floor and headed downstairs. This is getting serious, he thought. It wasn't just lights out, not just a broken window with a tarp lashing it. No power meant no water pump and no sump pump in the basement, water pouring down and seeping in.

He met Mae with Max and Arthur in the kitchen. "They were hiding in the bathtub," she explained. "I guess they were paying attention when we taught them where to go in a storm." She had the emergency kit with her: candles and matches, flashlights, food rations, light sticks, water purification tablets, playing cards, duct tape, a box cutter, ponchos, toilet paper, and tampons.

He heard something like moaning coming from the family room. The sound rose to a scream when lightning struck again—just one Mississippi away. Grabbing a flashlight, the duct tape, and the box cutter, he explained to Mae what had happened to the window. She said she'd work on getting the girls settled while he dealt with it.

In the basement, he looked for something, anything, to cover the broken sash. The best he could do was some plastic sheeting and cardboard. For protection, he donned his farm boots and barn coat, grabbed a broom, and headed upstairs. The glass-covered floor was slick. The wind and rain assaulted him as he reached through the hole left by the broken upper sash and struggled to grab the whip end of the tarp. He snatched a corner, seized the tarp with both hands, and began pulling it through the window. He had to lean back with his weight to make headway against the wind, which was pulling at the tarp like a sail. With three or four hard tugs, he was able to release the tarp fully from the roof and pull it through. He bundled it up as best he could and tossed it aside.

He retrieved the plastic, held it up to the window frame, and began trimming it with the box cutter while the wind slapped the plastic against his face. Eventually he managed to get four pieces of duct tape to hold the plastic over the opening, then fixed it in place with three more layers of tape. The plastic bulged inward but held. He repeated the process with the cardboard before sweeping the glass and wood into a corner. And he'd done it all in the small cone of light from the flashlight he'd wedged between a doorknob and a door frame. MacGyver would be proud.

I deserve a medal, he thought, the PAPI, the Paternal Award for Practical Ingenuity. He tramped down the stairs, trailing the ripped tarp like a fallen flag through the kitchen and family room. Mae had several candles lit and had distributed a couple of flashlights and some light sticks among the girls. In this odd illumination, Mae and Lizzie and her friends looked strangely vital, each one a candle flame, a rare bird. Either Mae had calmed them enough or they had grown so used to the storm they could talk with just an edge of worry.

When he returned from the mudroom, he saw that Mae had taken down a book from the top shelf, where novels were stored whose authors' last names begin with A.

"Until the power comes back on," she said to the girls, "we can't watch Jane Austen. But we can read one of her novels." She held up the cover so the girls could see. "This is *Northanger Abbey*—the perfect story for a night like this."

"Good idea," he said. "I'll grab a book myself and take the boys upstairs to bed." With his flashlight, he found what he was looking for and headed for the stairs with Max and Arthur. He heard Mae begin, *No one who had ever seen Catherine Morland in her infancy would have supposed her born to be an heroine. Her situation in life, the character of her father and mother, her own person and disposition, were all equally against her.* As he ascended, he thought of heroines and the six teenage girls listening to his wife, among them his singular daughter.

In his and Mae's bedroom, he tucked Max and Arthur in bed beside him. As they drifted off to sleep, he listened to the muted sound of reading below stairs. The rain and wind continued to pummel the house. He couldn't make out the words but felt the rhythm of the language, notes full of meaning and feeling.

When he was certain the boys were asleep, he pulled out his book and his flashlight. He flipped to the opening page and read, *It is a truth universally acknowledged, that a single man in possession of a good fortune, must be in want of a wife.* He smiled. Such a cheeky woman, that Jane Austen. He was certainly not a man of means when he met Mae so many years ago, and he had no idea he was in need of a wife. But as he listened to the murmur of Mae's voice and the boys' soft breathing under the rain and wind, as he thought of Alex's elopement and considered the young life of Lizzie, he realized this was exactly what he had lacked, precisely what he wanted.

The next morning, he was the first to rise, slipping out of bed without waking the boys. The power was still out. The May night had been cold, so the house was chilly. He peeked into the family room and found Mae and the girls bundled up in sleeping bags and blankets. He put on his worn running shoes and quietly went out the front door, letting the dogs follow him. The wind and weather were now calm. He surveyed the yard littered with tree branches. Low spots had become ponds. At the road, the ditch was full, water plunging through the culvert beneath their laneway. He walked a circuit around the house, checking for damage while soaking his shoes and socks. Loose and shredded tarps hung from the eaves of the front roof, exposing bare wood. He'd have to check for water damage in the attic. All in all, the old lifeboat had taken the battering pretty well. While he was outside, he checked on the animals. The horses were already grazing in the pasture, where pools blazed with the morning sun; the chickens were ready to be released into their run, anticipating a feast of worms.

He returned to the house, slipped quietly inside, and checked the basement. Without the sump pump running, the basement had filled with a couple of inches of water. Guess the lifeboat needs to be bailed, he thought. He'd have to assess the damage once the power was restored and the pump brought the water down.

Later that morning—closer to noon really—he was driving the girls home, retracing the path he took less than a day ago. They sat with their birdhouses in their laps and complimented each other's craftiness. Together they created names and calls and songs for their blingy birds. He thought about the birds he'd given over the years to Mae, beginning with a bluebird of happiness, including a pair of ivory swans she kept on her night table.

He was surprised to discover barriers before the stream crossing, with a sign reading "Flooding." Ahead, the road must have been damaged. He was unsettled, thinking of the detour he'd have to take today and maybe after the holiday weekend when he went back to work. He was a creature of habit.

"Can we take a look, Dad?"

"I'm not sure that's a good idea, Lizzie. Those barriers are there for a reason. It might be both dangerous and illegal."

"But Dad it's an educational opportunity. You know, to study the effects of flood water on roads."

"She's right, Mr. Mulder," another girl chimed in. "We could write a report on this for Geography. Does anyone have a camera?" The girls were already starting to open the van doors and he hadn't even put it in park.

"Okay. Hold on! You better let me go first. And when I say far enough, that's far enough." Evan put the car in park, turned his hazards on, and locked it up. He trotted to get ahead of the girls, who were almost at the barriers with the flashing yellow lights. "Proceed with caution. That's what yellow means," he said.

When they passed the barriers, he felt delinquent—as if he was leading the girls astray, helping them trespass and transgress. He moved forward cautiously and came to a stop with his arms out when he saw that the pavement ahead was filled with cracks and disappeared abruptly. From their position above the crossing, they could see the massive breach in the road. The culvert had been washed away; the rain had swollen the lazy stream to an enormous murky snake winding its way to the west, moving with the speed of a startled serpent. They stood silent before the sight until one of the girls started snapping photos with her 35mm camera.

Back in the van, he plotted out in his mind the detour he needed to take. He decided on the 401, given that more rural roads might be washed out. Soon the girls were sharing their amazement at the destruction they'd witnessed. As he sped down the highway, their conversation turned to other topics. They told family secrets—Lizzie sharing the open secret of his and Mae's elopement. Then the talk shifted to descriptions of their periods, opinions about their teachers, confessions of crushes (mostly on boys though one had feelings for a girl too), their plans for the rest of the weekend—and the rest of their lives. He marveled at their unfiltered talk. He was there and not there. Behind the steering wheel of this vehicle plummeting forward at 115 kilometers per hour, he felt his invisibility to these teenaged girls, even to his daughter. He was simply part of the machinery carrying them into their futures.

He wound his way through the subdivision of his own teenage years, dropping off the girls at their homes, birds to birdhouses. Each stop, everyone piled out and hugged the one they were leaving behind, finishing with cheek kisses, Jane Austen style.

At last, he was alone with Lizzie in the car and heading home. Through a yawn, she said, "Thanks, Dad." As she drifted off to sleep, he thought of Mr. Bennet with his five daughters, including Lizzy. Evan realized he too could not bear to part with his Lizzie but one day he must, that both he and Mae—who would bear the brunt of the hurt, he knew—would watch her drive off in some carriage conveying her into her future.

For now, though, she was here beside him. The distance—nothing but a small gap, really—had not yet widened to a gulf. He looked ahead. At home, there was a window to be replaced and a leaking roof to be covered, tree limbs scattered across the yard and a flooded basement. Then again, there was left-over birthday cake and ice cream to be eaten, Jane Austen's novels to read. He pressed down the Odyssey's accelerator.

BANDITS

For Sharon Klassen

The video footage was dark and grainy, but the shape exiting the coop door was unmistakable.

"Egg stealer! Chicken killer!"

Evan watched the video over and over on his laptop screen at the kitchen table as Arthur played it in a short loop. Arthur, just finished grade 9 that summer, had set up a small camera in the coop after Evan had complained of broken eggs and missing chickens, of missing eggs and broken chickens. For several days he'd gone out to the coop to find egg production way down, brown shells broken and hollowed out, feeders knocked over and raided. Worse, he'd found serious disturbances in the sand, feathers and down scattered about, plus the remains of a chicken wing in the outdoor run—clear evidence the hens in his flock were being picked off.

He asked Arthur to freeze the image on the dark shape exiting the small door he kept open during the day. "Little bastard!"

"It's probably a female, Dad."

"Bitch! You're going down."

"Calm your shit, Dad. It's just a raccoon."

"Watch your language." He looked at Arthur. "There's no such thing as *just* a raccoon. And what do you mean, calm my shit? My shit is calm, very calm." He turned his attention back to the screen. "Run it again." The video looped, the raccoon escaping again and again and again. "Bloody thieving bandit." He felt his twin, Evil Evan, expanding in his chest, blocking out Even Evan, his mild-mannered self.

He loved his hens, maybe a bit too much according to Mae. "You spend more time with them than you do with me," she'd say. "You might as well have a mistress." When he'd get a new batch of chicks—yellow, brown, or black puff balls with beaks and black-bead eyes, all perched on tiny legs and claws so large for their bodies—she'd complain he fretted more about them than he ever did about his own kids growing up, all four of them combined. "The chicks are less trouble," he'd reply. "They don't turn into teenagers." He got them day-old from the farm store in nearby Windermere and tended them carefully in the brooder under a heat lamp he constantly monitored until their feathers came in. That's when they were old enough to go out to the coop he'd built in the barn, where he'd keep them separate from the adult hens until the young birds could fend for themselves. His adult ladies were prone to pecking the little ones, even killing them—an old, old story about the female of the species, he thought.

He loved to feed the hens and fill their waterers, they seemed so eager to eat and drink and make merry and lay eggs. He'd walk carefully through the coop so as not to step on any of them, for they were skittish and flighty—bird-brained, after all—and were likely to get underfoot. When he brought winter snow into the coop on his barn boots, they'd gather around and peck at it. If he tried to gather eggs from beneath them, they were likely to peck his hand. He'd go back up to the house and complain to Mae. "Look at me. I'm hen-pecked."

"It must not be working very well, judging from the length of my honey-do list."

"I'll get to it after we finish everything on our honeymoon list." He liked to reference this list occasionally, inspired by the sexual adventures related to them by Larry and Caroline Laurence at the Talisman Ski Resort, as well as by a copy of *The Kama Sutra* he and Mae borrowed from the bridal suite. They hadn't returned it yet.

"In your dreams," Mae replied.

He'd share this hen-pecked husband joke with his kids and the rest of his family. They complained it was a groaner. He'd try it out on his egg customers. "Look at these scars," he'd say. "You can tell I bled for these eggs."

None of his hens were white—no boring Leghorns for him, no white eggs. Over the years, he rotated between getting Rhode Island Reds and Plymouth Rocks, along with breeds whose names seemed strange, like Black Sex Link. Such a hot name for a chicken, I have to get that breed, he'd thought.

And the brown eggs they laid were beautiful, not like store-bought eggs at all. No, his weren't blandly uniform in color and size, robotically manufactured at some factory farm. His hens laid eggs of different shades and sizes, some with odd shapes and wobbly ridges and spots, some pure brown and others dappled, occasionally one with a double yolk. They were all lovely variations of ovoid—he'd looked up the word for egg-shaped, from ovum for egg. He corrected people when they said *oval*. That's 2-d, he'd say. *Ovoid* is the real deal, 3-d. In his personal cosmology, the universe was ovoid. God had laid a giant egg and was brooding over it for billions of years. Any day now it might hatch into something heavenly. His hens' eggs were tiny replicas of this universe. They came out protected by a liquid sheen, a barrier against bacteria and antimatter. After the egg dried, he would just brush off any sand stuck to it. Maximum protection. No chinks in the egg's ovoid armor. Fragile armor, of course, easily cracked. But armor nonetheless, he chose to believe.

Occasionally when he scratched his ears or rubbed his eyes or ran his hand over the little bit of hair he had left, it occurred to him the human head was a bumpy ovoid container for the brain and its various attachments. Here was yet another mysterious connection between himself, the cosmos, and eggs.

His eggs did taste like heaven. It was true. Several people had told him as much. He had a sign at the road for neighbors and cottagers: "Free-Run Omega eggs. $4 a dozen." He brought eggs to coworkers at Wheel and Barrow Chartered Accountants. (He thought of them as his egg clients, not customers; he himself was their egg broker.) And he gave gifts of eggs to family when they came to visit. "There's no comparison," everybody said. "Your eggs are absolutely delicious."

He'd thank them and say, "Happy hens mean happy eggs." He did sometimes forget he wasn't the one laying them. It felt good to take credit—but a little weird.

He, Mae, and the kids had made a family project of it when he'd started talking about getting hens. Mae bought a couple of how-to books on chickens, which they studied together as a form of marriage counselling—growing closer by learning how to make a home for hens, rekindling the fire by raising fowl. Together with the kids, they framed out a coop inside their old barn and covered it with sturdy wire called hardware cloth. They covered every possible opening to make it an impenetrable chicken fortress, a Fort Knox to protect all those golden yolks. They'd installed a small door in the barn wall so the hens could go out during the day, built nesting boxes out of plywood and mounted them on the wall, and fashioned roosts out of an old wooden ladder. Mae read on the Internet—she'd found some interesting chicken chat rooms—that sand was the perfect litter and bedding for chickens. But it couldn't be sandbox sand, it had to be construction-grade sand. So they ordered a dump truck load, and filled wheelbarrow after wheelbarrow to cover the floor of the coop and bed the nesting boxes.

He'd learned the hard way the coop needed to be a fortress. The summer they started their chicken project, his daughter Lizzie was doing volunteer hours at a vet clinic in London. She'd just finished Grade 9. One day she brought home three young chickens from the clinic, abandoned birds dropped at the door in the early morning hours, probably by some urban farmer who thought he could raise chickens in an apartment. They decided to temporarily keep the chickens outside in an old wire dog crate until they could build a coop. But that night in bed Evan heard a commotion outside. By the time he'd pulled on some sweat pants and a T-shirt, grabbed a flashlight, and gone to investigate, two of the young chickens had vanished and the third was lying dead on the lawn outside the crate— all of them having mysteriously escaped the narrow bars, a sinister magic trick. He swung his flashlight beam in an arc across the lawn and caught the bandit waddling away with its plunder. In the light, it paused and looked back, its masked eyes aglow, then continued its escape.

While they were waiting for their first order of day-old chicks to arrive, they built their own brooder—a plywood box on wheels with a two-by-four framed lid covered in wire so they could watch the chicks but keep them safe from their dogs and cats, and hinged so they could lift it easily to feed and water the little peepers or catch and cuddle them. The inside bottom was protected by linoleum peel-and-stick tiles, a blue design left over from renovating the laundry room, plus several inches of pine shavings. They rigged up an arm from which to hang the heat lamp, the height adjustable so the warmth would be Goldilocks right as the birds grew.

That was about a decade ago, so the brooder had helped raise dozens of chicks into hens. To Evan each bird was vitally important, though he wasn't foolish enough to name them. They weren't just his hobby, not even just his passion. No, his free-run chickens were saving the planet, one egg at a time. He was doing his bit for animal rights, too—no cages for his hens.

He'd thought about installing cameras inside the coop and overlooking the run so he could live-stream his hens on the Internet. He'd considered writing a chicken blog, opening Instagram and Snapchat accounts, and setting up his own YouTube channel, becoming what the kids these days called a tuber. Who needed cat videos when you had chickens—hours and hours of entertainment. Could there be anything more comical than the way they ran to him when he brought them the kitchen scraps for a treat, racing like little feathered raptors, flapping their ineffectual wings. He'd open a Twitter account and send out regular tweets, real tweets from his chicks—hah! He'd be rich and famous, and so would his birds.

Never mind that he wasn't making any money selling eggs. That wasn't the point. He could figure it out if he wanted to. After all, he was an accountant. He knew he should probably charge more than he did just to break even, but he didn't care. He wasn't interested in a cost-benefit analysis. He sometimes said the egg money was his retirement fund, but that wasn't true. It disappeared into the daily errands of living. He loved the fresh eggs himself, that was true. But that wasn't quite it either. He couldn't really explain it. Maybe it was like adoption. His two youngest kids, Arthur and Max, were adopted. He and Mae had adopted rescue horses and dogs, too. Maybe he just felt this urge to adopt chicks, to be a chicken dad. Did that make him a rooster, a strutting Chanticleer? Or could it be that because he was a guy, it was a case of egg envy?

Maybe it was just the birds themselves, living creatures. The mystery of their growing up, the lives they led, their habits and behavior. The satisfaction of watching them flourish, the worry they wouldn't. Or it could just be about feeding them and seeing what magically popped out the other end, accompanied by some significant clucking.

But now the magic was threatened. A raccoon had discovered a weakness in Fort Knox, the little door to the run, and was breaching its defenses to plunder and pillage at will. The creature was trespassing. He'd been taught to pray, "Forgive us our trespasses as we forgive those who trespass against us," but he wasn't having any of that. His property was being trespassed; his world felt violated.

He shut his laptop and without a word to Arthur headed out to the barn. With a corn broom he shepherded the hens out of the run and into the coop. He closed the run door, then went inside and latched it with the sliding bolt. "Sorry, ladies," he said. "You're in witness protection for now."

Despite his initial anger and urgency, he took more than a week to get around to buying a live trap. His foe was cunning, and he didn't relish taking it on in battle. Instead, he looked for the easy way out. Keeping the hens in the coop permanently would solve the problem, but he couldn't stand the idea of taking away their freedom. They'd literally be cooped up if he did that. He considered hiring an exterminator or wildlife removal service, but he and Mae had moved to the country to be closer to nature. This solution seemed a copout, a city-slicker's solution. Besides, being Dutch-Canadian he was too cheap to lay out dough on getting rid of a pest. He seriously weighed poison or a shotgun as options—at least for a moment—but in the end rejected them. He'd studied just-war theory in university, but at heart he was a pacifist—though he did have to admit his principles were being sorely tried. He thought through these options, and discarded each in turn.

Each day, Mae asked him if he'd picked up a trap on his way home from work. She'd done the research for him, found one at the farm store in Windermere. Finally, on the Friday he did the deed and laid out the cash. It was almost two weeks since the video had caught the bandit on tape.

That evening he hardboiled a half dozen eggs. He didn't want to, but he knew he had to sacrifice some yolks for the greater good. He set up the trap inside the barn, right beside the coop. Inside the far end of the trap— a rectangular wire box with an opening on the near end—he placed two hard-boiled eggs in a paper bowl, then pulled back the handle on the top that set the trap. When the bandit walked into the trap, it would step on the metal trigger and release a flap behind it. Ingenious and humane, he thought, as he stood and examined the trap. Work your magic tonight.

The next morning felt like Christmas. He could hardly wait to get up and see what present the trap had left him. He was awake long before Mae and the kids, pulled on his barn clothes and his boots, and strode out to the barn while leaving tracks in the dew-soaked grass. He quieted himself as he approached the barn door, then peered in. In the early morning light the barn was dim, but he could see a dark shape in the sprung trap. An unmistakable shape.

He flipped on the lights and calmly approached the trap. He saw that both eggs were gone. The raccoon was sitting with its rear pressed against the trap's flap. Unblinking, it stared at him. He could swear the look on its face was one of patient resignation. It looked somewhere between calm and dejected, almost embarrassed having been caught wearing its bandit mask and prison-striped tail. But when he came closer it began pulling at the bars with its clever paws, its thin black fingers. He stopped, afraid. The phrase "primitive and irrational" popped into his head, but the fear remained.

He returned to the house, shook Mae awake, and explained they had a trapped raccoon to deal with. "You mean *you*, right?" was Mae's reply. "You realize I was having a lovely dream about horses. I was riding a sorrel mare on a Sable Island beach. I'd gotten special permission from the Prime Minister, who wasn't wearing a shirt. Now I'll never know how the dream ends."

"Sorry, but there's a nightmare out in the barn, and I could use some help figuring out how to get rid of it."

Mae emerged from under the sheets and followed him downstairs. While he made them some tea, she settled herself in the living room, opened her laptop, and started researching what to do when you have a live raccoon in a trap.

When he brought in the tea, she was ready. "It says here you need to relocate the raccoon at least five miles away, though ten is better—else it'll find its way back home."

"Clever critter. Guess I'll have to drive around and find a secluded spot. It wouldn't be neighborly just to drop it off at someone else's house or take it to the Timmy's in town."

As he sipped his tea he considered the possibilities. Most of the land around them was settled into farms—cash crop and dairy, some beef cattle, further east some vegetable fields and orchards, ginseng in what used to be tobacco country. Maybe he could release the raccoon in one of the few remaining tobacco fields so it could wreak havoc there. Perhaps he should take it to London, release it there under the cover of darkness. Lots of trees in the forest city, not to mention garbage cans and dumpsters. Wasn't the city their natural habitat now, not the country?

Better yet, why not take it to Toronto? They love raccoons there. The thought sent him on a wild, fantastic road trip. He saw himself rolling down Highway 401 in the fast lane, the raccoon in the back safely belted into an old car seat from the kids, peering out the window, enjoying the changing view from farmland to big city. He took the critter downtown, checked it into the Royal York. The next day, it did all the tourist stops. At the Royal Ontario Museum, it learned natural history. At the Art Gallery of Ontario, it enjoyed Group of Seven landscapes. It took in a Blue Jays ball game, rode the subway, visited some friends at the zoo, checked out some fish at Ripley's Aquarium, and scaled the CN Tower. City folk videotaped the whole climb, forgetting to turn their phones sideways, and posted it on the Web. The whole world watched as the little bandit made it to the Edgewalk deck and was invited into the restaurant for lunch. Later it checked out of the hotel without paying the bill and hooked up with some long-lost cousins. Together, they tore up the town—or at least several garbage cans with raccoon-proof lids. They were the new kings of Kensington.

Not a bad idea, Evan thought, to take it to the city. After all, the raccoon's dominion was now everywhere—east, west, north, and south, from sea to shining sea. How far north, he wasn't sure. Probably not to the Arctic Ocean, so not sea to sea to sea—but pretty close. Maybe he should start a campaign to make it Canada's national animal, replace the humble beaver. That might raise our profile around the globe, show a different side of the national character.

He imagined taking the raccoon to the beach instead—Port Stanley might be good, Port Dover even better. He saw himself on a Harley, the helmeted raccoon behind him holding onto his waist with its clever hands. They were on their way to a Friday-the-Thirteenth party. It could hang out with fellow *banditos*, clean those hands in Lake Erie, dine on smelt or Lake Perch, or sun itself on the beach while looking for a mate. He saw himself heading southwest from there and riding with it to Point Pelee, making it the southernmost raccoon in Canada. He would introduce it to Margaret Atwood, who'd invite it to have tea and biscuits. They'd share tips about bird watching and nesting sites before it swam to Pelee Island.

He came back to his senses as he took his final sip of tea. "I think I'll take it to Backus Woods," he said to Mae. "That's more than forty miles away. Plus, it's secluded and it's a conservation area. It's exactly where a raccoon should live—its natural habitat if it hadn't been for people."

"Just one more story of colonization."

"Colonization? You think we're the problem, not the raccoon?"

"I wouldn't put it like that. But you might look at it from the rac-coon's point of view."

The raccoon's point of view? Did it have one? "I suppose you mean live and let live. Coexist peacefully. But if we did that, we'd be overrun by them. The barn would be filled to the rafters and there wouldn't be one chicken or egg left—in the coop or on the planet. Life's most profound philosophical question—which came first, the chicken or the egg?—could no longer be asked, let alone answered. They'd colonize us, not the other way around. The raccoons will take over the world if we let them."

"I don't think you really have to worry about that, judging by the number of them that get hit by cars."

"Fair enough, but if we don't set up boundaries and keep them in their natural habitat, pretty soon we'll be just like Toronto. Before you know it, raccoons will outnumber people. They'll infiltrate city hall. I wouldn't be surprised if one day a raccoon was in the mayor's chair. Of course, it might do a better job of fixing Toronto's housing problems. But they'll stop at nothing. Queen's Park, the Parliament Buildings. Just look at politics south of the border. It hasn't gone to the dogs; it's gone to the raccoons."

"You're getting just the slightest bit carried away, don't you think?"

"Not a bit. You know what they say, 'Good fences make good neigh-bors.' There's wisdom in that thought when it comes to raccoons."

"If I thought you were being serious, I'd have to have you committed."

"You haven't looked into a raccoon's eyes. It's all there—thwarted ambition, criminal intent." He got up to go. "I should head out before the roads get busy. I'm not sure I want witnesses to this raccoon relocation."

"Good luck. If you're not back by noon, I'll send out a search party."

On his way outside he grabbed his barn gloves and coat for protec-tion, then found a tarp and a pitchfork. He'd decided to use Mae's hatch-back for the relocation. He told himself it was the only practical vehicle for the job, as the trap might not fit in his trunk and would definitely get his back seat smelly and dirty. Plus their old F-150 was low on fuel and reliability at the moment. He put the tarp down in the back of her car and carefully laid the pitchfork over the seats.

In the barn the raccoon appeared not to have moved. It stared at him as he walked over, adjusting its position only slightly to face him squarely. He picked up the trap by the handle and began walking as quickly as pos-sible to the car, holding the trap away from his leg, fearing those hands that could magically pull things through bars. The raccoon began lunging at the trap's back end, trying to break out. The force and weight knocked Evan off balance. He tripped and dropped the trap.

The door held. Thank you, Jesus, he thought. He found himself on the ground, eye level with the raccoon. For a startled moment, he met its dark eyes ringed in black fur. There, he saw an inscrutable life, as he had years before in the eyes of a rescued Percheron named Finnegan. Evan noted the brown-black stripe running between the raccoon's eyes from its nose to its forehead and was surprised by the white of its whiskered snout, more white around the bandit black, a rim of tan-white on the edges of its ears. The white gradually blended into the brown and black fur on its body, heavy all over until it smoothed out just above its hands and feet. The hands themselves were black, the fingers distinct—thin and clawed. The moment passed; the raccoon backed away from his face, hissing. Guess it didn't like what it saw. What did it see? He considered his balding head and big nose, his beard, his teeth, his eyes behind the barrier of his black-rimmed glasses. To the raccoon, a bandit's face?

He got up, brushed himself off, and looked down at the creature in the cage. He picked up the trap and now walked slowly and carefully to Mae's car. He gently placed the trap on the tarp and closed the hatchback without slamming it.

The roads to Backus Woods were quiet, but the trip was anything but restful for Evan. Before they'd even gotten down the long laneway to the road, he could hear scrabbling from the back of the car. He had a vision of the raccoon escaping the trap, its head popping above the back seat. The creature climbing over and jumping on top of his head, a living coonskin cap pulling off his glasses and nibbling on his ears. The rational part of his brain kept saying the trap door would hold, it was properly designed and manufactured. The irrational part wasn't convinced.

When he got to Backus Woods he looked for a secluded spot, a secondary road or trail that would give him enough time to release the raccoon without the interference of passersby or park rangers. For all he knew, what he was doing was trespassing since he wasn't using the park entrance. He pulled off at a spot where the woods seemed to have some dense undergrowth and put on his hazard lights. He got out, donned his barn coat and gloves, and opened the hatchback.

For the whole trip the raccoon had been scrabbling about in the trap, pulling in and shredding pieces of the tarp. Mae's car was a mess. Evan lifted the trap out and began yanking the tarp back through the bars. When he'd extricated the tarp from the trap, he placed the trap off the road's shoulder at the edge of the ditch, the door facing the woods. He retrieved the pitchfork from the car. Armed with the pitchfork in his left hand, his heart thumping in his chest, he placed his gloved right hand on the latch that opened the trap door. He pulled hard and the flap snapped up. The raccoon shot out, raced across the ditch, and disappeared into the undergrowth—all in a couple of seconds. Startled, Evan jumped back into the roadway. The last he saw of the raccoon were the shrubs rustling as it made its way into the forest.

Enjoy your new home, he thought. Y'all don't come back now, y'hear?

He looked around at the deserted road and the quiet woods on either side. Except for morning bird song, all was silence as he stood in the middle of the road, pitchfork in hand. No breeze stirred the leaves and needles. He felt watched. Quickly he placed the trap and the pitchfork back in the car, slammed the hatchback down, slid into the driver's seat, and pulled back onto the road, sweating in his barn coat and gloves. It was several minutes before he realized his hazards were still blinking.

That evening he reset the trap with more hardboiled eggs. Better make sure there aren't any more raccoons, he thought. Are they solitary or sociable creatures, possibly herd animals? He wasn't sure. When he returned from the barn, he called his son Alex and turned the day's events into a comical tale with himself as the mock-hero. "Picture me," he said, "armed with my pitchfork at the edge of the wild woods, the monster about to be freed at my feet. I'll tell you, that raccoon was a lot scarier than the killer rabbit in *Monty Python*. And there I was with no holy hand grenade in sight."

Despite such lighthearted tale-telling, that night Evan had nightmares. He was in the barn. It was murky dark with just thin ribbons of moonlight coming through the windows and doors. The hens were unsettled on their roosts. In his nightmare they too were having nightmares. There were nightmares within nightmares. The trap was sprung with a raccoon in it. As soon as he ran it to Backus Woods he'd come back and the trap had another raccoon in it, even though the trap was still in his hand. As fast as he removed raccoons, the trap filled up—sometimes with four or five squeezed into it at the same time. He ran out of room in the woods. The trees were full of them, the forest floor was crawling with them—the whole scene bathed in eerie moonshine—so he started putting them in the basement and the attic. In the nightmare, Mae told him he'd have to move out, their marriage was done, *finito*. There wasn't room for both him and the raccoons, and they were better company. She'd always liked bad boys, *banditos*.

He woke up in the dim light and looked at his sleeping wife. What was it about women and bad boys? Is that really what they wanted? Where had goodness gotten him, all these years? Of course, he'd gotten her pregnant when they were dating—going steady it was called then—and they'd eloped, running away to the Talisman Ski Resort in Beaver Valley. Didn't that make him a rebel? But that was pretty much it for his bad-boy behavior, and it was so long ago now—more than thirty years. He'd turned into a mild-mannered accountant, the Clark Kent of the spreadsheet. Maybe for the sake of his marriage he needed to revive his inner *bandito*. Should he buy a motorcycle, grow a ponytail with the wisps of hair on the back of his head, get one of his nipples pierced?

It was way too early for such questions. He was much too groggy to sort out the puzzle of his marriage, the tangled love knot he felt for Mae, a knot that went all the way back to a bike ride, their first date. Not to mention it was a knot threaded through with their four kids, with decades of being called *Dad*, that word still a mystery to him.

After this restless night, he was exhausted. He was afraid to go out to the barn. He needed to give himself a vigorous face wash before he could investigate what was out there on this quiet Sunday morning. When he put on his barn boots, his feet felt heavy; they swung like iron pendulums as he trudged to the barn.

He peered into the gloom before turning on the lights. The trap was once again sprung. He could see shapes moving within it. But what was that he heard? It sounded like the chirping of birds. When he flipped on the lights he was startled to see two baby raccoons huddled together in the trap. Above them he saw another baby crawling up the outside of the coop, the chickens on the roosts eyeing it curiously. One or two started pecking at the hardware cloth. The baby fell to the floor and starting climbing again. Hearing chirping to his right, he turned to see two more babies climbing up a post from one of the horse stalls, seeking higher ground away from him, a threat. All five were now chirping their alarm, calling their mother. It suddenly occurred to him, their mother was in Backus Woods. *It* was a *she*. He'd been thinking *it* all along, and here he was confronted with children, her babies.

He had to act quickly, before the three loose babies got up into the loft. He grabbed the metal dog kennel he'd used many years ago for those first doomed chickens and filled the bottom with pine shavings. Using a step ladder, he first climbed up to the two strays above the horse stalls. When he tried to grab one by the scruff of the neck, it turned and nipped his barn glove. He changed tactics, picking up the baby by its tail and holding it aloft until he could stow it in the dog crate. He repeated this procedure with the other loose babies before retrieving the two from the live trap. Now all five were chirping, exploring the crate's bars, and crawling over each other.

For the second morning in a row, he roused Mae from her dreams. What was to be done? He made such a commotion that Max and Arthur emerged from their bedrooms as well. When they got the story, they headed out to the barn to see for themselves.

"Leave them in the crate for now, until we decide what to do," Evan shouted after them.

Mae went on the Web, looking for answers. While she did that, he called Lizzie. By this time, she had started vet school after studying animal biology at Guelph and working summers at a nearby vet clinic.

"I was afraid of that," she replied when he'd told her about the appearance of the babies. "The babies are called kits, by the way. I figured you'd caught a female that had made a nest somewhere in the barn."

"So now I'm a home wrecker?"

"Sorry, Dad, it's the circle of life."

Mae interrupted. "Let me talk to Lizzie. I've got some information here I'd like to check with her." He passed Mae the phone and went into the kitchen, putting on the kettle and listening to one side of the conversation between his wife and daughter. He didn't want to participate in the circle of life. He wanted life to be ovoid, complete and contained with a rich yoke at the center.

By the time Mae got off the phone, the tea was ready. "All right. I've got some numbers here we can call. There's the SPCA and a couple of wildlife rescue centers in the area. It also says here kits that size can eat some dog kibble. Lizzie said to soften it and mix it with some scrambled eggs. Give them a dish of water too. While you're doing that, I'll make some calls."

He scrambled up a dozen eggs while the kibble was softening in a dog dish. When he'd mixed it all together, it looked like brown and yellow vomit. He took the dish of food, a pitcher of water, and an empty dog dish out to the barn.

Max and Arthur had taken kits out of the crate and were petting them. "What are you doing? I said to leave the kits in the crate."

Arthur answered, "What do you mean, kits? Aren't they pups or cubs or coonlets?"

"According to your sister, they're kits. You still haven't answered my question."

It was Max's turn. "They wanted to play, Dad. I mean look at how cute they are. They were begging to come out."

"I don't care if they said 'pretty please,' you shouldn't have taken them out. What if they're carrying diseases? Put them back in the crate. I've got food and water for them."

The boys popped their playmates back in, and held the door open for him. He first put the food in, followed by the water. Even before he'd gotten the door closed, the kits crowded around the dish of water and began dipping in and washing their hands.

"Look at that," Max said.

"Cool," Arthur added. "Why are they washing their hands?"

"They're known for doing that, but I'm not quite sure what it's for. Instinct, I guess, or maybe they've just got good manners, washing their hands before they eat. I know a couple of boys who could take some lessons from them."

"What do you mean? I wash my hands every time I go to the bathroom and before every meal. It's part of my religion." Evan knew Arthur's claim to be a whopper but said nothing. Max remained silent on the subject. As Evan and the boys watched the kits washing and drinking, he thought about the life contained within their small bodies. The bandit masks were already there, the ringed tails. Such tiny creatures, yet trespassers in training. How did they fit into the bigger scheme of things? Then again, how did he?

When he and the boys got back to the house, Max related what they'd seen the kits do. "Can we keep them, Mom? You know I've wanted my own dog for years, and you've always said no. But you didn't say anything about a pet raccoon."

"Are you nuts? What are they going to eat, your dad's eggs?"

"What's wrong with dog food and scrambled eggs? I'd make it for them."

"You do realize that dogs and raccoons are enemies?"

"I'd train them to get along."

"Kinda like you and Arthur get along?"

"That's different. We're brothers. Brothers are supposed to fight."

"The answer's still no. Raccoons don't make good pets. That's what the Internet says, and your sister agrees. They're hard to raise and they pretty much stay wild. Not to mention that they're ingenious with their hands. You'd never be able to keep them out of the kitchen cupboards. Every time I turned around, they'd be in the fridge or the garbage can."

Evan had to agree with Mae. The house had already gone to the dogs and cats, and sometimes to the chicks when they were in the brooder. It would be disastrous to bring raccoons into the mix. "Besides," he added, "you boys will be off to college in a few years. Your mother and I would be stuck with them."

Max turned to Arthur. "It was worth a try." The boys headed back outside to check on the kits.

"Any luck with your phone calls?"

"Not yet. That's no surprise though on a Sunday morning."

When he went to church he couldn't keep his focus on the service. His mind kept wandering to the dog crate full of kits in the barn. He could hear their noisy chirping, the racket of little furry birds. They're what he saw when the little kids went forward for children's time and headed off to Sunday School. He prayed to God, the creator of this beautiful ovoid universe, for wisdom. He prayed that the God of children and sparrows and lilies of the field would also be the God of chicks and kits.

That afternoon, Mae got through first to the SPCA and then the wildlife refuges. The news wasn't good. The SPCA didn't take in raccoons, and the ladies at the refuge centers both said they were full. Worse yet, they said the rescue centers all over Ontario were full of raccoons. There was no room at the inn, an old, old story. They did offer the best advice they could under the circumstances. Evan would have to take the kits to the spot he dropped off the mother and hope for the best.

So he scrambled a dozen more eggs, depleting his supply almost to zero, and filled a bucket with dog kibble. He loaded the crate full of kits into Mae's hatchback and retraced his route through the lazy Sunday afternoon countryside, the summer fields of wheat and corn and soybeans, the woodlots, the orchards and vegetable patches, the little towns and crossroads sleeping in the heat. All the way to Backus Woods the kits kept up their chirping.

When he arrived at the same spot where he'd dropped off their mother the day before, he pulled over and put on his hazards again. He grabbed the bucket of food and waded through the ditch grass and the curtain of undergrowth. On the other side he found the woods, with open forest floor, spongy with humus and green growth. He looked around nervously, certain he was now trespassing the boundaries of the park. He tossed the bucket of food onto the ground and returned to the car. Without gloves or a pitchfork, he pulled out the crate full of scrambling, noisy kits. He carried it awkwardly down into the ditch and through the undergrowth, snagging his clothes and the crate, scratching himself on brambly branches. When he broke through to the open woods, he put the crate down by the food and opened the door. The kits clung to the inside bars. He tried shaking the crate upside down to dislodge them. In the end he had to reach in and pull them out. But once out they all headed for trees and starting climbing to the safety of branches.

I guess that's a good sign, he thought, as he latched the gate and carried the crate back to the car. He pulled back onto the road and the chirping faded away.

When he got home he called Lizzie and described the kits' climbing into the trees. "That's good, Dad. It means they're old enough to find safety. Hopefully, their mother will hear them. Either way, there's nothing you could do. Either their mother will find them, or a predator will. It's not pretty, but that's the nature of things. It's the circle of life."

"You mean the circle of death."

"Remember the mother was stealing your eggs and killing your chickens."

"To feed her own young, though."

"True, but think of it from the prey's perspective, not just the predator's."

"Hmm…your mom suggested I look at it from the raccoon's point of view."

"She's right, but so am I. You're talking about a whole ecosystem, the biome our little farm's part of, us and our species included. Look at it from both perspectives and throw in your own—homo sapiens, you know, wise person."

"Wise person? Does the name really qualify for our species? Personally, I'm not sure I'm smart enough for that. It might be more than I can manage. I just want the world to be simple and whole, a perfect ovoid."

"Ovoid?"

"Yeah, egg-shaped." And he launched into a description of his beautiful cosmology until Lizzie was laughing. "Ovum, ovoid, oval, ovary— they're all part of one beautiful eggy world."

"You're such an egg-head, Dad."

"Especially now that I'm bald."

"Problem is, you've forgotten about the pesky sperm."

"True. The intrepid little swimmer who crosses oceans just to break an egg. He's a necessary evil, I guess. Come to think of it, he's the one who started it all between your mom and me. The little troublemaker got her pregnant, which led to eloping, which led to your oldest brother."

"Nothing but trouble."

"Don't forget a little swimmer led to you too."

"Like I said, nothing but trouble."

"Then there's your younger brothers."

"Double trouble."

"All because of that little swimmer. Guess we can blame everything on him."

That evening, Evan reluctantly reset the trap. He'd come to see that using a live trap could lead to unwanted encounters, complications. But if there were more raccoons he needed to face them.

The next morning before heading to work he was relieved to find the trap empty, but he kept the hens inside, just in case. At work, he told a white lie, said he had an appointment that afternoon so he could leave work early. He did think of it as an appointment as he drove out to Backus Woods. He felt foolish, didn't want Mae to know about it because he wasn't sure how to explain what he was doing. He was still haunted by the chirping of the kits.

He found the spot, pulled onto the shoulder, and put on his hazards. They were necessary now, given the traffic flowing in both directions. He realized he wasn't dressed properly for trespassing the park's boundaries again, in his dress shoes and dress pants, his shirt and tie. But he needed to see. He paused until the traffic let up, sheepish under the curious stares of passing motorists. He descended into the ditch, slipping in his shoes and landing on his elbows, staining his sleeves green. He crouched and worked his way through the undergrowth, stumbling onto his knees and muddying his trousers.

When he emerged beyond the curtain into the open wood, all was quiet. He looked up into the green canopy but saw no movement. He heard no chirping of furry birds. Where he had thrown the bucket of food was now ordinary forest floor. He wondered for a second if he was in the wrong spot, but no. This was the place. The food had all been eaten. Nature in some form or other had consumed it. He hoped Nature had taken care of the kits, too. But there was no knowing what had happened to them. The woods remained silent on their fate.

At that moment a breeze stirred up the canopy of leaves and found his sweating face. A dozen or more birds erupted noisily from the branches above him, where until that moment they had been silent and still. He wondered at their fierce and fragile life within the shelter of the anchored, ancient trees. He knew little about the types of trees he was looking at, even less about the birds. Perhaps he could still learn. It wasn't too late.

At home, he put his dirty clothes in the laundry. Days later, Mae would notice and ask him how he had soiled his elbows and knees. He would do his best to explain why he had to go back. "Okay," she said, "but you had me worried. I thought you'd had some kind of outdoor rendezvous. You know, *au naturel* with some wild woman, one of those single-breasted Amazon warriors you're always talking about."

"It was a rendezvous, I guess, just not that kind." He tried to laugh off her worry and his own behavior.

In the days before Mae's discovery, he kept the hens in the coop and the trap set. Each morning, the trap was empty. On the Saturday morning—a week after taking the mother raccoon to Backus Woods—he opened the coop door and released the hens into the run. He treated them to piles of fresh grass clippings and kitchen scraps he'd saved up, along with a couple of cabbages he'd bought. For a good while he watched the frenzy of pecking. It was good to feel hen-pecked again.

He went to the library in Windermere and signed out a book on birds and another on trees. Next he picked up a poultry catalogue from the farm store. At home he spent time paging through the books, looking for the birds and trees from Backus Woods, others from his own farm. He spent some time paging through the catalogue, studying the equipment he could buy and the breeds he could raise. Later, he'd talk with Mae and they'd fill out the order form together. After all, he had to bring his flock back to its optimum size. Eggs were needed. People were depending on him. And so was the ovoid universe.

RIDE
For Ray Louter

Evan was riding his lawn mower, a John Deere X300, on the large front lawn of his and Mae's hobby farm. He was cutting the grass, once again following the rectangle pattern imprinted on the lawn from about twenty-five years of mowing. With each counter-clockwise circuit, the rectangle kept shrinking toward the center. He was making rectangles, but he felt like he was going in circles.

He was wearing his Blue Jays ball cap, a T-shirt that read "I admit it. I ate the last cookie," paint-spotted farm jeans, and worn Under Armor running shoes. For protection and pleasure, he wore over the cap and his ears a set of headphones attached to an iPod Shuffle clipped to his shirt. His kids had put together his playlist—Supertramp and Styx and Boston, some bluegrass, a little bit of Bruce Cockburn and a lot of ABBA. Everything he was wearing, down to his socks and underwear, was a gift from Mae and the kids, though the iPod was a digital hand-me-down from his oldest, Alex. Most days, this thought would have made him feel like a lucky man.

It was a Friday the thirteenth in July, and it was late morning. For hours now, a steady stream of motorcycles—Harleys and Hondas and Kawasakis, three-wheeled Spyders and crotch rockets—had been blasting past on the county road, headed for the party at Port Dover, east of where he and Mae lived, outside the mid-sized and middle-of-the-road city of London. The constant roar had unsettled both the dogs and himself, so Mae kicked him out of the house and onto the mower while she disappeared into a mystery novel in the living room.

Normally, he loved mowing. It was as if he was giving the lawn a haircut to tidy it up, to keep the humble weeds—Chicory, Queen Anne's Lace, dandelions, and crabgrass—in their place. He loved the sound and feel of the mower, even though the lawn was so bumpy his belly and little man boobs jiggled up and down. Every time he mowed, he reminded himself he should roll the lawn next spring. And that he needed to get more exercise. Damned middle-aged metabolism, he thought. He hadn't gotten to either of these resolutions yet.

It's true, he reflected, nothing runs like a Deere. The mower rolled forward in a satisfyingly straight line. The spinning blades spat a swath of clippings to the right, over his previous circuit, making a soft blanket. He watched the barn swallows, a dozen or more, circle him, performing their aerial acrobatics. He was a moving star—a heavenly body—around which they turned elaborate orbits. One moment they skimmed the surface of the lawn, feeding on the bugs the mower had disturbed. The next they swooped up and around. They darted towards the mower, veering at the last second to reveal their tan underbellies. They flew figure eights around him. They were a feathery halo following him around the yard. The phrase *symbiotic relationship* popped into his head, *companion animals*. A saying also surfaced in his mind. *Consider the birds of the air. They neither sow nor reap.* Lucky ducks, he thought.

In his circuit, he came to a mature maple in front of their house— what had once been a sapling growing in their eavestrough, transplanted to this spot their first summer on the farm. He circled the tree now towering above him, then continued toward the road. Ahead, the branches of a massive weeping willow drooped to the ground, creating a curtain that he needed to penetrate. He and Mae had planted this tree the same year. Normally, he would have trimmed the branches by now, though Mae liked them this way and had made her feelings known. Parting the curtain while mowing was problem enough, but his front wheels sometimes ran over the branches, yanking them downward. If he wasn't quick enough to back up, they'd whip him in the face when they were flung free of the tires. Other times, low branches would knock him in the head, dislodging his headphones and cap, dropping leaves and twigs and bugs down his neck and into his shirt.

And this was what happened when he entered the curtain now. He didn't duck far enough and the thin leafy branches wrapped around his face and neck. They were thin whips, or a tangle of hair choking him. His hat and headphones tumbled off. His glasses were pulled from his face. He stopped the mower before he was pulled back over the seat and began frantically extricating himself from the branches, stripping them of their leaves. When he was done, he carefully began feeling around on the mower for his glasses. No luck. He got off and did the same in the grass, hoping he hadn't run them over, given how nearsighted he was. He found them lodged just in front of the rear tire, slightly bent but still wearable. Relieved, he retrieved his cap and headphones from behind the mower and brushed himself off.

He listened to the roar of bikes on the road. The sound held him, now that his headphones were off. He walked through the curtain of branches toward the road. It was noon and the summer sun was a hot cap on his head. Sweat surfaced all over his body. He watched in the harsh sunlight as the motorcycles rumbled past without casting shadows. Men in leather jackets wore stoic, impenetrable faces. A tattooed woman in a tank top rode by, her bare arms deeply tanned, eyes hidden behind sunglasses. Often, it was a man and a woman together, on separate bikes or snugly together on one, a man and his biker babe holding onto his waist, pressing her chest against his firm back, spooning their way down the road.

What Evan noticed was that except for the occasional young guy on a crotch rocket, most of these bikers were grey beards, like himself. And here they were riding hard, riding defiant against an unlucky day and an unlucky number, against the conjunction of the two. Why is Friday the thirteenth unlucky? he wondered. He vaguely recalled an explanation connected to the party of thirteen at the Last Supper, followed by a Good Friday not so lucky for the man being crucified.

As the bikers roared past, an image of the Port Dover beach surfaced in Evan's mind—the cliffs, the sand, the water stretching to the horizon. Obeying an impulse he didn't understand, he returned to the mower, started it up, and left the shelter of the weeping willow. His rectangular circuit unfinished, he directed the machine up the slight incline to the laneway, headed to the road, and joined the parade of bikes. He had his Deere in full throttle rolling down the gravel shoulder, going eight kilometers per hour and getting passed by bikes going eighty plus. He didn't look back to the house where Mae sat reading, not once. He'd joined the pilgrims. He too was on a mission.

Of course, at the speed he was going he wouldn't get to Port Dover until it was dark. He didn't think of that, but it was okay because the party would still be going strong. Besides, his mower had headlights. Through his headphones sounded Supertramp's "Take the Long Way Home." Classic, he thought. So right. He belted out the lines he knew by heart, the words somehow saying what he couldn't about his life at that moment. The rest of the time he hummed along, feeling the lyrics sink into his soul. The road stretched ahead of him as he repeated the last line to the song's closing.

When he was a kid, his dad loved to take the family for drives. He'd sometimes say, "Let's go see if the lake's still there." They'd pile in the car, squished because Dad insisted on buying stylish coupes rather than family sedans, and head to Port Stanley. Other times, they'd just hit the road with no destination in mind. Evan would ask his dad where they were going. "I'm just following my nose," he'd reply. It was a big Dutch nose, a nose Evan inherited. What was it they said about a big nose, and the size of a man's penis? Must be a myth, he thought, as he contemplated what was hidden in his own pants.

The motorcycles thundered past and he kept rolling down the gravel shoulder, passing fields of ripening wheat and knee-high corn, cut fields of hay and cool-looking woods. He rolled by a graveyard with thin black tablets leaning at odd angles. The ditches were filled with tall grass, bulrushes, and flowering weeds. Or were they wildflowers if they were in a ditch rather than on his lawn? He wasn't sure. He waved at neighbors giving him quizzical looks and at migrant workers in orchards and fields of vegetables.

About a half hour out, he passed a man walking in the opposite direction on the other shoulder. He was heavy-set, bald, and carrying three cloth grocery bags in his right hand. He held out his left thumb signaling to anybody going in his direction he needed a ride.

Evan slowed, removed his headphones, and shouted out, "You taking the long way home?"

"What d'ya mean?"

"You're heading the wrong way!"

"Looks like it, don't it? This Friday the thirteenth shit. The whole world's gone crazy."

"For some it's a short trip."

"I can see that, Bud. Interesting mode of transportation."

"The wife won't let me buy a bike."

"Smart woman! Ain't that the way, though. The female of the species is generally a heap a trouble. Always gotta be in charge. Bossy britches, every one of them. That's why I never got hitched myself. You're looking at a free man, free as a bird."

"What's in the bags?"

"All my worldly possessions, Bud. Everything." He placed the bags on the gravel and pulled out an alarm clock, a canteen, an all-in-one camping dish set, a roll of duct tape, a Swiss Army Knife, a hatchet, a sleeping bag, dental floss, toilet paper, and a change of clothes—one complete set. "Everything a man needs," he said after holding up each item for Evan to see, underwear and all.

"You sure that's everything a man needs?"

"You know what they say. You can't take it with you, when the bell tolls and all that." Having shared this bit of wisdom, the man was about to pack up his possessions when he stopped, dove his hand into one of the bags, and pulled out a snow globe. "Shit. Almost forgot," he said as he shook it up. "I've got this memento of my travels. Keep it for sentimental reasons—from when I went to Banff." He seemed to be tearing up as he said this.

"That's beautiful," Evan replied. "I've always wanted to go there." As the man starting loading his bags, sniffling loudly, Evan thought about the Talisman snow globe sitting on the jelly cupboard back at home, the one he and Mae had picked up on their honeymoon. It gave him a momentary pang, wishing he could be there to shake up the scene with the little horse-drawn sleigh carrying the miniature family through the woods.

"Good luck, Bud. I got places to go and people to see." The man's words brought Evan back to his mission. The fellow picked up his bags, put out his left thumb, and started walking. A pickup barreled by without slowing or moving over. Evan heard "Bastard" shouted as his mower picked up speed again.

It had been a month since his dad died, three weeks since the funeral and burial. His dad had made it to eighty and then suffered a catastrophic stroke. Catastrophic, catastrophe—it was the word the doctors used. Evan had taken some bereavement leave, for he was bereaved. It was an ordinary catastrophe, the death of his father, one suffered by many, but it was his own catastrophe.

He was going back to work at Wheel and Barrow Chartered Accountants on Monday. He'd be working the numbers once again, crunching them, measuring assets and liabilities, managing wealth for the firm's clients, but it had become nothing but a numbers game. He felt like the math didn't work anymore, the numbers didn't add up.

A couple of hours into his trek, he passed a sign pointing right to Candyland and straight to Mt. Salem. Just beyond the sign his mower sputtered, the engine died, and he rolled to a stop. He was out of gas. He hadn't thought about the gas tank when he started down the road. He had no wallet or ID, no money in his pockets, no phone. Guess this makes me a failed Boy Scout, he thought.

He got off the mower and studied the empty gas tank, as if looking at it would make a difference. He cleaned his glasses on his T-shirt and then looked around. Ahead he saw an abandoned farmhouse with a decaying barn behind it. He decided to stow the mower there. He began pushing the machine, but it offered heavy resistance. He was either really tired or the mower was a lot heavier than he thought. He suddenly remembered that he had to pull the lever at the back so the mower could roll freely. That's better, he thought, as he and the mower headed to the laneway. Some guys and girls in a jeep honked as they went by, startling him with the blare and their laughter. The stream of bikes continued to rumble on as he turned the mower into the laneway and pushed it up the slight incline. When he was parallel with the house, he paused to look around, checking if anyone with criminal intent might be watching him. Seeing none, he brought the mower around the back of the house and stashed it behind a lilac bush.

He used his shirt to wipe the sweat from his face and looked at the barn. He read "Knox and Sons" in faded white paint on the front. Guess all the sons flew the coop, he thought, studying the broken windows of the house. The back door was holding on with just one hinge; the steps were rotten.

He noticed that the cellar doors were open. Cellars are cool, he thought. Maybe I'll take a minute to get out of the heat. He peered into the gloom and began descending the stairs. As he bent his head to clear the ceiling, he heard chittering and hissing and smelled something foul, even rotten. As his eyes adjusted, he was confronted with a family of raccoons. He climbed back out, stumbling, only to hear the same scolding coming at him from above. A bandit face appeared in an open upstairs window.

"Eggs stealers! Chicken killers!" Evan had had run-ins with raccoons. He wasn't a fan, but he regained his composure. "I get it. This place is already occupied. I'll move it along." With that, he backed away, pocketed the key from the mower, grabbed his headphones, and trotted down the laneway to the road. For future reference, he checked and remembered the house number—666.

He shaded his eyes and looked along the road to the horizon. He checked over his shoulder to make sure the bikes were still coming, and they were—a loud cluster of twenty to thirty bikes was bearing down on him. Though hot and tired and thirsty, he began walking the gravel shoulder that would take him to Port Dover, headphones around his neck to keep the sun off. He adopted a pedestrian perspective.

An hour later, he was getting close to Mt. Salem. He was coming up to a picturesque farmhouse with an expansive front porch. On the porch were three women in flower-print sun dresses, two of them sitting on either side of a table that contained a plate of cookies and a sweating pitcher of amber liquid and four glasses. The third woman leaned against a post. Their feet and shoulders were bare. Music floated through the windows and reached him at the road—bluegrass filled with banjos and fiddles. He was certain he heard the angelic voice of Alison Krauss. The porch was an alluring island in an ocean of heat.

He could see that the women were beautiful the way country women were beautiful—healthy from hard work, firm of flesh, sun-kissed skin, buxom. Does anyone use that word anymore? he thought. I like it. I'm going to use it every day. Their hair was auburn, like Mae's before the grey set in. Long and free plumage. Their eyes were a warm brown, like Mae's. Dark chocolate. The woman leaning against the post stepped down into the sunlight. She glowed with life like a wild, colorful bird. The fiddles and banjos played on.

"Hi there. You must be tired. Why don't you come on over for a drink? We've got something delicious to quench your thirst. You can start with some sweet tea, homemade. After that, we'll attend to all your troubles." The other women rose and with a wave and a smile beckoned him to come over. And he felt powerfully beckoned. He had a sudden image of himself in a sunny bedroom with flower-print wallpaper, hands and feet tied to an iron bedstead with feathered boas. He was naked upon a Tree of Paradise quilt. So were the three women, and they were having their way with him.

The image didn't lack attraction for Evan. Then he remembered that he was a very hairy man, that he came from a long line of hairy men, his father included. Evan had taken to calling himself Sasquatch with Mae and the kids. It was a joke that betrayed the self-consciousness he felt about his follicles. He was even hairier than the illustrated men in *The Joy of Sex*. About the time he turned forty, the hair started vacating his head and migrating to other parts of his body. It was one thing to have some chest hair and a healthy nest in the pubic region, but when your ears and your back and your butt turned positively furry, that was man-animal territory. He'd become a manimal. During sex one night, Mae called him her Wookie. He responded with a pretty good impression of Chewbacca, but outside their bedroom it was a different matter. She'd been cutting his hair since university days, but now it was getting hard for her to know where to start and where to stop.

He was thirsty. He was tempted. The music was soothing, the porch steps inviting, the women beautiful. And those cookies were calling. But no. He covered his ears with his headphones and began running toward Mt. Salem. Only once did he turn to look back. The women were standing at the road, still waving, still beckoning him with a glass of cold sweet tea and a plate of cookies, with themselves.

He'd been faithful to Mae for more than thirty years, ever since they eloped and did a runner to the Talisman Ski Resort in Beaver Valley after finding out she was pregnant. Or at least faithful in the most technical sense if not the biblical sense, in the sense that counts. He looked at other women, but he was careful not to leer or ogle or stare at their breasts, especially not to look at teenage girls. For God's sake, he was old enough to be their father. Soon he'd be in grandfather territory. He worked hard to avoid becoming that most despicable of men, an old letch. But he felt himself close to danger territory, where women found a man creepy, or worse, pathetic.

Where had such faithfulness gotten him, and Mae for that matter? They were growing old together, facing what other couples faced. Soon their nest would be completely empty. There was Alex in his thirties. He'd been married to Selene for a decade, but they had no kids. Something didn't feel right between them; it hadn't for months. Lizzie was half way through vet school—stressed about her studies and her wedding. Next month she'd marry Tomás on the farm; they were in the thick of preparations. Given the death of Evan's dad, they'd talked about postponing but decided it best to go ahead, saying he'd have wanted them to. They planned to pile joy on top of grief, if they could pull it off. And then there were Max and Arthur, whose faces and lives seemed to be getting sucked into their smart phones, he saw so little of them. They'd struggled through grade 10. He didn't know what their options would be in two years; he was worried they were headed for choppy waters. Now he was wondering if this trip he was taking was a second elopement, a running away from what he'd run toward so many years ago in a borrowed 1972 Chevy Nova.

In recent years, he and Mae had had to deal with the health scares of middle age. For Mae, it had been the mystery of Bell's Palsy, the right side of her face falling in the course of a day. She'd gone through extensive rehab, but she'd lost half her smile. She still lamented it. She'd had bouts of the blues, especially as her oldest children had grown and moved away. Each morning, he dispensed colorful pills into colorful containers for morning, noon, supper, and night.

After his dad's stroke, Mae had gotten worried about Evan and made an appointment for a physical. Just yesterday, his body was studied by their family doctor. Her gloved fingers told her that his prostrate was enlarged. He supplied his blood and urine for testing. He would get the results next week. Right on schedule, given his age. He was looking the big C in the face.

As he walked into Mt. Salem, he came up to a church that was serving refreshments for bikers. The sign at the road read, "Bikers of all denominations welcome. We're all in God's gang!" They had bottles of water and sandwiches. He might not have a bike and he might not look like a biker, he thought, but hell they were a church, and he was hungry and thirsty. He tried his best to put on that stoic face he'd seen on the bikers riding by and grabbed a bottle of water and a sandwich off a table. He accepted a free WWJD bracelet, grumbled a raspy "thanks," and wandered out of the church hall.

When he'd finished downing the sandwich and water, he noticed two bikers, a man and a woman, watching him. They nodded in his direction and he tipped his cap. They wore black leather vests over tight white muscle shirts, and fingerless riding gloves. Their vests were covered in badges, their arms tattooed with fantastical creatures—dragons, griffins, and sea serpents. They had a matching mermaid and merman on their left forearms.

Their rides were trikes, three-wheelers. Evan and Mae had talked about getting one of these in their retirement—she thought three wheels were okay, not two. They would bomb around the country lanes, go on road trips, and haunt their kids for weeks on end. That was their retirement plan, three months with each kid and then hit the road. Alex was trying to bribe his sister to take his three months.

"Didn't we pass you a while back?" It was the man who asked.

"That's likely. My ride broke down. Had to leave it with some party animals at a farm. But I'm determined to get to Port Dover. I'm on a mission."

"Well, why don't you ride with us?" the woman offered. "We'd be happy to help, wouldn't we Phil?" Phil grunted in reply. "The name's Sally."

Evan hesitated. After all, he'd told his kids for years not to accept rides from strangers. But surely Phil and Sally weren't strange. They were trikers heading to Port Dover on Friday the thirteenth. "You sure it's no trouble?" He walked over, shook their hands, and introduced himself.

He was about to board Phil's trike when Sally interrupted him, handed him her spare helmet, and said, "You can ride with me, Sugar." The helmet was deep purple with a peacock feather design, a constellation of eyes. It was tight on his head. Good thing I have a small, bald one, he thought. She opened one of her saddle bags so he could stow his cap and headphones. He tucked them in among the liquor bottles Sally was carrying to the party, and climbed aboard behind her. He was careful where he put his hands. Though he was tempted to lock his fingers around her waist and hold himself snug to her back for safety's sake, he thought of Phil and decided it might be wiser to sit up straight and place his hands lightly on her hips.

With that, they were off. Evan felt himself flying above the asphalt, his shirt pressed against his chest and rippling in the wind. He kept his mouth closed to avoid bugs in his teeth. He now understood the reason for the stoic expression and effortlessly adopted it himself. He felt fortunate to have met Phil and Sally. The tune to "Ride, Sally, Ride," ran through his head. The landscape rushed toward him and receded behind. They travelled through Froggetts Corners and Walsingham. They wended their way through Backus Woods and passed signs for Long Point, Turkey Point, and Port Ryerse.

And then they arrived. Port Dover on Friday the thirteenth. A town of 6,000 hosting more than 100,000 pilgrims. Both Main and St. George were packed with bikes and partiers, so they ended up parking on a side street, Grace.

When they dismounted, Sally took the helmet from Evan and pulled out a bottle of whiskey. Phil produced three shot glasses and Sally deftly filled them, passing one to Evan. "Was a barmaid in an earlier life," she said, winking. The three lifted their glasses and downed them. Before Evan could catch his breath from the burn, Sally filled the glasses again for a second round. "Down the hatch," she said. Evan was holding up his hand to stop Sally when she filled it a third time. When they finished, Sally and Phil raised their fists in the air and let out a hoot that was quickly answered by other nearby bikers. "We're here. We made it! Time to party!" Phil hollered.

"Thanks for the ride," Evan said. "I think I'll head down to the beach now." The whiskey was having its effect. It had been a while since he'd had so much whiskey this fast. When his dad came for a visit, they'd have one drink together. "I take it for medicinal purposes," his dad would say each time. Nevermore. Evan had a bottle he hadn't touched since his dad's death, except once on the day of the funeral to toast him on his way. The last time Evan drank too much whiskey, he was a teenager away on a class trip to Ottawa. Some of the rowdier kids had brought booze and drugs—it was the seventies, after all. While a classmate smoked some oil, Evan tried some whiskey. It was his first experience with a spinning bed and violent retching. It cured him: he'd been careful with the drink ever since, with the exception of some honeymoon Margaritas.

"What's the hurry, friend?" Sally put her arm around his waist. "This could be your lucky day. Me and Phil would love to have you party with us."

"But I need to get down to the lake. Besides, I wouldn't want to get in the way."

"The more the merrier. Just look around. By the way, have you got a place to stay tonight? Me and Phil have a spot at a campground outside town, The Shady Shore. You'd be more than welcome to join us. There's room for three in our tent, if you know what I mean. Me and Phil have an open marriage."

Phil sent him a crooked smile, something close to a leer. Evan found it hard to look at either of them. He was imagining himself in a double sleeping bag, sandwiched between them, spooning and being spooned in return.

"The kids went ahead of us and have the campsite all set up. Like I said, the more the merrier." She squeezed his waist tight, then pinched his butt.

He jumped in reply. "Your kids?"

"Yup, got four. Two of them Phil's, the other two not sure. Ages 8 to 18. Two girls and two boys, a complete set. See this tattoo. That's a mother and child design. They mean everything to me."

"And they're okay with your open marriage?"

"Hell, yeah. It's the twenty-first century, man! We've taught them to live and let live, to give and get all the love they can. None of that Puritan bullshit for us."

"That's very progressive thinking." Evan was tempted to attach himself to this family, with their wild and free ways. "I'll have to think about it."

"Don't think too long. We're at site thirteen. Lucky number. Lucky we got it. Had to book it more than a year ahead." With that, she hugged Evan hard, dipped him low, and kissed him, sticking her tongue into his mouth. He tasted the whiskey. God, this is a strong woman, he thought, as she pulled him back up.

Slightly stunned and more than a little drunk, Evan thanked them again for the ride and hurried off into the crowd.

"Don't be a stranger," Sally yelled after him. "There's more where that came from."

A few moments later, he heard Phil and Sally let out another hoot. He was tempted to turn back for another shot and maybe another kiss, but pressed forward. He was in the thick of it now, as he tried to get his bearings and find the beach. He was surrounded by a crush of people. Living on the farm, he wasn't used to it. Maybe I've developed agoraphobia, he thought, checking his pulse. Or claustrophobia. Or both. I'll have to consult Dr. Google. He was intoxicated by smells—a blend of suntan lotion, sweat, cigarette smoke, weed, spilled beer, and roasting meat. In the distance, a tribute rock band was playing heavy metal favorites. People were raising beer bottles and lighters in the air, even though the late afternoon daylight made the flames invisible.

As he made his way to St. George Street, he came across a booth set up by an outlaw biker gang. They were handing out promotional literature, with a command center of cops watching them carefully from a block away. Evan focused on the flier pressed into his hand by a heavily tattooed arm. It was a recruitment pitch. For every new member who joined, his or her partner could join for half price. Minorities and members of the LGBTQ+ community were especially welcome to apply. How progressive, he thought. It was so good to see biker gangs get with the program, though he wondered if any of them rode Indian bikes. Maybe he should warn them about this non-PC territory.

As he passed the command post, a cop stepped forward and cautioned him about getting involved with the gang. "Don't worry," Evan replied. "I just took it to be polite." He watched the cops send drones aloft to monitor the party. "Stay safe," he said to the cop and walked on.

When he was out of view of the gang and the cops, he folded the flier into a paper airplane, using the intricate design he learned when he was a kid. After church, he and his friends would fold the bulletin this way, making a squadron of planes, and fly them off the balcony in the sanctuary. They'd get five points for hitting the organ, ten for the pulpit, twenty-five for the communion chalice, and fifty for splash landing in the baptismal font. When his flier was folded he launched it into the air above the crowd. After a decent flight, it dove sharply, and he heard, "What the hell?" followed by laughter. He watched as the paper airplane was sent aloft again. And then again. And again.

He could have watched it fly all day, but he was on a mission, so he began making his way through the crowd on St. George toward the beach. He passed a news crew interviewing a man on the street. Above the blare of the heavy metal, Evan heard the man say, "The bikes are great, but I'm here for the short shorts and the sexy women." A woman beside him chimed up, "Don't listen to him. He's a sexist pig." Then she laughed and hugged and kissed the man. She turned back to the reporter. "I just feel so lucky to be here, so blessed. There's just so much love on the streets right now. You know, I didn't think I'd even be here. I had an operation just a month ago. Had a lump removed. You know, in my private parts. Can I say that on TV? Thank God, it turned out it wasn't cancer. What's the word again? It was benignant. Or benothing. Something like that." The woman and the man laughed into the camera.

Evan moved on. He could see the water of Lake Erie now, sunlight glittering off its surface, as he rounded the corner onto Walker Street. How appropriate, he thought, I'm walking on Walker Street. I've walked part of the way to Walker Street.

He weaved his way through sunbathers and partiers on the sand until he found a small open spot near the water. While the town was abuzz with noise and activity, the lake was calm. The water extended to the horizon, smooth and cool. To the right Evan saw the towering cliffs that inspired the town's name.

The lake looked so beautiful, so inviting, he stripped off his shoes and socks, his sweaty T-shirt and farm jeans. His hairy body was exposed, back and all, but he didn't give a damn—about all his furriness or the farmer's tan on his arms or his lily-white legs. He placed his ball cap and headphones on top of the pile of clothes as he felt the hot sand burning the soles of his bare feet. Aside from the WWJD bracelet, he was wearing nothing but a pair of boxer shorts that said "Kiss Me!" in front and "Bite Me!" in back. The fabric was covered in big red lips smiling to expose bright white teeth. Close enough to a bathing suit, he thought. No one will notice.

He began walking out among the swimmers, the children and teenagers and men and women enjoying the water. He retrieved a Frisbee that landed near him and tossed it back to a boy playing with his dad. He kept walking against the resistance of the water, past most of the swimmers, until the water was up to his neck. His eyes almost level with the lake, he felt there was something magical about the horizon line where sky and water met, where the water seemed to lift to the light.

He'd made it, missioned accomplished.

He dropped to his knees on the sandy bottom and looked into the murky water. He realized he was still wearing his glasses and grabbed them before they floated away and disappeared. His whole body felt embraced by the water. He could stay here forever. He could open his mouth and swallow the entire lake. He could start swimming across the lake, like a merman. If he was lucky, he'd meet a mermaid or catch a ride on someone's pleasure yacht. If not, he'd go too far to ever turn back. He just might reach the horizon and be lifted with the water to the light.

The murkiness reminded him of a childhood memory, one of his earliest. He was in the darkness of a shed. He and his friend Ross had plucked carrots from the garden of Ross's mother. They'd washed the black soil off the beautiful orange carrots under an outdoor faucet and were now hiding in the shed, eating their stolen carrots. He still remembered the smell and the crunch and the taste. He thought, we were simpatico, Ross and I. We were symbiotic.

More images floated through his mind—a dinner when he spilled peas in his lap and Mae laughed so lovingly at him, a bubble bath in a heart-shaped tub while a woody fertility god looked on, the light of a honey moon shining down on him and Mae. Hospital rooms where birth and death took place, a Percheron in the belly-deep grass of the pasture, swallows flying around the mower. Companion animals. Simpatico. Symbiotic.

A fish—he thought it was a Lake Perch—floated into view only inches away. It hovered before him, shimmering in the dull light—an intricate mesh of yellow and black scales, an array of fins, a glassy eye. He raised his hand to touch it, and it darted away, disappearing into the murk. He felt strangely bereft, alone. He thought suddenly of Mae, alone at home.

His lungs were beginning to ache. He rose from the bottom, his head emerging and shedding its cap of water as he gulped the air. He put on his glasses and took one last look at the horizon, then turned back to the shore. What he saw and heard was a carnival, a party in full swing. He imagined himself on a swing, reaching peak height.

The gulls wheeled and cried above the water and the shore. *Consider the birds of the air,* he remembered. *See how the flowers of the field grow.* So beautiful, their little lives. What did worry get you, he thought. Not a damn thing. He felt all his sadness, the disappointments and hurts of his little lifetime, float down within him like autumn leaves. There, they settled onto all the joy he'd been granted, a gift, like green grass. Perhaps time, like sun and rain, would turn it all to soil. In the coming days and years, what would come of it? What seeds might sprout still? God only knows, he thought.

He looked again at the strangers on the shore. It was time to go home. He began walking out of the water. Maybe he'd plant more trees on the lawn to disturb those rectangles. Better yet, let it all grow into native grass and wildflowers. Well, at least some of it. He couldn't quit mowing cold turkey. As for him and Mae, they'd live a little, like take up curling, join the club in Windermere. They'd look into buying one of those trikes when he got home. They could ride to the Alberta foothills, see the wild horses, and check out Banff while out there. Or head east to Nova Scotia, park their trike and take a tour boat to Sable Island.

When he emerged from the water, his boxer shorts clung to his skin. Front and back, he was exposed—his junk and his hairy butt. He was the sole contestant in a wet underwear contest. A teenaged girl in a pink polka dot bikini yelled OMG to her friends, and they started laughing. She was taking pictures with her phone; he instinctively moved his hands to his crotch. A father scowled and covered the eyes of his young daughter.

Evan hurried to the spot where he'd left his clothes, but they were gone. He looked around frantically, thinking he'd lost his bearings. Nothing. He heard his name called from a distance, and when he located the sound he saw Phil and Sally waving his clothes in the air like flags. Sally was wearing his Blue Jays ball cap. The nerve of it.

"If you want these back, you know where to find us." It was Phil who shouted this invitation.

Sally added, "But Sugar, you've got to party hearty with us before you get them back!" With that, Sally and Phil disappeared into the crowd.

Evan was sobering up fast. He wondered if Sally had said "party hearty" or "party hardy," and whether there was a difference. He also thought, so much for live and let live. It would be really liberated if they'd show him some brotherly love right about now.

He did his best to make sure his boxers weren't clinging to his skin and hurried across the burning sand, trying to catch up with them. Instead, he encountered a police officer on St. George. She didn't look much older than Max and Arthur; she must have been fresh out of the academy. Her blond hair was pulled back in a tight bun, and her eyes were hidden behind mirrored aviator sunglasses. The lenses flashed the sun in his eyes.

"Excuse me, sir. But are those your underwear?"

"Yes, they are. They're boxers—a gift from my wife. But I can explain."

"You know I can arrest you for indecent exposure."

"But I had clothes. Someone stole them."

"Are you saying you've been sexually assaulted, sir?"

"No, no. At least, not yet."

"But someone has threatened you?"

"No, it's more like an invitation I can't refuse."

"You've lost me, sir. I think you better come with me so we can get this sorted out. Have you been drinking?" She stepped closer and leaned in, within range of his breath.

"No, no. Well, yes, the same people who stole my clothes gave me three shots of whiskey, just three. You see, I just need your help. Can I borrow your phone to call my wife?"

She stepped back and crossed her arms. "Three shots of whiskey? I'd say you've been engaging in risky behavior. I might have to add public intoxication to the charges, maybe even drunk and disorderly. It explains why you've lost your phone, too. Is your wife lost? Did you get separated from her? We could put out an APB."

"No, she's not here. She's at home. Our home is near London. She's probably worried. She doesn't know I'm here."

"She doesn't know you're here? Is this some sort of domestic dispute?"

"Not exactly. I just wanted to come to the party."

"I'm sure she would have understood if you wanted to ride your bike here today, of all days. Why don't we find your bike and figure out how to get you home safely?"

"I don't have a motorcycle. That's not how I got here."

"So you drove your car? What's the make, model, and license number? I'd like to see your driver's license, sir." She pulled out her notepad and a pen.

"No, no. I didn't bring my wallet. I left it at home."

"Driving without your license. That's a serious offence. We'll add that to the list." She began scratching on her pad.

"No, I didn't come by car. That's what I'm trying to tell you."

She continued writing. "Then how did you get here?"

"I came by mower, foot, and trike." Evan paused when he saw the stunned look on the officer's face. Her pen was now still above the pad, hovering. "It's a long story. I was on a mission."

She recovered her composure and spoke soothingly now. "Sir, we can get all of this fixed back at the command post. There's a lost-and-found, so we can look for your clothes. You'd like that, wouldn't you? There are nice paramedics who can help you. They can find you someone to talk to."

"I really just need to call my wife. But I'll come peacefully, officer." With that, they walked side by side through the crowd to the command post. Strangely, he was enjoying it a bit, as it was the only perp walk he'd ever made. Maybe this was his lucky day, after all. The stares and hoots and laughter of the drunk revelers embraced him like the water in the lake.

At the command post, he sat and told the story of his day to a circle of listening cops as the evening light began to settle on Port Dover. When he was done, he was sure he heard a voice outside the circle jokingly remark, "The old greybeard is a bit of a loon, isn't he? Belongs in the loony bin, if you ask me." Old loon? Loony bin? Evan was indignant. He thought his explanation was clear and sensible, but maybe it wasn't. Maybe they were all in the loony bin, right here, right now.

He spoke to the cop who'd brought him here. "Officer, can I have my one phone call now?"

"You're not under arrest, Evan. You can borrow my phone to call your wife."

He thanked her as she passed him her phone. He dialed home. After one ring Mae picked up. "Evan, is that you?"

"Yes, it's me, Mae."

"What happened? Where the hell are you? I was worried sick. After I finished my book, I looked for you everywhere. You were nowhere to be found, and I was all alone. I was just about to call the police."

"I'm here. I need a ride. Can you come get me?"

There were several moments of silence at Mae's end before she asked, "Where's here?" And so her questions began. He told her his story. He tried to explain. He wanted them to be simpatico again. He offered her the only thing he had left to give, his symbiotic love.

"I'm coming for you," she said.

Refuge

"Lizzie and Tomás are having their periods at the same time again," Mae said to Evan as she put down her phone. Their daughter and her husband had been married for about a year, so their periods—her menstruation and what Lizzie called his manstruation—were now in sync, kind of like what happened when women lived together for a while.

Evan and Mae were sitting in the family room watching *Life of Pi*, on pause in the middle of the Pacific Ocean. Evan mused, "So they're demonstrating all-around general irritability leading to bouts of crying? She's experiencing some physical cramps, while he's being tormented by the emotional kind?" He then quickly added as the thought came to him, "They're not coming for a visit this weekend, are they?"

"Not exactly," she replied.

"You mean they're going away for a couples counseling weekend, don't you? They're just dropping off their dogs, aren't they?" Lizzie and Tomás had two moose, not dogs. Evan called them the monster meese, the drool dudes.

Mae was indignant. "It's not couple counseling. Don't be ridiculous. They just want to get away for the weekend. You know, they're young and in love. They're still in the honeymoon period. You probably forget what

189

that's like. Plus, they've got sand in their shoes. They like their freedom."
Mae paused, then added, "And what's wrong with their visiting? We don't
see them nearly enough since the wedding."

He loved his son-in-law, but he didn't want to get in the middle of
any fireworks between Tomás and Lizzie. There were enough fireworks
between himself and Mae, though the displays had become more fes-
tive now and less dramatic than earlier in their marriage. They engaged
in recreational fighting, just to keep in shape. You never knew when it
would be time for a big blow-up.

He loved his son-in-law, but he especially loved his son-in-law's full
name—Tomás Fernando Esteban Ospina. It just rolled off the tongue,
even though Evan didn't speak Spanish. It was Tomás's second name Evan
especially loved. Every time he saw his son-in-law, a switch flipped in his
head and the tune to ABBA's "Fernando" became an ear worm burrowing
into his brain. Some of the lyrics too. All that youthful passion willing to
risk itself for freedom. He'd sing as he strummed an air guitar, and belt
out the chorus. Such sweet liberty, he thought. Something to fight for.

Lizzie met Tomás in university. Mae liked him right away, so Evan
realized he better get with the program—though, as the saying goes, no
man was good enough for his daughter. His role required that he play it
up a bit, at least for show.

Lizzie had a few dating disasters before Tomás. There was the Dutch
boy in high school, Jan, tall and thin and blond, no butt whatsoever. Before any dating happened, Jan's parents wanted to meet Lizzie, Mae, and
himself. At the Timmy's where they got together, Jan's parents were polite,
but Evan sensed in them a reserve he recognized in some others from
his clan—a reserve bordering on coldness. He felt their judgement like a
blunt nail pounded in by a religious hammer. When Jan first came for a
visit, Max greeted Jan by punching him in the nuts—Max was only four
at the time, so his behaviour was easy to excuse. Still, it was another sign
for Evan, a subconscious judgement by son *numero duo*. He and Mae
were happy when Lizzie parted ways with Jan, calling him a cold fish and
a bad kisser.

In her first year of university, Lizzie encountered a wider world and
started dating a young Black man named Derek. He was from Nova Scotia, Africadian heritage. On spring break, she travelled to Halifax to meet
his family. By the end of the school year, though, Derek had dumped
her. Apparently, he wasn't feeling it. When he came back in the fall, he

came out of the closet and started dating a guy. Lizzie worried she had the power to turn guys gay.

Until she started dating Tomás. With Tomás, things were different. What started as friendship grew into romance. Mind you, Evan learned later that Tomás worried he might be just the gay rebound boyfriend. One of his earlier girlfriends had been jilted in the same way as Lizzie.

When he came to meet Evan and Mae, Tomás was polite and funny. That compensated for drooping drawers, his pants hanging low to expose a good portion of his underwear. Evan noted with approval, though, that Tomás was a fruit-of-the-loom man, boxer style. Tomás obviously had a great sense of humor, too, because he laughed at Evan's puns and punished everyone with his own. They both got accused of groaners.

Tomás was a gentle soul. Before proposing to Lizzie, he sought out Evan and asked for his blessing. Evan thought about the beautiful babies Lizzie and Tomás might have, how they would diversify the gene pool when the world seemed hell-bent on ethnic cleansing. He gladly gave it.

Tomás has a big heart, Evan thought now. Over the years, they gradually pieced together Tomás's story. His family were Colombian refugees, fleeing the civil strife and drug wars of their homeland in the mid nineties. As a child, Tomás saw corpses in the street, bodies wearing the notorious Colombian necktie. His parents received threats, so they fled. Evan knew little of the journey, except that eventually Tomás and his parents crossed from Buffalo into Fort Erie, seeking refuge, settling in Hamilton.

In his mind, though, Evan has created an imaginary journey for Tomás. He forgets that Tomás came as a child with his parents, likely on a plane or by car, and sees him instead as a young man on a boat alone on the ocean, having lost his beautiful twin sister Antonia to the deep. He made his way across the Gulf of Mexico and up the Atlantic coast, at the will of the Gulf current, unable to find safe harbor in the States, even at the Statue of Liberty. Tomás was a Colombian Pi Patel, sharing his boat with the tiger Richard Parker, with hunger. After drifting past Sable Island where they saw the beautiful wild horses, they landed at Pier 21 in Halifax. Richard Parker entered Canada as an illegal alien and found a home in Point Pleasant Park at the tip of the Halifax peninsula. He survived by eating the occasional tourist. In between meals, he performed a public service by snacking on Canada Geese, thus keeping under control the surplus population. After parting from Richard Parker, Tomás began his trek to Ontario, finding shelter at stations on an underground railroad for refugees. The journey turned his joints into those of a much older man, tied permanent knots into his muscles so that he needed regular massage therapy for the rest of his life.

Refugees had been in the news lately—so many millions on the move, so many people unwanted. Evan remembered that his mom's entire family arrived at Pier 21 in the early 1950s, refugees from post-war Europe. He himself carried that experience inside his bones, within his collective memory. When he was in his teens, their church sponsored a family of Vietnamese refugees—Boat People, they were called, adrift like Pi Patel. He remembered this generous family inviting his family to dinner, doing them the honor of serving them snake soup. So many refugees throughout history, he thought, even baby *Jesús, Santa María,* and Uncle *José* fleeing to Egypt to escape King Herod's baby-killing fear and wrath.

Tomás, too, had grown up with this flight inside him. He studied politics and international studies in school; he majored in environmental science. He knew the land; he was a student of the soil. If anyone would listen, he had ideas to make the Earth a better place, if not to save it.

"When are they going to be here?" Evan asked Mae. "Maybe they'll stay for dinner. It would actually be nice to have them home, even if they are PMSing."

"I'm glad to hear you've changed your tune," she replied. "They'll be here with their moose in an hour."

"Good. I've got a new pun to share with my favorite son-in-law, the illustrious Tomás Fernando Esteban Ospina."

"He's your only son-in-law," Mae replied, as she unpaused the movie, releasing Pi Patel back into his journey.

Borrowed

"Honey, have you seen my water bottle, you know, the green metal one?" Evan was trying to get himself ready for work on a Monday morning, his brain and body sluggish still from the weekend.

"I saw it on the counter where you always leave it," she replied. "You know, where I tell you not to leave it because it clutters up my work space."

He ignored the dig. "It's not there. I need it for work."

Mae got him the bottle so he could take some reverse-osmosis water along for his commute to Wheel and Barrow Chartered Accountants. She also wanted him to drink more water at work, and the green bottle— his favorite color, the hue of nature and intelligence—was a reminder. He'd recently had his annual physical and their doctor—a Portuguese woman who brooked no nonsense—told him to walk fifty minutes three times a week and drink eight eight-ounce glasses of water every day. He didn't want to use plastic water bottles for this. He and Mae were trying to shrink their carbon footprint down to baby shoes. The planet was on borrowed time; they'd come to believe each generation had it only on loan, in trust.

"If I were you, I'd text your son. You know, the borrower." Mae was talking about Max. He and Arthur had gotten on the school bus about fifteen minutes before, leaving behind a wake of dirty dishes, discarded clothes, and forgotten textbooks. They were both in grade 11, on the cusp of something approximating manhood.

He grabbed his phone and texted Max. "Do you have my water bottle?" He used proper capitalization and punctuation—every encounter with his children an opportunity to teach. Even when they asked him simple questions, he gave them long, involved answers. His kids called them "Dad's lectures."

A few moments later, he got a reply. "who me I wd never do that I dont know what ur talkin about LOL."

Evan typed in capital letters, "YOU TURD." He hit send, then added "Have a good day at school."

Max sent back a poop emoji followed by a smiley face with a huge toothy grin and squinting eyes.

Evan suppressed his aggravation and slapped together his usual lunch—a PB and J sandwich on whole wheat, a banana, and a yogurt. He pecked Mae on the cheek and wished her a good day. She volunteered at the local grade school where Max and Arthur once went, where they'd never be forgotten. He then bustled out into the chilly March sunshine and his cold car, a hybrid. He bought it on the advice of his son-in-law, Tomás, who did the research for him.

That Max, he thought, as he drove the country backroads on his way into the city. No respect for other people's stuff, no respect for personal boundaries. Poster boy for the sharing economy. Borrowing my sweaters without asking and wearing them to school—my favorite Blue Jays hoodie, no less. For God's sake, taking my argyle socks, even filching my underwear, my favorite Kiss Me Bite Me boxers—the ones I wear just for Mae. Using my deodorant and shaving cream, dulling my razor. I'm sure he's responsible for my missing nail clippers. Because of him, I'm growing claws on my hands and feet, for crying out loud.

And Evan did cry out loud all the way to work, one long tearful vent on wheels.

He missed his green metal water bottle all through the day and complained about it—and about his children, especially about Max—to any co-worker who would listen, even to clients.

But as he drove home from work, he remembered Max as a little kid, always a little-shit grin on his face. Once when the boys were about six, about a decade ago now, Evan went to an accountants' convention in Ottawa—the normal number-crunchers' wild time in the nation's capital.

On the way back, he was about a half hour from home, carrying some beaver tail pastries for Mae and the boys, along with some convention swag, when Mae phoned him. "You might as well go straight to the hospital," she said. "Arthur needs stitches."

"What happened? Is it serious?"

"I'll explain when you get here."

When he arrived at the hospital in Windermere, the doctor had just finished up the stitches on Arthur's forehead. Great timing, he thought, remembering trips to the hospital with his daughter Lizzie.

"Look at what Max did to me, Dad. He hit me in the head on purpose."

"Did not. Anyways, you were cheating."

"Was not. I never cheat."

Evan interrupted. "What are you talking about? What do you mean, he hit you in the head?"

Mae explained. "They were playing dodge ball with a metal water bottle."

Evan was momentarily stunned, then resigned. "Dodge ball with a metal water bottle, of all things. It's not even a ball, for goodness sake. That means you were playing dodge bottle, a game that doesn't exist. Knowing you two, the bottle was probably full, too, wasn't it?"

"Half full," said Max.

"Half empty," said Arthur.

They hustled the boys out to their cars, Arthur to Mae's and Max to Evan's. Mae wanted him to have a stern talk with Max, while she lectured Arthur on his cheating ways.

"Wait a minute," Evan said. "I brought you guys gifts from Ottawa." He looked at Mae, then pulled two metal water bottles out of his swag bag, red for Max and blue for Arthur. Each bottle had a picture of the parliament building's Peace Tower on the side.

"You're kidding," said Mae.

"Now you boys can play dodge bottle and do double the damage," he suggested as he got in his car.

A lot has changed and nothing has changed since then, Evan thought as he crossed the stream that meant he was a few minutes from home. Max still wore that little-shit grin, just on a bigger face and a taller body, and he was still causing trouble with metal water bottles. Whatever happened to that red bottle I got him? he thought. Never mind. Max was both a borrower and a lender, generous with not just other people's stuff but his own.

Some days, Evan thought, I don't know whether to hug that kid or dope-slap him. He's definitely living on borrowed time, that one. As he pulled into the laneway, he was considering whether he should throw his water bottle at Max when he got it back. He thought twice, though. It could mean another trip to Emergency.

He parked the car and grabbed his gear out of the back seat. As he began walking toward the house, there was Max in the doorway with that little-shit grin on his face, Evan's green metal water bottle held up beside his cheek. Max then took a long, long drink from the bottle. When he'd finished, he smiled again and started running.

When Evan got in the door, he found his bottle sitting on the nearby table with a note underneath it. It read, "Remember I'm your favorite son. Black is beautiful! Black lives matter, too, especially mine!" Max was mixed race, a person of color, their colorful child refusing to live in a black-and-white world. Evan smelled the bottle to make sure it was just water and then took a swig. Refreshing, he thought. On loan from planet Earth to his body, like everything. It occurred to him that Max, that all their kids, whether by birth or adoption, were simply on loan to him and Mae, that he and Mae were in fact on loan to them, on borrowed time.

After placing his water bottle on the kitchen counter, he went to the bathroom and filched Max's hair pick. Max was fussy about his afro, spending hours on it. Evan took the pick into the living room, greeted Mae, and ran the pick over his bald head.

"What in the world are you doing?" she asked.

"Taking my revenge," he replied. He pulled out his phone and texted Max, "I'm using your hair pick to groom my hairy ass." He followed the sentence with a happy face sticking out its tongue, and showed Mae the text.

"You're so mature," she said.

"WTF!" Max replied, followed by a crying face emoji.

Faint of Heart

"Lizzie was kicked by a horse today." These were the words that greeted Evan when he arrived home from work. Mae was sitting at her desk in the family room with her laptop open in front of her.

"Is she alright?" He was not especially worried because he knew if it were serious Mae would have called him at work. Lizzie was accident prone. She'd been a klutz all her life. He was used to one mishap after another, to what felt like plain bad luck.

"She's fine, but she's got a nasty bruise on her thigh. I told her to go to the hospital to get it checked out just in case." Mae clicked her mouse a few times. "Come take a look. She posted a picture." Peering at the screen, he saw in the photo that Lizzie had unzipped her vet scrubs to reveal a massive welt on her right thigh. His stomach seized at the sight. He imagined Lizzie working with the horse in a barn, the creature afraid or high strung or annoyed or in pain, Lizzie walking behind it at just the wrong time—and whack, hoof making contact with flesh.

He knew her job could be dangerous and gruesome. She'd posted pictures and told stories about wrestling cows and performing surgeries on them. Blood and guts, literally. But it was what she'd wanted to do since she was little.

The photo took him back to her childhood misadventures—tumbling down stairs, sitting on a roll of barbed wire, doing a face plant off a swing. She'd literally tripped over her own feet so much she got in the habit of yelling out with every clunk and bang, "I'm fine. Everything's fine!" Even years of dance class didn't seem to help, though sometimes he wondered how much worse it might have been without them.

One evening when she was three, she ran around the house after her bath, wearing nothing but a towel as a batman cape, copying her older brother Alex. As she ran full tilt through the family room playing tag with him, she stepped on the edge of the towel, lost her footing, and smacked her forehead on the edge of a large clay planter. By the time Evan and Mae got there, blood was on the floor, her face, and her chest. Mae put a wet cloth to Lizzie's forehead. They stuffed her in her pajamas, grabbed her favorite stuffy Hamlet the pig, and rushed her to Emergency.

The waiting room was hot and crowded. Evan stood for much of the time, while Mae was able to find a chair and sit with Lizzie in her lap. Other parents sat with their pale and coughing children wearing masks. Elderly men slumped in their wheelchairs. Twice paramedics wheeled in accident victims on gurneys. One was a moaning young woman, her face bloodied and her head held still in a cage. The other was a man who looked to be about his own age, unconscious. He heard the paramedics say to the nurse, "suspected heart attack," as they rushed him down a corridor.

By the time they got to see a doctor, Evan was hot, his stomach empty. He watched the doctor use a metal probe to examine the wound as Mae held Lizzie's hand. He watched the needle puncture her skin with local anesthetic. He watched the threaded needle, a curved steel hook, pierce the skin and traverse the wound, which was still oozing blood. Lizzie was crying in pain. Why wasn't the anesthetic working?

He felt the blood empty from his face and his hands, wooziness take over, his legs buckle. He tried to find a seat behind himself but missed, fell to the floor instead, his last thought before fainting a flood of embarrassment.

When he came to, he found himself clutching Hamlet to his chest. A nurse was holding a bottle of smelling salts near his nose. She helped him sit up and then offered him a glass of water. Mae was just getting Lizzie down from the examination table. He was relieved to see that her wound was completely covered with a bandage.

The doctor joked with Lizzie, "Should we give your daddy a needle? Maybe that will make him feel better."

"Yup," Lizzie said, "Daddy needs a needle too."

"No, no, I'm quite alright. Everything's fine, except my dignity of course. That's taken a beating."

When Lizzie's stitches had to come out—a simple trip to their doctor's office—Evan made sure he had a work commitment. He had to work hard to schedule an important meeting for that time slot, but he managed it in the end so Mae would handle this appointment by herself.

When he got home from work that day, Lizzie was excited to show off her now uncovered, thread-less wound. He wasn't eager to see it, but decided he had to man-up—he couldn't have his three-year-old daughter knowing he was squeamish. What he saw on her head was a jagged line, still an irritated red but also with a whiteness that promised to be a scar. It looked like a slightly tilted Z. When a few years later he started reading the Harry Potter stories to her, they decided her scar was a lightning bolt—just like Harry's.

Now more than twenty years later, he realized that lightning just kept striking. He looked again at the photo on Mae's screen, studying his vet daughter more closely. On her forehead, the lightning bolt still blazed, memento of a childhood misadventure. His own bruised ego, reminder of his faint heart, remained a tender spot still.

"Show me some more of her photos," he said to Mae. In several of them, Lizzie was on horseback—maybe the one place she was perfectly at ease. He was taken back to all the riding lessons and the horse shows, the grooming and the feeding and the barn chores. Lizzie pole tilting and barrel racing, trail riding and galloping through their field. Horse and rider naturally graceful. How lucky they'd been, all of them. How lucky they were.

HAM

Evan was sitting at the head of the dining room table or its foot, with Mae at the other end. It all depends on your perspective, he thought. He was a husband and a father, had been for thirty-odd years, and still wasn't comfortable with the trappings of patriarchy, even if they were largely symbolic in his home. Occasionally, Mae humored him.

It was Christmas Eve, and his kids were gathered for their traditional dinner. Alex was there on Mae's right, minus his ex-wife—she who must not be named. Lizzie was here with her husband Tomás, on Mae's left. On his own right, beside Tomás, was Max, wearing Evan's favorite Blue Jays hoodie. Probably my underwear, too, he thought. And on his left next to Alex was their youngest—just by two weeks—little Arthur, a king in his own mind.

The table was set with the traditional red table cloth and red napkins, and Max had filled it with scented candles. They used to have the lights off in earlier years, but now Evan and Mae needed the light to see their food. As in past years, there was a large casserole dish of scalloped potatoes—scalped potatoes, Arthur used to call them—along with another casserole dish of peas, Alex's favorite. At the center of the table was the "piece duh resistance," as Evan called it each year, a large spiral ham with a golden glaze.

Arthur had the Costco-size squeeze bottle of mustard ready beside him. He had to go first with most things, the mustard included, even though he was the fussiest eater in the family, with Alex a close second. Come to think of it, Evan reflected, Lizzie was a close second, too. With this traditional Christmas meal, the only part Arthur really liked was the ham. He'd take three or four large slices, preferably with a lot of fat on them, and fill up the rest of his plate with a large blob of mustard. Evan and Mae knew he was hoping they wouldn't notice the absence of potatoes and peas.

At least he uses utensils now, thought Evan. When Arthur was younger, he was a tactile kid. He had to touch his food with his hands, to use them to shove it into his very slobbery mouth. He gave very moist, open-mouthed kisses. When he went outside to play, he often came inside with dirt smeared around his mouth. Sometimes Evan wasn't sure it was dirt. They lived on a farm. It could be something else. One time when he was about eight, Arthur was playing with a vinegar packet in the car. He twisted it hard so that it popped open and squirted into his left eye. He then rubbed the vinegar in for good measure. Evan had to take him to Emergency, where the doctor laughed at the story before sending them off to the optometrist.

"Pray, Dad, before the food gets cold," Arthur said. And Evan did so, remembering to thank God for the pig in the stable when Jesus was born and the pig that gave its life so they could enjoy this meal. He'd read *Charlotte's Web* to all the kids when they were little, and they'd watched the movie *Babe* when it came out on DVD. They were all mindful of the sacrifices that pigs made, though each year they debated whether there would have been a pig in the stable. Evan argued yes, though he'd never seen one in a crèche. He knew it wasn't kosher, but he'd added a toy pig to their nativity years ago.

"Amen," Evan said and turned to Arthur. "Now, son *numero tres*, are you sure you want some ham? You want to risk it after what happened?"

Arthur groaned. This was another tradition on Christmas Eve. Evan recounted Arthur's misadventure with a ham many years before, while they enjoyed their current piece of pork. "Yes, Dad, I'll risk it—just like last year." Evan had prepared for this moment by having a couple of glasses of wine before dinner—after the Candlelight Service at church, of course, not before. The wine sat there in his empty stomach like inspiration. He had another full glass in front of him. And he launched into the tale as the dishes got passed around and the sound of clashing cutlery filled the room.

When Arthur was three, he was a little monkey with a round moon face and a billiard ball head covered with blond hair, trimmed short by Mae. He and Max loved to hang out at their play center. There they often collected oddities from the house and around the farm as part of some game with elaborate rules only they understood. When Evan mowed around the play center, he had to be careful not to run over chunks of metal, tree branches, nests of baling twine, and colorful rocks.

He came home from work on a Friday afternoon in July and noticed as he parked the car that their dogs were pawing at something under the play center platform. I hope it's not a dead rabbit or something worse, he thought—and then proceeded not to think about it anymore. This negligent forgetting was consistent with his parenting philosophy.

When he got in the door, Mae said, "Arthur's really sick. He's been throwing up all day, and it's coming out the other end, too—diarrhea. He's got a fever of 102. I've been giving him water, but he can't seem to keep it down."

"Sounds like the flu," Evan said. "But it's an odd time of the year for it."

The next morning, the Saturday, Arthur was no better. He was now complaining of bad stomach cramps as well. From Arthur's window, Evan could look down on the play center. The dogs were back at it, scratching and digging at the ground. Every once in a while, they went up on their hind legs trying to get at something on the platform. What's there, he thought. What have Arthur and Max been collecting now?

He put down Arthur's puke bucket, and headed out to the play center, calling the dogs off and dragging them in the house by their collars. When he got back out, he could smell and hear the play center collection before he could see it. Flies were buzzing over the rotting corpse of an unpackaged spiral ham—the ham Mae had bought on sale for the next Christmas Eve, still months away. Arthur and Max had taken it out of the freezer in the mudroom, along with a frozen pizza—now sitting open on top of its box, pepperoni curling in the sun; a package of hot dogs—still closed, thank God, but the color of white socks gone gray with age; and a large bag of French fries, reduced to slime. The boys had been making a meal of their favorite foods.

Before he cleaned up the mess, he rushed into the house to tell Mae what he'd found. She looked up the number for the nursing hotline and called it right away. After describing Arthur's symptoms to the nurse who answered, Mae told the story of what the boys had done, what Evan had found. He could hear the nurse's laughter as Mae held the phone away from her ear.

They followed the nurse's post laughing-fit advice and took Arthur to the hospital in nearby Windermere, leaving Max with Lizzie, fifteen at the time.

The Emergency room was busy with summertime injuries—sprains and heat stroke and concussions from soccer games, the old accompanied by caregiving children and the young with their caregiving parents.

After an hour of sitting, it was Arthur's turn. Mae repeated the symptoms and re-told the tale to the same effect—laughter, this time from the doctor. Arthur didn't seem nearly as amused. He stared sternly at the two of them, his face deadpan. The doctor wiped away her tears and said, "Given what I'm seeing and what you've told me, I'm pretty sure it's salmonella. We'll test for it to make sure, and then I'll give you a prescription for antibiotics. Keep him drinking plenty of fluids, and it should clear up within a week."

As Evan did every time he finished this story, he turned to Arthur and said, "Now, are you sure you've fully recovered? Some days, you're pretty crabby, so it's hard to tell. I believe general crabbiness is one of the long-term effects of salmonella, along with an aversion to salmon and other healthy foods, of course, and an addiction to mustard—the hard stuff straight from the bottle."

Arthur replied through a mouthful of ham, "Yes, Dad, I'm fully recovered. I'm just crabby because of your annoying stories." Evan smiled and took a gulp of wine, his paternal duty to spread Christmas cheer successfully completed for another year. Of course, his own ham was now cold—the price he paid to be the head—or the foot—of the family.

FLOTILLA

Evan and Mae were perched atop the Peace Bridge between Fort Erie and Buffalo, and he was ill at ease. They were just on the downward side heading into America, but they had a long way to go before they made the booth. There, they'd need to explain themselves to the border guard, indicate the purpose of their visit. Evan saw the water of Lake Erie far below, converging into the Niagara River on its way north to the Falls, where the currents of an enormous mid-continental watershed plummeted endlessly over the escarpment on their journey to the sea. Even though it was early May, the water still looked cold, a chilly slate blue.

Evan hated heights. He liked to joke it wasn't falling that scared him, it was landing. But that wasn't exactly true. He needed solid ground under his feet, *terra firma*. That was why they weren't flying—that, and the expense, of course.

He was fighting the urge to pull a U-turn. He wished he could put the car in park, abandon Mae, and walk back to home soil. He'd keep to the center line, as far from either railing of the bridge as possible, threading the two-way traffic of cars and pick-ups and campers and transport trucks. Instead, he gripped the steering wheel hard and kept his right foot firmly on the brake of Mae's aquamarine Honda Fit. He focused on the license of the car ahead—New York plates, Empire State—not the water to the left and the right, the water far below. Lately he felt as if he'd lost his sure footing. Some days even with Mae he felt he was stumbling along in their marriage—after all these years.

Before they crossed into America, Mae tried Alex's number one more time. After a few moments, she said, "Nothing. Again. No answer and his damn message box is still full." They were going to America in search of their son.

Evan looked for comforting or optimistic words about Alex, but found none. At home, Lizzie had taken some emergency leave from work to watch her younger brothers Max and Arthur. Evan and Mae had enough on their minds without having to worry about the boys, home alone. Two weeks ago Alex had called Evan and Mae from Georgia to tell them his divorce was final. He sounded happy, or at least relieved.

But three days ago Mae saw a post from her cousin Gabby congratu-lating Alex's ex on her wedding. "Why the hell is she still friends with his ex," Mae said. "I'm going to let her know how pissed off this makes me. What was she thinking? I mean, she should know better. She's gone through a divorce herself. As far as I'm concerned, she's stabbed him in the back."

Gabby's post included a photo Alex's ex had shared. Mae raged. The last thing she needed was to see a wedding photo of that bottle blond in a white mermaid dress, her bold blue eyes staring straight into the camera as her new husband hung all over her. Indignant, Mae had deleted the picture—but not before showing it to Evan.

Alex had mentioned nothing about his ex getting remarried after the divorce. They were pretty sure she hadn't told him. They were afraid he'd had to find out through a social media post. Typical.

Evan and Mae had been trying to reach Alex for the past three days—phone calls, texts, emails—nothing. Alex and his ex broke up two years ago, the summer Lizzie married Tomás on the farm. After the cer-emony and reception, she who must not be named ran off with her musi-cian lover, the keyboard player in the wedding band. She was the one who got the gig for him and his mates. The two of them landed in Vancouver after a few days. From there, she sent Alex a selfie of her and her lover, with the caption "BYE!" They looked like they had their tongues down each other's throats. The Lions Gate Bridge was in the background, sus-pended above the Burrard Inlet.

When a shocked Alex showed him and Mae the picture, he remembered thinking, that's quite the talent taking a selfie while necking. He wondered how many takes it took. He remembered cursing her, hoping she and her lover ended up down and out in East Vancouver, living rough and hooked on oxy. He was not proud of it. In fact, he was ashamed. But that was what he felt looking at her. She'd abandoned Alex. She'd abandoned ship that easily, put a whole continent between them.

After Alex's marriage fell apart, he needed a change. Meaning he needed to get away. Meaning he needed to leave the country. In his mid-thirties by then, he quit his job as a web designer for a firm in downtown Toronto, cashed in his RRSPs, and enrolled in grad school in Savannah, Georgia—about as far from Vancouver as he could get and still be on the same continent. He was studying film and animation. He said it was where the future was. The word is dead, he said. The image is king. Long live the king. Evan had argued with him about that one, called it regicide.

That was last year. Evan recalled that difficult conversation as he and Mae continued to inch forward on the downside of the Peace Bridge. They were on American soil, land of the somewhat free and home of the gun-toting brave. There was just one car ahead of them now and it was pulling up to the booth. He and Mae got their passports ready.

When it was their turn, Evan and Mae got through without incident. After all, they were a White couple—moving past middle age—taking a little vacation to visit their son at school—nothing suspicious about that. They said nothing about being on a missing-person case. What the guards didn't know wouldn't hurt them.

They were cruising now—down 190 and then onto 90 West for a bit before they got off and started heading south on 219. Evan was surprised to discover they were climbing steeply away from Lake Erie—the furthest they had gone by car before was the Buffalo airport. That was to pick up Alex this past Christmas. They were now on *terra incognita*. Evan had mapped out the route without really understanding they would be travelling through the Appalachians. He didn't use an atlas anymore, just printouts from Google Maps. He wasn't comfortable—at least not yet—with simply using the app on his phone, its digital female voice telling him what to do. He preferred to have a map in his mind of where he was going, a mental atlas that helped him know where in the world he was, at what precise point on the spinning globe. Being lost was being at sea, as far as he was concerned.

The fact was that he and Mae were not well-travelled, in spite of talking over the years about trips they'd love to take—especially out west to the Foothills to see the wild horses, and east to Nova Scotia, maybe even as far as Sable Island. Between the seemingly never-ending renovations to their farmhouse and the demands of their hobby farm, including their menagerie of animals, they never found the time to get away. They'd started their married life by running off to the Talisman Ski Resort in Beaver Valley. Since then, they'd stayed close to home. So many years later, he no longer felt intrepid, if he ever had; travel unnerved him. Perhaps over time he'd developed a fear of strangers, which was a problem since strangers were everywhere.

Mae navigated as they threaded two-lane highways through western New York and into Pennsylvania. Here spring was further along than at home. There was more green on the trees the further they drove. Shrubs were bursting with yellow flowers. He and Mae skirted a large forest and came upon a resort town, quiet now with the snow gone, ski slopes light green ribbons draping the mountain slope.

Roadsides were dotted with collapsing houses, electric poles topped with old-fashioned glass insulators. Suddenly out of the hills and forests appeared factory towns, homes fanning in rows on slopes above the industries by which the towns lived or died. Everywhere, American flags reminded him they were on foreign soil.

As they drove, he and Mae occasionally revisited what went wrong between Alex and his ex. The subject was a toothache that flared up when touched and then faded. As far as Mae was concerned, the amount of time the ex took in the bathroom to get ready for anything was a sign. Especially when that one bathroom was being shared by upwards of twenty people at Thanksgiving or Christmas. He and Mae were sure it hadn't helped that Alex and his ex eloped—she didn't want a church wedding, no family there. Of course, he and Mae had also eloped, which Alex's ex mentioned repeatedly. But that was different. Mae was pregnant with Alex—they'd eloped to make things right, maybe to avoid the embarrassment of a shotgun wedding.

When Alex's ex left him, they'd been married for more than ten years. Evan and Mae tried to find out from Alex how long the affair had been going on. He said he had no idea. He said there weren't any signs that he could see. He said he didn't want to talk about it.

Privately, Evan said to Mae, "It could be that her piano-playing lover really knew how to tickle her ivories, if you get my drift. Maybe that was

Alex's problem. He'd quit his music lessons, and wouldn't play her instrument anymore. It's hard to have a marriage without some of that music."

Mae replied, "If that's the case, he was probably right to quit playing. He was likely getting frostbite from that ice queen."

At one point the highway they were travelling ran alongside a small river for many miles. As he and Mae entered a river-valley town, they came across a crowd, the first real crowd they'd seen. A large banner across the highway read "Welcome to Allegheny Cinco de Mayo." A second line on the sign read, "Come float your boat!" Both sides of the highway were filled with people carrying kayaks.

"That's right," Mae said, "It's May 5th today. Happy Cinco de Mayo!"

"I don't get it. What's the connection with kayaks? Kayaks are Inuit, not Mexican. Cinco de Mayo celebrates a victory Mexico won in some battle, not a boat trip down a river. I'm pretty sure they didn't use kayaks in their navy." He had a kayak, a gift from Mae and the kids for his last birthday. He'd asked for it with the hope of getting more exercise—and of becoming more intrepid, adventurous enough to set out on rivers and lakes, maybe even one day the Great Lakes. He was signed up for lessons in June. His goal was to one day navigate the Thames River from its source to its mouth at Lake St. Clair, paddling through Woodstock and London and Chatham, through farmland and the remnants of the vast Carolinian forest, the northern edge of the forest they were travelling through now.

"It looks like fun," Mae replied. "You're becoming a real curmudgeon, just like your dad was." His dad died two years ago. He had a catastrophic stroke a couple of months before Lizzie's wedding, a blood vessel leaking into his brain.

Evan stopped to let people cross the road and get down to the river. They waved thanks to him with their paddles. When he got through, he and Mae drove further alongside the river. For several miles, they watched the colorful flotilla making its way downstream. Outside the town, the road curved right and crossed a bridge over the river. People were watching from the bridge and waving as several kayaks floated beneath it.

"Look," he said. "It's all water under the bridge."

"Maybe to you it is. That's 'cause you don't give a dam."

"Hah. Good one. But you know that's not true. I do give a damn. Look at how stubborn I was waiting for you to commit." It was now a joke between them. After fifteen years of marriage, Mae had finally admitted she was ready to commit to their relationship. They'd survived the seven-year itch twice over. When she told him, a reservoir full of worry and uncertainty drained away.

"Yeah, and I've regretted it ever since. Some things you just can't take back. Like you said, water under the bridge."

"Too true. What's that song? You know, it's too late, baby, so you'll just have to fake it. No going back, my dear."

"I'm pretty sure you screwed that up. It's about dying inside. That's something you can't fake—or hide."

"Close enough."

As they crossed the bridge, Evan saw to the left that the stream opened out into a lake—clearly the destination for the kayaks, as several were paddling about already. As the road curved and headed back up into the hills, he saw a large tent set up on the near shore, along with all the makings of a party about to start.

He and Mae were now travelling south into spring, south out of the Appalachian Plateau and into the true Appalachian Mountains. It felt as if Mae's little Fit was riding the waves of the hills. When they reached each crest, they saw the forested mountains spread out around them to the horizon. At times, he felt they were alone crossing this sea of trees.

"I understand now why people believe in Sasquatch," he said to Mae at one point. "He's what mountain men turn into after years of living alone in this wilderness."

"And what about mountain women?"

"They become single-breasted Amazon warriors. I think I see one in the trees over there with her compound bow."

"The Amazon's in South America, dummy."

"They're migrant workers. Illegal aliens. Trump's trying to deport them. He calls them sickos and criminals. That's why they're hiding in the mountains."

At one point, they were surprised to see a sign for Washington, DC. "Look," he said, "we could turn here and go to Trumplandia, in the District of Corruption."

"No thanks," she replied. "I'll take this wilderness over that political jungle."

"What? You don't want to be there for the Trumpocalypse?" He tried to remember how many times the Donald had been married and divorced, how many affairs and prostitutes had come to light. He heard Trump's voice on that tape, saying, "When you're a star, you can do anything. They let you do it. Grab them by the pussy. You can do anything."

Was that the measure of the man—husband, father, leader of the free world?

As the sun started setting, they decided to stop in Roanoke. After booking into the Lost Colony Motel, they ordered some Olive Garden. In the dark, he decided to try the map app on his phone. He listened intently as the digital female voice navigated him through the unfamiliar maze of highways, boulevards, and shopping centers on a moonless night. He was unnerved, feeling he wasn't in charge, but she got him there and back again.

In the bland room, he and Mae sat on the bed and ate pasta and salad. There was a *Family Feud* marathon on the Gameshow Network. For a couple of hours, they listened as the host started each show saying "Welcome to *Family Feud*. I'm your man Steve Harvey, and like always we got a good one for you today."

"Didn't he write a book a while ago about relationships?" Evan asked.

"Yes, he did. *Act Like a Lady, Think Like a Man.*"

"Wonder if it's any good."

Over and over, Steve Harvey asked questions beginning, "We surveyed 100 married women." Evan and Mae kept guessing what these married women said, no matter how ridiculous the question. Mae was good at this, he had to admit, but of course she had the advantage of being a married woman herself for more than thirty years.

They'd lasted that long. Why hadn't Alex and his ex? Why didn't so many people? Growing up, he'd heard the phrase "unequally yoked" in church. What did it mean? As a kid, he pictured two oxen or a pair of heavy horses yoked together pulling a plow. Was that what marriage was? If the pair were unequal, did it mean one animal was big, the other small, so they couldn't pull together? Or was the yoke not attached right? It was Saint Paul who said that to warn believers about making bad marriages, to consider staying single if they could hack it. A single saint. Great advice coming from a dude who never married. As far as Evan could tell growing up, in his church unequally yoked meant marrying someone who wasn't Dutch. Once he'd heard a cousin say, "If you ain't Dutch, you ain't much." The phrase seemed to say it all.

Of course, he now understood that it was pretty much the same everywhere. People were expected to marry inside the tribe, however it was defined. It might be region or race or religion or class—or some mixture of these. No messing with the gene pool. No dilutions. You folks stay in your pond over there. We'll stay in ours over here. No bridges. Don't dig a channel between them; don't let the waters mix; don't let the stagnant waters flow free. Of course, he might be completely wrong. It might just be a matter of like attracted to like, perfectly natural. Then again, he'd fallen for and married Mae—a woman as far from Dutch as he could imagine.

Marry in haste; repent at leisure. Is that what Saint Paul was on about? Evan and Mae had married in haste—eloping and running off to the Talisman, ending up in that honeymoon suite that felt like the inside of a womb. Had they forgotten to repent? Did they need to repent after all this time—of the premarital sex and the stain of an out-of-wedlock pregnancy? In his world at that time, this was almost the unforgiveable sin.

Wedlock, now there was a strange word—to be locked into the wedded state. Is that what it meant? A trap or a safe space, maybe both? Or maybe something kinky—like furry handcuffs. Years after they'd eloped, he learned that his family tree was full of shotgun weddings—his grandparents on his dad's side, an aunt on his mom's side, for starters. Rampant with wild growth.

Alex and his ex hadn't married in haste. They'd eloped in haste, but by then they'd been going out for almost seven years. Evan didn't get it. Why wait so long, then run off alone? They'd always said they didn't want kids. He and Mae had thought with time they might soften up, but no. Had it become a problem, a stone of discontent dropped into the waters of their marriage, stone after stone leading to divorce?

Recently, he'd heard a new phrase for splitting up—conscious uncoupling, invented by celebrities who seemed to swap partners as easily as they changed their wardrobe each fashion season. He imagined a man and a woman—faceless celebrities—their hairless, naked bodies entwined and writhing on silk sheets they'd wasted their ill-gotten gains on. Mid-coitus, they stopped dead and looked each other in the eyes. They started thinking and couldn't stop. They consciously uncoupled their groins, dressed mechanically, and smoothed their hair. They shook hands, exchanged business cards, and went their separate ways. They left behind their subconscious minds, peas tucked beneath the mattress.

On the TV, the Majumber family from Minneapolis had just won $20,000. They were jumping up and down and hugging each other in a huddle on the stage, while Steve Harvey was saying they'd be back again with another chance to win more money and maybe a brand-new car.

Before lights out, Mae tried Alex again. "No answer," she said.

The next day they were up early and soon into the Carolinas. Each mile took them further and further into the green-clad mountains, deeper and deeper into spring until it was suddenly summer. It felt as hot as an August day in Ontario. As they descended the eastern side of the Appalachians they found themselves on four-lane highways taking by-passes around cities. The drivers were urbanites—in a hurry, lane-weaving, aggressive.

"It must be the NASCAR effect," he said to Mae. "Of course, it's still not as bad as Toronto."

When they stopped for lunch at a fast-food joint, he felt the heat like a cap on his head, the air heavy. Inside, he noticed that all the employees were African American, every single one. How was he supposed to understand that? Was that a good thing? A bad thing? Affirmative action, or its failure? As a foreigner, he didn't have the tools to make sense of it, maybe to make sense of America at all. He should be wearing his Canada T-shirt, the one with the beaver on it, letting everyone know he was Mr. Multiculturalism, a peacekeeper-type. Though he sometimes suspected that was simply a disguise.

The land began leveling out over the course of the afternoon. He and Mae were surprised to see palm trees and large beds of wildflowers in the strip of grass between themselves and the northbound lanes. Just yesterday, they had the heater going. Today, it was the air conditioning blowing Arctic air at them. By late afternoon, they were getting near the coast. He could sense water to the east. There was a wetlands feel around them.

In a long flat stretch of watery land, they passed a low, square building without windows. A large neon sign at the road proclaimed "Southern Gentleman's Club" beneath the outline of a reclining, busty woman with long legs and long hair. Ladies and gentlemen, he thought. When he built the jelly cupboard so many years ago, his instructor—Bob Wright—called him and that dink-eyes Brad Reynard and the other students "gentle men." What did the phrase mean? He thought too of Elizabeth Bennet accusing Mr. Darcy of proposing to her in an un-gentleman-like manner. What did it take to be a proper gentleman today? Did it matter anymore? Did anyone care? Most importantly, had he been one to Mae?

As he mused on these questions, they left South Carolina without fanfare and entered Georgia, crossing water on a flat bridge. Mae got out the sheet with the directions he'd printed off for getting to Alex's apartment. Looming ahead now there was a large, high bridge. As they approached, a sign announced it was the Talmadge Memorial Bridge. He wondered who or what Talmadge was, and why Talmadge needed to be remembered with a bridge. Was he perhaps a true gentleman? He'd ask Alex when they found him.

Then they were climbing and crossing the bridge, the Savannah River flowing far below, as far below as the Niagara River was the day before. The city and its port, with its enormous cranes like robots, were laid out below them. They passed the crest, and he felt himself falling back to earth. He broke out in a slight sweat chilled by the cold air blasting from the fan.

As they descended toward the city, Mae read off the exit he needed to take. Problem was, he was feeling dizzy and disoriented. He missed signs and flew by exits, caught in the traffic flow of Friday rush hour. Before he knew what was happening, he was heading west away from Savannah. He saw a sign for Macon. Rhymes with bacon, he thought. Macon bacon—Georgia's finest. At the next exit, he turned around and headed back. Mae repeated the exit he'd need, now coming from the other direction. He decided it would be better to backtrack, turn around, and come at it from the right direction. But then he realized it meant going back across the bridge. He panicked and jerked the wheel to catch the last exit. They entered the city, where he was confronted with too many choices—left or right, straight. Go back, go back, he thought. He fought the urge to reverse back up the ramp, a manoeuver his dad once pulled when driving in his seventies.

"Let's stop," Mae said. "You need to calm down and get your bearings."

"I don't know. This part of the city looks pretty rough. Let's go a little farther. Maybe we'll connect with one of the streets listed in the directions." What he didn't say was that he was afraid to stop. What was more frightening was that he didn't know why.

"You know I'm not going to be much help. I get lost in a phone booth."

Soon they were right downtown. The river was off to their left. "This can't be right," he said. He made a quick right turn to head away from the waterfront. Now he was going the wrong way on a one-way street. A car was coming straight at them. Mae shouted his name. The sound mingled with a blaring horn. He made another quick right into an alley and came to a stop. "Shit," he said "That was close." He was shaking.

"You almost destroyed my car," Mae said. "Do you need me to drive?" The fact that she offered told him how worried she was.

"No. Everything's fine." He drew out the final word into a whole-note of doubt.

"It's not fine. I'm not sure you're fit to drive my Fit."

After some moments, he released the brake. He followed the alley and turned left at the next street, looking first for any one-way signs. Right away they ran into a square park blocking the way. It was populated with gardens and monuments and park benches, with people and their dogs. But what he noticed most were the enormous trees. Their lower branches reached far out horizontally from the massive trunks, and most branches were draped with a light green vegetation, like tinsel. He'd ask Alex what they were if they found him. When, not if. When.

A car behind him honked. He decided to treat the square like a rotary, turned right and then left. "It's kind of pretty," he said. "Let's go around." He went all the way around and then made another half cir-cuit until he was heading up the street, where he found another square. He repeated the circuit before heading up to the next and the next. In a tour-guide voice he commented on the architecture of the buildings, the historic churches, the iron works, the gardens, the statues, the magical trees with their beautiful tinsel.

After the fourth square and the fourth circuit, Mae said, "I appreci-ate the tour, but we're going nowhere fast. Not to mention you're making me dizzy. Can't we stop now?"

"Just a bit further."

"I have no idea where we are and where we're going. And I'm pretty sure neither do you."

"After all these years, you've got no faith in me?"

"I'm not sure faith is what this situation requires. A map would be more useful."

"Faith is exactly what's needed. A mustard seed of faith, a cup of hope, and a bucket full of charity on your part."

"You know you've been my charity case for almost forty years now. That's a long time for a woman to suffer."

Ignoring the dig, he headed up to the next square. It turned out it was the last one. From there he made a straight run up a boulevard com-pletely arched over with these magical trees. Then he hit a major artery, Victory Drive. "Sounds promising," he said as he turned left.

"You're so bloody stubborn. Just like your dad." She looked out her window at what was turning into the outskirts of the city. "You remember we came here to find Alex. I need to see my son. We have no idea what's happened to him and you're wandering aimlessly around a city we've never been in before."

"This isn't wandering. It's sightseeing." He paused. "And I'm not stubborn. I'm indecisive. They're two very different things." Had he driven all this way just to avoid finding out the truth, whatever it was?

"What you are is lost, hopelessly lost."

"I'll just drive a bit farther. I need to clear my head." They were now out of the city, and they saw a sign for Tybee Island. They were crossing more bridges over more water—the Wilmington River, the Bull. People had built piers out into the rivers with cabanas and boat houses at the end. He saw houseboats and speedboats and fishing boats. Some seemed to be coming up the river after a day of boating. Ribbons of wake crisscrossed the river as the vessels headed to their home docks.

They were driving along the Savannah River now. They crossed Lazaretto Creek and were suddenly in a resort town. He followed the signs for the beach. When he could see the Atlantic Ocean, he brought the car to a stop. He put it in park and killed the engine.

He turned to Mae. "Okay, I'm lost. But just look what I found."

"An ocean is pretty hard to miss. If you drive a bit further, we can see if my car floats."

He looked out over the beach. It was now early evening. He was surprised to see how many people were there, but then he remembered it was early May in Georgia, not Ontario. Some families were packing up, probably heading off for dinner.

"Well, we're here. I'm going to have a look while you figure out what to do next." Mae exited the passenger door and stretched. Then she leaned back into the car. "You coming or what?"

They headed to the boardwalk. He reached for her hand as they strolled out over the Atlantic. He didn't want to get too close to the railing. "Tell me everything's going to be okay," she said.

"Everything's going to be okay," he replied.

"That was really convincing."

"We've made it this far." They were at the railing now. The sun was low behind them, over Savannah. The ocean spread before them, like wrinkled fabric. Looking down from this height, he watched the waves roll in over the swimmers. Couples jumped into the breakers, holding hands. Couples lay side by side on beach towels, propped on their elbows. Laughter drifted up to the boardwalk. Further out, a windsurfer glided across the water, angling toward shore. Evan gripped the railing with his free hand.

Back at the car, he pulled out his phone and opened the map app. "What's Alex's address, again?" Mae read it off. "I think we crossed that street back in the city," he replied. "Maybe I can find it myself."

"No way. Type it in and do what she says."

"Am I going to spend the rest of my life being told what to do by women?" He was half joking, half complaining.

"If you know what's good for you."

He was now obedient to the app's digital female voice. She led them aright, navigating bridges and boulevards, squares and one-way streets, until they arrived at a three-story walk-up apartment building in what was called the Victorian District. "Your destination is on the right," the voice said with satisfaction.

Mae took out her phone and tried Alex's number one more time. "Nothing," she said.

"I assume he has a buzzer. Let's see if he answers that."

They entered the building's foyer and looked for his name and apartment number. Mae pressed and held the buzzer. She released it for a few seconds and then pressed it again in a series of short, sharp bursts. The silence dragged on. He felt he was in a deep pool of worry in which frightening possibilities surfaced like fish—injury, amnesia, murder. It was the water off Tybee Island with shark fins slicing the waves, chasing the windsurfer.

"Hello?" He recognized the tinny voice as Alex's.

"Alex, this is your mother. Your father and I need to speak to you."

Silence. Then, "Mom? Dad?"

"Yes, Alex. It's your parents, remember us?"

"You're here?"

"Yes, Alex. This is your father. Let us in."

More silence. And then the buzz of the door lock being released.

He and Mae climbed to Alex's third-floor apartment. They entered the long hallway—slightly out of breath—and saw Alex standing in his doorway, half in and half out, waiting for them. He yelled out to them, "Mom. Dad. What are you doing here? Is something wrong?" When Mae reached him, she hugged him hard, then released him and smacked him on the back of the head. "Is something wrong? Is something wrong? You tell me. What's wrong with you? Can't answer your phone? Can't reply to a simple text? Your dad and I were worried sick."

"You were? Why? It's no big deal. You know what I get like in school. It's not like I'm ever quick to get back to you."

Alex had grown a bushy beard since his Christmas visit. His hair was standing up on his head. He'd put on some weight, rounded out in the face and belly. His eyes looked a bit puffy, his skin pale. He was wearing baggy gym shorts and a T-shirt with a rainbow on it and the slogan "Love is love."

"That's quite the beard," Evan said. "You look like the mountain men we saw in the Appalachians."

"I needed a break from shaving."

"You're not turning into a hipster, are you? One of those fake mountain men."

"No. You won't find any beard balm in my bathroom. And no, I haven't taken up vaping." He led them into his apartment. Evan was surprised to see pizza boxes on the coffee table in the living room, drink glasses on the floor, microwave popcorn bags on the couch beside a bed pillow, chocolate bar wrappers on the end table. The curtains were closed against the evening light. He could see through the bedroom door that Alex's bed was unmade, a jumble of sheets and blankets on the floor. Alex was always such a neat freak, he thought. What happened?

Alex took them into the galley kitchen. "Sorry about the mess," he said. "I've been kinda busy with school and stuff." The counter had five or six empty vodka bottles on it; one remained half full. A couple of plates were covered with the remnants of pizza crusts and the bones of ribs and chicken wings. Alex picked up a large baggie filled with rice and rolled it around in his hand until a cell phone appeared, as if this was all the explanation that was needed.

"What happened?" Mae asked.

"Drowned, I'm afraid. I was out with some school friends a few days ago. We were walking home through a park and messing about by the fountain. Actually, we decided to cool off in it. To be honest, we were a little drunk. Okay, a lot drunk. I forgot my phone was in my pocket, and before I knew it, it was at the bottom, sitting on all that shiny change people throw in. It's been drying in this rice ever since. I was thinking of trying to turn it on today." He was eyeing the phone somewhat wistfully.

"That still doesn't explain why you didn't answer my emails," Mae said.

Alex looked at her a bit sheepishly. "Actually, I haven't checked my email since my phone went in the drink."

"Why not?" Evan asked.

Alex turned to him. "Would you believe I'm doing a digital fast?"

"Not bloody likely," Mae said. "You've been on your devices 24-7 for years."

"Okay. That's true, but I did think about it. For a few minutes."

"Then why haven't you been checking your email?" Evan asked.

"I'll show you." Alex led them out to the living room and picked up a rectangular device sitting on the couch among the popcorn bags. "Look," he said. "It's a Nintendo Switch. Thought I'd celebrate my divorce by giving myself a present. I've been waiting months, until a break between terms. I needed to get my mind off things—everything—studies, relationships, life."

"Okay." Mae's word was really a question.

The words came out in a rush. "So I've been playing Zelda kinda nonstop for the last few days—maybe a week at the most—ever since I drowned my phone." His thumbs were twitching a bit as he showed them the screen. The pull of it. Evan remembered playing Super Mario Cart with Alex so many years ago, this child he once carried on his back along the sidewalks of London's streets, pushed in a stroller through its parks alongside the Thames River.

Mae said, "You mean we've been worried sick about you and the whole damn time you've been playing a video game?"

"But I had no idea you were worried. That's not my fault, is it? You've never worried before when I haven't phoned back right away. What's different now?"

Mae looked at Evan for a moment. "So you haven't heard?" she said.

"Heard what? You're kinda scaring me."

"Your ex got remarried—just last weekend. She posted photos. Barely a week after you got divorced."

"Selene? Married?"

"We don't use her name anymore. We call her other things, starting with 'she who must not be named.'"

Alex dropped onto the couch. Mae moved aside some popcorn bags and sat beside him. Evan found a chair across from them.

"It is her name, though. She deserves at least that consideration."

"You really think so? You're not pissed off about this?" Mae was not convinced.

"I am surprised. Hurt she didn't tell me. I mean, I would've hurried up with the divorce if I'd known she wanted to get remarried that badly.

I thought they were just shacked up. To be honest, I really believed she'd gone completely sour on marriage."

Mae replied, "I just don't get it. She cheated on you, ran off with a musician, for God's sake. Of all the bloody clichés. Why the hell aren't you furious with her?"

"It's not that simple."

"Then what the hell happened?" Mae asked.

Alex put his Switch down on the coffee table. Mac turned so she could look more directly at him, and he slumped back deeper into the couch. "Shit happened," Alex said. "Both of us were working all the time, trying to get ahead, like everybody in Hogtown. We spent less and less time together. Given my job, I was online all the time, even when I was home. She complained I wasn't really home when I was home. She started going out nights with girlfriends from work, sometimes staying out all night. I got mad about it. She said why did I care. I wasn't really here anyways, always on my computer working or playing video games. We had a big blow-up. When the dust settled, I agreed to a trial separation."

"How come we never knew about this?" Mae asked.

"I never told you about it 'cause I was embarrassed. You and Dad have been married forever, and you were mad about us eloping in the first place." He paused, his eyes lowered. "My guess is that's when she met her piano player, but I don't know for sure." He looked up for a moment at both of them before studying his hands again. "I did something really stupid while we were separated. I got lonely. I met a woman online. You can imagine the rest. We never actually met in person, but it might as well have been an affair. I felt like shit, was stupid enough to tell Selene about it, and begged her to come back. I told her I'd change, and I tried. We did get back together for another half year before she took off. I thought things were fixed. Obviously, I was wrong."

Alex paused and looked up at both of them. He intertwined his fingers and lowered his eyes to study his hands.

"That explains a lot," Evan said.

"You're blaming yourself?" Mae asked. "You didn't change enough? Bullshit! Look at what she did to you. Did you never think her affair was revenge? Running off without a word—knifing you right in the eyeball with that picture?"

"I can't believe that. That's not the Selene I know."

"And apparently still love," Mae said. "I just don't know why."

"Not bloody likely," Alex replied. "Well, maybe." His eyes began to leak, his throat to catch, just as they did when he said goodbye to them at Christmas. Parting as sweet sorrow.

"You need to let her go," Evan said. "Just let it go." He paused. "Forget it, that's just a stupid Disney song. What do I know?"

Alex collected himself and said, wiping his eyes, "I wish it were that easy. To let it go." But his voice was lighter; it carried a musing tone that was on its way to amused. And all three of them did muse—a grown child, a mom, and a dad—sitting silently for some moments. Evan's mind wandered, strangely, to the two-person kayak he and Mae saw as part of the flotilla yesterday, paddlers in sync as they reached the open water of the lake. What work and practice were needed to achieve such harmony?

Eventually, Mae broke the spell. "So are you going to feed us, or what? You go have a shower and get dressed. Your dad and I will tidy up a bit. Then we'll get some supper. Your choice, our treat. Whether you're celebrating or grieving, it's best not to do it on an empty stomach."

"You can let a lot go when your stomach's full," Evan added. "Just belch it out."

"That's terrible, Dad."

"Or let it out the other end."

While Alex was in the shower, Mae phoned Lizzie. "Yeah, he's alive," Mae said, "but I wouldn't say he's well."

The next morning was a Saturday. They told Alex they'd need to head back the following day so Lizzie could return to work.

"That gives us a whole day," Alex said. "Let me show you around Savannah." For the morning, he took them into the old part of the city. They strolled through the parks they'd driven around just the day before. They lounged on park benches, watching tattooed men and women in shorts and muscle shirts walk their dogs and carry poop bags like treats.

"What's with these trees?" he asked Alex.

"They're amazing, aren't they? They're called Live Oaks, and the stuff hanging from them is called Spanish Moss."

"Like green tinsel."

"Pretty, but you don't want to touch it."

"No?"

"The moss is filled with chiggers, bugs that bite. They'll leave you covered with red welts."

"Still looks beautiful, though. Does the moss hurt the tree?"

"Not a bit. They just hang out together."

"They're symbiotic," Evan said. "Simpatico."

As they walked the streets and admired the architecture, they came across a house with a plaque in front of it—the childhood home of Flannery O'Connor. "The name's familiar," he said as he read the plaque. "She wrote a really weird story I had to read in high school English, 'A Good Man Is Hard to Find.'"

"That's the truth," Mae quipped.

"This family from Georgia is going on a vacation to Florida. Then the grandmother does something to cause an accident. This guy called the Misfit comes along and instead of helping them he murders them all. The whole family, baby and grandmother too."

"I'm not sure I want you living in Georgia much longer," Mae said to Alex. "When are you coming home?"

"I've got to finish my program first," he said. "Then we'll see. We'll talk about it later." Evan could sense some evasion in the answer. He knew it wasn't what Mae wanted to hear. It wasn't what he wanted to hear either. He was certain Mae would like to take Alex home in the morning, put him up in his old bedroom until he recovered, feed him comfort food. They had talked about the possibility on the trip down.

Evan saw that Flannery's childhood home was kitty-corner to a large cathedral. A flier he'd grabbed from a stand outside the front door said she was a devout Catholic and went there almost every day for mass—her spiritual home close by her physical home.

After lunch in a downtown café, Alex took them on a boat cruise of the Savannah River. As the guide described some of the waterfront buildings, he rattled off his spiel about Savannah's history, Georgia's history—the original plan that it would be a colony free of slavery, and how that was thwarted. When they went beneath the Talmadge Memorial Bridge, he explained the controversy over the name, Eugene Talmadge being Georgia's governor in the middle of last century, a man whose policies were openly racist.

The tour took them upriver a ways and then back down past the city on the way out toward Tybee Island and the Atlantic, open water. Evan felt drowsy in the warm sunshine and tuned out the drone of the guide. He had no sunglasses with him, so he squinted out over the brilliant water. It was populated this Saturday afternoon with all manner of vessels, from catamarans to yachts to fishing boats. A couple on a jet ski zipped by. Closer to shore people lounged in paddle boats, legs pumping in rhythm. A half dozen kayakers were arrayed around their instructor, listening to her directions. Floating, he thought. We're all here together, floating along.

By the time they docked, it was late afternoon. They decided to have an early supper, followed by an early night, since he and Mae were planning to head out "when dawn cracked," as he said to Alex. They wanted to make the trip back in one long day.

It was warm enough to eat at the outdoor patio of a restaurant. Their server was a woman Alex knew from school—a person of color, and she was a warm and colorful person. He introduced her to them, and she welcomed them to Savannah, hoped they were having a good time, said to Alex, "You didn't tell me your mom and dad were coming for a visit."

"They surprised me," he replied. "They're like that."

Mae said, "We thought we'd see for ourselves what kind of trouble Alex was getting into, but we have to head back tomorrow."

"That's a shame. It's such a beautiful old city, lovely and romantic."

Alex went over the menu with her, and she made suggestions she thought Evan and Mae might like. She leaned over Alex's shoulder, close by his ear, pointing to items. They spoke familiarly with each other, joking, talking about their break between terms. What they were doing, Evan realized, was flirting. As blind as he was, he could see it.

With a smile, she headed off with their order. Mae said to Alex, "What a lovely young woman. So, when are you going to bring her home?"

"Really, Mom? We're just friends. She's an international student, like me—from Costa Rica. We're in the same program. We get together as part of a study group, and sometimes we work on projects together."

"Friendship is always a good place to start," Mae replied. "Don't wait too long. Remember, you're a free man now."

The next morning, as dawn cracked the Sunday sky wide open over the ocean, he and Mae wended their way out of the city. Church bells sounded, marking the hour and calling people to worship and rest. He'd programmed the map app with their home address and was trusting the digital female voice to get them there, back to familiar territory. He knew he and Mae would have to drive in shifts to make it. He'd have to give up control of the wheel.

They began climbing the Talmadge Memorial Bridge, and Mae asked, "Do you think he's going to be alright?"

"He'll find his feet. I'm sure of it."

"But what if he doesn't? What if he doesn't find someone, if someone doesn't find him? Billions of people in the world, but it can be such a lonely place. When he's done his studies, what then? He could just end up drifting further away from us."

"Then we'll have to come back. We'll find him wherever he goes."

At the peak of the bridge, Evan saw the wide world before them—an intricate network of land and water laid out to the horizon in morning glory. They passed the crest and descended to the ribbon of road ahead.

CYCLES

For the past hour, Evan and Mae had been cleaning their bikes, covered with a winter's worth of barn dust. They oiled the chains and checked the gears, adjusted the brake pads and tightened the seats. They'd bought the bikes last summer, intending to pick up cycling again. In their late fifties now, they kept saying to each other they needed more exercise. It was like the refrain to a melancholy song. "The Sound of Silence" came to mind for Evan. But somehow the bikes were banished to the barn, sitting inert over the winter like his and Mae's bodies. The tires went flat and flabby, just like their muscles.

It wasn't always this way. Decades ago—lost in the prehistorical mists of time, Evan liked to say, or many, many moons ago—their first date was a bike ride. After circling and circling her street on his ten-speed, he worked up the courage to stop at her house, a red-brick semi-detached structure set among many duplicates along the street, a hall of mirrors. A Happy Hearth Upholstery and Furniture Repair van occupied her driveway. He'd met her through his sister—Mae and Annalise were building a model rocket together. Mae had set off vibrations in him; he felt like a tuning fork she'd struck. He was still vibrating as he pressed the button to her doorbell, extinguishing for a moment the little light. The seconds dragged on until a man he assumed was her father opened the door and spoke through the screen.

"Can I help you?"

"I'm wondering if Mae's home."

"She is." Silence and a military man's stare, a close and hard study. Evan felt self-conscious in his Supertramp T-shirt and frayed cut-off jeans. He brushed the sweaty hair off his forehead.

"Can she come out to play?" This is what he thought and almost said, he felt so small in front of this man. Instead, he said, "I'm Annalise's brother Evan. Mae's doing a project with her. Could I talk to Mae for a minute? It's not about the project though. It's about something else. It won't take a minute. Maybe a couple of minutes." He felt himself babbling and shut up.

Without answering, Mae's father turned away and disappeared into the house. Left standing there on the threshold, Evan wasn't sure what to do. Was that a no? Would it be best to retreat to his bike and pedal out of sight, pretending he'd never risked the doorbell? He decided to count to sixty, while keeping his feet planted on the steps.

As he counted, he heard the murmur of voices inside. He couldn't make out the words, though some of the notes sounded masculine and firm, others feminine and saucy. When he'd reached fifty-nine for the second time, there was Mae at the door, looking at him through the screen.

"Hi, it's me," he said.

"I can see that."

"Would you like to go for a bike ride?"

She stepped out onto the porch. There was about a foot between them. She was wearing a white T-shirt with red piping around the V-neck and the sleeves. She was wearing red shorts, short shorts. Her arms and hands and legs and feet were bare and beautiful. Her bobbed hair was brown, her eyes brown behind big tortoise-shelled glasses, seventies style. Her lips curved into a smirk as she crossed her arms. "With you?"

His heart thumped hard in his chest. It really did. Surely she could hear it, too. "Yeah. I mean if you'd like to. If you're not doing something else. If you're not with someone else. Are you?"

She hesitated. "No."

"No, you're not with someone else, or no, you don't want to go for a bike ride?"

"Depends. Are you saying I *need* to go biking? Like, do you mean I need to lose some weight? Are you saying I'm fat?"

"No, no, that's not it. You're not fat." He paused, trying to play it cool. He wanted to say something like "You're not. You're hot," but he worried about the cheese factor. Instead, he said, "Doctors recommend regular exercise for its health benefits. Studies also show that people are more successful at sticking with an exercise program if they do it with a partner. We could be like, you know, exercise buddies."

"Buddies? Alright. Let me get my bike. It's in the shed around back."

That afternoon they rode around their subdivision's crescents and avenues, the streets lined with young, staked trees in front of bungalows, semidetached homes, and row houses. They ventured out into the industrial park between the houses and the highway. On the busy streets he rode behind her, a gentleman. He admired the view—and said as much—her bottom perched on the narrow saddle, the shape and rhythm of her hamstring and calf muscles, the slope of her back ending at her shoulders and neck, the shadow of her bra visible beneath her shirt.

Back at her house, they sat side by side on her porch steps. Her skin that he dared not touch was glowing. A map of their future was there, though he could not trace the route. In less than a year, he would get her pregnant.

"Did you know," he said, "that it used to be considered scandalous for a woman to ride a bike? It's true. Some people claimed it was morally dangerous." This was his idea of small talk.

"I guess we'll find out if they were right."

That was almost forty years ago. Now it was June again, and they were determined to get back on their bikes. He retrieved their helmets from the mud room, dusted them off, and passed Mae hers. Their plan was to go around the block—a large block of country roads. They'd left behind their subdivision long ago.

They snapped their helmets onto their heads and mounted their bikes. His was a black trail bike, Mae's a purple and white classic roadster with large balloon tires and a comfortable saddle seat. "Here goes nothing," she said as she pedaled her bike into motion. He followed suit, riding behind her.

Mae began picking up speed down their long laneway, but she hadn't gone far before both she and the bike began to wobble. She turned the handlebars back and forth as she tried to keep her balance on the gravel. She veered off the laneway onto the lawn in a large curve and capsized. She was on her back with the bike on top of her.

He dismounted and ran over to check if she was okay. Because of the lawn's downward slant, her head was lower than her feet. She laughed as she struggled to extricate herself from the bike. She couldn't get up, a turtle flipped on its shell.

"I need your help," she said. He grabbed her bike and set it on its kick-stand in the laneway beside his, then grasped her hands to right her. "That was graceful," she said. "I think that's enough for today. Tomorrow I'll see if I can fall over a little further down the laneway."

They parked their bikes up at the house and eased themselves down onto the porch steps. He pressed his arm against hers as she caught her breath.

"It's a start," he said. "Progress. Before you know it, we'll be booking down the road."

"Getting passed by little grey-haired grannies and toppling into ditches."

"As long as I get to ride behind you, I don't care."

Somewhere inside, they were still a couple of school kids, he was sure of it.

For a few moments, the world felt still. Inside, he mirrored that stillness. He listened to the chickens clucking in their run. He thought of the horses grazing in the pasture, tails swishing, heads shaking, and skin twitching against the flies. He imagined the barn cats sleeping in the hay he'd stacked just last week, the dogs dozing in the family room on the other side of the door. Still life. Life still.

"Tea?" he said eventually.

"I'd love a cup."

"Yes, tea heals all wounds."

"I thought that was time."

"Time's too busy flying, keeping company with the sun and the moon. He doesn't have time for doctoring, too." He rose and helped her to her feet.

In the kitchen, she filled and put on the kettle. While she got out the tea bags, he retrieved the teapot cottage from the jelly cupboard. He paused, holding the pot in his left hand, to study the framed picture on top—the two of them with Larry and Caroline Laurence, forever joined together cutting a cake in the dining room of the Talisman Ski Resort. There, he and Mae had celebrated the moonshine promises they'd made to each other when they eloped. He'd learned that almost a decade ago the resort had closed down, bankrupt. He wondered what happened to all the fixtures in the honeymoon suite. Maybe he and Mae could have gotten a memento or two at auction—a Venus-on-a-clamshell soap dish or that woody fertility god, if not that hot-pink heart-shaped tub.

He picked up the Talisman snow globe with its miniature horse-drawn sleigh carrying the miniature family through the miniature forest while tiny skiers went down the little slope beyond the woods. As he often did, he shook the globe, put it back down, and watched the blizzard swirl until it settled.

The jelly cupboard was no longer stained maple. Over the years, Mae had changed it, one time sanding it down and painting it Chinese red, another time removing the trim around the top to give the cupboard a more contemporary look. Twice they'd replaced the glass after horse play by the kids cracked it. Recently, she'd had him paint the cupboard a satin black on the outside, a soft blue on the inside that set off nicely their good company dishes. Beside it on the wall the photos of wild horses from the Foothills and Sable Island kept vigil.

"The kettle's almost boiling," she said. "Got an ETA on that teapot?"

He turned toward her. "How about now?" he replied. "Soon enough?" He carried the teapot cottage to her, holding it out with both hands, like an offering.

CPSIA information can be obtained
at www.ICGtesting.com
Printed in the USA
LVHW012234191221
706663LV00002B/33

DATE DUE

PRINTED IN U.S.A.